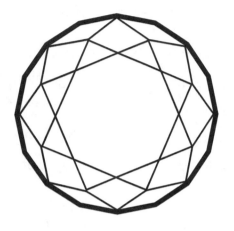

Books by Will Wight

CRADLE

Unsouled

Soulsmith

Blackflame

Skysworn

Ghostwater

Cradle: Foundation
(collects books 1-3)

THE TRAVELER'S GATE TRILOGY

House of Blades

The Crimson Vault

City of Light

The Traveler's Gate Chronicles

THE ELDER EMPIRE

Of Sea & Shadow

Of Dawn & Darkness

Of Kings & Killers
(forthcoming)

Of Shadow & Sea

Of Darkness & Dawn

Of Killers & Kings
(forthcoming)

GHOSTWATER

CRADLE : VOLUME FIVE

WILL WIGHT

HIDDEN GNOME PUBLISHING

www.WillWight.com

will@willwight.com

twitter.com/willwight

To my grandfather,
the first William Lawrence Wight.

1934 - 2017
Thanks for lending me your awesome name.

PROLOGUE

Mu Enkai had been nothing before the egg.

He was born a servant, following just enough of a fire Path to allow him to operate a furnace for a low-ranked refinery. He'd spent his days shoveling coals and choking in smoke, making barely enough scales to live on.

Then the sky had turned red. He and his fellow servants had taken shelter in the cold furnace, huddling together for days before the earth stopped shaking and the air was no longer flooded with blood aura. When they emerged from hiding, shaking but alive, *it* had been waiting for him.

The egg was a glossy, polished orb the size of a man's head, waiting among the debris of the refiner's shop. Unlike the building, it was unharmed. Spotless. Beautiful.

He could feel its promise in his soul; the blood aura that had drowned the world for days was concentrated here. Enkai had never considered himself an ambitious man, but in the egg's sleek shell, he'd seen his future.

His reflection was not a servant. Not someone who followed a half-remembered, incomplete Path that wasn't considered good enough for the sects and schools. He'd seen a king, crowned and baptized in blood, and that promise seized something dark in his soul and pulled it forward.

When he'd stepped forward, the others had too. He looked to his left and to his right and saw that he was surrounded by thieves.

It had been a brief, ugly fight, not a showdown between honorable sacred artists. The egg had gloried in the blood spilled, and when he stood victorious, he didn't think about his wounds or his fallen friends.

The egg was *all his.*

He'd drawn it inside him without quite knowing how. It nestled inside his soul even now, warm and safe beside his core, and its power blazed in him like a bonfire.

Enkai had been nothing but a Lowgold, and not an especially powerful one at that. But now, what did advancement mean to him? Highgold was nothing compared to the power of the egg.

Now, he sat in the highest floor of the top-ranked restaurant in town. The strongest sacred artists in the region now knelt before him, trembling, daring not even to look him in the eye. Now, *they* were the servants.

Before the egg, Mu Enkai would never have dared speak up in the presence of the three Highgolds who now bowed before him, each with a different Goldsign and a different set of robes. They all represented different Paths, but none of theirs could stand against his.

The egg changed his body as much as his spirit. Before, he had been small and hunched; as a boy, he had often been compared to a rat. Now, he was lean and sharp, like a hungry wolf. His Goldsign—a shifting flame pattern on the back of his hand—had been stained red as blood. Veins of crimson stretched from his hand and up his arm as the egg's power radiated out, infusing more of him.

He gestured to one of his Highgold servants, and the young woman flinched as she raised a slice of rare spirit-fruit to his lips. Even younger than him, she was already a Highgold. No wonder she'd had such a high opinion of herself. She had required a number of demonstrations of his new power before she understood his strength, but now she respected him. He could read that respect in her trembling fingers and the veil she kept around her spirit.

Enkai bit into the fruit and savored its icy flavor. It carried a soothing power into his madra channels, though little of it went into his core. Most of it went to nourish the egg.

That was even better. The egg had begun to show cracks, and once it hatched, he could barely imagine the power he'd control.

He opened his mouth for another bite, but his servant's hand was frozen. She stared off into the distance, eyes growing wider.

She could *still* ignore him?

Weak sparks of fire kindled in the air around his head, formed by his irritation. The egg echoed him, releasing fist-sized balls of blood-red fire. The egg's copies were stronger than his own, but that only excited him. The egg's power was his.

Before he could pull the young woman's attention back by force, he noticed that the other two Highgolds—an old man with a trio of horns on his head and a motherly woman with iron-gray skin—were staring off in the same direction.

He extended his balls of fire to the backs of their necks. All three of his servants fell to their knees with cries of pain as his power scorched their skin.

"Tell me what it *is*," he demanded. He may have had power beyond any Highgold, but he was still only Low-gold. Their spiritual perception was beyond his.

They looked at each other, which only stoked his rage further. The balls of fire trembled, ready to drive through their bodies. Blood aura affected flesh, so the flames of the egg burned men more easily than wood.

"We feel someone," the young woman said. She glanced at the ceiling and licked her lips.

That was all she said.

He wanted to slap her—the egg's power could boost his basic Enforcer technique into a blow that would crush her skull. Instead, he stood and gripped her by the chin. Her face paled, and her eyes slid to the side so she didn't have to stare into his eyes.

"When I ask a question, do you think I want half an answer? Tell me—"

"It's the Skysworn," the older woman blurted from the floor. She bowed more deeply. "They must be here to recover the town after the great battle."

The old man had also not dared to stand after Enkai forced him to kneel. "They will be pleased to know that you have already restored order."

Despite their reassurance, or perhaps because of it, alarm spiked in Enkai's heart. The Skysworn were more than just a police force; they were wandering judges, empowered by the Empire to punish criminals. He had been raised on stories of independent sacred artists being inducted into the Skysworn and going on to become some of the Blackflame Empire's greatest heroes. Even the current Emperor had served as a Skysworn for years.

They could take away everything he'd earned for himself. They might even sense the egg in his spirit, and they would surely kill him and take it from his Remnant.

The thought of losing the egg made him sweat more than the thought of his death.

Enkai released the Highgold's chin and began stalking away, his fireballs blinking out of existence. He had created a room reinforced with scripts just for an occasion like this. He would hide until they went away. "Keep them away from me," he commanded. "Tell them nothing."

Someone rapped on the window.

As one, all four pairs of eyes snapped toward the sound. A man stood outside on a dark green cloud, arms crossed, in robes of deep blue. It looked almost like an Arelius uniform, but there was no way he was there to clean the windows. Broad-shouldered and powerfully built, he loomed over the room, glaring like an executioner about to pass judgment. His right arm was a Remnant prosthetic, a skeletally thin limb of white light. Despite his young age,

he gave off an oppressive feeling, as though he were deciding which of them to destroy first.

Enkai shivered at the sight of him, afraid to extend his
spiritual perception lest he be punished. Though the egg
had made him a conqueror, now he felt like a servant once
again, flinching whenever an expert passed.

Without waiting for instruction, the old man hurried
over to the window and pushed it open. Only then did
Enkai notice the pin on the stranger's chest: a green cloud.
That was the emblem of the Skysworn, though a full
member would be wearing a suit of jade armor. Perhaps a
disciple? Or a subordinate, deputized to help deal with the
emergency?

Whoever the stranger was, Mu Enkai decided it was
time to slip away before he was noticed. The Skysworn
would assume the Highgolds were in charge anyway, and
he gave off the air of a man looking for someone to punish.
Let his anger fall on them while Enkai snuck away. The egg
would serve him just as well in some other town.

"Pardon," the young stranger said, "but could you tell
me which of you is in charge here?" His voice was apolo-
getic, and he bowed slightly as he spoke.

Enkai stopped at the top of the stairs.

All three of the Highgolds glanced back, but the old man
coughed before he spoke. "I am happy to represent my
master before the Skysworn," he said, and Enkai breathed a
little more easily.

"Your master?" the Skysworn apprentice asked, looking
surprised. "Is there a Truegold in town?" Now that Enkai looked at him further, he saw that the man was even
younger than he'd first appeared. And not quite so intimidating as his frame would suggest.

A shiver passed through Enkai's soul—the stranger had
scanned him. But it was soft as a brushing feather. The scan
of a Truegold's perception might have weighed on him,
but this was lighter than a breeze. Either the stranger had
withheld his power for the sake of respect, or...

Delicately, ready to withdraw at a moment's notice, Enkai extended his own perception toward the stranger. With only a strand of his awareness, he touched the young Skysworn's spirit.

It was no stronger than Enkai's own.

With such a light touch, he couldn't tell many details, but he didn't get a sense of fathomless strength he would expect from a Skysworn. In fact, the quality of the stranger's madra felt like a child's: like a pure, untainted spring. He couldn't sense the extent of the man's core, not without a more thorough inspection, but his madra was no more dense or potent than an average Lowgold.

Shame crept into Enkai's heart, quickly followed by anger. To think, he had allowed one of the Skysworn's *servants* to frighten him. He hated himself for his momentary weakness.

Their exchange of scans took less than a breath. The stranger with the Skysworn pin turned to Enkai, eyebrows raising. Instead of drifting away on his cloud, the boy held up both hands to show he held no weapon—his Remnant hand looked less threatening with fingers spread.

Enkai conjured a ball of blood-red fire, contempt fueling his madra. "I rule here," he said harshly. "If the Skysworn need to speak to me, they can come themselves."

Still hovering outside the window, the stranger pressed his fists together and bowed over them in a sacred artist's salute. "Forgiveness. We did not intend to disturb you. It is an honor to meet you; we were wondering who had done such an excellent job of protecting this town after the Dreadgod's attack."

The crimson flame still drifted around Enkai's head, but he paused. He *had* defended the town, but he had never expected the Skysworn to recognize the truth.

Enkai straightened his spine and faced the stranger head-on. "They had no Skysworn to protect them. They needed a strong leader."

"They're alive thanks to you," the Skysworn deputy said,

radiating sincerity. The more Enkai saw of the man, the softer he looked. "How did you do it?"

The honest admiration in the question cracked through Enkai's suspicion. He swelled with pride; it was about time *someone* asked him that question.

"People love to follow the strong. You have to show them your power...but not *just* show them. They have to feel it. You have to grind it into them, so that your strength is as present and undeniable as the sun."

Two of the three Highgolds flinched back at the reminder. Not the young woman. She frowned up at a high corner of the room as though staring through it. He didn't spare her a thought.

The stranger nodded seriously, rubbing his chin with his hand of flesh, with the attentive air of a man taking notes. He still wore what Enkai would call a glare, but he didn't seem angry. Well, a man couldn't help the face he was born with. He was clearly reasonable, no matter what he looked like.

"Well, if your approach worked so well here, I can't wait to see how it will help the next town."

Enkai hesitated, the fire around his head sputtering. "The next one?"

"In the wake of the crisis, we have more citizens in danger than we have capable leaders. I'll have to report this to my superiors, but I'm sure we'll want to put another town or two under your jurisdiction. If you are willing to serve the Empire in this way, of course."

The egg. This was all thanks to the egg.

The townsfolk had given him tributes: more scales, elixirs, and treasures than he'd seen in his lifetime before the egg. Another town would make him rich beyond his dreams.

But more than the riches, it was the people that captured his imagination. Even more people, bowing to *him*. Sacred artists taking *his* orders.

He cracked a smile for the first time, and two of the Highgolds joined him, though their expressions were a little too shaky for his taste. The young woman was late, still staring at the corner of the ceiling, but she eventually shook herself awake and smiled even more broadly than the other two.

A thread of suspicion crept back in, and he extended his perception. The egg had lent him some of its bloody power, which helped his madra burn through flesh, but it had done nothing to extend his spiritual awareness. He stretched his spirit as far as he could, feeling nothing but the spirits of the remaining townsfolk huddled in their homes...and one presence high in the sky. A Truegold, headed this way.

The *real* Skysworn were coming.

Their servant was just stalling for time.

Fear and rage and pain crashed over Mu Enkai in one dark wave, and he fed it all to the egg. Tendrils of its power extended more deeply into his soul, and he welcomed them. The ball of fire over his head swelled to life, turning a deeper red, and the stranger stumbled back. He held up his white arm to shield his face. He had realized his mistake...but too late.

Enkai swirled madra through his body, stepping forward and lashing out with a Striker technique. The fireball that he'd created streaked forward like a shooting star, followed by eight lesser lights. This technique had once been used to light firewood, but the egg had transformed it into a new level entirely. It had evolved, becoming a true weapon.

Fused with fire madra, the blood power would allow it to burn flesh like dry tinder. It could devour the body of a Lowgold in seconds.

Though he hadn't thrown it at a Lowgold.

The young Highgold cycled her spirit quickly, raising icy mist as a shield, but his technique burned through hers without slowing down. For an instant, she had a shocked look on her face and a scorched hole in her belly.

Then she went up like a torch. She opened her mouth to scream, but the fire had swallowed her breath. Her chest was a blackened ruin before the eight smaller sparks landed, trailing after the initial fireball.

As a Highgold, she took a second or two longer to burn.

With everything he'd done for this town, they still dared to call the Skysworn. She had sensed them coming and failed to warn him; no matter how many demonstrations he gave, they all still plotted behind his back. The truth felt like a knife in his back, and black hatred rushed out of the egg.

Though it didn't use an audible voice, the egg seemed to whisper to him.

You have no choice. They pushed you to this.

Before a breath of time had passed, while the first Highgold still had half her flesh left, he had already taken aim at the second.

The old man kicked off a movement technique, sparks flying from his feet, as he dove for the window. He still presumed to run; that stoked Enkai's fury even hotter. If he had to burn through the Skysworn servant to reach the old man, so be it.

But the stranger wasn't outside the window anymore. He was dashing across the wooden floor, focused on Enkai like a man staring at a blood enemy, pulling back his arm of flesh as though he was about to drive it into Enkai's stomach.

Enkai drove his red fireball down instead of forward, slamming it onto the Skysworn servant's head.

The man dropped to one knee, ducking to the side, forced to drive his strike up to meet Enkai's wrist. His palm struck, but not hard enough to stop Enkai's move. He seemed even weaker than a normal Lowgold. Pure madra rushed into Enkai's wrist without ruffling a single hair on his arm, but it did flow into his spirit and disrupt his technique.

...about as much as a gentle breeze disrupted a bonfire.

The bloody fireball fell undeterred, burning through the servant's blue robe in an instant and entering his body. With the bloody power of the egg fueling it, he was dead already.

He screamed, but Enkai had already moved past him. He should have *known* what would happen when he tried his tricks. They wouldn't work on Enkai.

The real Skysworn would arrive to find nothing of this town but ash.

He leaped out the window and landed on the stranger's green Thousand-Mile Cloud. From his vantage point, he could see the old man almost to the edge of town, sprinting down the dirt road and past the half-destroyed buildings that had remained after the Bleeding Phoenix's passage. Another few seconds, and he would be beyond Enkai's range.

But he wasn't there yet.

Enkai hurled another ball of fire flanked by eight lesser echoes, and it hurtled toward its target. The egg's hungry power would draw it to the scent of blood.

He would have watched, but a twinge of danger turned him around. Six green daggers floated around the old woman, and her spirit had latched onto his. She paled when he turned around and launched her Forger technique early.

Familiar with her madra, Enkai knew that this technique contained a life-poison that was all but impossible to stop. It would devour his life just like his own fire devoured the body, but leave him with an unmarked corpse.

A wash of bloody flame consumed all the daggers. He could barely call what he'd done a technique; it was nothing but pure power flowing out of him. As such, the red flames that landed on her skin didn't consume her instantly.

Or quietly.

She screamed loud enough to wake the dead as he hopped down from the Thousand-Mile Cloud, landing on the ground two stories below. He felt the first aching pain of exhaustion in his spirit, drawing more deeply on the egg to quench it.

The town was nothing more than a collection of homes flanking a single wide dirt road. Most people lived above their businesses, and more than a few faces peeked out of upper windows at the sound of the screams. When they saw it was him, they slammed the windows shut.

Cowards. They all disgusted him.

Filled by the egg, he poured one ball of fire after another into the air around him, keeping them in orbit around his body. He was relying so much on the egg now that they looked more like fist-sized droplets of blood that were shaped like flames rather than actual fire madra. Eight smaller lights hovered around each one, until he was surrounded by a swirling constellation of power.

The energy within him was thirsty. He could feel it. Each technique strained against his control like a dog against a leash, begging to go hunt its prey.

Someone slammed to the ground beside him, kicking up a ring of dust.

It was the Skysworn stranger.

His skin was undoubtedly scorched, his face tight with pain, but he had not been consumed. Enkai's hatred raged hotter; the Skysworn must have wasted valuable defensive constructs on their servants. They spent so much money just to defy him, when they could have had him as an ally.

He would show them the truth of the choice they'd made.

The stranger spread his hands, watching the fireballs encircling Enkai. "You don't have to hurt anyone else," he said, voice smooth and calming. "This isn't what you want. This is what the Blood Shadow wants. Let's just slow down, and we can talk about how to get you what *you* want."

A peal of laughter boiled up from inside Enkai, loud and venomous. "I'll show you what I want."

He released his techniques.

Sixteen balls of fire, each trailing eight sparks, streaked away from him in lines of red light so that he was surrounded by a crimson web. There were sixty-two spirits left living in town.

It went down to forty-six in an instant.

The egg's power wasn't exhausted yet. After those first people died, their bodies burst into hungry red fire. That flame craved flesh, and it jumped from victim to victim in a second. The second wave didn't die so quickly.

The screams rose from a solo to a chorus.

Enkai whirled on the Skysworn servant, rage so great his body couldn't contain it. He filled his palm with bleeding fire, but it felt just like blood.

"It's mine!" he shrieked, and even he wasn't sure whether he meant the egg or the town. *"You don't get—"*

Enkai froze, throat locking up.

Something had changed.

The stranger stood with his eyes widened in horror, mouth half-open as he stared at the blackened holes burned in village walls. He looked like a man watching his own home burn.

But he *felt* like a monster.

His spirit suddenly loomed like the shadow of a dragon flying overhead. Rage replaced by icy dread, Enkai scanned the stranger's spirit. His core still wasn't dense or bright enough to be a Highgold. For a moment, Enkai wondered what had changed. Then he realized: the man's madra wasn't pure anymore. His channels were filled with black fire.

Darkness flooded into the stranger's eyes like ink, his irises kindling into circles of burning red. That horrifying gaze locked onto Enkai.

"Why?" the Skysworn servant asked, and the word was a plea.

Enkai drew even deeper on the egg. Its power was the ultimate counter to fear.

He hurled the ball of red light in his hand, packing twice as much madra into it as usual. The lights following it looked like stars, and each could consume a tiger like a torch.

When the technique left his hand, the Skysworn servant's body erupted in a black-and-red haze. It was like an illusory flame, burning all around him, but it put a heavy pressure on Enkai's spirit.

The stranger waited, motionless, until the bloody fireball had almost reached his chest.

With explosive force, he leaped straight up.

Enkai's fireball blasted through the cloud of dust he'd left behind, which trailed up into the air. The Striker technique looped in the air, swirling up, nine orbiting lights chasing after the stranger.

He'd already started falling, gathering red-streaked black fire into his human hand. It gathered slowly, taking far longer than Enkai's technique had, but it carried a great sense of danger.

Enkai reached behind him, pulling a twisted green-tipped knife from his waistband. This was a Highgold treasure, one of the most valuable weapons in the town. The blood-fire was rising to meet the falling servant, and even if he landed safely, this dagger would be waiting for him.

A green cloud swept in from the left, catching the stranger mid-fall. He flew away on his Thousand-Mile Cloud, and once again Enkai's technique swept through empty space where his target had once been.

Enkai's fireballs were Striker techniques. They were not Forged, so they ran out of power quickly. This one had already diminished to almost nothing, and Enkai could feel it unraveling. He snarled, forcing his spirit past its exhaustion again, digging deeper into the egg for another technique. He locked his eyes on the Skysworn's emerald cloud.

There was no one on it.

A great, hot, overwhelming power loomed up from behind. Enkai turned, dagger raised, and a white fist caught him in the jaw.

In his conquest, Enkai had taken blows from Highgolds before. The power of the egg had strengthened his body until he felt like he had leather for skin and stone for bones. He could catch a hammer-blow with one hand, standing as firm as though his boots were nailed to the ground.

This time, he felt nothing but a flash of pain and a tremendous rush of noise. Then he realized he was lying on the inn's floor in the middle of a pile of splinters. Groggy, he tilted his head up; there was a hole in the front wall big enough to ride a horse through.

The stranger stood there, a silhouette against the sky holding a ball of black fire. More flame blazed around him in a hazy corona. His shadow fell over Enkai like the specter of death.

No. Enkai would not allow himself to die here. Not to a Lowgold.

The power of the egg was much greater than this.

In an instant, Enkai drew his core dry. He pulled so hard that it might cause permanent damage to his madra channels, but he was beyond caring. He pulled up all the power of his spirit, drinking thirstily from the madra of the egg.

Between his hands, a red light bloomed. This didn't look anything like flame; it was a pure crimson light that hung in the middle of his palms like a red sun. *This* was a technique worthy of the egg. It sang with power, an echo of the Phoenix's song that had turned the sky red.

In triumph, he pushed forward, releasing the technique on the Skysworn's servant. A river of light, straight as an arrow and thick as a man's leg, blasted forth with all his rage and fury.

The stranger lifted his left palm in response, his ball of dark madra hovering in front of him. It erupted into a bar of liquid fire, black streaked with red.

The two streams of fire clashed head-on, only a foot from the Skysworn apprentice's outstretched hand.

Enkai was prepared for a direct clash of their spirits, pushing the egg's madra into the technique so he could blast through the stranger's technique.

It wasn't enough.

The dark flame devoured his, melting through an inch at a time. By the time Enkai started to panic, the stranger's power was almost at his chest.

"You can't—" Enkai started to say. Then the bar of black fire burned through his stomach.

And the egg was gone.

Dark flames spread through him, and he collapsed to the floor like a straw doll. It didn't hurt like he would have expected. It only tingled, as though he faded away like a Remnant.

He had time for one last, jealous thought. This stranger had so much power, but he acted like a servant. If Enkai had sacred arts like that and combined them with the egg, he could have ruled the world.

Seconds later, Mu Enkai was nothing more than a pile of ashes.

Unsatisfied, dark fire spread from his body, consuming the ruined inn. The screams coming from around town slowly died while the survivors huddled in silence and darkness, hoping to be overlooked.

In the midst of the black flames, the apprentice Sky-sworn stood alone.

CHAPTER ONE

On their clouds, Lindon and the two Truegold Skysworn returned to Stormrock, the black city in the sky. They alighted in the tallest tower, presenting entrance codes to the Skysworn on guard.

This was Starsweep Tower, headquarters of the Skysworn. For them, it must be like coming home.

It was only Lindon's second time inside.

Numb, he followed the two green-armored figures inside, past a few other scattered Skysworn. They all looked as exhausted as he felt, and the smell of blood hung heavy in the hallways. More than once, he saw a servant in the dark blue uniform of the Arelius family mopping up a puddle left by a bloodspawn. Or one of its victims.

The Bleeding Phoenix hadn't even attacked directly. It had only risen for a few days.

They would be cleaning up the aftermath for years to come.

All the Skysworn were either on a mission, preparing for a mission, or too injured to work. They were stretched so thin that even the Lowgolds didn't have a moment to rest.

Without a word, the two Truegolds brought Lindon to a single, sparsely furnished room behind a black door. It was lit by a stark white circle of script on the ceiling, and filled with only one round table and nine surrounding chairs. There was a three-foot gash in the wooden table, and it looked fresh.

Lindon slid his bulky brown pack into one of the chairs, then turned to leave the room.

Bai Rou held up one armored hand, his eyes burning yellow in the shadow beneath his hat of woven reed. "Stay here," he commanded.

Lindon wanted nothing more than to sink into a chair, but he had more pressing concerns. "Pardon, but I will return. I'd like to go see Yerin."

Renfei, a slight woman with a resolute air and a black cloud hovering in the air over her, jabbed a finger at the table. "Sit. We'll be back. Do not leave this room."

"I would like to check on her for myself, if you don't mind." The last he'd seen her, her soul had been exhausted, but her Blood Shadow was stable. That was the main reason why he wanted to make sure she was all right; the Skysworn were not likely to leave someone with a Blood Shadow to herself. Especially not now.

Bai Rou stepped forward. He was a brick wall of a man, and the armor only added to his silhouette.

"Sit," he said.

Though, as big as Bai Rou was, he only had an inch or two on Lindon. Compared to the difference in their spirits, that didn't seem like much.

How would that armor help him against the Path of Black Flame?

Lindon realized he was meeting those yellow eyes glare for glare, and dark madra was creeping into his vision. Blackflame flowed through him, angry and defiant.

He looked to the side, blinking his eyes clear, and focused on his pure core. With the clarity came the cold shiver of reality setting in; he had almost started a fight with a pair of armed and armored Truegolds in their headquarters.

"Apologies. I have been...stressed."

Lindon couldn't have called Renfei's expression sympathetic, but at least she hadn't pulled the hand-sized hammer hanging at her hip. "Don't be. The target is dead, the parasite neutralized. Mission accomplished. Don't think about it more than you need to, just *do as you're told.*"

He sunk into the nearest chair, trying not to just collapse and sleep. He tried to brace his right arm on the table, but he forgot to cycle madra through it, so his Remnant arm sank right through the wood. "I apologize for my disrespect, but I am concerned about Yerin. Please, I need to know that she is being treated well."

Yerin was being treated like a prize pig hauled in front of a bunch of butchers.

Her hands were manacled in halfsilver and chained to the stone wall behind her, while a bunch of unarmored Skysworn prodded her spirit with theirs. It was hard not to shake like a shaved bear in the snow under the tickle of their scans.

"And you feel that you were treated...poorly by the Skysworn?" the voice of this green-hooded man made it clear that he thought a knife across the throat and a shallow grave was better treatment than she deserved.

"What put that in your head?" Yerin asked, glaring at him.

She didn't say any more, but one of the hooded figures in the back scribbled onto a little board. She figured they were making sure she was still herself, and not a shell the Blood Shadow happened to crawl into. She just wasn't sure how they were doing that, when they didn't know her from a bullfrog.

"Have you had any urge to harm or kill your fellow man?"

"Having a few of those urges right now."

"What color is this card?" He held up a paper with a splash of yellow paint on it.

Her Goldsigns twitched, the silver blades hanging over each shoulder eager to cut her free. She calmed them—they wouldn't be able to cut through the halfsilver, made of madra as they were, so she would have to dig through the script-reinforced stone behind her. And the second she started trying that, they would cook her like a side of bacon.

Still, she was stone certain they were doing nothing but burning up her time. "What does that tell you? Is a Blood Shadow blind to color?"

The Skysworn examiner looked like he was struggling not to spit at her feet. "Answer the question."

"Yellow. You want me to tell you the shapes next?"

This time, he held up a green card. "And this one?"

"...if you can't tell what color that is, you need a new line of work." Every Skysworn in the tower wore green robes when they were out of their green armor.

He paused for a second as though deciding whether he could backhand her or not, but accepted the answer. He pulled out a card with a triangle painted on it.

"Do you know what shape this is?"

She stared at him. "Are you pulling my chain right now?"

"Answer the question."

She shook her wrists, rattling the chains. "You're welcome to kill me now if it'll bring this to an end."

He stepped closer, wind madra swirling green around him. He wore a thin beard and he looked at her like she'd killed his children and made him watch. "Don't *tempt* me, Redmoon."

She grinned at him. "Not Redmoon. Arelius." Eithan Arelius was the only reason she was tied up at all, instead of facing the business end of an axe.

If he touched her without the stamp of his Emperor, or at least another Underlord, Eithan would wear his skin like a scarf.

He reddened and turned away as the door opened. When Bai Rou entered, the examiner and note-taker buzzed over to him like vultures to a corpse. They muttered to him for a while—telling tales about her, she was sure.

The big man's burning yellow eyes flicked to her, and she turned her smile on him like a blade. He gave no sign whether she'd drawn blood or not, but raised his voice so she could hear. "She's clear?"

"It's in a stable condition," the note-taker said, "but there's no telling how long that will last. It's largely up to her."

"She'll turn against us before the sun sets," the examiner said, glaring at her.

Bai Rou folded his arms and leaned against the wall, and he was watching her too. "She comes with me."

Yerin rattled her chains again. "We're wasting breath. You got a key, or am I going to go gray in here?"

They freed her in spite of the examiner's protests, but left the halfsilver shackles on her wrists.

Bai Rou pulled her into the hallway and began marching her down without a word. She caught more than one hostile glare, rough search of her spirit, or flare of a half-formed technique.

What a spine that took, to shake swords at a girl in chains. They had better hope she didn't remember their faces. Not only did she have the power of Redmoon Hall inside her, she had the will to use it against them. They'd dropped her off a cliff and left her to die.

Well, *one* Skysworn had.

Smartest thing to do would be to kill her flat-out. If they let her hit Truegold, they'd regret it.

"You looking for somewhere to drop me?" she asked.

He said nothing.

"You can't kill me, so you want to put me to work. Lindon isn't cutting it on his own?"

She tried to conceal the real worry she felt, after she'd been forced to leave Lindon in the care of the two Truegolds. She'd only had a fingernail's weight of trust in the Skysworn to begin with, and now even that much had dried up and blown away. They wouldn't draw swords on him, not with Eithan's name hanging over him, but they wouldn't step quick to help him either. He needed her help.

"The Blackflame completed his mission," Bai Rou said. "We will speak to you both, and that's all you need to know."

"That so? Last I checked, there were three of us. What about the new girl?"

She thought she saw a shadow of worry pass over his yellow eyes, and that cheered her.

"She's coming too," he said, scowling.

Renfei stood in front of the room where she'd left Akura Mercy to recover. It swung open soundlessly, revealing a mass of darkness so thick it was almost palpable. If she stuck her hand past the doorframe, it looked as though it would be swallowed by endless night.

Only one thing was visible in the inky murk: a bright purple book, hovering in the center of the room. It glowed, but somehow cast no light. Only the book itself was visible, a single distinct figure in an ocean of black.

The book was spread open, its pages thick, and it pressed on her spirit with an impression of overpowering might and incomprehensible age.

Then it vanished, and Mercy hopped out of the dark.

If not for her wide purple eyes, Mercy would look more like a friendly innkeeper's daughter than a child of the mighty Akura clan. She beamed at Renfei, clasping her hands behind her back and leaning forward with a twinkling smile. "Sorry, sorry! I know it's gloomy. I heard you knock, but you know how it is when you're deep into cycling. You just lose your head!"

A staff fell out from the darkness. Made of what looked like polished black roots, the staff was taller than Mercy, with its top carved to resemble a snarling dragon with purple pinpricks for eyes.

...or perhaps not carved. Though its eyes didn't move, Renfei was sure they'd fixed on her, and she thought she heard a hiss.

It was enough to get her madra cycling and send a hand to her hammer.

Mercy grabbed for the falling staff, fumbled it, tried to catch it with her other hand, almost lost her balance, and ended up seizing it in both hands. She raised it triumphantly. "Got it!"

Renfei's eyes moved from her to the shadow behind her. "What were you doing in there?" she asked. She didn't intend to, but she was using her Skysworn voice: the tone of a career authority figure.

"Cycling," Mercy said, waving one hand as though she meant to blow away the darkness like smoke. "It's not my favorite aura to cycle. Hard not to fall asleep."

It was deep shadow aura in there, laced with some other, darker aspects that dissipated even as Renfei tried to sense them. It was a tapestry of black.

Some of the rumors about Akura Paths flashed through her mind, and she could feel her expression harden. This was a fine nest of vipers she had to babysit.

Mercy was watching her, and slowly she stood up. Renfei felt an instant of what she could only call a premonition: she was about to see beyond the mask of the cheery, innocent girl.

The Akura Lowgold reached up with one hand—gloved in slick black, as though she'd dipped it in tar—and placed her fingers on Renfei's arm.

"You must be *exhausted*," she said.

Renfei searched her face for anything mocking, but found only sympathy. A trainee shouldn't speak to their Skysworn with such familiarity, and a Lowgold should express more respect to a Truegold.

But she was an Akura, so that much was to be expected. She would have grown up around people who could evaporate Renfei with a thought. Sometimes, Renfei wondered why any Akura stayed only Lowgold, even one as young as Mercy.

"You don't need to worry about me," Renfei said, turning to walk down the hall. "Follow me, we have to meet your...partners."

Mercy followed without protest, walking side-by-side. She twirled her staff and almost dropped it. "I can't imagine a more trying time to be a Skysworn," she said idly.

"I certainly can't remember one," Renfei said. Or the last time she'd actually sat down for a meal, instead of taking it on her feet or on her cloud.

"I don't know how you find time to *sleep*."

"Sleep?" Renfei said dryly. "Never heard of it."

Mercy nodded along. "You can work every hour of the day, and there's still more to do."

"We'd be short on staff if we had twice the Skysworn we do. Recruitment will be up next year, you can bet on that, but that means even *more* work for the instructors and recruiters..."

Renfei and Mercy arrived first. Lindon looked up hopefully when the door opened, but when he saw it wasn't Yerin, he sank back down into his chair. The respectful thing to do would have been to rise from his seat, but he couldn't make himself move.

The green-armored Skysworn gave him a quick look that suggested she noticed. He winced.

She didn't spare him more than a glance, though, continuing to talk lightly with the girl at her side. Mercy held her tall black dragon-staff behind her back, and the piercing purple gemstones it used for eyes seemed to fix Lindon with a glare. The Akura girl hopped into a chair opposite Lindon. She almost tipped over backwards, grabbing onto the table for support.

Renfei chuckled, and Lindon wondered if that was the first time he'd seen her laugh. She had always seemed stern and professional, if not cold, to Yerin and Lindon. Even before they'd come into direct conflict. Now she treated them like suspects she might have to execute at any time.

Maybe she treated Mercy differently as a daughter of the Akura clan. But then, it was hard to stay on guard against someone who was struggling to pull her chair down to the ground before she spilled over.

Once she settled at the table and sighed in relief, Mercy gave Lindon a wave. "You've been working hard too, haven't you? I've caused you trouble," she said apologetically, bobbing her head.

She had been recovering from madra exhaustion and a collection of light injuries, after their fight against the bloodspawn and subsequent days in a basement. The spiritual healers of the Skysworn had determined that she was unfit for duty, so she had remained here to recover. She had actually protested Lindon being sent out alone, trying to struggle out of her bed before Bai Rou restrained her.

No, the strange one was Lindon, having been proclaimed fit for duty so quickly. Part of that was the speed of his physical recovery, thanks to the Bloodforged Iron body: after three days in that basement, he had already recovered almost entirely. The touch of Little Blue, the Sylvan Riverseed, had helped ease the burden on his spirit.

But there was nothing she could do about spiritual fatigue, and Lindon *still* felt a deep ache in his madra channels from overuse. He wondered if he had really been in any better shape than the other two, in terms of his soul.

Or if the Skysworn had simply sent him out without caring if he lived.

"No, no," Lindon said hurriedly, "I hope you're all right. I couldn't—"

"Quiet," Renfei said, cutting him off. "You want to chatter, do it on your own time."

He couldn't help but notice that she hadn't interrupted Mercy.

The door swung open again, and Bai Rou ushered Yerin in ahead of him.

Seeing Yerin in one piece was a deep breath of relief for Lindon. Her skin was covered in thin scars and her black robes were tattered, but that had always been true. Two arms of Forged silver madra extended from her back, their ends flattening into blades: her Goldsigns.

The halfsilver manacles around her wrist bothered him at first, but he understood the necessity. Her Blood Shadow was made of living madra, like a Remnant, so it wouldn't be able to manifest through halfsilver without carving a chunk of it out. Yerin wouldn't be able to cycle her own madra through her hands without great difficulty, and using a technique of any kind would be much harder than usual. She was effectively hobbled.

But without such precautions, she might not be able to leave this place alive.

Her face cracked into a half-smile when she saw him, and she started to speak, but Renfei repeated her line about chatter. Yerin rolled her eyes, then took a chair next to Lindon. Mercy waved at her, smiled, and mouthed the word 'Hello!'

Looking somewhat confused, Yerin nodded back.

Bai Rou slammed the door and leaned against it, the brim of his hat tilting down to cover his eyes. Was he standing guard against an escape attempt, or just generally being intimidating?

Renfei dropped a cloth sack onto the table. Its string was drawn shut, but a watery blue light spilled from its mouth. She surveyed them as though looking over a host of enemy troops. The cloud hanging over her head seemed darker and more solid than ever.

"You're all Golds," she began. "I won't spare my words. We all know why the Captain put you all together."

Because a Blackflame, a Blood Shadow, and an Akura were all potentially dangerous liabilities, but their backing was too strong. The Skysworn couldn't kill or imprison them without cause.

"Because you don't give two plucked hairs if we live or die," Yerin said, propping her chin on her hand.

That was also true.

"I wouldn't put you on the same team if the Captain hadn't ordered it," Renfei continued without acknowledging Yerin. "And even so, we had never intended to give you assignments. Keeping you out of the public eye and under our supervision would have been enough."

She really wasn't sparing her words. Lindon was almost impressed, but her sudden frankness made him wary. What was she leading up to?

"Now, the situation has changed. We're going to use every asset we can lay our hands on, and if it turns out we can't use you, we'll throw you out."

"Seems to me you tried that already," Yerin said, but before her statement was halfway out, dark fog boiled out from Renfei. Cloud Hammer madra. Though it looked like mist, Lindon got the spiritual impression of a great fortress wall.

"Do not take this lightly," Renfei said, nailing Yerin to the spot with the force of her stare.

Yerin didn't back down or look away, but she did shut her mouth.

"We will put you to use for the Empire, or we will throw you in a cell. At best. Now, under ordinary circumstances, Skysworn teams select from the available missions together. But the three of you have to stay isolated from the public. Rumors about a Blackflame loose in the Empire are bad; rumors about a Blackflame under the command of the Skysworn are good. But only if he *is* under the control of the Skysworn. Understood?"

That went for all three of them, of course. The Skysworn might not trust Yerin because of her Blood Shadow, but if she did eventually earn their faith, it would look as though they'd captured a member of Redmoon Hall and compelled her to work for them. And an Akura working for the Empire, instead of the other way around, would make the entire Blackflame Empire look stronger.

No one said a word, but Mercy nodded eagerly.

"I will be brief, because we have a cloudship to catch on the hour." She activated a script on her armored wrist, and a beam of light streamed out, projecting lines of violet light on the air. They sketched a ghostly model of an island, hovering in the middle of tossing waves.

Lindon was less than impressed. A White Fox binding could have made an illusion that looked real, and suggested sound and even smell.

"We're headed for a three-day journey into the Trackless Sea. It will be cramped and uncomfortable, and I expect you to silently cycle the entire way unless we need you to fight. Our destination is a pocket world called Ghostwater, created by the Monarch Northstrider."

There was a general intake of breath all around the room.

"Pocket world?" Yerin asked, leaning forward eagerly. Her bladed Goldsigns tapped the table beside her. "That's where sects keep their treasures."

Mercy rubbed black-gloved hands together. "I've always wanted to visit one! Our family has one, but it's too dangerous for anyone less than a Lady."

"I'm sorry," Lindon said, "but...a pocket world. That means..."

"It means a pocket-sized world. A self-contained space much smaller than our own, but separate. Exactly like it sounds."

He wished he hadn't had to ask.

Renfei continued, pointing to the image of the island. "This world, Ghostwater, was designed to contain a research facility. The honored Monarch abandoned it almost fifty years before eventually losing his life."

According to Eithan, most believed that the Monarch had died seven years ago. Not even two years ago, Lindon had seen Northstrider alive with his own eyes. At least that much of the Skysworn's information was inaccurate, though they wouldn't believe him if he corrected them.

Besides, the Monarch wouldn't mind them entering a world he'd abandoned decades ago. Would he?

"Now, the battle between the Akura Matriarch and the Dreadgod has damaged the anchor binding that world to our own. If our experts are correct, it will crumble within the next few months."

Lindon was dying to ask about this "anchor," but he suspected Renfei didn't know herself. And wouldn't appreciate further interruptions even if she did.

Reaching into the bag she'd brought, Renfei produced a jewel. A sapphire, which shimmered like sunlight filtered through water. White and green lights flickered at its heart, though it cast blue illumination on the walls and ceiling.

"We were alerted to the current problem by *this* artifact: the Eye of the Deep. It was left to the last Emperor in the Blackflame family for safekeeping by one of the Monarch's Heralds. It grants access to main facilities of Ghostwater."

She held up the gem. "I will carry this and guide us around, so stick with me. Without this, you will die alone as space itself crumbles around you."

"Forgiveness, but what is our assignment?" Lindon asked. He was actually eager to see something Northstrider had built, but there had to be a purpose for their presence there. Lindon and Yerin didn't know how to stabilize a world.

"We go as scouts," Renfei answered. "We will determine if Ghostwater is really damaged. If it is, we will secure as many treasures as possible for the Empire and then report back. At that point, the Emperor will decide what to do with the time we have left."

One of Yerin's sword-arms raised. "And how heated do we expect this to get?"

Bai Rou's yellow eyes narrowed on her, and Renfei's brow furrowed in confusion. "It's a relatively cold sea, and it's almost winter. Bring a coat."

"Not what I meant."

This time, Bai Rou answered her. "The world's defenses are down. Could be scavengers."

Yerin nodded, as though that was exactly what she'd wanted to hear.

"Is there anyone living inside?" Mercy asked.

"No," Renfei said, tucking the Eye of the Deep back into the bag. She gestured to Bai Rou, who stepped away from the door. "Now, we are entering into an unknown situation with an unknown number of enemies outside the boundaries of the Empire. If you aren't prepared, feel free to stay in a cell."

Before leaving the room, she turned to Lindon. "We need all the boots we can get on the ground. Go get your turtle. Half an hour."

Then she was gone.

The flight to the island was quiet, boring, and more than cramped. Their cloudship was covered, but hardly large enough for six people. Orthos took up most of the upper deck himself, and he spent most of the journey tucked away in his shell, pretending they weren't in the sky.

Yerin and Mercy, at least, could cycle aura on the ship. There was no way to start a fire without killing them all, so Lindon just focused the Heaven and Earth Purification Wheel on his cores. It felt like spending three days with iron bands around his lungs.

After the first full day of being packed into the cramped, dark confines of the cloudship, Mercy scooted over to Yerin and Lindon. Orthos snored behind them, and the two Truegolds were up on deck.

"What do you think the pocket world is like?" Mercy whispered, full of excitement.

Lindon exchanged glances with Yerin. She was sitting next to the wall, Goldsigns curled down over her shoulders to avoid scraping the ceiling.

"I suspect you know more about that than we do," Lindon said politely. He and Yerin hadn't figured out how to handle Mercy yet. She had acted like they were all friends almost from the moment they'd first met. It was disconcerting.

"Oh, I don't know anything about our family's pocket world. And now we get to see one!" She clapped a hand on Yerin's shoulder, and Yerin shrugged it off.

"Have to wonder what Eithan would think about us getting hauled away," she muttered to Lindon.

"If he didn't want us here, he'd show up and take us away." Eithan had left them to the Skysworn for a reason, and he rarely explained himself. Lindon relished the chance to make decisions for himself, but at the same time, the Underlord still hadn't taught him any pure madra techniques.

"My master used to leave me to take risks for myself too," Yerin said. "Can't make it far without taking any risks." She hesitated, then added, "Especially if you're trying to make it...so far."

Lindon knew what she was referring to. Eithan had shared his ambitions with them in the form of a vision from the heavens. It had sharpened Lindon's aims, but he hadn't had a chance to discuss the vision with Yerin yet. Even now, Mercy was with them all the time.

She leaned closer, eyes sparkling. "What are we talking about?"

Yerin ignored her, and Lindon made up a flimsy excuse.

Finally, they reached the island.

It was larger than Lindon had imagined from the sketch in the air; big enough that from their vantage point hovering just above the trees, he couldn't see the opposite shore. It was heavily forested except for the beaches, with one prominent hill in the center doing a decent impression of a mountain.

Renfei put them down on the beach, the dark green cloud beneath their ship hovering inches over the sand. Withdrawing the Eye of the Deep, she headed for the treeline.

Lindon, Mercy, and Yerin leaped out of the ship at the first opportunity, all groaning at the chance to stretch their legs. Orthos followed them a moment later, landing in the sand like a boulder. He didn't stretch his head out. In fact, after falling, he pulled his legs in as well.

A shadow lay across the turtle's spirit. Lindon could feel it through their contract. He needed Little Blue to balance out his spirit, and soon, or he would become a problem for all of them.

Lindon pulled his pack from his shoulder, slinging it around, intending to pull out the Sylvan Riverseed.

"Here it is," Renfei called. She swept out a hand, and a bolt of dark cloud slammed into a tree in front of it, crushing it and sending it tumbling into the forest.

In front of her stood a jade doorway, not surrounded by any wall. The door was rectangular and covered in script, and it shimmered blue-green like a murky pond with its surface disturbed.

Renfei pulled out the Eye of the Deep, glancing at it and then back to her partner. "Bai Rou."

The huge, green-armored man had already left the ship, his hat of dried straw shading his face. He strode over to her, where they exchanged an animated discussion.

"What's crawled up their armor?" Yerin asked, nudging him with the side of her silver Goldsign.

Mercy stumbled in the sand, but braced herself with her staff of smooth black. Its dragon head hissed at her, glaring with violet eyes. "The door wasn't supposed to be open."

Lindon rested his hand on Orthos' shell, considering.

"They're going to separate us," Lindon said, keeping his voice low. The other two turned to him, Mercy looking resigned, Yerin's face darkening. "One group goes through to scout, and the other stays out here until the first reports back. They'll divide us so that each of them can handle a group on their own."

Yerin's hand moved for the hilt of her sword. She'd been allowed to have the weapon back when none of the Skysworn could sense anything exceptional about it.

It was the weapon of a Sage, but neither Yerin nor Lindon had said anything. It seemed the Sword Sage's blade could hide from lesser artists.

"Let them try to split us up. Now's our chance; we fight them out here." She nodded to Orthos. "Big guy ties up the big guy, and the other three of us take Renfei."

Lindon exchanged glances with Mercy, and both of them extended a hand in a calming gesture.

"We don't need to go that far," Mercy said.

"It's too much of a risk. We don't need any more enemies than necessary."

Yerin gave them a sour look. "You two got in step awfully quick." She took her hand away from her sword, but her Goldsigns twitched as though ready for action.

"Wei Shi Lindon," Renfei shouted. "You and the beast are with me. Ladies, you stay with Bai Rou. We will observe the situation and report back within the hour; I can relay a message to Bai Rou at any time."

Unsurprised, Lindon rapped his knuckles on Orthos' shell. "It's time, Orthos."

The turtle's limbs slid out slowly. He didn't feel tired. Quite the opposite; it felt as though Orthos were wrestling to keep himself under control. The rings of red in his black eyes were bright, but he nodded to Lindon.

Lindon and Orthos joined Renfei, facing the portal. Its rippling surface gave no indication of what waited on the other side.

"We walk through together," the Skysworn said, cloud rolling over her head.

Lindon took a deep breath and stepped forward. Yerin

stopped him, hand on his left arm.

She looked as though the words had gotten caught as she tried to speak. She cleared her throat. "...stay sharp," she said at last.

Mercy gave him a wave.

"Gratitude," Lindon said, dipping his head to them both.

Then, with Orthos on one side and Renfei on the other, they stepped into the jade doorway.

As he'd experienced before, the world was swallowed by an endless expanse of blue light that looked thick, as though he could reach his hand out and run his hand down it as though down a veil.

But this time, it only lasted an instant.

CHAPTER TWO

The air ripped like a torn page.

Lindon stepped through the portal into a bubble of air the size of a castle. His shoes crunched on the dry sand of the ocean's floor, which spread out in front of him to the edges of the bubble. Twisted rock formations and bunches of brush-like weeds rose in irregular patches, with tiny crabs skittering from shadow to shadow.

The water outside the bubble was black as ink, but the space was brightly lit by...Lindon hesitated to call it a "tree." It looked more like a glowing, abstract sculpture meant to represent a tree: a bunch of blue tubes spread out like roots coiled together to make a trunk, and at the top—where he would expect leaves—were clusters of glowing yellow lights. They weren't too bright to stare at, but all together they lit the bubble like late afternoon.

This ocean clearing was silent in a way the land never was. No wind brushed these plants, and no waves crashed nearby. Only the occasional scuff of sand or the soft drip of water disturbed the stillness, and the air tasted of salt and green plants.

A sense of awe hung heavy over the space, like Lindon had trespassed on an ancient tomb. Invisible pressure pushed on him as though he'd shouldered the entire weight of the ocean above.

It was only a moment before he realized that the pressure wasn't his imagination. By then, he'd noticed that Renfei had stopped, one hand on her hammer, her cycling madra drawing wisps of dark cloud around her armor. Orthos growled so low and loud that the sand shook.

They weren't alone.

A young man sat with legs crossed on top of a nearby boulder. His robes were white, his unbound hair spilling down his back, and his features so delicate that at first Lindon mistook him for a woman. A disc of shadow hovered behind his head like a dark halo.

There were others that might have drawn Lindon's eye first, but this man drew his spiritual perception like a magnet. He was a deep, dark weight, and Lindon had to pull back his perception before he touched the young man's spirit. He was cycling now, eyes closed and breath even, but Lindon feared that even the slightest touch would wake him.

Far at the other end of the clearing, where the edge of the bubble met the sand, a sprawling miniature palace of golden madra glittered in the light. A pair of servants in plain, identical white coats stood at attention in front of the curtain that served as the door. A...creature...peeked out of that curtain, shimmering even more than the palace.

It looked like a woman merged with a dragon, covered in gold scales and with a face closer to that of a lizard than of a human. She wore strings of jade, silver, and pearls in layers around her neck, and rather than a sacred artist's robe, she had wrapped herself in silk of every color. As she saw the newcomers, a smile stretched across her leathery lips, and she casually manifested a shining drop of gold madra between her claws.

Lindon began cycling Blackflame. Once, he had caught a Truegold off-guard and burned away the man's hand. If he could injure Sandviper Gokren so badly, he might have a chance against these strangers. So long as they didn't notice him first.

His attention was drawn by a deadlier threat: a flash of red from the left, far away from both the cycling man and the dragon-woman.

He recognized that color. He recognized that sensation in his spirit, a shivering impression of a thousand corpses drowning in a crimson sea.

A young woman stepped up, Blood Shadow covering her like a cloak. Her hair fell into her eyes, shrouding her expression, but blood madra trickled away from her feet, steadily spreading across the sand. She didn't bother to veil her spirit, so she blazed like a bloody torch to Lindon's perception. She was Truegold, without a doubt, and a strong one at that. She gave Lindon the same impression as Renfei or Bai Rou, and she looked to be at least ten years younger.

The Redmoon woman made three, but there was a fourth presence nearby.

He cast out his perception and immediately noticed a tiny hut to his right. It looked like it had been slapped together from mud and bundles of dried grass, though he could see neither of those materials anywhere around him.

Another young man, about Lindon's age, pulled himself out of the hut's doorway like a corpse crawling from a grave. His eyes were bloodshot and half-lidded, his gray cloak stained and dirty. Two emerald horns rose from his forehead, pointing up.

Lindon accidentally brushed the man's spirit with his spiritual perception, and he hurriedly pulled it back. The man seemed not to notice, but his aura felt as strong and steady as the roots of a mountain.

He took in the situation with the look of a man who would rather be anywhere else. Though he had done nothing that Lindon could tell, the golden-scaled woman stopped in her tracks, looking nervously in his direction. The girl from Redmoon Hall watched them all.

"Who are you?" the horned man asked the Skysworn, wearily.

Renfei was muttering under her breath. "Bai Rou, do not

follow. I repeat, maintain your position and call for reinforcements. Multiple enemies. We will try to disengage."

When the man addressed her, she drew up straight and consciously drew her hand away from her weapon. The black cloud over her head rolled and rumbled.

"We are the Skysworn of the Blackflame Empire," Renfei announced. "We are responding to reports of a disturbance around this facility after the passage of the Bleeding Phoenix."

Her voice was smooth and practiced, but her tension infected Lindon. He withdrew Blackflame, changing his breathing pattern and pulling power from his pure core. Blackflame would serve him better in combat, but in a fight between Truegolds, could he even make a difference? Anonymity would serve him better.

The man's perception moved over their group, slow and careless. He dismissed Lindon in a blink, but his spirit lay heavy on Orthos and Renfei. "Who is backing you? The Winter Sage?"

Orthos snarled, smoke and red light rising from his shell. "We need not answer to you."

The stranger stared at Orthos with absolute disinterest, as though replying was too much effort. Based on Lindon's feeling of the horned man's spirit, his confidence was entirely justified.

A woman's voice piped up over his, airy and amused. "When you're done, leave me their trinkets," the golden dragon-girl said. "It's so exciting to see a pack just bulging with who-knows-what treasures. And I like the look of that armor."

The green-horned man sighed. "Not every fight needs to be to the death, dragon. What could they possibly have on them?"

"They shouldn't be here," came an eerie whisper from the Redmoon Hall girl. The liquid form of her Blood Shadow had almost reached the base of the portal. "They are not bound by the rules. Who can know who sent them?"

"We are here on behalf of the Blackflame Empire," Renfei said loudly, "under the protection of the Akura family." She shot a glance to the man cycling on the boulder. "If we have disturbed the honorable representative of Redmoon Hall, we apologize and will withdraw."

"Back," she said under her breath to Lindon. "Back through the portal."

Lindon turned immediately, but a tendril of blood raised itself from the ground and poised in front of him like a snake coiling to strike.

"Hold, Lowgold," the young woman commanded. "We wait for instructions."

"No need to bother your Sage with this," the golden dragon said. She was approaching by then, strolling closer to the portal, though Lindon noticed she gave the cycling man's boulder a wide berth. "Strip them and send their bodies to the ocean. What is that behind your back, Skysworn?"

For the first time, Lindon realized that Renfei was gripping the Eye of the Deep behind her back in her left hand. Her fist tightened around the gem, but she still edged backwards.

"I salute the honored representative of the Desert Monarch and King of all Dragons, and I assure you, if we are allowed to return to our empire, we will send you a greeting-gift that far outstrips any of our meager belongings. Furthermore—"

The world went silent as the young man on the boulder opened his eyes. Like Mercy's, they shimmered like a deep amethyst.

Shadow flashed out from the seated man as though it had been unleashed, dimming all light. His right hand drifted up, then down, like a painter leisurely adding a stroke to canvas.

"Silence," he said, as his hand lowered.

In a blink, so that Lindon thought he'd imagined it, a thin line of shadow flickered down, passing through the middle of Renfei's body from the top of her head down.

The Akura representative closed his eyes.

Renfei fell apart.

Her armor was still untouched, but her body collapsed in a pile of blood. Lindon stared, too stunned to be horrified, and before he could avert his eyes, the Blood Shadow covered Renfei's corpse.

An instant later, a towering giant of black clouds slid out of the Shadow with an explosion of force that sent both Lindon and Orthos tumbling away from the portal. The Remnant punched two fists of dark fog together with explosions that cracked like thunder, launching itself forward.

The golden dragon-girl met it with a tinkling laugh, sending a wrist-thick river of golden liquid punching through the spirit, but Lindon didn't have time to watch. The Blood Shadow was re-forming, gathering itself up to engulf him.

A massive boulder plunged from above, slamming into the sand, cutting off the Blood Shadow and shielding Lindon.

The green-horned man stood staring at a hole next to him, where that boulder had once rested. He gave no sign that he had even moved, his dirty cloak hanging dead from his shoulders.

"He is not your opponent, Yan Shoumei," he said wearily.

"But you are," she said, gathering her Blood Shadow around her and dashing forward."

The young man walked to the other side of another boulder, kicking it lightly. A green ring flashed as his foot made contact, and the boulder shot forward as though launched from a catapult.

Whether by design or coincidence, it landed inches from the first boulder, between Lindon and the portal.

Lindon ducked behind the stones, leaning around them to look at the place where Renfei had fallen. He was choked by a complex mess of emotions when he saw her half a face—relief that she was gone, regret that he couldn't bring her body back to her family, and fear now that she wasn't around to protect him. Though he'd never trusted her, at least she'd been on his side.

But he wasn't looking for her body. He was looking for a way out.

Her armor was still unharmed; it seemed that the shadow-sword had struck her *through* the green Skysworn plate without damaging the metal. He wanted to take it with him, but it was still half-engulfed in Yan Shoumei's Blood Shadow, and Lindon wasn't foolish enough to stick either of his hands anywhere near that. Maybe his Remnant arm could feed on it like it fed on the bloodspawn, but he wasn't willing to bet his own safety on it.

Her hammer was nowhere to be seen, which he regretted even more than the armor. As the weapon of a Truegold from the Cloud Hammer sect, it would have been invaluable.

But most importantly...

The sapphire she'd been holding behind her back rolled free, darkened with spots of her blood.

Lindon snatched it up, stuffing it quickly into his pack. If he had the Eye of the Deep, he could deactivate the portal after leaving. Maybe he could lock these others inside to fight it out amongst themselves.

Orthos roared, launching dragon's breath at the gold-scaled girl engaged with Renfei's Remnant, but she ducked to one side of his Striker technique and avoided it with ease. The Cloud Hammer Remnant reared back, preparing to drive a dense fist into the girl's head.

A sigh cut across the battle, and the Akura young man opened his eyes again. The shadow returned.

"I asked for *silence.*"

Flickers of black, like feathers in the night.

Renfei's Remnant was split into two clouds, which drifted apart as it began to dissolve into essence.

The dragon-girl skidded to a halt, scattering sand into the air. The shadow-blade passed in front of her, leaving a perfect line sliced into the ground.

The horned man raised a hand, and a circle of green script flashed into existence in front of him. The edge of shadow cut into it, and the script flickered at the contact before shattering like glass.

His shield must have weakened the attack, because he didn't fall into two pieces like Renfei had. Instead, the skin on his hand split open, leaking blood. He stared at the wound with lifeless eyes, as though watching someone else's hand.

Yan Shoumei's Blood Shadow cloak was split in half, revealing deep red sacred artist's robes beneath. She hissed and backed away, her Shadow drawing itself together, but she seemed unharmed.

An instant of pain flared through Lindon's soul, and Orthos howled.

His shell split open, spraying dark blood and ruddy light in equal measure. He staggered back, letting off flares of Blackflame madra out of sheer panic and instinct. His pain dimmed Lindon's mind, but it also stoked the rage of the Path of Black Flame. Without thinking, Lindon tapped back into his Blackflame core, and the Burning Cloak sprang to life around him.

Everything had taken only a few breaths, and the battle was so far above Lindon's level that he had unconsciously shrunk back. But now he had a task he could handle: get Orthos back through the portal. If the rest of them could make it out alive, that would be a victory.

It took the strength of his Enforcer technique to restrain Orthos, who was lashing out with blind pain, but Lindon hauled him to a stop and started pushing toward the portal. He glanced back at the Akura man, only to see him lifting his arm again.

That gesture was enough to fill Lindon with terror now, but the purple eyes weren't fixed on Lindon.

He was looking at the portal.

Following his gaze, Lindon noticed with a jolt that the portal was transparent from this side.

Bai Rou was holding Mercy back with one armored hand, dragging her away from the portal. He was clearly trying to retreat. A handful of yellow madra droplets blasted out of his other hand, striking at Yerin.

Who was darting for the gateway.

She slashed back without turning, her white blade casting a storm of invisible swords that shredded Bai Rou's Striker technique. Her eyes were fixed on the portal.

Sometimes it felt like it had been a lifetime since he'd left Sacred Valley. Other times, he felt like a child who had just left home. The reality was, he had been outside the Valley for a year and a half. He was overwhelmed by the weight of so much time. Surely it couldn't have been that long. But at the same time, he wasn't sure how he'd crammed so much into such a short time.

But through all of it, he'd been with Yerin. By now, he knew her as well as he knew anyone. Seeing her face as she ran, he knew in a split-second what she was thinking. In that moment, he understood her thoughts better than he understood his own.

She was coming for him.

Whether she had sensed something from the other side or whether she'd heard Renfei's report to Bai Rou, she knew something was wrong. She was headed into the hands of these Truegolds, and she didn't even know it.

But if she did know, she would only run faster.

Ever since Lindon had first adopted the Path of Black Flame, he'd lamented how long it took him to gather dragon's breath. Never had every fraction of a second burned him like they did now, as he shoved his hand of flesh in front of him and poured madra into it.

Dark fire gathered in his palm, pointed at the portal. Was it faster than the shadow the Akura was calling? He didn't know. He *couldn't* know without turning, and that would take him precious instants.

Yerin kicked off from the stone floor. Lindon scorched his madra channels, pushing power in a loop through his soul with every breath, Blackflame burning his body and his soul as he forced it to move *faster*.

The world darkened. Shadow flickered.

And a bar of Blackflame madra tore through the thin, green metal frame of the portal.

Instantly, the window into another world winked out. A blade of darkness sliced a smooth gash in the sand where the portal had once been.

The sand was bare. No Yerin.

Lindon's breath of relief disrupted his cycling technique for a moment.

Thick, choking spiritual pressure fell on him like a weighted net, but he still couldn't look back. His Remnant hand didn't pass through living beings like it did through objects, so he pushed Orthos with both hands, struggling against the huge sacred beast's strength.

The Akura could cut him down at any time from behind, but he shoved Orthos through the sand. The Burning Cloak worked in bursts of strength, so it was easier to punch or kick than to carry something heavy, so he could only push Orthos a few yards at a time, moving him toward the nearby boulder. He didn't know if it would stand up to the young man's shadow blades, but at least they wouldn't be so close.

The pressure faded before Lindon reached the boulder, and he was so surprised that he couldn't resist a glance back.

The Akura man had closed his eyes again, returning to his cycling. He had taken the destruction of the portal as nothing.

But he was the only one.

The other three all stared at the damaged portal frame, their battle forgotten. The Redmoon Hall girl stared out of the veil of her hair and trembled like she was watching her own home burn down. The man with the emerald horns looked from the portal to Lindon and passed a hand over his face. And the dragon-girl had both clawed hands in front of her mouth, eyes wide.

Then she and Yan Shoumei turned to Lindon. Rage of red and fury of gold pushed against his spiritual senses.

Black-and-red haze flared around Lindon as he heaved Orthos with all his strength, sliding the turtle behind the boulder. Orthos' struggles had gotten weaker and weaker, and Lindon could feel his consciousness fading. It sent a spike of alarm through Lindon—he hoped this was just exhaustion caused by exertion and injuries, but it felt like a slide into death.

Hunkered down behind the boulder, Lindon felt the flares of madra recede. It seemed they were trying to keep all disturbances to a minimum to avoid waking the cycling Akura again.

Which gave him a window to find a way out.

Suppressing his dread and alarm, he scanned the darkness of the water around him. He was only steps away from the bubble that separated him from the cold, black water all around them.

However the fight among the Truegolds fell out, it wouldn't bode well for Lindon. He needed somewhere to escape. He'd closed the portal, and that fact hung over him like a sword suspended by a string: he had destroyed his *only way home.*

But he shoved that panicked thought to the back of his head for later. There had to be another way home, and now that he had the Eye of the Deep, he held the key to the entire Ghostwater facility. If there was a way, he'd find it.

He just needed to get out of here now.

He scanned the black water along the ocean floor, looking for other spots of light.

A gold sun rose behind him, and his Enforced jump sent sand spraying behind him. His Burning Cloak surged, his madra channels still shrieking in protest after he'd abused them to force out the dragon's breath.

Lindon twisted in midair, bringing his white arm up in front of him as a shield.

The golden dragon-girl stood before him, necklaces

hanging against her golden chest, her silks shimmering in many colors. She held out a claw.

"The sapphire, the pack on your back, and anything you have in your pockets. You have no idea how expensive it will be to return home without that doorway."

So there *was* a way out, and these Truegolds knew it. Lindon tucked that fact away.

"If you compensate me for my expense and give me something that is worth more than your life, I may leave you unharmed." She was keeping her voice low, shooting frequent glances at the spot where the black-haired man meditated.

Lindon ducked his head toward her, raising his hands and letting the Path of Black Flame fade from his spirit. The Blackflame urged him to fight her for dominance, but he shoved it down and drew from his pure core instead. He needed a clear head.

Orthos growled and stumbled next to him, but fell to his belly. His eyes fluttered shut.

"Please, forgive this one for his rudeness," Lindon said, sliding his pack off one shoulder. "This one believes he has something that may please you, but please spare the lives of this unworthy one and his companion."

The ridge of scales she had in place of eyebrows raised, and she said nothing, allowing him to continue. Lindon reached into his pack, pulling out the biggest box he'd brought with him on this trip. The case of the Thousand-Mile Cloud the Skysworn had lent him.

Before he could open the box, Orthos' eyes snapped open and his spirit seethed with the same insane anger that had possessed him when Lindon had first met him.

Lindon stared at him, shocked, as Orthos rose to his feet with the Burning Cloak flaring around his shell. Lindon's was a pear-shaped aura around his body, but Orthos' shell rose as high as a horse's back and he was almost as wide as he was tall. He looked like he was surrounded by a black sun.

Even in the grip of his temper, he only growled and didn't roar as he had before. Lindon couldn't tell if that was because he was still partially in control of himself or if he simply didn't have much energy.

The dragon-girl bared her fangs and gathered lines of liquid gold madra in both hands. "Black dragons," she said quietly, snapping one hand forward. "Little better than dogs." A whip of madra unfurled from that fist, cracking in front of Orthos' head. Though the attack flashed like lightning, it made only as much sound as a man snapping his fingers.

Orthos didn't flinch, ducking to the side and then extending his neck to snap at her arm.

Lindon wasn't there to watch a fight. As soon as Orthos rushed forward, he cast the Thousand-Mile Cloud's box aside and let the dense, grass-colored cloud unfold in front of him. He clambered onto it, merging his madra with the construct and urging it forward. Into the water.

There was a glimmer of yellow light in the distance. It could have been a reflection from this bubble, and Lindon would have preferred to find one that was clearer and closer, but he wasn't quite spoiled for choice. As he reached the bubble, he carefully reduced his speed and ran his fingers through the water.

They pierced the bubble easily. As he'd hoped, this bubble was created by a massive script-circle that manipulated aura into holding the water at bay. He should pass through without obstruction.

"Orthos!" Lindon turned behind him to shout, hoping the sacred beast had enough mind left to hear him.

He saw a line of gold descending on him like a curved blade.

Lindon twisted at the last second, taking the madra whip on his pack. The attack caught him over the ear and on the hip, burning like a heated brand, but the pain wasn't the worst of it.

The worst was the lurching sensation he felt when the cloud vanished from beneath him.

The Thousand-Mile Cloud, given to him by the Sky-sworn so he could follow them on assignments, dissipated into green wisps of mist as the whip struck the construct's core. A shattered ball covered in script fell to the ground, singed. The rest of the construct faded into essence of cloud madra.

A split second later, Lindon hit the sand too. He rolled, ignoring the pain, trying to put some distance between himself and his attacker.

After rolling a few yards, he noticed he was leaving a trail behind; his pack had been torn apart. Burned, torn cloth that had once been part of his spare clothes. Fragmented scripts, broken stones. His heart caught in his throat as he saw water and broken trees spilling onto the ground between two cracked halves of a transparent case. Little Blue's tank.

He dove for the twin halves of the case.

A quick glance showed him that Orthos was keeping the golden dragon-girl busy, but he couldn't tell what the other two were up to. Apparently their silent truce remained.

The first half of the case was empty. Nothing but mud and sand left after it had fallen from his shredded pack. He dumped it out, just to be sure, but there was no sign of the Sylvan Riverseed.

And nothing but garbage in the second half.

Lindon's eyes moved from one to the other as flashes of gold and red played over the glass. Like a rising tide of heat, Blackflame crept into his veins. His strained channels ached, but he pulled more.

Before the rage of the Path of Black Flame took over, he gathered himself and released his spiritual perception.

A sensation from behind him, like a fresh breeze, released his tension. With a breath, he let Blackflame go, and leaned to see behind a tiny mound of sand.

Little Blue huddled behind it, clutching her hands on her head as though trying to shut out sounds. She looked like a woman made of deep blue madra, only a little taller than his hand, in a flowing dress that was really part of her body.

Lindon extended his hand to her, and she turned to him with wide eyes that seemed to be filling up with tears. Lindon was fairly certain the spirit couldn't cry, but her gaze trembled. She ran to him with arms outstretched, chiming like a bell, and clambered up his arm. Each footstep was an ice-cold pinch of static, and each was a reminder that she was still alive.

A wave of sand sprayed into the air as Orthos crashed down next to him. His spirit was dwindling as he ran out of madra, and his consciousness was starting to fade again—it almost felt like he was sleepwalking, but the turtle shook himself and flipped over from his shell, growling at the golden dragon-girl.

Holding Little Blue to his shoulder, Lindon dashed over to the box he'd discarded from the Thousand-Mile Cloud. He started shoving everything that had survived into it: the leather roll that contained his Soulsmith tools, the polished wooden case holding his badge collection, the notes on hunger madra, and his Heart of Twin Stars manual. He was especially relieved when he found that in one piece.

The Eye of the Deep went inside too, but it must have taken a hit from the woman's whip. The jewel had a single long crack down one side, white-and-purple dream madra drifting out in wisps of mist.

If the physical vessel burst, the construct inside would dissipate. Lindon couldn't worry about that now; he just had to hope it lasted long enough.

Lindon slammed the lid shut with his left hand and tried to fasten it shut with his right, but the Remnant arm passed through the latch like a ghost. Hurriedly, he used his left hand to seal the box. This would be big enough to hold all his surviving tools, but more importantly, it was waterproof.

He rushed past Orthos, seizing the turtle by the tail. Orthos dragged him forward for a moment, ready to run at his opponent, but eventually noticed the human clinging to him.

Lindon pointed to the light in the water and shouted, "Run!" Then he ran through the bubble.

Black, icy water swallowed him.

CHAPTER THREE

Yerin passed through the jade doorway sword-first.

And out the other side.

She stumbled into the underbrush and whirled, looking back to see Mercy and Bai Rou on the beach behind her. Bai Rou held Mercy against the sand with one arm, the other extended toward Yerin, yellow madra swirling around his gauntlet. His eyes glowed the same color from within the shade of his hat.

"Return, recruit."

Yerin stared at the door. She walked through it again, sweeping it with her perception.

The portal was gone.

Lindon was inside.

Cycling her spirit, she pushed all the madra she could into the script. The runes around the frame flared silver, then tinted a shimmering blue-green before dying out. The door stayed empty.

She stared at the artifact, trying to think, but her brain was stuck in the mud. Renfei's message to Bai Rou had played loud enough for them all, and the phrase "multiple enemies" was all she needed to hear.

But the Skysworn had held her back from passing

through the portal. He had stopped her.

Endless Sword madra flowed through her. Her white blade was in her hand.

Bai Rou's fist tightened, and his madra broke into a rain of droplets that came at her sideways, like rain blown by a gust of wind. She'd faced his power before; it ate through the mind as it did flesh. The Path of the Amber Well, Renfei had called it.

It would be as useful for questioning as it would for restraining targets. One drop on her skin, and she couldn't be sure she'd be able to keep her sword in her hand. He'd tried this technique on her only a moment ago, to stop her from going through the door.

If he hadn't, maybe she'd have made it.

She could have dispersed the technique with sword aura using the Endless Sword technique, but she compressed silver madra in the edges of her blade instead.

Yerin chopped her sword down, unleashing the Rippling Sword Striker technique. The slash unleashed a surge of silver light, a crescent storm of sword madra and aura that rushed at Bai Rou, tearing through his technique and sending sand spraying to either side as it blasted toward him.

He was a stage more advanced than she was; his techniques should trample hers rather than the other way around. But how could a spray of rain stand up to a full sword-slash?

Bai Rou raised his forearm and the technique slammed into his armor, breaking like a wave on a rock. It took a chunk out of his hat, sending straw drifting on the wind.

He'd gathered his madra together for another technique, but Yerin had known she couldn't break through that green armor so easily.

She rushed in, closing the gap.

The Path of the Endless Sword didn't have much of a full-body Enforcer technique, but her Steelborn Iron body took care of that. It drew madra from her and she dashed forward with speed equal to Lindon in his Burning Cloak.

And she showed Bai Rou the Enforcer technique she *did* have.

Her blade shone silver with the power of the Flowing Sword. The technique gathered both aura and madra, growing more and more powerful as the battle continued. Eventually, she would hit hard enough to break this True-gold's armor.

It would be a struggle to hold it for so long without losing control of the technique, but she was angry enough to try.

The shining blade descended on him like the judgment of the heavens, and he had to take it on his raised arm once again. His other was occupied with a struggling Mercy.

This time, the blow slammed him into the ground. Her next strike sent a chip of green metal spinning into the air. Her third cracked one of his vambraces.

She was screaming by the time he released Mercy to use both hands. She could let him off for dropping her off the city and leaving her for dead. In a way, that had been merciful; he could have killed her himself while she was helpless under the control of her Blood Shadow. She could let him off for his threats, for the way he treated them like enemies, for his never-ending reminders that he would kill them at the first sign of defiance.

But he had held her back from saving Lindon. That was too far.

Yellow madra gathered around his hands, and with an instant of freedom, he'd turn the tables on her with his superior strength.

She didn't give him that instant. She reversed her last slash, slamming her sword up into his chest.

He flew back so fast that he tore into the surf, sending up a plume of water.

She stuck to him like a leech, sprinting after him, leaving Mercy behind. Her shining blade hit him again before he righted himself, knocking him into the water, and a Rippling Sword followed him into the ocean, slicing through the waves.

She began sinking herself, but she didn't let up with the Striker techniques. She hit him with two, then three, before the water swallowed her.

With the strength of her Steelborn Iron body, she hauled herself through the water, but she saw only clouds of sand and murky water. Her spiritual perception caught his general direction: he felt like a liquefied nightmare. She swam toward him.

The water around her lifted, like someone had scooped her up in a giant, invisible bowl.

She felt herself, and the chunk of ocean around her, rising into the air. She lunged forward, but the water shifted so she went nowhere, tumbling in a chaotic storm of bubbles and dust.

She sent her perception out, trying to sense what was happening even as she strained her eyes to catch a glimpse through the rolling ball of water.

It was only when the dust settled that she got the full picture.

Bai Rou had used a Ruler technique to command the water. The aura lifted a globe of the sea with her trapped inside. He stood on the surface of the ocean beneath her, reaching down to pull his soaking hat from the surf.

His yellow glare cut through the water, and his spirit released its full power like a crashing tide. He had to use half his madra to hold this Ruler technique in place, but the rest of his spirit was focusing itself in his palm.

In only a breath of time, he'd either spear her like a fish or fill this water with his madra and dissolve her. Maybe both. But his rage couldn't compare to hers.

Which made her drop her guard.

Yerin's relationship to her unwelcome guest had changed in the last week. It was free now, but she'd shown it whose sword was sharper. It was quieter, but she couldn't shake the thought that it was smarter now too. It had been a caged wolf before, and now it was a lurking killer, biding its time.

And now it slipped its collar.

The Shadow boiled out of her, a mass of blood madra that stretched out of her back and formed into a copy of her swimming by her side. The Blood Shadow wasn't an exact reflection; it looked almost like a Remnant version of her, built of all sharp, jagged angles and covered in red paint. Two thin arms stretched from its shoulders and flattened into blades, matching her own silver Goldsigns. It carried no sword, but its fingertips sharpened into points.

She tried to restrain it, but it had already passed her control. At this second, they wanted the same thing.

The Shadow melted, oozing out of the water globe and falling toward Bai Rou. It didn't care much for anything that would hold a regular body back. Madra would have stopped it, but normal water did about as much good as a screen umbrella.

Bai Rou pushed his technique toward the Shadow, and this was more than just a fistful of rain. It was a stream of Amberwell madra that coiled like a dragon, diving at the blood spirit. It cut right through the Blood Shadow's left arm, which sent a spike of pain through the parasite. Yerin could feel it, but she wouldn't say it hurt her. It was more like hearing about someone else losing an arm.

The Blood Shadow took the injury as the cost of doing business, turning its fall into a lunge without a care.

The blades on its shoulders struck like a pair of scorpion stings, carrying Striker techniques with them. Its Rippling Swords were stained red, carrying as much power from blood as from the sword.

She hadn't known it could do that.

Any other time, she would have been disgusted and horrified to see her Path of the Endless Sword techniques used by this creature, but now...now she just wanted Bai Rou to hurt.

He slipped to the side, feet sliding across the waves as though he stood on slick stone, dodging the first at the same time as a burst of yellow madra dispersed the second.

Her Blood Shadow landed on him.

It clung to him like a monkey to a tree, driving its clawed hands and its Goldsigns into his body. He twisted his head, pushing blades aside so he took everything on his armor. But Skysworn armor was famous for a reason.

Green light flared within the plates, and a pulse of emerald wind madra blasted out from him, shoving everything away. The Shadow was thrown backwards, splashing into the ocean.

But he'd tried to split his concentration too many ways. His Ruler technique fell apart.

Yerin dropped as the water around her rained back down. Cycling underwater was like trying to push gravel through your channels, so she hadn't bothered using any other techniques while she couldn't breathe. Her lungs were on fire, but that wasn't even close to the top of her mind.

And she'd never released her Flowing Sword. The blade shone like a silver star in her hand, a bonfire of madra and aura. It carried power like a Truegold's weapon, and she was about to see how it stacked up against his armor.

She angled herself to fall next to him, raising her sword for a strike. He was just turning away from the Blood Shadow, his perception sweeping through her spirit with a shiver. She gave a cheer in her heart; he was too late. She had him.

Then a black spear pierced her through the chest.

She'd set her eyes on Bai Rou, so she had no warning until she felt the hot pain beneath her collar. A black point, thin as a finger, stretched from her robes.

Her lungs seized up. Her spirit fought against the dark madra passing through her, which was a contest her spirit easily won. The black branch dissolved within a second, but it had enough to disrupt her techniques. The power blew away from her sword like dust on the wind, and she splashed into the sea.

The pain vanished when the madra did, and she touched her skin with her fingertips. No wound. It didn't even feel bruised.

Her fury surged again, and she twisted in the water, pushing madra back into her sword. Her core was all but empty, with only scraps left, but she'd go at Bai Rou with her teeth if she had to.

A black tendril, like a burnt tree root, wrapped around her. She slashed it away, but three more replaced it, cradling her and hauling her back through the waves. She struggled, but she wasn't far from shore. The branches pulled her back to shore, and she rolled onto her feet, pushing her way free.

Mercy stood there panting, covered in sand, her ponytail undone. The dark madra extended from her oil-gloved hand. She had taken *his* side.

Yerin cycled the last of her madra through her weapon, preparing the Endless Sword, but Mercy released her own technique and collapsed back onto the sand, panting. "That's... harder than...it looks," she said through labored breaths.

The Blood Shadow faded to red light, which streamed out of the ocean and into Yerin's back. It slid into her spirit, coiling around her core weakened and unsatisfied. Yerin felt about the same.

She paced to the side, keeping her sword on Mercy and her perception locked on Bai Rou. He hadn't moved. Why?

Mercy's staff lay next to her, the eyes of its dragon-head glowing violet, but she didn't reach for it. "We can't fight each other," she said quietly.

Yerin gave a weak, angry laugh. She reversed her sword, plunging it into the beach an inch from Mercy, but the Akura girl didn't flinch.

"*We?* You've *buried* me." She jerked a thumb over her shoulder. "You think he'll let me walk away now? That's my one chance gone." Yerin stood over Mercy, rage and the frustration of failure boiling inside her.

Mercy held up her hands, showing them empty. "I thought we should be more worried about them." She pointed both hands up at the sky.

Since the portal vanished, Yerin had kept her spirit locked on Bai Rou. Now, she finally noticed the rest of the world.

A golden cloud hovered only a hundred feet over them: a Thousand-Mile Cloud big enough to hold several houses. How had they not seen that when they arrived? How had they not felt the ones riding it? In her spirit, they shone like burning lamp-oil.

One of those questions was answered as another veil dropped on another side of the island. Its presence felt wild, savage, eager for battle. A thousand beasts roared along with the rising power, shaking the forest. Winged creatures took to the sky in a cloud.

But she could understand veils. She didn't understand how the air could part only a few yards from her, revealing a towering black castle that stretched from the beach into the forest. It cast its shadow over her and Mercy both. It looked like it had been dropped from the sky, with half-crushed trees emerging from its foundation, but she didn't hear the crunch. Had they been like that all this time, and her eyes had been tricked?

The whole palace was surrounded by a smooth rectangular outer wall, its only visible opening a pair of tall, spiked gates. From behind those gates, Yerin sensed darkness, fear, and endless despair.

Veils continued to drop all around the forest, so powerful that she was sure some of these forces had to contain Underlords at least. From the far shore, she felt a familiar feeling of nauseating slaughter: a Blood Shadow. Maybe more than one.

Powerless, Yerin dropped to the sand next to Mercy. They had never been alone on this island. They were surrounded.

The instant the portal was destroyed, Yan Shoumei was overcome with anger. Her Blood Shadow picked up on her agitation and started to flow toward the Lowgold.

It wasn't just *her* agitation. Something about his thin, white replacement arm stoked her Shadow's appetite, which was a complication she didn't need.

She remembered herself just in time and pulled it back. Ziel, the horned boy from the Wasteland, was nearby, and she knew him by reputation. He was known to wait on the sidelines for an advantage. The second she struck at the Lowgold, he would take advantage of her distraction and hit her while she was distracted.

There was no love lost between Redmoon Hall and the sacred artists of the Wasteland. Especially not now, after the Dreadgod's rampage.

Instead, keeping an eye on Ziel, she drew her Shadow back into a cloak around herself and began backing away. Contrary to her expectations, he wasn't looking at her at all. He was staring at the broken portal frame with a dead look on his face.

Maybe he didn't have a gatestone. Shoumei had no doubt that the gold dragon and the Akura did, so if Ziel did not, he might end up as the only one trapped here in this pocket world. If so, she might owe that Lowgold thanks.

...though her anger returned when she thought of having to crack her gatestone. Each of those represented days of work from a Sage or better; they were not handed out frivolously.

It was meant to save her life from a situation of certain death. Breaking it to replace what should have been a free trip home was frustrating at best.

She backed up until she felt the cool air coming off the wall of water behind her. Ziel was staring at the portal, either lost in despair or in contact with his master. Harmony was cycling still, and thank the heavens for that. He even made her Blood Shadow shiver. Ekerinatoth and the turtle were engaged in battle, while the Lowgold scrambled around to recover something in the sand.

According to the truce, none of them were allowed to leave this habitat until all six faction representatives arrived. They were still waiting on the young prince of the Tidewalker sect and the delegate from the Ninecloud Court.

However, without the portal, there was no point in waiting. The treaty had been decided by the higher-ups in each faction, so Shoumei should never violate it on purely her own judgment, but...

She slipped into the dark water.

The Sage of Red Faith would applaud her decision. Even if some supervising Heralds could sense what was happening here, they wouldn't blame her when she wasn't the one to break the pact.

No one followed her, or even noticed her leave. She was free to hunt.

Ekerinatoth snapped another whip at the retreating dragon-turtle. It cut a satisfying chunk out of his shell, but her opponent didn't turn. Instead, he used that Enforcer technique of his to dash away and follow his human through the bubble of water aura containing the vast ocean of Ghostwater.

She lashed her golden tail in irritation. A black dragon's Remnant could fetch a pile of high-quality scales if you knew the right buyer, and she did. Its shell would have made a decent decoration, or the foundation for a seventh-grade refinery. That was at least a hundred medium-grade scales. And who knew what was left in that box the human was carrying?

He at least had that sapphire construct, which she suspected was connected to Ghostwater. If that were true, the Heralds would pay her in *top*-quality scales. Her tongue flickered out involuntarily.

She would have had them already, if not for Harmony.

Ekeri glanced back at the young Akura on the boulder. It singed her pride that she had to restrict her techniques to avoid disturbing a human, but pride was nothing before the reality of strength. She had to admit, she'd never personally seen a Truegold sacred artist with as much skill as this Akura elite. She'd known Underlord-level dragons who didn't put as much pressure on her spirit.

She almost drooled at the thought of what riches he must be carrying on him. He'd have a void key on him somewhere, which might even contain treasures from Akura Malice herself. Her master would be pleased with her if she could turn over something that embarrassed the Akura clan. He may even bestow his smile upon her in person.

Ekeri brought herself back to reality. She'd gotten lost in daydreams again, which was a long-time habit of hers.

Drawing one claw down the wall of dark water, she snapped her tail. Immediately, her two attendants—in their plain white robes—appeared behind her. They were only Lowgold, but their Path was designed specifically to serve leaders like her.

"Contact the Herald," she ordered. "Describe to her the situation, and tell her that the others won't be arriving. The portal has been destroyed. I request permission to begin immediately."

The two attendants bowed, but before they could do anything, Ekeri's world softened to white.

"Ekerinatoth of the gold bloodline," a smooth, overwhelming voice echoed in her very soul.

This was not the voice of a Herald.

She fell to her knees in awe, tears hot on her face to hear her name spoken in this voice. *"I see you,"* he said. *"I am with you. You may begin."*

Ekeri took the time for one last bow, wriggling in the sand to show her deference, and then shot off into the water.

She did not dare to delay the orders of the Monarch of Dragons even a second longer.

Akura Harmony breathed darkness.

This habitat was bright, but endless night pressed in from all directions outside. With concentration, he could filter shadow aura from the water outside and draw it into himself, purifying and refining the shadow in his core.

He was at the peak of Truegold, only a small step from Underlord. His soulspace was filled, and a spark of soulfire waited at the heart of his soul. This sort of ordinary cycling would do very little for him until he broke through to the Lord realm.

But Harmony was not a man who skipped steps. If he had to wait, he would cycle. When he had a moment free, he would train. When he finished training, he would train some more.

There were others of his relatives that were closer to becoming Akura Malice's heir than he was, but they were generations older than Harmony. And they might decide to ascend, to wherever it was that Sages and Heralds went instead of staying and becoming Monarchs.

Harmony intended to face that choice himself one day. And to get there, he couldn't waste a single breath.

These others had disrupted him with their noise, so he had struck out at them. That was as far as he allowed them to occupy his attention. He hadn't even bothered to reach out his spiritual perception and scan them; it would be too much of a distraction from his cycling.

His grand-aunt's voice echoed inside him, though it sounded younger than his own.

"Begin," the Sage of the Silver Heart ordered him.

Without a second's hesitation, Harmony opened his eyes and stood, marching into the darkness. Even Ziel of the Wasteland had departed already, so he was the last to leave. That did not bother him.

Only the Akura family knew about the true prize at the heart of Ghostwater. While he feasted, the others would fight over scraps.

He had no rivals here.

Eithan kept his smile on for the Imperial clerk, trying not to show the woman his irritation.

"I don't want to inconvenience His Imperial Majesty, of course," he said. "That's why I'm doing it this way. He requested that I not show up in his chambers anymore without an audience, so I'm requesting an audience."

The clerk sniffed. A Truegold woman of seventy, she reminded him of a taller Fisher Gesha; her gray hair was pulled up into a bun, and she looked like she was strict on her grandchildren.

She sat behind a desk in the Imperial palace in Blackflame City, inside an unassuming office that would have looked more at home in one of the Arelius family's administrative centers. As an Underlord, he was allowed into the palace uninvited, but he was still supposed to request an audience with the Emperor.

He had expected this part of the process to be simple.

"During this time of emergency, all Underlords are expected to contribute to the defense of the Empire. The Emperor will not see any Underlords unless they have information contributing to the emergency effort, or unless they represent the interests of a major family or clan." She looked him up and down. "You are no longer the Patriarch of the Arelius family, so you do not have the standing to make such a request."

Eithan had known this would cause him no end of trouble. Cassias and his father had taken the title of Patriarch away from him in order to bring him to heel. When the threat of Redmoon Hall was behind them, he would have to make his irritation *abundantly* clear.

He calmed himself, focusing on the cycle of his madra. "Ah, I see the confusion. I have information that is vital to the fight against Redmoon Hall. But it is very sensitive. I'm afraid I can only speak to the Emperor himself."

She narrowed her eyes. "She said you'd say that."

He could have asked who she meant, but he had a good guess. Eithan turned, calling out to the hallway. "By *she*, I'm guessing she means you."

There was a moment of hesitation as Naru Saeya struggled with herself in the hall. After a few seconds, she straightened her spine and walked straight up to the door.

The Emperor's younger sister was a famous beauty, and she bristled with barely contained energy. Her wings were folded behind her back, and she wore a fan of peacock feathers over one ear.

Saeya marched up to Eithan without another moment of hesitation. "If you really have information, you can give it to me. I'll take it to His Imperial Majesty."

He gave her a deep bow, complete with a flourish of his outer robe. "Your generosity moves my spirit, but I'm afraid I can speak only to your brother."

She pushed the heel of her hand against her forehead as though struggling with a headache. "I've been in the city for no more than a day, and I'm back out to the battlefield tomorrow. While I've been here, I've dealt with emergency requests from every sect, school, and family in the Empire. My patience is long dead. If you don't want me to kick you from here to the Trackless Sea, then tell me what you want."

"I want a spot in the Skysworn," he said immediately. "I have two promising students that I believe can become Underlords for our Empire, and I'm hoping to scoop up a third. They're gaining some experience as part of the Skysworn, but I have to be there to guide them personally."

She lowered her hand, giving him a puzzled look. "You'll never take my uncle's place."

"Surely the Skysworn could use a second Underlord who isn't in command. Especially now."

Saeya chewed on that for a moment. She started to turn, then she shook her head, then she threw up her hands, then she folded them again. It was like watching two women have a debate in one body.

In the end, she gave a frustrated sigh. "Fine, listen. Here's what I'll do. After you help me hunt down the last Underlord emissaries, I'll get you in to see my brother."

"Or I could slip in there myself," Eithan countered.

"You're fighting one way or the other. You know he's just going to tell you to get back out there. Do it, make yourself look good, and he'll listen to you."

That made some sense. It was a large part of the reason why he'd tried to get an audience instead of popping up in the Emperor's home; he needed to stay on Naru Huan's good side.

Eithan turned and saluted the Imperial clerk with both fists pressed together. "Excuse me, madam. It seems that I will no longer need your assistance."

She sniffed at him and turned back to her work.

He gestured for Naru Saeya to lead the way out; not only was it polite, but he couldn't push past her without shoving her wings out of the way.

"We'll be taking the fight to them," Saeya said eagerly, wings trembling. "We might be able to rid ourselves of them for good."

That reminded Eithan of an idea he'd been toying with for the last few weeks. His smile widened. "I would like to make a quick stop first."

CHAPTER FOUR

Lindon burst through the next bubble, shivering and gasping for air. Spots of color blinded him as his lungs heaved. Another second, and he would have been breathing water.

Little Blue trembled on his shoulder. There were *things* in the water. Long, serpentine creatures with patches of glowing blue running down their sides. He had thought they were schools of fish from far away.

At least no one had followed them. He'd kept his perception behind him the whole way, and he hadn't sensed anyone behind him. No one except those massive spotted serpents. He shuddered again.

Now his Blackflame core was all but useless, and his madra channels felt like sunburned skin that he had rubbed with sandpaper. He desperately wanted Little Blue to soothe him, but when she raised a hand to try, he stopped her.

She was weak, and her powers were needed elsewhere.

Orthos had stumbled out of the water after him, the light spilling from his cracked shell dim and weak. The instant he emerged onto dry land, his eyes rolled up into his skull and he collapsed.

Lindon dropped his box, carrying the Sylvan Riverseed over to him. She touched him, sending her soothing power into his channels; Lindon felt it through his connection to Orthos. He couldn't tell if it made a difference.

Limbs and spirit trembling with exhaustion, Lindon took his first look around at their new bubble. It didn't take him long.

All he could see was a forest of tall, drifting grass. He called it "grass" because he imagined this was what grass would look like if he were the size of an ant. Each blade was dark green and rose to the height of a tree. They swayed in an invisible ocean current, as though they were still submerged in water. There was plenty of room between each stalk, so Lindon could see some distance away, but all he saw were more plants.

Compared to the entrance, this place was dim and shadowed. Most of the light came from yellow discs rising in bunches from the sand. He thought they were scripted runelights at first, but upon closer inspection they looked more like naturally glowing plants. Surrounded by tree-sized stalks, the illumination cast a maze of drifting, dancing shadows.

A blue glow passed over the sand like a brief flash of starlight, and Lindon looked up. In the dark water overhead, a train of blue lights slid lazily past. It looked like a serpent constellation come to life, and Lindon shuddered, scooting farther from the wall of water. If the bubble hadn't stopped him from entering, he had no reason to think it would stop one of these massive snakes.

Little Blue chimed in his ear from her spot on his shoulder, and he turned to Orthos. His spirit was still weak, his breathing unsteady. Before anything else, he needed to get Orthos some help.

He had to cycle pure madra to his limbs just for the strength to stand up, and his Bloodforged Iron body was hard at work repairing scrapes and bruises he never knew he had. He had the Eye of the Deep, so he just needed to find a door. Behind that door would be something that could help him. He didn't know what exactly that would be, but he had to believe it.

The forest of sand and waving sea-grass didn't suggest any direction, but it stood to reason that any exit would be against a wall. If it turns out there was no wall, and he was trapped in a bubble at the bottom of an endless ocean world...well, then he would have to wait for the others to find a way to save him. Yerin, at least, wouldn't leave him here.

As long as there *was* a way for them to find him, with the portal destroyed and the key on this side. That was the sticking point.

Lindon set off walking away from the wall of water, carrying his boxed possessions in his arm of flesh. He didn't have the madra to spare to run it through his Remnant arm and prevent it from passing through the box, so he just carried it one-handed.

Lindon was counting on his footprints in the sand to lead him back to Orthos. He would prefer to take the sacred turtle with him, but Orthos' bulk made that easier said than done. He had to scout the way first, and just hope that Orthos could hang on until he made it back.

Dread and panic pushed in like darkness outside the bubble, but he pushed it aside and reached into his box for the Eye of the Deep.

The round, cut gem was slightly larger than his fist. It felt warm in his hand, although that could have just been in contrast to the icy chill of the water outside. He glanced from side to side as he walked, trying not to miss any movement in the drifting shadows of the sea-stalks, but a thread of his madra plunged into the sapphire.

The crack in the sapphire leaked another breath of dissipating madra. The internal construct was damaged. He needed to seal the breach in the sapphire or transfer the construct before it lost structure entirely; every puff of escaping madra was another piece of the construct lost. It would dissolve eventually, but it would be useless to him long before that.

This time, the construct activated. A spiritual tug pulled his attention in one direction, where a spark of blue light only he could see hovered over the stalks. He wasn't sure exactly *what* the construct was showing him—he wasn't trained in the use of this construct, so he could be headed for an exit, a broom closet, or anything in between.

But it was something. He returned the Eye to the box and trudged on.

Lindon marched with eyes open and senses stretched. He kept his spiritual perception light and close, to avoid accidentally brushing across any enemies, but he couldn't march forward blind. The air smelled like fish and salt water with a few hints of flowers, as though he trucked through a seaside garden.

There were no prints on the sand besides his. He hoped he was alone down here; Ghostwater was supposed to have been abandoned until recently, after all.

A sudden, harsh noise echoed in the distance, like a whispered scream.

He froze, weighing the risk of extending his spiritual perception. Whatever it was, it wasn't close, so he cautiously took another step forward.

Blue light flowed around the shadow of a nearby stalk.

He expected another of those luminous serpents in the dark water overhead, but his spiritual senses screamed a warning and his eyes snapped up.

From behind the nearest blade of grass emerged a fish the size of a bear. It swam through the air as though through water, and its fanged mouth couldn't close fully over its needle-sharp teeth.

A quick flash of his Copper sight showed him blue-green aura gathered into a cushion beneath its fins.

It was swimming through water *aura.*

The fish's silver scales rippled as it swam by only two feet from Lindon's head. His scalp tensed at the discomfort of having those teeth so close, but the creature gave no sign that it had seen or sensed him. It drifted along, vanishing into the towering grass.

Back in the direction Lindon had come from.

Carefully, with no idea whether these things even had ears, Lindon turned and crept after it. He hated to be the kind of idiot who would follow a tiger back into the jungle, and he was haunted by images of the fish flashing out from behind a stalk in front of him with jaws open, but it might be headed for Orthos.

After a moment, that harsh shriek came again, but it was much closer this time. It stabbed his ears, followed by a shuffling sound like something digging through sand.

Lindon ran.

He hadn't traveled far; it only took him a few seconds to retrace his footsteps to the gap in the stalks where he'd left Orthos.

The fish was eating him. It had the turtle's shell in its massive fangs, and was working itself back and forth, trying to chew through the hard plate. Orthos' body shook like a rag seized by a dog, spraying sand everywhere. The fish wasn't getting anywhere with the shell, but it quickly bit another spot, and Orthos' body turned a little more. Getting that much closer to exposing his underbelly.

The last of his Blackflame madra raged through Lindon's channels.

His power gathered in his palm of flesh, a ball of dark, liquid fire. It would take a breath or two to condense enough that he could use it as a Striker technique, but as soon as Lindon began gathering power, the fish released Orthos. It spun around, baring its fangs and hissing at him.

Then, with an abrupt silver flash, it struck.

Lindon couldn't split his concentration to ignite the Burning Cloak, but his right hand came up without his order. The skeletal, bone-white arm flew up eagerly, seizing the creature.

Slightly pointed nails met the creature's scales and clawed for a grip. Madra flowed through the sacred beast, so his Remnant arm could seize it easily, but it wasn't satisfied with only a handful.

His arm held the fish in place for an instant, dragging it

to a halt, though the force of its resistance dragged Lindon through the sand. He almost lost his hold on the dragon's breath technique, but he didn't have the mental energy to wrestle his arm for control.

At last, black fire lanced out from his left hand. The bar of dark flame speared the fish through the middle, burning it from the inside out, and emerged from the fish's tail in a spray of smoke and burning chunks.

The madra continued at an upward slant, eventually hitting the water overhead and vanishing. His right hand drew on the handful of madra like a mosquito drawing blood, and it seemed to grow a little brighter. A brief impression of sated hunger passed through his spirit as the madra dissolved to essence.

A chorus of shrieks, identical to the one the fish had let out, rose in the distance.

Drawing from his pure core, which still shone bright as the moon in his spirit, he funneled power through his body and tucked the box under his left arm. Madra flowed through his replacement arm as well, and he seized the underside of Orthos' shell in his white grip.

Box under his arm, Little Blue on his shoulder, Lindon dragged Orthos forward step by step.

Silver-blue light rose behind him, casting more waving shadows as he passed through the stalks, but he concentrated on pushing ahead. He didn't have a hand to spare to pull out the Eye of the Deep, but the general direction was straight away from the wall where he'd entered.

Which was perfect, because a sacred fish's Remnant was rising back there.

He pushed himself faster, though it felt like his knees would buckle with every step. This was where he needed the Burning Cloak, but not only had he totally exhausted his Path of Black Flame, his madra channels were at risk of serious injury if he kept straining them. Pure madra was far easier on the channels than Blackflame was.

He needed Little Blue's help to recover. Better yet, he

needed a spiritual healing elixir, a few good meals, and three days of rest.

More fish, identical to the first, darted out of the forest of stalks. The Remnant was nowhere to be seen, but the others circled him curiously one time. Then, with the single-minded unity of a school, they all turned to Lindon.

He extended his spiritual perception over them. The fish felt like furious whirlpools, and the Remnant like a raging river. But there was something else moving toward him, something that emerged from the darkness like dawn breaking.

Before the fish struck at him, a golden whip emerged and struck it on the scales, leaving a scorch-mark on silver.

Deafening shrieks rose once more, and the three fish turned in a fury on the source of that heat. Lindon didn't stay to watch the sacred beasts fight the dragon-girl; as soon as they moved to attack, he hauled Orthos away.

He'd never developed a full-body Enforcer technique for his Path of Twin Stars, so he had no way to efficiently cycle it to his limbs for strength. He was wasting madra like this, but without the power of his spirit, he would never have been able to haul Orthos' weight. Sweat beaded on his forehead, his elbow trembled where it met the white of his Remnant arm, and every breath was a labor.

Still, he pushed himself faster. She had chased him. He was certain she hadn't followed him immediately after he left, because she hadn't bothered to veil her spirit. He would have felt her approach.

Which meant she had waited before chasing him. Why? He wasn't sure why she cared to chase him at all, but if she did, why give him a head start? Fair play?

Her voice rose to match the shrieking fish, shouting insults at them and promising punishment for their insolence. She had started mocking a group of fish.

Well, considering that they gave off the same pressure as a Highgold and they were undoubtedly sacred beasts, maybe they were intelligent enough to understand her. Regardless, he could only hope they stalled her long enough for him to reach his destination.

And that this destination would actually save him.

Every step in the sand cost him another fraction of his pure madra, and Orthos' presence in his mind was a constant, dark well of weakness and suffering. Every time Lindon pulled on his shell, he worried that he would soon be pulling a corpse.

But his exhaustion didn't leave him much room to worry about others. Soon, his vision had narrowed to nothing but that point on the horizon, and his mind was filled with nothing but the next step.

He almost didn't realize when he arrived.

A huge shadow washed over him, and he jerked his sight up, certain for a moment that a fish was descending on him from overhead.

A rocky tower rose from the sand, slightly taller than the waving weeds all around. Wearily, Lindon dropped the box in his left hand and the giant turtle in his right. He fumbled for the latch, but his white hand passed right through it again. This time, he focused, cycling pure madra through his hand and flipping the box open.

After another moment of exhausted flailing, he came up with the fist-sized sapphire. When he poured another trickle of madra into it, he realized exactly how low he was; the construct drew out fully half of the power he had remaining.

It pointed him to the base of the stone tower.

Though he called it a tower, it looked natural, like a rough pillar that had been left standing after a river eroded the rest of a cliff over centuries. Only one aspect of its construction seemed artificial: a bowl-sized scoop out of the rock surrounded by delicate lines and barely perceptible script.

The Eye of the Deep showed him a blue light hovering over that indentation. It took a moment for his exhausted thoughts to click together, but once they did, he recognized the bowl for what it was: a keyhole.

Lindon stumbled forward, dropped to his knees, and pushed the sapphire inside.

With a sound like milk slurped through a straw, the rock melted. Even the keyhole disappeared, leaving him holding the Eye and staring into a dark tunnel.

Dry wind whispered out, carrying the scent of dust... and a hint of coppery blood and something sickly sweet, like a whiff of garbage. The tunnel extended down, beneath the level of the sand outside, and the walls were covered in long scratches. Another keyhole rested in the tunnel wall to the right.

The wind from the tunnel whistled, and Lindon realized that he could no longer hear the fish shrieking.

A bland, unremarkable-looking man in pressed white appeared out of nowhere to Lindon's right, hands folded behind his back. He looked down on Lindon and spoke in a quiet voice.

"Shall I detain him?"

With the last of his madra, Lindon pushed Orthos down into the tunnel. He could barely fit, and he slid a few feet down the smooth, sloped floor before coming to a halt. His consciousness didn't flicker.

"I think we have a moment to bargain," the golden dragon-girl said airily, stepping from among the stalks. A disc of shining gold liquid floated behind her head like a halo, she held a whip of the same madra in one hand, and her footsteps hissed on the sand. Some sort of Enforcer technique, he was certain.

There were long, pale scratches across her golden scales. The fish must have tried to bite her, but failed to penetrate her hide.

She pointed with one claw to the jewel. "Give that to me, and you may live. Give me your box without complaint, and you may follow me as my attendant until I withdraw."

Lindon tucked the box under his left arm and gripped the Eye of the Deep in his right. He had to hope his Remnant arm didn't decide to disobey him now. "I apologize, honored lady. Perhaps once I have had a night's sleep."

Then he jumped backward, slamming the Eye into the keyhole on the wall.

As he'd hoped, the wall reformed immediately.

But not before gold madra sprayed into the tunnel, filling it with burning heat. He flinched back, but then the wall finished forming, blocking the rest of her attack.

All sound cut off.

He turned back to the tunnel, with the only light coming from the dim red glow of Orthos' shell. He fell to the ground, catching his breath, letting the box slide down the slanting floor until it came to a rest against Orthos' side.

He crawled over to it, leaning against Orthos' leg. If he touched the wrong part of the sacred beast's shell, his hair might catch on fire. Orthos could control that while he was awake, but not sleeping.

Propped against the turtle's leathery skin, he looked into Little Blue's face. She seemed concerned, reaching for his forehead.

"Just need a minute," he said. "Just a minute." He leaned back, breathing heavily, trying to soothe his spirit.

He didn't notice when he slipped into sleep.

第五章

CHAPTER FIVE

Lindon woke some time later to a bright light glaring into his eyes.

He shot up, sending shocks of pain shooting through his joints. His breath came in uneven, painful gasps, but he pushed it into rhythm so his madra would *move.*

They're coming for me, he thought. *I can't be here. I have to run.* He felt another spike of panic. *Where's Yerin?*

He spun, an Empty Palm gathering in his left hand. Over Orthos' bulk, he could see nothing but a sloping hallway lit in blue, long scratches leading down the wall. He turned back the other way: an empty stone wall. His ragged breathing echoed in the tight hallway.

When his mind woke up, he remembered where he was. Alone, trapped in a Monarch's pocket world.

Slowly, he let the aches in his body drag him back down. His throat was dry and painful, his ribs bruised, his back aching. He covered his eyes with trembling fingers and looked between them at the ceiling.

The circle of runes glowed blue, bathing them in a watery light. He should stand up and check out his surroundings. He could sense that Orthos was still alive, but still unconscious and weak. They could all still be in danger.

Breathe. He had to keep his madra under control.

As a matter of habit, he focused on the Heaven and Earth Purification Wheel cycling technique. It dug at his spirit like he was trying to drill a hole in his own heart, and it felt like metal bands were tightening around his lungs, but it gave him something steady to focus on.

He inhaled and exhaled in revolution after revolution until he could make himself believe that the fight was over. The enemies were gone.

Now that he had a moment to think, the memories closed over him like the icy cold ocean of Ghostwater.

Yerin's scarred face as she tried to reach the portal to save him.

Renfei, poised to speak, as a red line grew down from the top of her head.

His Thousand-Mile Cloud dissipating to mist.

The two halves of Little Blue's habitat lying in the sand.

Renfei's death hit him harder than he'd expected. He hadn't known her well, trusted her, or particularly liked her. But seeing her killed in front of him, so casually...so easily...

She was a Truegold in full armor, and she went from alive to dead in a moment. She didn't deserve that.

And that could have been him, just as easily. More so.

Then there was Yerin.

What was happening to her on the outside? It couldn't be worse than what was happening in here, so at least she'd been spared that, but he couldn't help but run through the possibilities. Without Renfei, Bai Rou could have decided he'd be better off without his apprentices. Mercy and Yerin wouldn't be a match for him, even together; Mercy was only a Lowgold. He could kill them both and say they'd all died with Renfei, and Eithan was the only one who would ask any questions.

Ever since losing his arm, he would sometimes wake up and forget. He'd try to reach for something and see the skeletal stretch of white madra and the sight would strike him as wrong. That wasn't *his* arm. It would take his brain a moment to piece together the truth.

Separating from Yerin felt the same. Looking down the hallway without seeing her was like glancing down and seeing his arm missing.

A worried chirp shook him out of his cycling trance, and he pulled his hand away from his face. He was surprised to discover his fingers were damp, and hurriedly swiped at his eyes. His father would have given him a lecture for crying in public. There was no one here to see, but it was hard to shake the old fear that he'd be caught in a shameful position.

Little Blue was barely visible against the ground, looking up at him in the azure light. She was pale and thinly spread; he could see right through her.

Only then did he realize that his soul felt much better. He still had almost nothing in either core, but his channels had been scrubbed and cleansed. While he wouldn't want to fight, at least he wouldn't risk permanent spiritual injury with a single Empty Palm.

Carefully, Lindon lowered himself back down to the floor and held out his palm to Little Blue. "Gratitude," he said, as she clambered up to his wrist.

She'd done what she could for him. And Orthos would not recover on his own.

Yerin might not be with him, but he wasn't alone. These two needed his help.

"Are you hungry?" he asked softly. The Sylvan Riverseed let out a long, slow tone that sounded like a flute.

"I'll find us something," Lindon said, glancing over at Orthos. "This place was built by a Monarch. There are treasures in here we can't imagine."

His voice echoed back to him in the corridor.

He picked up the Eye, but pouring madra into it didn't do anything useful. It only pointed him to distant locations; too far away to be any help. Still, he carried it with him just in case. The rest of his belongings stayed with Orthos.

He felt naked without the pack on his back, but the

almost imperceptible weight of Little Blue on his shoulder gave him comfort.

Together, they walked down the sloping hallway.

Very quickly, he discovered that the corridor was not empty. There were keyholes like the one at the entrance every few yards. His first few discoveries were causes for excitement; if these were all exits, then he would be able to leave without risking an encounter with the dragon-girl or the fanged fish.

Excitement gave way to disappointment every time. The first time the wall melted away around his gemstone, it revealed a closet packed with buckets. Many of the metal buckets were rusted through, the wooden ones rotted away. There was a puddle of something that smelled metallic in one corner.

The next door was empty except for a pile of shredded and half-burned paper.

The next was a broad storage room with hooks dangling from the ceiling. That was all; just empty hooks.

The fourth contained bedframes. No beds, only frames.

He found a food closet with all the packages torn open, their contents devoured. There was a massive, empty warehouse that looked like it was sized to hold whole ships. But no matter how he explored it, he found no other exit.

He'd been exploring for what he guessed to be an hour by the time he spotted the end of the hall. It had stopped sloping downward long before, so now it was just a straight hallway with a flat wall at the end.

It was distant enough that he guessed there were sixteen more doors between him and the end. He had been trying to visit every door in order, so that he could easily keep track of which ones he'd checked and hadn't, but so far he'd found only garbage and rot.

By this point, his thirst weighed on every thought, his stomach growled, and even this short walk had left his legs soft and trembling. If he couldn't find anything in these rooms, he'd have to return to Orthos and go out the front door. If the gold dragon-girl was still waiting for them... well, he'd have to risk that.

With time pressing on him, he skipped the last rows of doors and moved right to the one at the end of the hall. If there was any one door that might have something in it, this would be the one.

He opened the door, and purple light radiated out, clashing with the endless blue.

The light in the room came from a knee-high well of worked stone, which overflowed with some glowing purple liquid. It spilled over the edges, pooling on the floor, trickling away into grates. As Lindon watched, a single drop of the purple liquid fell from overhead and landed in the pool with an audible plop.

The room wasn't large, perhaps ten paces to a side, with floor-to-ceiling shelves against each of the three walls. All of the shelves were packed with piles of...junk.

There was a chaos in the air that he felt in his spirit, a mix of brief impressions with conflicting purposes. Random light flashed from one junk-pile or another, giving off colored sparks.

As he moved closer, he saw that some of the piles were metal, others wood. Still others were smooth and thin, as though made out of eggshell. Most of the surfaces had script-circles inscribed in them: mostly to contain madra, but others for a dozen other functions. Only when he turned one over and exposed a last trickle of madra fading to essence did he realize what he was looking at.

Constructs. This was the storage room for constructs.

Their spirits had all faded away over the years since Ghostwater had been closed, except for a few bits of madra preserved by scripts. The fully spiritual constructs would have vanished entirely, leaving only the physical vessels of those bound to some material.

Excitement warred with disappointment. He felt like he should be looking at shelves of treasure, the key to his escape from Ghostwater...but realistically, it had been too long. Some functions of these constructs might be intact, but they wouldn't last long and probably would accomplish nothing like their intended function.

As though to prove it to himself, he flipped over one of the most complete constructs, in which he could sense flickers of madra that reminded him of the Path of the White Fox. With a tendril of pure madra, he activated its script.

"...first success of its kind," a cold, flat voice emerged from the construct. "There were thirty-one other elixirs refined in the Life Well habitat. Which one would you like to see?"

A beam of light emerged as though to project an illusion in light, but it showed only a meaningless jumble of images.

Lindon grabbed the somewhat functioning construct—if nothing else, he could perhaps learn from its construction—and turned instead to the well.

The liquid inside, which he was careful to avoid with his shoes, was not opaque, as he had first imagined. It was clear water, tinted purple, and it radiated a spiritual sense of focus and determination. Every minute or so, another droplet fell from the ceiling into the pool, which had overflowed over the years and ran down the sides, draining into grates in the floor.

A few dark blobs at the bottom of the pool told him that some pieces of a construct must have fallen from the high shelf overhead. Bracing himself, he opened his Copper sight. The well was a dense concentration of shifting violet images that he associated with dream aura, though it had an equal concentration of blue-green water aura. The two powers flowed harmoniously, and from what he could tell, the water aura might even be stronger.

He closed his sight, thinking. Was this involved in the Soulsmithing process for these constructs, somehow? The one he had examined definitely had a dream aspect to it.

"Oh, don't worry about the water," a bright male voice echoed through the room. "It's just water." Lindon wasn't startled by the sudden noise—one of the constructs must have activated because of his presence.

"At least, chemically," the voice went on. "I know it's glowing and purple, and it would be very reasonable to think 'I will not drink this, because it will melt my insides,' but I promise you, it will not melt your insides. Not quickly, at any rate. Technically, everything erodes your insides slowly, doesn't it? Worth thinking about."

None of the constructs on the shelves were giving off any lights, so Lindon examined the one in his hand. Still dark.

The voice piped up again. "You should give it a drink. The master used to reward workers with a sip from the Dream Well when they had pleased him. Or when they, uh, needed to complete a project and didn't have time for sleep. Or when they had angered him, and he wanted them to be fully aware of the punishment. Total focus, that's what it gives you."

Lindon turned his attention to the well.

A cracked and rusted metal ball sat at the bottom of the liquid, in the middle of the other garbage he had dismissed earlier. With every word, light flashed from the cracks in the iron.

Lindon rummaged on a nearby shelf until he came up with a couple of arm-length rods that had once been part of a mechanical construct.

"You're ignoring me, that's what you're doing. A bit rude, isn't it? I mean, don't you think? First person I've spoken to in...however long I've been down here, and I was hoping for a better conversationalist. How long *have* I been down here, do you think?"

Using the two rods, Lindon seized the metal ball and carefully raised it out of the pool.

"Oh! Wait, what are you doing! Careful, there! Careful! If you drop me, I will take...revenge...on you. Such sweet revenge, like...hitting all your...toenails."

Lindon lowered the flashing ball to the ground. Now that it was out of the well, he could see that the light coming from the construct was the same purple shade. Now, had the liquid taken on that color because of the construct, or vice-versa?

"Oh wow, I can see so much more from out here. Thank you, giant stranger. Giant...glaring stranger. Are you angry at me, or do you scowl at everyone you meet?"

Lindon almost dropped the ball. "...are you talking to me?"

Everything else had *sounded* like a conversation, sure. But constructs only said what you told them to say. All of those responses had been recorded illusions, scripted to be played under the proper conditions.

The ball shifted in his hands, as though looking around for other people. "Nobody else in here has much to say, really. Although I suppose I was like that before, too, wasn't I? That's embarrassing."

Lindon had to ask something that couldn't possibly be a predetermined response. "What is your favorite flavor of pie?"

"...I'm not a pie-construct, am I? What I know about pie could fill a...a little...the tiny scoop you use to eat soup."

"A spoon?"

"No, that can't be right. That's ridiculous. *Spoon.* Get out of here with your nonsense words."

Lindon knelt down next to the construct on the ground, staring intently through the cracks in the metal, aching to pick it up but still afraid of touching the purple liquid. "Are you a Remnant that they bound like a construct?"

"I am the Keeper of the Dream Well!" the construct intoned from within its rusty shell. "I was built right here. Well, not *right* here in this room, obviously, but down the hall a little. A guide-construct, that was me, made to give people the rules of the Dream Well. 'Congratulations, favored servant! You have been chosen to drink from the Dream Well, so that your labor might serve the great work!' That sort of thing. That's why I have such a pleasant voice."

"But you're...thinking," Lindon said, still peering into the construct. In the purple sparks making up the construct's true body, he saw what looked like the spokes of a slowly turning wheel.

"That's a relatively new development. Some time after I fell in the well, I realized I could put words together in new combinations. Then I realized I'd realized it, and that was the beginning for me, wasn't it? The 'realization cascade,' that's what I call it! I don't call it that."

Incredible. Was it only long exposure to this Dream Well that brought the construct to life, or did this reflect the advanced craft of a Soulsmith skilled beyond his imagination?

"Do you have a name?" Lindon braced himself and seized the rusted construct, cycling madra to resist the effects of whatever the dream-water did.

Nothing. It felt like ordinary wet metal against his fingertips.

"Before landing in the well, I was basically a big ball of memories with the ability to produce sound, so I didn't have much in the way of casual conversation. But they did *call* me things, let me see if I can remember...garbage, that was a common one. Defect. Junk. Chaff. Waste. By-product of a failed experiment. Failure, that was another favorite. Dregs. Slag. Scum. Refuse. Dross. These aren't very flattering, are they?"

"Pleased to meet you, Dross," Lindon said, dipping his head slightly to the construct. "I am Wei Shi Lindon."

"Oh, you have a name too! That's exciting. This is the first real conversation I've ever had. And I am *loving* it, by the way. Less...intellectually stimulating than I had imagined. I was picturing myself debating with great minds, you know, but this is still exciting! I'm still excited to be talking with...you."

"Forgiveness, but a minute ago you didn't know what a spoon was."

"Yes, but I know how to say 'intellectually stimulating' and 'refuse.' Let's call it a tie."

Lindon nodded to the glowing purple water. "You changed after falling in the well?"

"It's designed to boost focus and eliminate mental fatigue in humans," Dross said. "One sip, and you'll be able to work all night at peak efficiency! That was part of my pitch for the water, back in my prime."

Lindon moved a little closer to the pool. "Well then, I think I might try a taste." There were elixirs that refined the mind, and they were expensive.

"If anything, it will make you more alert and focused. Might even make you smarter, which ah...no offense, but...I mean, you should just take a drink. Let's leave it at that. Vials are over there on the shelf to your right."

Lindon found a rack of thumb-sized metal vials, capped in a substance that felt like wax. He pulled off the cap and dipped it into the well; a small amount splashed on his thumb, but it still felt like normal water.

He still had his misgivings about drinking a strange purple liquid, but he felt nothing sinister from the well. And it was obviously here for a reason; to water the workers made sense. If others had drunk from this, he could as well.

Also, the thirst was starting to get painful.

He tipped his head back and swallowed the mouthful of water from the flask. He expected a stronger flavor, somehow, or some rush of power, but it was just water. It had the mineral taste of spring-water.

An instant later, the effects kicked in.

His thoughts sharpened. The mental haze of exhaustion was swept away. The world around him was clear, like his eyes had been cleaned out, and he took a breath of air like it was his first.

Little Blue scurried up his back and onto his head, leaning over to give him a pat on the forehead.

"I told you," the construct said. "Invigorating power to keep those motivated movers moving and those tired thinkers thinking. That was one of the mottos I was working on for the Dream Well, what do you think?"

"It's like a full night's sleep in a bottle," Lindon said, staring into the empty vial.

"Oh, that's a good motto for the well. I'll use that. The water also helps you focus when you're distracted, approach complex problems with new inspiration, or you can freeze it into little bits of ice and use it to make an ordinary drink glow purple."

Lindon filled the vial.

"Now, it is *incredibly* valuable. I'll have to check and see if you have authorization to take a second...oh, you're drinking it. You're already drinking it."

The second draught didn't seem to have much effect. It was mostly like taking a refreshing drink of ordinary water.

"I didn't get much from that. How long before it will have the same effect again?"

"However long it takes a human to get tired, I guess. When you're already focused and alert, I'm not sure what else it could possibly do for you. That's a thousand high-grade scales per dose, by the way. In case you were wondering."

There was a whole shelf of similar vials, and Lindon was already filling them. When he looked at the purple rivulets on the floor, it physically pained him to imagine how much of this precious elixir had been wasted down drainage grates over the years.

"Has no one else been down here?" He couldn't imagine that other sacred artists would leave a treasure like this alone.

"I'm not sure, to be honest. No one's been in here since I've woken up, but it's not as though I could see much from inside the well."

Lindon stoppered a vial and grabbed the rusty ball. "You're a memory construct, aren't you?"

"You're carrying me. What's happening? This is a rush! But maybe slow it down."

Lindon took him to a shelf where a half-crushed wooden box waited. "Do you know what sort of construct this was?"

"It stored visual records from the rest of the facility. Most of these did, actually."

Lindon extended his spiritual perception through the box. It felt like Dross, so this should work. "Do you think you could read these fragments?" When he'd inspected the room before, none of the constructs had been intact enough for him to use. Maybe Dross could get something out of them.

"I'm not, ah...well, you're putting me on the spot, aren't you? I could give it a try, but I don't perform well under pressure."

There was one intact circle on the remaining half of the wood, and Lindon scratched it with his thumb. Instantly, a ribbon of half-formed images drifted up through the box in a cloud, dissipating into the air.

"Wait, we're starting? Put me over it, quick! Quick!"

When Lindon held Dross over the smoke-like memories, the construct made a gasping sound. Instead of blowing apart, the images drifted into the cracks in the construct shell.

Lindon pressed his eye against one of the cracks, fascinated. As the images soaked into the purple light that made up Dross, they merged *into* him. New lines formed in the purple cloud, and new lights sparkled inside the construct.

"Mmmmmm ah, that goes down smooth."

"Does it feel like you're eating it?" Many constructs of similar function could merge with one another, but it had never occurred to him to wonder what it might *feel* like for the construct.

"Didn't have too many memories left in that one, actually, so there was nothing too special about it. It's like when humans share blood."

"Humans don't share blood."

"They should. Anyway, I now have access to some facility history records. After Ghostwater was sealed away, some Heralds came and looted the place. They had a few sips from the well, but it didn't matter to them. They're Heralds, aren't they? Probably don't ever sleep anyway. Oh, I see it now! One of them is picking me up! Hello, me!"

He was silent for a moment, then added, "Well, that's a bit disappointing, isn't it? He tossed me into the well. Ouch. Rejection. Never feels good. I wasn't *me* back then, but even so: painful."

"When did you wake up?"

"Take me over to the one that looks like a...shelled pinching beast." Lindon carried Dross over to the crab-shaped construct he'd set aside before, and once again Dross inhaled the remainder of the construct.

Again, Lindon watched Dross' internal mechanisms grow more complex as he breathed in the dream madra.

His mother would have given five years of her life to see this.

"...fifty-six years," Dross said quietly. "That's how long I've been stuck in that well alone. Wow. Best I can tell, I've only been myself for the last five or so. That's the oldest memory I have."

Lindon looked over the shelves upon shelves of other memory constructs. "These all have information about Ghostwater?"

"Sure they did, once. This habitat was the headquarters of a project meant to design and improve memory constructs to accomplish the grand work. Never succeeded. Turns out, when they put a memory construct into your head, you just end up with a better memory."

"I'm going to want to hear more about the 'grand work,'" Lindon said, staring up at the shelves. "But first, do you have room for more?"

"I think I could grow to like you," Dross said. "You know, eventually."

Half an hour later, as they hiked back up the hallway toward Orthos, Dross sighed. "Well, that was disappointing."

Lindon carried a full rack of twenty-four filled vials in one hand, and a bucket half-full of glowing purple water in the other. He'd found the bucket in one of the abandoned maintenance closets, and the handle was even scripted so that he could carry it in his Remnant hand without having to focus madra to the fingers.

"I mean, I knew I could hold more information, but I have staggered even myself. I feel like I could swallow another whole room full of information. Did you know that a thunder eagle was a *bird?* Birds fly through the air, not through the water, I don't know if you were aware. This is a fascinating area of study. Why don't *you* fly?"

Dross' rusted metal ball was tucked into the waist of his robes, while Little Blue sat on his shell. She kept peering down through the cracks, staring at Dross' construct form, though he didn't seem to enjoy it.

"Oh, she's...she's looking in here again. That's embarrassing. Could you...I mean, if you don't mind, could you please stick to yourself? Yes, thank you. No privacy here, I tell you."

"You were telling me about the grand work," Lindon prompted, as the ground started to slope upwards.

"The grand work is the whole purpose of Ghostwater, isn't it? Northstrider built this whole pocket world to find a way to enhance his mind. You know, sharpen it up. He had all the power he could handle, so he figured the way forward was to improve his *use* of that power. Fight smarter, not harder, as they say. There were three branches of research down here. This was where the Soulsmiths tried to develop an advanced memory construct that could take over some of his mental processes. Total failure. Their memory constructs never grew to be anything more."

"That room was still full of constructs," Lindon said. He could only imagine what treasures had filled this place before; if only this facility hadn't been looted, it might have been packed to the brim with Soulsmith research materials.

"Yes, well, after the first few Heralds left, they took everything valuable with them. All the advanced memory constructs, as well as the tools and techniques for making them. After that, they decided that this pocket world was still a good place to train their disciples, so every ten years they send some Truegolds in here for training. I learned all this from those security constructs, by the way. They saw more than I would have believed. And while I was stuck in a well! The world is unfair."

When he reached Orthos, Lindon knelt and placed everything on the ground next to the wooden chest. Reaching behind him, he pulled out the Eye of the Deep, which was still slowly leaking essence from the crack in the gem.

"Aaaaahhh," Dross said, "now *that's* a vessel. Pretty to look at, and only one crack! Luxury. Hey you! You in there! Do you even know what a life you have?"

The Eye, of course, didn't respond.

"This is the key to Ghostwater, but it's losing cohesion. If you will agree, I could link you to this construct. It should help repair damage to the Eye, give you a better vessel, and expand your capabilities." Lindon hefted the gem in his hand. "Personally, I'd love to see what a self-aware construct could do with greater powers."

Dross made a thoughtful humming sound. "That's a taller hurdle than just drinking in more information, you know. I'd need to be bound to the gem just like the original construct. Once I am, though, I don't see why I couldn't show you around. Give you the tour. I'd love to see the whole place myself, to be honest. But you'd need to find a Soulsmith to perform the operation."

Lindon reached into his wooden chest and pulled out the tightly packed bundle of leather. He untied it, unrolling it on the ground. Soulsmith tools hung in pouches and from loops.

"I am a Soulsmith," he said.

Apprentice, he added, but only in his head.

"Oh, are you? Brilliant, then! Let's do this!"

CHAPTER SIX

The gates at the front of the black fortress swished open, trailing through sand. Yerin pushed herself to her feet, her empty core making her dizzy.

Bai Rou stomped up to them in his heavy armor. He stayed far enough away that Yerin couldn't reach him. Not that he needed to. She had less fight left in her than a caged rabbit.

Didn't stop her surge of hate and anger at the sight of him. If he hadn't held her back, she wouldn't be out here right now.

Mercy brushed sand from her hair and robes, moving toward the gates. She tripped in the sand, stumbling a few steps forward to the entrance.

An old, balding man in a pressed purple uniform scurried out. When he saw Mercy, he slowed, bowing to her with every step.

"My apologies, Mistress, my apologies."

Mercy brightened, hurrying up to him. "Old Man Lo! Do you remember me?"

Old Man Lo cringed, dropping to his knees and pressing his forehead to the beach. "I cannot apologize humbly enough, but I am forbidden from answering any of your questions. I can't be sure what answers might be considered...aiding you."

The cheer on Mercy's face faded. She looked down. "Oh, that's...that's all right. Don't worry."

Lo looked like he was about to cry as he stood up. With trembling hands, he brushed himself off, eyes locked on Mercy.

But after a few deep breaths, he'd composed himself and turned to the rest of them. He dismissed Yerin with an up-and-down glance, looking to Bai Rou. "You and your attendant will answer to my mistress. Come."

Yerin jerked her head to Mercy. "Her?"

Lo acted as though she had not spoken, turning back to the still-open gates.

"Not me," Mercy said sadly. "We should go in."

She started walking, but Lo froze. "Ah...please, Mistress, forgive me. Exercise the quality for which your divine mother named you, and have mercy upon me." He was still facing away from her, which Yerin thought might be considered rude, but he was also trembling. Maybe he was too scared to see her reaction.

"I cannot allow you inside," he continued. "Giving you shelter, you see."

Mercy's face contorted for a moment. "I can't even visit?"

"The divine command was...difficult to interpret. We cannot give you assistance, but how could my mere judgment be enough to decide what *she* would consider assistance? Please spare me and wait out here."

Mercy slumped, bracing herself with her staff.

Yerin was starting to see a bigger piece of the picture. Mercy's mother, the Monarch who had fought with the Dreadgod, had kicked her out. Without the help of her family.

Seemed cruel. She'd have expected a Monarch to kill a rebellious daughter straight and true, which would be the end of it.

Bai Rou still had not moved, but finally he spoke. "Do you speak for the Akura family?"

Old Man Lo turned to give him a withering stare that plainly said he thought the Skysworn didn't have the brains to rub two sticks together. "The mistress of this castle is Akura Charity, Sage of the Silver Heart. *She* speaks for the Akura family, your empire of children, and humanity itself. Your hesitation in following her commands will be noted."

Bai Rou fell to one knee. "I apologize and hurry to obey," he rumbled.

Lo continued through the gate without a response, but as he did, a gold light grew like a second sunrise. Yerin had already drawn her sword at the feeling of a flame passing overhead, though exhausted as she was, there was little she could do.

The giant golden Thousand-Mile Cloud blocked out the sun, but glowed brightly enough that they didn't see much of a difference. A woman's voice billowed out from its surface.

"We all have questions for the intruders," the voice said. "Show some respect for our master and let us ask questions together."

Old Man Lo was so short she could see the top of his balding head, but he looked up at the cloud as though at a noisy bird bothering his meal. He spoke in a normal voice, so he was putting a lot of trust in the other person's ears. "My mistress will disclose all answers after the questioning, as she sees fit."

He continued walking and Bai Rou followed him.

"You give no consideration for the King of the Sands?" The woman sounded angry now.

"Be content with your scraps, *dragon*," Old Man Lo snapped, spitting the last word. "You can thank your grandfather that my mistress hasn't torn you from the sky already."

There was a series of roars from the cloud that were even louder than the woman's voice, and she spoke through a mouthful of anger. "I will remember this."

Lo snorted and released the veil around his spirit. For an instant, an overwhelming pressure pushed down on the spirits of all around him before he veiled himself again.

Yerin caught her breath when the pressure vanished. He was an Overlord.

The dragons clearly felt the same as she did, because the Thousand-Mile Cloud vanished more quickly than it had arrived.

Old Man Lo brushed his sleeves out and led the way into the fortress at last.

It was like the whole place was designed to give strangers a case of the shivers. The only light came from dancing blue flames caged on the walls, and the hallway leading in from the gate was drowning in shadows. Spikes hung from the ceiling, and in the darkness, it was hard to tell how far overhead they were.

She tried to extend her perception, but she might as well not have bothered. Darkness covered the halls, blinding more than just her eyes.

They wound around the fortress until Yerin lost track of the way they'd come, which she imagined was the point. After a winding journey, Lo pressed his hand to a heavy metal door that barred their way. It dispersed to fog, and he strode through.

Bai Rou and Yerin followed, staying as far away from each other as the width of the room let them. The fog carried a chill with it, and Yerin shivered.

When they were through, the door reappeared, solid as ever.

The room inside was lit by globes of frosted glass all over the walls, floor, and the ceiling many yards overhead. They cast everything in shades of gray, but it was clear that they weren't meant to be helpful to visitors.

The lights were there to show off the statues.

Stone statues the size of buildings towered over them, lined up in rows on the sides of the room. The one closest to Yerin was an ape with feet braced on the ground and arms held wide, mouth open in a vicious roar. She could have used its toe as a table.

The statue across from it showed a figure in full armor, sword in one hand and shield in the other. The sword was pitted, the shield cracked, the armor dented, and the figure's knees were bent in the process of rising. But still it raised its weapons to meet the ape.

It was a theme among all the statues in the room. Along one wall, giant sacred beasts leaping to battle. Along the other, battered human figures met them.

There were nine figures in the room. Eight complete statues and one block of stone in the sacred beast row. It stood opposite an empty pedestal.

A woman sat in front of the stone, her hair tied up and gathered in a rag, her sacred artist's robes covered in a smock. She held a chisel in one hand, sitting in a cycling position, eyes closed.

Yerin couldn't feel the force of her power, but she could see the aura around her. All the vital aura stilled like a held breath. The Sage's spiritual perception overwhelmed the block of stone, submerging it and buffeting it like the ocean's waves.

Lo held up a hand. "You will wait," he said quietly. "You will die on your feet, patiently waiting, if she requires it."

"I don't require it," said the Sage of Silver Heart, slowly coming out of her trance.

Her eyes were a deeper purple than Mercy's, and they carried a depth and an insight that reminded Yerin of her master.

But her master had looked like a man in his thirties. This woman looked like she might not be twenty yet.

She rose, gesturing to the block of stone. "What do you think this should be?"

"We would not dare to guess," Old Man Lo said.

Bai Rou dipped his head down, silent.

"A dragon," Yerin responded. "It's the one you'd expect."

Akura Charity nodded, as though she had expected as much. "Would that not be too obvious?"

Yerin looked from one statue to another. "If you don't want them obvious, don't make them so big."

"On the scale of what they represent, they are no more than figurines."

Yerin didn't follow that, so she grunted.

Purple eyes moved to Bai Rou. They waited a moment, then the Sage said, "Take him from me and question him separately. I will question her."

Lo moved in a blur, and in less than a blink, he had soundlessly moved Bai Rou out of the room and shut the door behind him. It was over so fast that it felt like a dream.

"We may release him when we learn what we need," she said. "It depends on him."

"Keep him," Yerin said.

The Sage looked at her, expressionless.

"I'm stone-serious."

Charity flipped the chisel like a coin. It flew up to the ceiling, spinning end-over-end. "We need to know what happened to the portal," she said. At the very tip of its flight, the chisel brushed softly across the stone of the ceiling. Then it fell.

"Don't have a hint myself," Yerin said.

She caught the chisel, still watching Yerin.

"We're working with the Skysworn," Yerin said. "Black-flame Empire. Something was going wrong out here, something with Ghostwater, so we came to lay eyes on it. Three of us went in." Her voice caught briefly as she added, "Three of us stayed out."

"There was a transmission from one Skysworn to the other," Charity said, flipping the chisel again.

"Multiple enemies. Told us not to run in."

"And you tried to run in anyway," the Sage said.

"...yeah."

Charity caught the chisel on one extended finger this time, perfectly balanced.

Now she was just showing off.

"I have monitored the situation on the inside," said the Sage. "I know exactly what happened in there. What I'm trying to decide is whether you are here, now, by coincidence or by design."

"Not my design," Yerin said, but what the other woman had said caught her ears. "My...fellow disciple ended up in there. I'd give two fingers and a pile of gold to hear what happened to him."

Charity flipped the chisel up and grabbed it again. "After the great Northstrider withdrew his presence and protection from Ghostwater, six of the great Heralds in the world gathered to inspect the pocket world. They represented a significant portion of the world's military power, and were they to do battle inside Ghostwater, they might have torn the world apart. So they bound their spirits to a truce.

"Once they had taken the greatest treasures, they departed, but they added one more restriction to their agreement. Every ten years, each could send a promising student to hunt for treasure themselves."

The Heralds must have cleaned the place out, but a Herald's trash might drive a dragon wild with greed.

"What about my Lowgold?"

"All the students we send are Truegold," she said, ignoring the question. "They enter at different times, but to preserve a spirit of fair play, we have them wait in the entrance until all participants have arrived."

She tapped the edge of the chisel against her arm, and for the first time, Yerin felt the sword aura around the tool. It was so condensed that it felt solid.

"The Blackflame Empire is not one of the contestants. When we realized who you were, we experts held a conference among ourselves to decide whether you should be permitted to enter."

Yerin clenched a fist to keep from putting a hand on her sword. It wouldn't help, but it would make her feel better. They had been a hair away from getting killed by a Sage, and they hadn't even known it.

"As you were too weak to be a real threat," she went on casually, "we decided to allow your entrance. At best, you may have served as training for our students. At worst, you would affect nothing, and perhaps have a few fortunate encounters of our own."

She pointed the chisel at Yerin. "So, tell me why the Lowgold destroyed the portal."

Yerin lost her breath.

"I understand *how*. The Path of Black Flame has one of the most famous variations of dragon's breath. But he clearly targeted the portal with intention. I wish to know why."

Akura Charity folded her arms and waited.

"...couldn't tell you why Lindon does half the things he does," Yerin muttered. "But I could throw out a guess or two." She wanted to ask if Charity was sure Lindon hadn't done it on accident, but the woman was a Sage. She knew.

"Sounded like he was fighting?" Yerin said, with a questioning tone.

Charity inclined her head.

"Then he could have been trying to lock the enemy inside. 'I'll take you down with me,' that sort of feeling."

The Sage waited for her second guess, but this one was harder to say.

"I couldn't swear to it, but he might have...if I had to guess...been stopping someone from...getting in."

"Stopping you," Charity said quietly.

Yerin gave her one nod.

"My grand-nephew is inside. If I thought the Blackflame Empire or the Sage of the Endless Sword were making a move to upset the balance, I would move to maintain order."

Yerin squared her shoulders, meeting the Sage's eyes. Usually no one recognized her Path, even if they recognized her master's title. Only those who had known her master.

"However, I suspect it is no more than coincidence," Charity allowed. "We were not scheduled to return to

Ghostwater for another year, but the Phoenix's rampage assures that the pocket world will not last so long. We were not supposed to be here. Anyone who intercepted our plans and then sent *you* to disrupt them would be...beyond inept."

Yerin couldn't contain her question any longer. "The Lowgold. Is he still alive?"

"The last time I checked, he was." The Sage watched her reaction, so Yerin kept it dull. "If he continues to survive, he could reap great rewards. But he will need to find a way out."

"So there *is* another way?"

"There is another entrance to Ghostwater on this island. Map." She extended one hand, and Old Man Lo appeared briefly, pressing a weathered sheet of paper into her palm before bowing and disappearing again. Yerin couldn't track his movements.

Pinching the paper between two fingers, the Sage extended it to Yerin. "This is a rough map of this island, including the second portal."

Yerin pressed both fists together and bowed to the Sage of the Silver Heart. "My thanks. You've been...so helpful." Too helpful. It was suspicious.

The Sage pointed to Yerin. "Helpful to you. *Not* to my niece."

"Ah." That eased Yerin somewhat. Whatever was going on inside the Akura family, she could take advantage of it. "One last question?"

The Sage inclined her head.

"Why are *you* here?" Yerin asked. "I'm sure your grand-nephew is a generation's star genius, but putting a Sage on guard duty is like sending a tiger to hunt rats."

A smile ghosted across Charity's face. "There is a larger competition coming. One with far more at stake than this one. I suspect we are all here for the same reason: to catch a glimpse of our opponents and stop them from stealing a march on us."

"A larger competition?"

The Sage of the Silver Heart reached out. She didn't seem to move quickly, but she had a finger on Yerin's forehead before Yerin could react. Suddenly, Yerin knew the way out as though she'd walked the path a thousand times.

"A tournament," Charity answered, and turned back to her statues.

When Yerin returned to the beach, she found Mercy sitting on a picnic blanket eating noodles from a bowl. The noodles were hot. Where had *that* come from?

Mercy scrambled up, setting her bowl aside and almost spilling it. "Yerin! I thought you might not...well, I was going to give you another hour, and then I was coming in."

Yerin didn't see a Lowgold forcing her way in anywhere that an Overlord and a Sage didn't want her, even if they didn't use direct force. "Lindon's still alive," Yerin reported.

Mercy let out a long breath. "And the others too?"

"I...didn't think about them," she admitted.

"Well, the others are stronger than he is. If he's all right, I'm sure they are too."

"She said her grand-nephew was in there. Someone you know?"

Mercy scratched her head, looking away. *"Probably*, yes. She has more than one grand-nephew, but uh...it's a good bet that she's talking about Harmony."

"Your cousin?"

"No, no, we were from entirely different branches." She twirled hair around one finger, still looking away. "He was my fiancé."

Yerin's eyebrows raised. She had hoped that Mercy might recall some little bits and pieces about her distant cousin. She hadn't thought she'd hook a shark on the first cast.

"It ended before I left the family, though," she added.

"You called it off?"

"He did. He's very competitive, and he doesn't take losing well."

That could be bad, if he saw Lindon as a competitor. But he was supposed to be a Truegold. And if the Akura chose him to represent them here, he'd be one of their best. "Losing...to *you?*"

Mercy winced. "When I was younger, I didn't hold back very well."

"Well, he wouldn't have to worry about that now. You're still a Lowgold."

She shrugged, leaning her staff against her shoulder. "Depends on the competition."

While Yerin was still thinking that through, Mercy continued. "I don't think he would even notice Lindon was there. Orthos and Renfei maybe, but only if they bothered him."

That only increased Yerin's worries. If Lindon stumbled on whatever prizes the Truegolds were searching for, he might not fight for them, but he'd try to snatch them somehow. Sure as the sun rose.

Yerin set off for the woods, marching through the sand.

"Where's Bai Rou?" Mercy asked.

Turning, Yerin glanced from side to side. "I don't see him, and I don't see anybody who cares. The Sage said there's another way into Ghostwater somewhere on this island, so I'm finding it. The Akura aren't the only ones out here."

She continued into the forest.

After another few breaths, Mercy followed.

Lightning flashed and thunder rolled, and Eithan leaned over the deck of the cloudship to watch. There was something endlessly fascinating about watching a storm *beneath* him.

Naru Saeya, the Blackflame Emperor's little sister, gripped the railing next to him. Her wings—the Goldsign of the Path of Grasping Sky—glittered like emeralds in the lightning flashes. They were smaller and sleeker than most on her Path, and she was correspondingly faster.

She shouted to be heard over the thunder. "I'm going in myself," she bellowed. "He'll die!"

"No, he won't," Eithan said, watching the lightning roll behind him.

Of course, he was also watching everything else.

He and Saeya were not the only Underlords present. Chon Ma, the top-ranked Underlord in the Blackflame Empire, did battle in the sky all around them. He was a bear of a man, and he raged like the storm, carrying a black one-handed hammer in each hand. Black clouds appeared beneath his feet with each step, so he ran through the air, another black cloud hanging over his head like a picture of dread.

He bounded in three long steps over to his opponent, pulling one weapon back. It drew dark gray Cloud Hammer madra with it, until it was shrouded in a dense fog.

The Blood Shadow raised one arm to meet the blow.

The hit cracked as loud as thunder, blasting the Shadow to liquid madra. It splattered away, losing its wings and falling through the air.

Chon Ma had overextended himself for that strike, and the Blood Shadow's host wasn't about to let that opportunity pass him by.

He was a serpentine man, tall as though he'd been stretched, wearing the black-and-red robes of Redmoon Hall. He raised a sword, so thin it was almost a needle, and gathered razor-sharp aura at its point. His strike was as swift and precise as one would expect from an Underlord, driving at Chon Ma at the exact moment he was distracted by the Blood Shadow.

But the head of the Cloud Hammer school was not the first-ranked Underlord for his beard. He continued his blow, letting the momentum spin him around, his second hammer meeting the sword-strike instantly.

Eithan was always impressed with such predictions.

Those born without the ability to see behind them certainly learned to adapt.

Both hits crashed against each other, sending the two men flying backwards. Clouds formed under Chon Ma's feet, and he stayed hovering in the air, while his opponent landed on the flat side of a flying sword.

Eithan couldn't remember the Redmoon Hall man's name. *Gergen?* he wondered. *Gergich. Gargol. It doesn't matter; I won't need to remember it for long.*

The peacock feathers that Naru Saeya wore behind her ear were sodden with the rain they'd flown through to get here, but she looked as though the heat of her fury would dry them in an instant. "Get *out* of my way."

Her wings swept back, pushing him aside, and she gathered up wind aura. As she was about to launch herself into the air, she froze. Then she spun around.

"See?" Eithan said, staring into the storm.

Saeya's senses were almost as honed as someone from the Arelius family. Her attunement to wind aura was truly impressive, and she could sense movements in the air from miles away. This storm would strengthen her Ruler techniques and aid her cycling, but it would also interfere with her senses. Ordinarily, she wouldn't have noticed so much later than he did.

"What are you saying?" she spat. "Now we're *all* going to die!"

A red Thousand-Mile Cloud rose up the side of their ship like a shark breaking the waves. He looked like he was in the middle of his twenties, his pale face framed by black hair that fell to his waist. He wore a dark, shapeless coat that covered him from shoulders to feet, and a blood-red hook dropped from one loose sleeve.

Longhook, Underlord emissary of Redmoon Hall.

Eithan's shoulder throbbed as he looked at that hook. It had been restored by the greatest healer in the Blackflame Empire, so he wondered if it was still wounded, or if it was just the shame of losing blood. He tried not to be embarrassed about taking a blow from a man named Longhook, but it was hard to restrain his shame.

When the Bleeding Phoenix vanished, the emissaries of Redmoon Hall had been caught even more off-guard than everyone else. They were deep in enemy territory, surrounded, and their master's departure left them purposeless.

Unfortunately for the citizens of the Blackflame Empire, that largely meant they killed their way through the population in whatever direction they thought led to safety.

The Emperor had whipped his Underlords into hunting them down. Except for one minor detour to pull his disciples out of a basement, Eithan had spent the past several weeks hunting emissaries. This was a huge opportunity for the Empire; they would never have another chance to deal such a blow to Redmoon Hall. The Akura clan would reward them handsomely for each Underlord head.

But their strategy was all dependent on their advantage of numbers. Each Redmoon emissary counted as two opponents, since their Blood Shadow could fight independently. So they operated in teams of three Underlords apiece.

They only had three such teams, along with one Overlord, but it had been effective so far. They had collected two Underlord heads out of a presumed six remaining in the Empire.

However, now the weakness in their plan was revealed. Instead of three-on-two in their favor, it was now four-on-three against.

Naru Saeya drew a sword of transparent, shimmering light from her soulspace. It looked like it was made of crystalline stained glass or fractured rainbows; whatever Soulsmith had made it, Eithan appreciated their aesthetic sense. "And you had to drag a Highgold into this," Saeya said. "I just hope you can fight."

"What if I couldn't?" Eithan proposed. "Boy, that would be embarrassing in this situation, wouldn't it?"

Longhook noticed him, and his lips tightened. Eithan couldn't read what that expression meant—was he excited to see Eithan, as an opponent he'd beaten before? Disappointed? Angry that he couldn't finish Eithan off last time?

Before Eithan could decide, there was a red hook rushing at his face.

Longhook's long hook was his Blood Shadow wrapped around an actual sacred weapon: a long, heavy chain with a thick meat hook at the end. It carried enough force to punch straight through their ship, and Longhook could manipulate it with shocking grace and speed. As Eithan had learned last time.

Eithan met this attack with the same strategy he'd used last time. He poured madra into his iron fabric scissors and slammed them into the hook.

He wasn't using a proper Enforcer technique, but he was using a *lot* of madra. The hook stopped, the chain rippling like a sea in storm. Eithan was pushed a few steps backward, but he took them gracefully.

And this time, Eithan wasn't alone.

Saeya swept in as a green blur, her rainbow sword flashing. Longhook's weapon coiled back of its own accord, blocking her sword, but her free hand came up and made a fist. Loops of green madra wrapped around him, locking him in place.

Eithan followed up with the simplest Striker technique anyone could use: a pulse of madra focused in a line. In his case, the pure madra passed through the chain of Longhook's weapon, weakening the Blood Shadow and causing it to falter for a second. Saeya was coming around for another pass.

So far so good. They were keeping Longhook under pressure.

Which meant...

The red on the emissary's hook oozed back, revealing dark gray metal. It boiled away as Longhook drove Saeya off with one fist, pulses of force madra pushing her back.

In an instant, he'd gathered up his Blood Shadow. His hook started to slide back up his sleeve, one link at a time, and he looked from Eithan to Naru Saeya.

"Go home," he said, the words scraping out. They were barely audible over the rolling thunder. "We are leaving your lands. You will not see us again."

"You *dare* ask us for mercy?" Naru Saeya's voice was hot. Her bright green madra took Longhook in the gut like a fist, carrying him off his Thousand-Mile Cloud and into the wind.

His Blood Shadow caught him.

It formed into his copy, standing on the railing, its hand grabbing him by the leg and pulling him back onto the ship. Longhook didn't even look surprised, his coat fluttering in the wind as he landed.

"This will be worse than last time," the emissary promised, locking eyes with Eithan.

Eithan drew himself up, cycling madra through his channels. He let his power as an Underlord blaze forth, matching Longhook face-to-face.

"It will," he declared. "Last time, I did not reveal to you my ultimate technique."

A flare of chaotic madra from below his feet was all the warning Longhook had. Eithan had scripted the veils into the cloudship's cabin himself.

Then a beam of deadly madra, thick as a barrel and bright as the sun, blasted through the cabin of the ship and washed over Longhook. The light streamed out in a bolt like condensed lightning, too bright to watch directly, streaking from the ship up into the sky. It faded out as quickly as it had emerged, the light fading to a thin line.

Longhook fell from the ship, smoking and unconscious. He would probably survive the impact with the ground, but he wouldn't be happy.

"I call it the 'ambush,'" Eithan said.

Fisher Gesha poked her head through the ragged hole in the ship's deck. She held in her hands a smoking, twisted launcher construct. It looked much like one of the simple, physical weapons some lower sects used for defense: a cannon.

"I didn't miss! Hm. I told you I wouldn't miss."

Fisher Gesha, a shrunken old woman with gray hair tied up into a bun, looked like she shouldn't even be able to hold the cannon. Spider legs stuck out from beneath her, as she stood on her drudge construct for transportation. And to reach things on high shelves.

Most Gold-level techniques couldn't do much more than scratch an Underlord's skin. But she had come up with a plan for a compound launcher construct that used six Striker bindings at once. If they were properly contained and focused, she had theorized, they could produce an effect that was greater than the sum of its parts.

Under normal circumstances, the weapon would be too unwieldy to set up and use. The enemy would sense it coming a mile away, and activating six Striker bindings at once put too much of a strain on the construct's vessel. It was the sort of method that sounded better than it was.

But Eithan had found her plans, and had wanted to see them in action.

"A lovely strike!" Eithan called. "How did the script hold up?"

"Strained." Gesha tapped a ring on the metal of the cannon's outer layer. "Warping already. And the Song of Falling Ash binding is an inch from falling apart, if you ask me. Not that you did."

"We'll need more goldsteel plating," Eithan mused aloud. He couldn't afford that himself—not without the resources of the Arelius family. That irritation still threatened to prod him to anger. He would have to deal with that, when he was done mopping up Redmoon Hall.

Of course, he could save up top-grade scales and eventually afford most of anything in the Empire. But it would have been so much easier with the family behind him.

He pushed that annoyance aside and returned his attention to the battle in the sky around them.

"What was that?" Naru Saeya asked, holding her rainbow sword to one side, staring blankly into the rain. She ended up repeating herself: "What *was* that?"

Chon Ma was bleeding from a cut on his face now, delivering a speech about honor to the remaining Redmoon Hall emissary, whose arm hung broken and bruised from his shoulder.

"You skulk in the shadows," the Cloud Hammer Underlord proclaimed. "You rely on power that will never truly be your own. This is why you are weak."

Eithan turned to Fisher Gesha. "Do you think you could squeeze out one more shot?"

The construct flared to life.

CHAPTER SEVEN

There were any number of reasonable objections that Dross could have made to the Soulsmith operation, but since the construct seemed happy enough going along with it, Lindon certainly wasn't going to say anything.

First, he moved the bucket of Dream Well water in front of Orthos. Then he forced the turtle's mouth open and poured a vial of the purple water down his throat.

It didn't quite wake him, but Lindon could feel his consciousness smooth out. His sleep went from rough and fearful to soft and deep. When he woke, he'd need some water, so hopefully the bucket would be enough. He'd always had trouble wrestling his thoughts, too; maybe the Dream Well could help him.

With Orthos settled, Lindon sat Little Blue on the turtle's head. She gave a chirp, and he patted her with one finger. "When I'm done here, I'll have some food for you."

Then he got to work.

Binding a spiritual construct to a physical vessel was one of the basic skills of the Soulsmith. Essentially, he had to hold the construct into the exact shape of the vessel, then merge the two while using his own madra to tie them together. To stuff a ghost back into a body, both ghost and body had to match.

There was only one complication that mattered: the sapphire already *had* a construct in it. So he was trying to meld two constructs *and* fix them both to the gem.

Fisher Gesha would tell him to extract both Dross and the Eye of the Deep construct, then break them down piece by piece until he could rebuild them into one construct with the functions of both. Then he could bind that *single* construct to the gem or, preferably, another suitable vessel without a hole in it.

Then she would have hit him for trying to do this without guidance.

But Lindon had neither the time, nor the experience, nor the equipment to do it that way. He wasn't sure that a living construct like Dross could even be safely deconstructed. He'd have to roll the dice.

Not that he would put it to Dross that way.

He extracted a pair of gold-plated tongs from the roll of tools, holding them up to show Dross. "I'll be using these to remove you from your vessel," he explained. "Then—"

Dross zipped out of his rusted container.

He hovered in the air, a purple cloud filled with violet sparks. Within the cloud, Lindon could see patterns of crossing lines, like Dross was made of a structure of ghostly timbers.

"Done!" the construct said cheerily. "Now what?"

Lindon put the tongs down. "Now...try not to resist."

He put his left hand on the Eye, pouring pure madra into the construct. It was already filling most of the vessel, so he only had to focus on holding it still. That was easier said than done; it felt like trying to keep hold of a living heart that tried to escape his hand with every beat. Essence drifted out of the crack more quickly.

Lindon reached out with his inhuman right hand, then hesitated. He needed his hands free to project the madra, which meant he couldn't hold the tongs.

Of course, strictly speaking, he didn't *need* the tongs.

After a moment of hesitation, he reached out for Dross

with his white grip. "Please don't move."

As Lindon seized Dross, he actually *felt* the construct in his Remnant hand. It felt like gripping a handful of cotton. A pang of hunger ran up the arm into Lindon's soul, but he kept the limb under control. An instant of lost focus, and the arm would devour Dross.

"That gave me a tingle. Is everything all right?"

Sweat rolled down Lindon's face, but he forced a smile. "Hold still, please."

Now came the hard part. He had to project *more* pure madra around Dross to hold him in place. And it had to be exactly the right shape of the sapphire.

Well, one step at a time.

His madra still hadn't recovered much, so he needed to do this quickly. With a rough grip of madra, Lindon contained Dross' cloud-like form into a jagged form roughly the shape of a cut gem.

"It occurs to me," the construct said, "to wonder about my identity. You know what I mean? Was I *me* before I could think freely? Now, when you merge me with this key, I'll be taking on...who knows what memories and functions."

In order to get this part of the process exactly right, Lindon should have made a mold of the sapphire. It was too late now, so he Forged Dross to match the cut sapphire. As closely as he could, he tried to get every ridge and facet in exactly the right place.

His spiritual grip was slipping, and he was essentially bleeding madra. Even with the added focus from the Dream Well, he was having trouble holding both constructs in the right shape at the same time. Dross kept shifting gradually.

"Will I think of myself differently? How will I see the world? Will I even be able to think anymore, or will I be like I was before?"

Heavens help me, Lindon thought to himself. Then he shoved the constructs together, hoping they would match.

"Will I be *myself?* What if I hate being a key, but it's too late?"

There was resistance. Lindon had to push the last of his madra into the effort and shove them together until he forced them to click.

It was a good thing Dross didn't have a physical body, or this would have been excruciatingly painful.

"On second thought, I'm not sure I..." Dross' voice froze halfway through the sentence.

The light in the gem flickered and rippled. Lindon's spiritual grip tightened; had he failed?

Motion passed through the light, as though something were swimming inside the sapphire. The light started to change, staining the vessel purple.

"...want to do this," Dross continued. "It's too risky, isn't it? Who would gamble their very self on a game of chance?"

Lindon fell back, leaning against the wooden chest, holding up the gem that now shone purple.

"We're done," he said, swiping sweat from his brow.

"We are? Oh, that's good then. Now you mention it..." Dross flew out of the crack in the sapphire, leaving the jewel dull and dark. He looked very different than before: his nebulous cloud-form was more of a defined orb, and instead of simple lines, now he was a complex interlocking mechanism of what looked like gears. The sparkling lights whirled in a deliberate, complex cyclone.

"I feel good. I feel *great,* actually. It's like I've had one eye closed all my life, and now I've opened the other five." The drifting matrix of phantom machinery drifted around Lindon's head. "You've got quite a complicated soul, don't you? *Two* cores, I feel like that's an unusual number. And I can see your face so much more clearly now! It's...well, at least you have a wonderful spirit. Yes, indeed. That spirit of yours, wow."

That was a little alarming. After this one operation, Dross had gained senses like a Jade's. Had the Eye of the

Deep always sensed what was going on around it?

Lindon folded his legs into a cycling position and fixed his gaze on Dross. "Now, maybe you can help *us*. We need to find a way out of here."

"That's right in my wheelhouse. A guide *and* a key, that's me. Everything you need to find your way, all in one convenient bundle. Are we talking out of the Ghostwater world entirely, or out of this room?"

"Both."

"Ah, okay, right. Hmmm...there's a portal outside, which—"

"Apologies, but that's no longer an option."

Dross drifted slowly in a circle, like a man pacing. "There's another portal just like that one, but I won't lie to you: it's a *little* deeper in the facility. It's located in...*North-strider's*...personal quarters." He said the Monarch's name in a hushed whisper.

A stone sunk into Lindon's gut. "Can you open a Monarch's door?"

"I am the Eye of the Deep now," Dross said confidently. "No problem at all. And this Monarch was of the opinion that the best security was his presence. I can open his door, don't you worry, but *getting* there is the trick."

Lindon's tension eased slightly. "And how about out of this room?"

"Even easier." He bobbed over to the keyhole and flashed brightly. "Here it is! I'm astonished you didn't notice this before, actually."

"I'm afraid there may be someone out there waiting for me. I admit, I was hoping for another exit."

Dross whirled in the air and then swooped over to the keyhole. Half of him dipped into the wall. His insides shone, a mass of phantom gears, and the clouds of sparks within him flickered and rolled.

"Ekerinatoth of the gold dragons," he announced as he emerged. "She goes by Ekeri, which is good, because that's faster to say. She is waiting just outside for her prey to surface. That's you, by the way. You're the prey."

Lindon looked from the construct to the keyhole. "How did you know that?"

"This whole place is a network of constructs. Just lousy with 'em. I popped in, sampled their memories for the last few hours, then popped out. Turns out there's all kind of records in there; the same factions have been coming back every ten years for over fifty years now, so we've piled up quite the hoard of juicy gossip."

Lindon's interest spiked. This was something he could use.

"What can you tell me about her?"

"Well, she's close enough to Underlord that she can take on a humanoid form, can't she? By the time she reaches Archlord, she'll look even more human than you do. And there's every reason to suspect she will. She's the heir to the richest family on the continent, and they didn't get that way by *not* stealing everything that isn't nailed down, if you understand me. She practices the Path of the Flowing Flame, which involves dragon-fire behaving like a liquid. I imagine that's what she sprayed onto the door for about an hour after you vanished. Didn't do any good, of course. Those are high-quality rocks."

The thought of fighting another Truegold made him feel like he was backed into a corner again, but he set that feeling aside. This was an opportunity to push himself forward.

"Can you help me figure out how she fights?"

"I don't know everything, do I? What do I look like, a... know-everything construct? That's a terrible name, I'm sorry, I'll try again. What do I look like, an omni-codex?" He brightened. "That sounds pretty good, actually. Omni-codex. Call me that from now on."

"The only way we're getting out of here," Lindon said, "is through her."

A deep, gravelly voice rumbled from behind him. "Now *that* is the path of a dragon."

Orthos' eyes were dim, but they still smoldered with orange-red light. The black turtle shifted his bulk, and he let out a cough. On his head, Little Blue jumped up and down in excitement.

Tension he hadn't even noticed melted from Lindon's shoulders. He'd been so concerned that Orthos would never wake up.

The turtle nodded to the bucket. "That's some good water. But I'll need more than that if I'm going to walk out of here. I need meat."

"Then I need a way to get past Ekeri."

Orthos laid his head on the ground, eyes sliding shut again, but his mouth crooked open in a smile. "Here's a lesson for you: dragons can be sneaky too."

Ekeri rested in her portable shelter only ten yards from the hidden entrance in the stone. The device could make a home out of nothing in only an hour, but it was designed for convenience, not comfort. The rooms in the shelter were bare Forged madra, and she had to carry around all her furnishings herself. She pulled a chair out of her void key and had set it up so she could watch out the second-story window.

She had tried everything she could to force her way into the stone, but it was either dense with earth aura or protected by formidable scripts. Or both. The rock wasn't even scorched after her...perfectly calm and controlled assault.

When that hadn't worked, she had vented her considerable irritation on the nearby vegetation. Now the seastalks around the shelter had been burned away, leaving nothing but sand. There was nothing blocking her view of the entrance.

For the first hour, she watched with perfect patience. In the second hour, she began running her claws down the wall. By the third hour, she had clawed her window significantly wider.

"Where are they?" she demanded of her attendants, and there was more dragon than human in her voice. She calmed herself an instant later—her Monarch lived in human form, and she strove to imitate him in all ways. She couldn't wait until her soulfire was strong enough to change her body completely.

"Replying to the noble lady: they could stay inside until their supplies run out. Surely there would be greater prizes of more interest to milady in another section of the facility. Our maps indicate there is a sacred garden full of natural treasures only a short swim from here."

Ekeri stopped herself when she realized she was growling. Her attendant was a bland man, younger than twenty, whose expressionless face was almost identical to his counterpart's. Or maybe she was just bad at telling them apart.

"There are secrets in there," she said, chewing on her claw. "A Lowgold doesn't come in here with a black dragon-spawn for nothing. They have secrets on them, and I want them."

The two attendants exchanged glances, but their faces were so blank she could read nothing in them.

"Allow me to make a proposal, if it pleases the noble lady. Let us scout out the nearby habitats, and we can report back to you whatever we find. Perhaps we might find something even more valuable than this black dragon-spawn's secrets."

Ekeri kept gnawing on her claw for a moment as she thought. She didn't like the implication that she was pursuing the wrong prize, but at the same time, she didn't want to give up the other treasures of Ghostwater by focusing on one. Especially if the world was really collapsing soon.

"One of you stay with me," she said. "I can't allow them to escape, and I won't watch this window on my own all day."

"It would be my pleasure to stay," one of them said, voice empty of anything that resembled pleasure, "but surely they cannot escape your perception."

That was true. There was virtually no chance that a black dragon-spawn or the human borrowing his draconic power could evade her, especially in this area full of water aura. Their madra would stand out like a bonfire in the snow.

Irritably, she waved her hand to dismiss them. It was hard to give in when they were right. Plus, this place scraped her scales the wrong way; she couldn't even cycle aura here, as the power of water drowned out everything else.

"Watch out for the wildlife," she called back to them as they left. The fish had been a handful for her, a Truegold, and her attendants were much weaker.

Ekeri curled up on a couch, which she also produced from her void key, and tried to feel like she wasn't wasting her time by staying here.

Several hours later, she had almost drifted off when she felt something pressing against the edge of her spiritual perception. It felt warm and welcoming. Like a roaring fire.

She leaped up and dashed out of the house.

At first, it had gone so well.

Lindon had already known the basics of veiling his spirit; essentially, he just kept the movement of his spirit slow and quiet, so there was little for an enemy to sense unless they scanned him directly. It was one of the simplest principles in the sacred arts, but as it turned out, Lindon had never had much cause to perfect the technique. He was always so much weaker than everyone else that he was difficult to sense anyway, and pure madra was perhaps the 'quietest' form of power he could practice.

As a result, his veils were sloppy. For eight hours straight, Orthos forced him to practice veiling his power over and over until Orthos could feel the difference from only a yard away in the cave. Lindon pointed out that if

Ekeri was nose-to-nose with him, she would be able to *see* him, which only earned him a lecture about how useful veils were. Especially for him, with his two cores; he needed to be able to hide anything unusual about his spirit at a moment's notice.

On the bright side, the water from the Dream Well made the training practically paradise by Lindon's usual standards. Anytime his concentration wavered from its peak, or exhaustion started weighing him down, he took another vial of purple water and it was like starting over fresh. Lindon was starting to think he'd get addicted.

Dross told him that he was the only sacred artist in the history of the facility to be able to use the Dream Well so lavishly, but as Lindon saw it, the water had been left to pile up for the past fifty-six years. It was about time someone used it.

When Orthos was confident enough in Lindon's veil, Lindon made Dross check the situation outside. He contacted the security constructs and found that Ekeri had blanketed the area in her spiritual perception...but she wasn't physically watching his entrance anymore.

So he'd snuck out quietly to go fishing.

Orthos had declared his veil exceptional; not because of his hasty practice, but because pure madra was difficult to detect by nature. Any veil he made was twice as effective. Which brought up another problem: Lindon couldn't switch cores.

He wasn't skilled enough to veil Blackflame, and that Path was hard to hide anyway. As a fellow dragon, Ekeri would be able to discover Blackflame anywhere within this *habitat*—which was what Dross called the pockets of air within the giant bubbles.

Which meant Lindon had to catch one of these Highgold-level fish, kill it, and bring it back without using Blackflame. He had a plan for that too, but not one he liked.

He felt like he saw eyes on him with every crunch of his shoes on sand, but a golden dragon-girl didn't leap out of her two-story fortress of Forged madra and burn him to death, so he had to assume he was still hidden. After creeping around, it had only taken him a few minutes to locate one of the drifting fish.

The bear-sized creature slid lazily over Lindon's head, silver scales glinting in the dim yellow light. Its fangs clashed like spears, but it didn't seem to notice him at all. As Dross had said, they seemed to hunt by spiritual perception alone.

Dross, tucked away in the now-purple gem stuffed into the pocket of his outer robes, started to say something. Lindon slapped him. He muttered to himself, but stayed quiet.

Now it was time to execute Orthos' plan, which—in its entirety—consisted of one step: "Hit it with your arm."

Lindon couldn't help but feel a little nervous about that advice.

Without a full-body Enforcer technique, Lindon had to use basic Enforcement on his entire body. The spirit had a strengthening effect on the body, with or without the guidance of a technique, and all he was doing was pouring effort into that. It was horribly inefficient, and it would exhaust his madra more quickly and provide worse results compared to a real Enforcer technique.

However, it did make him stronger.

Lindon jumped ten feet straight up, seizing the fish's tail in his left hand. He dragged it down to the ground, though the fish fluttered and strained to stay in the air. As it fell, it gave off a deafening shriek.

Now he had a deadline.

According to Dross, the fish screamed to one another every once in a while under natural conditions, so its cry shouldn't alert Ekeri, even if she heard it. However, the other fish would start coming immediately.

He didn't sense any other sacred beasts within a hundred yards, so even in the worst-case scenario, he had a few seconds.

Lindon threw his whole body over the creature to pin it to the ground, though it was still *strong*. Its flailing and flopping nearly bucked him off. But in a moment, he had locked his legs around it.

Now it was time to execute Orthos' plan.

He pulled back his white arm, filling it with the power of his pure core, and began slamming it into the fish's head.

The sacred beast screamed and screamed. Dross assured him they weren't any more intelligent than normal fish, just more powerful, but the shrieks bothered him anyway. Lindon hammered until the silver scales began to crack, and dark blood splattered his face.

This is why I need a weapon, he thought. Of course, there was every chance he would have lost a weapon at the same time he had lost his pack.

When the fish's spasms began to weaken, he gripped the sharp tips of his white fingers into its newly exposed flesh.

Then he triggered the binding in his arm.

Gladly, the limb started gulping down the creature's madra. The arm seemed to grow more dense as it fed, more real, though strangely enough it seemed to get a shade darker as well. Like it was shading to gray instead of its normal, pristine white.

When Lindon had gotten the arm, he'd hoped that the hunger binding would allow him to steal madra from other sacred artists. That, he reasoned, would help him to learn more Paths.

But other than the obvious practical downsides to such a plan, he'd since learned that the hunger binding was not as simple to use as the Ancestor's Spear had been. Maybe there would be a day when he *could* use the arm to pull madra into his core.

Until then, he had at least learned one trick.

When the arm had absorbed so much water madra from the fish that it started to tint blue-green, Lindon vented the excess power. Aquatic madra sprayed from his forearm, splattering like rain on the sand before it dissolved into essence.

The arm could swallow some madra of any aspect to strengthen itself, but anything more than that amount would start changing the aspects of the limb's madra. Unless Lindon wanted the limb of a water-Remnant, he had to vent the extra madra before it corrupted the arm too much.

The Ancestor's Spear had a similar feature, and Jai Long had used it in his battle against Lindon. Based on that principle, Lindon had a few ideas for using it in combat, but he had yet to test any of them.

Without its madra, the fish had lost the will to resist. It flopped once or twice more as Lindon drove his fist into its skull until he heard something crack.

Then, at last, the creature was still.

Without missing a breath, Lindon grabbed the creature in both hands and started dragging it across the sand. It wasn't quite as heavy as Orthos, but it still wasn't light.

And silver-blue light bloomed as a Remnant began to rise from the body.

The Remnant looked like a wire model of the same fish, and it pulled itself free of the body as Lindon continued marching. He kept an eye behind him, hoping to lose it, and let out a breath of relief as he passed around a clump of tree-sized stalks. The Remnants didn't seem as dangerous as their living forms.

When he turned back to the front, he was standing face-to-face with a wall of fangs.

This new fish gave a shriek that stabbed his ears, and Lindon ducked just in time. Even so, the fish's scales scraped against his scalp as it swam past his head.

Lindon turned, following the fish...only to see the shining form of the Remnant drift straight through a stalk.

There was no time to think. Without considering it another instant, he changed the pattern of his breathing and drew from the Path of Black Flame.

Blackflame madra surged through his veins, filling him with heat. His channels still burned, despite Little Blue's healing touch, and he hadn't cycled aura to refill his core. There were only a few dim sparks of madra left in his core.

Though it was enough for a few seconds of Burning Cloak.

Lindon leaped at the Remnant first, kicking off in an explosive burst fueled by the Enforcer technique. He swept his Remnant hand down on the wiry spirit, clawing through its structure. His white fingers seized the pale blue wires that made up the Remnant's outer layer, and he dragged the Remnant down by its strings.

Then he tore away a chunk of madra.

The Remnant's scream sounded like a crashing wave, but Lindon didn't have time to waste. A Cloak-powered fist punched through its head like a spear, then he turned to catch the living fish that was darting at him.

He caught a lower fang in one hand and an upper fang in the other. The force of the creature's charge pushed him backward through the sand, and its breath stunk like dead fish and rotting vegetation. Nearby shrieks told him more of its school was coming.

Orthos was always telling him that he needed to think more like a dragon. Eithan seemed to agree with him, considering his talk about tiger-chasing.

That was always easier to do with Blackflame raging through him.

Even as his madra started to die, Lindon met eyes with the sacred beast. A dragon could not be defeated by a fish. *He* was the predator here. He had the power.

The last of the Burning Cloak surged through his limbs, and his arms burned. He roared as he pushed power through both hands.

In a massive rush of strength, he tore the fish apart.

He stood with its body in his left hand and its lower jaw in his right, panting, blood coating the sand. As his Blackflame core winked out, he threw his head back and let out a shout of victory.

Then he switched back to his pure core and instantly broke into a cold sweat. What had he been thinking?

"See," Dross said from his outer robe, "you're not being stealthy at all. What you're doing there is being loud. You see? You see the difference?"

Before the Remnant could rise from the new body, Lindon grabbed the old one and started running through the trees. Even his pure core was almost out of madra, and he silently thanked Eithan for the Heaven and Earth Purification Wheel; if he hadn't been practicing that technique for the last year, he would have run out of madra long before.

By the time he could see the door, he knew he wasn't going to make it.

CHAPTER EIGHT

He could feel Ekeri even before she leaped from the second floor of her shelter, landing in a puff of sand around her golden claws. Her tail swept behind her, and even though he found it hard to read any expression on her reptilian face, he was sure she was glaring at him.

"The key," she said, holding out her hand.

Lindon was tempted to give it to her. He could have Dross leave the Eye, then hand over the worthless sapphire, and use it as a distraction to dash for the door.

But he'd have to abandon the fish if he did that, and Orthos was going to need to eat *something*. Lindon had seen him munch on everything from chairs to boulders, but there must be a reason the turtle hadn't just taken a bite out of the wall. He needed something more substantial. It was Lindon's job to bring it to him.

Lindon dropped the fish, balanced on the balls of his feet, and raised his right arm. "Forgiveness, but I have to get past you."

Her eyes flashed like a flare of sunlight, and she gave a cruel-edged laugh. "You've got a mouth on you, Lowgold."

He pushed pure madra through his channels, sharpening his focus. He knew he couldn't actually defeat her here, especially not with an empty Blackflame core and a dying pure core. He was here to see how she fought.

She would open the same way everyone else did: with a Striker technique. If he could drain some of its power away with his Remnant arm, then he could hopefully land an Empty Palm when she closed the distance. That would be his chance.

The dragon rushed at him. He reached for her, but she moved like water, flowing around him. Her tail slipped around him, and her fist flashed out.

Pain exploded in his chest like a hammer crashing into his ribs. His back felt like he had slammed into a brick wall, but he hadn't actually moved anywhere.

Her golden scales glimmered from an inch in front of him, her fist buried in his chest. She'd punched him into something solid, but he was sure he hadn't been standing against anything. His eyes widened and he coughed up a mouthful of blood, turning his head inch by agonizing inch to see what was behind.

Her tail. She'd wrapped her tail around his back to keep him from flying away.

His madra stuttered as he tried and failed to take a breath. Light rippled around her feet: the Enforcer technique that she'd used to shorten the distance.

Reptilian teeth flashed as she smiled. One of her hands snaked around his waist and seized the gem, pulling it out. It glinted blue in the dim light.

"You could have handed it to me, you know," she told him.

Despair clutched his heart as he was reminded of a simple truth: most people who chased tigers ended up killed by tigers. For a moment, he'd forgotten.

With a speed that looked like a blur, her tail withdrew and slapped him across the top of the head.

Lindon slammed into the ground in an explosion of sand. His memory blurred, and his world turned to sand and darkness.

He woke when a clawed foot kicked him in the cracked ribs. It wasn't fueled by an Enforcer technique, or he would have exploded like a sack of blood, but it still caused him to scream in pain and curl up around his knees.

"What is this?" she demanded. He looked up through teary eyes to see her tossing the dull sapphire next to his head. "It's dead. Is this a fake?"

Through the haze of pain, Lindon couldn't understand what she was asking him. But he still flailed with one hand until it closed around the sapphire, pulling it back into his pocket. She didn't stop him, but the air around her grew hot. She drew back for another kick, and Lindon flinched.

A bar of black dragon's breath tore through the air, blasting at Ekeri's chest. She slid out of the way, ducking with the boneless agility of a serpent. She glared in the direction of the technique, hissing through her teeth.

Orthos, surrounded by a Burning Cloak, came to a halt next to Lindon in a spray of sand. He was panting heavily, his spirit a mask of pain, and the crack in his shell vented red light.

A liquid, golden whip spooled out from Ekeri's hand. "Stay still. Answer my questions, and I will spare you all."

Orthos didn't say a word. He bit down on Lindon's outer robe.

Lindon reached out with both hands, grabbing the tail of the fish. His thoughts were fuzzy, but he still knew he couldn't leave empty-handed.

He Enforced himself as best he could with his remaining madra, but he ended up doing little but holding on for his life as Orthos kicked his way over to the tunnel.

"Ghost!" the turtle said through clenched teeth.

Dross, a floating ball of purple light, zipped over to the keyhole. A flash, and the stone wall melted.

Golden light bloomed as a Striker technique shot at Lindon, but Orthos slid sideways. He grunted as he took it on his shell, but kept running.

A second later, they were through the wall, and Dross

was closing it behind them.

"Let's look on the bright side," the construct said. "We have most of a fish. And we've learned so much. An educational opportunity, that's what that was."

Lindon and Orthos lay on the stone, panting and groaning. Painfully, Lindon inched his neck over to the side to see the fish he'd grabbed.

Half of it was gone. He held a chunk of silver-scaled meat on the end of a wiry tail.

He spoke around his cracked ribs. "We need a new plan," he said.

Ekeri stood watching the stone, tapping her claws together and thinking.

There had been a construct in that gem yesterday. Today, it had escaped its vessel and opened the door independently. Meaning it could operate on instructions and had a measure of control over Ghostwater.

Even more interesting, they had evidently known she was here. The Lowgold had come out wrapped in a veil, and hadn't retreated at the sight of her shelter or shown any surprise at her attack.

Was the construct spying on her? Or could they send their spiritual perception out from the tunnels, even though she couldn't send hers in?

Most importantly of all, they didn't have another way out of the tunnel. Otherwise they would never have fought in and out of this entrance, knowing she was here.

Together, this convinced her that she was right. That construct was the key to Ghostwater—if she could take it for herself, it would lead her to greater treasure than anyone else. She might leave this world stronger than Akura Harmony.

And she *could* have it. The black dragon-spawn was dying, and the Lowgold wasn't worth mentioning. They had risked her wrath for the sake of food, which meant they had no provisions in there.

So they would be coming out of this door. Soon. And she was in no hurry.

Lindon didn't sleep. Instead, he drank from the Dream Well.

The world sharpened, which in turn drew his attention to his robust catalogue of aches and wounds. He was covered in cuts and burns, his madra channels still gave him sharp pain, and his ribs were definitely cracked. He'd even coughed up blood, and his Bloodforged Iron body was concentrating his madra on healing internal injuries in his chest and stomach.

"Oooh, that looks painful," Dross said, from back in his seat in the jewel. "I'm sure you're looking for a way to restore your spirit, eh? Of course you are, every sacred artist is. Lucky for you, *I* have the perfect solution!"

Every time he left his vessel, he lost a little essence, but thanks to what he'd taken from the other information constructs in the storage room, he shouldn't be in any immediate danger.

"There is a Spirit Well," the construct continued. "Oh, it's beautiful: blue as a summer sky. So I'm told. I've never seen it myself, and for that matter, I've never seen the sky either. Or summer. Anyway, it promotes growth in the soul, stimulating recovery and increasing madra density. That was another reward for the workers: a glass or two could take a Highgold to the brink of advancement. Quite a coveted bonus, I can tell you, and I'm sure it's been piling up just like the Dream Well. This is an opportunity not worth missing, I can assure you."

Lindon pushed himself up to a sitting position, leaning against the wall. "Where?"

"Ah, that would be in the tablet library. It's where the dream artists pursued *their* project: they thought that they could condense a type of mental madra that, when focused on the brain, increased performance."

"It didn't work?"

"In small doses, it worked like a charm. In less-small doses, it drove all test subjects *violently* insane."

"And how do we get there?"

A brief violet light flashed, pointing straight out the door. "It's roughly five hundred yards in *that* direction."

Right through Ekeri. Of course.

In any case, if he wanted to recover, he needed to keep his strength up.

Lindon looked to his fish. He would love to start a fire—not only would he prefer to cook his fish, but he needed something to generate Blackflame aura. If he simply waited on his soul to recover madra naturally, it would take weeks to refill his core, and that would be without refining or adding to his power in all that time.

But he wasn't sure he was capable of rising to his feet. Instead, he used his Remnant arm to peel the skin and scales away from a stretch of pale blue-white flesh. Ripping off a stretch of meat, he popped it into his mouth raw.

It exploded with flavor in his mouth, a sweet but metallic taste. It wasn't unpleasant, but it was intense. He almost spat it out in surprise. The meat was tender, melting like butter on his tongue, and he swallowed it without having to chew.

He gasped with relief after swallowing, reaching for a flask of Dream Well water to wash it down. "That has quite a taste to it," he said.

Orthos cracked one eye. "Bad?"

"It's...a lot." His right arm flopped to the ground instead of grabbing the nearest water vial. With an inward sigh, he reached out with his left arm.

When that didn't follow his directions either, he knew something was wrong. Little Blue, who had been curled up on the floor nearby, piped a questioning note.

"Orshoth," he mumbled, "shere's shumfing..."

Heat crawled out from his stomach and slid through his blood. Sparks of lightning danced inside him, and his muscles started to tremble. A moment later, they began to dance.

His eyes rolled up into his head as he felt his body shake against the stone.

Poison, he realized. He'd been poisoned.

That was exactly what the Bloodforged Iron body was meant for, but he'd used up all but a fraction of his madra fighting Ekeri. He could feel it draining his spirit, but once he was dry, he'd be helpless.

"Cycle it!" Orthos demanded. "Take control!"

Cycle it? Lindon wondered. The heat from the fish wasn't traveling through his madra channels, but through his bloodstream.

He tried anyway, forcing his lungs to inflate and focusing on the warm, crackling energy. He pushed out a breath, and the energy moved through his body a little more.

It was like trying to push a millstone uphill one inch at a time, but he stuck with it one breath at a time.

As he did, he noticed something: he wasn't running out of madra. His Iron body should have been pulling from his spirit to heal him, but instead, it was feeding on the power from the sacred beast's meat. Now he focused on the cycling process eagerly.

Some time later, he lay on his back, staring up at the blue lights of the ceiling, breathing slow and even. His Bloodforged Iron body had seized on the last of the fish's energy, dispersing it through his limbs. Even his Remnant arm fed on it with relish.

Lindon sat up. His ribs were still tender, his spirit still aching, and his cores as empty as ever...but much of the pain had vanished. Not only that, but his arms and legs felt tense, and somehow lighter than usual.

"...was I poisoned?" Lindon asked.

Orthos took a huge bite out of the fish, tearing away half the remaining flesh and raising his head up so it fell down his gullet. Lindon could see the lump of meat sliding through his throat.

The huge turtle let out a breath of satisfaction a moment later, shaking himself like a wet dog. "Now *that* is meat fit for a dragon." He eyed the remaining chunk of fish tail. Extending one nail, he slid off a hand-sized piece and slapped it skin-down on the ground next to Lindon. "Make that last," he said.

Then he snapped up the rest of the tail, bones and scales crunching between his jaws.

"You know, I've thought of something that you might have wanted to know a few minutes ago," Dross said, his gem flashing. "It's not too big of a deal. Hardly worth mentioning, really. But those fish? They're called Silverfang Carp, and they are not meant to be eaten by humans. They were raised here like cattle, you know, to feed some of the, ah, larger specimens of Ghostwater."

Lindon felt a sick feeling in his gut. He hoped it was his nerves and not some sort of horrifying parasite.

"Their meat promotes physical vitality and muscle growth," Dross went on. "So it's not as though it's unhealthy! The opposite, really. So you see, good for you! And you survived, so...no harm done!"

Orthos belched so loudly the floor shook. "I haven't had a meal like that in decades. The Arelius family could not afford meat of that quality. You're lucky; this is the sort of food the Emperor eats."

"He probably has his cooked," Dross pointed out.

"So Overlords can eat this safely?" Lindon asked.

"Underlords and above have their bodies reforged by soulfire," Orthos rumbled. "Something of this level is no problem for them, but it also doesn't provide as much of a benefit. The earlier you start eating like this, the better it is for you. If you did nothing but gorge yourself on those

Carp for the next month or two, you'd have the strength of a lion and the endurance of an ox." He barked out a laugh. "Maybe soon, I can stop calling you human."

Dross added, "That is, *if* you survived. And if there were no crippling deformities caused by uncontrollable growth of your muscles and organs. Which, none so far so...yay! Let's all celebrate and not, you know, cast blame on anyone who didn't warn you."

Lindon hurriedly scanned himself with his spiritual perception.

If anything, he seemed to be healthier than before his fight with Ekeri. A quick glance through his Copper sight showed that the line of green life aura running down his spine was brighter than ever, and the blood aura in his body was rich and dense.

He was no healer, but he imagined that was a good thing.

Mentally, Lindon thanked Eithan for leading him to the Bloodforged Iron body. If the Underlord had done nothing else for Lindon, that favor alone would have deserved Lindon's gratitude.

He started eyeing the remaining piece of Silverfang Carp meat. He wasn't exactly eager to go through that process again, but...

"I couldn't match her," he said. "Physically, at least, she was stronger than Jai Long."

Orthos coughed up a laugh. *"She* is a dragon." He seemed in much better spirits now, after a meal; Lindon hoped the fish would give him the strength to heal his wounds.

"And she eats like this?"

"Gold dragons eat meat of this quality from the moment they hatch." He bunched his shoulders in his version of a shrug. "By now, she will have reached her limit. Her body can be improved no further, while you have room to grow."

With his right hand, Lindon skinned the meat, tossing the skin and scales to Orthos. Then he crammed the remaining fistful of Carp into his mouth.

When he recovered, he could stand. Shakily. He hobbled down to the lower level and withdrew everything flammable he could find, piling it together. Orthos lit it on fire, and Dross activated vents in the ceiling that drew away the smoke.

At first, Lindon was concerned that the smoke would be visible to Ekeri outside. But she already knew they were in here, so what harm could that do?

The fire consuming the fuel released destruction aura, and the blazing flames generated fire aura. It was out of balance—there was far more fire aura here than destruction, and all of it was muted and suppressed by the overwhelming power of water—but there was enough for Lindon to cycle.

At Orthos' instruction, he simply drew the aura in and converted it to madra. He spent very little time cycling it for advancement or operating the Heaven and Earth Purification Wheel to push for a deeper core. This basic aura cycling technique of the Path of Black Flame wasn't anything fancy, Orthos told him, but it was better for recovery than the Purification Wheel.

"Purification Wheel?" Dross asked. "That sounds intriguing. Is that your cycling technique?"

Lindon didn't answer him. Eithan had emphasized that others might kill him in the hopes of pulling his cycling technique from his Remnant, so he tried to draw as little attention to it as possible. Not that he expected Dross to be spreading rumors, but it was better to be safe.

In three days, during which they had nothing else left to eat, Lindon had refilled his Blackflame core and begun to train. At first, he worried every hour that the world would disappear suddenly, taking him with it. But it was supposed to last for a few more months...and besides, it wasn't as though he knew how to escape. The fastest way out *was* to train.

No one slept—Dross and Little Blue didn't need to, and Orthos and Lindon were sustained by the Dream Well water. Which was the only thing they had to drink.

"A Path is designed for one purpose," Orthos growled at him. "You must learn to see that purpose." The turtle's mental state had been improved by the Dream Well water, so he hardly lost himself anymore, but his spirit was still scarred. Physically, he'd recovered enough to limp around the hallway, but he rarely moved more than that.

He didn't cycle either. There wasn't enough aura to sustain them both, so Orthos left it to Lindon.

"What is the strength of the Path of Black Flame?" Orthos asked, locking red-and-black eyes onto him.

"Overwhelming power," Lindon said. He had heard Orthos talk about this often enough to know what answer he wanted to hear.

The sacred beast grumbled, dissatisfied. "But why? What does that accomplish?"

Lindon thought for a moment before he answered. This reminded him of discussions he'd had with Yerin.

"Pressure," he said. When he trained against Yerin, it felt as though he was always on the back foot, so that he couldn't launch an attack without losing a hand.

Orthos grunted approval, snapping up a mouthful of rusted metal. Lindon was starting to wish *he* could digest old iron as well; it had been three days since his last taste of food.

"When your opponent defends, he is not attacking. And the first mistake he makes will be his last. Now, Ekerinatoth's Path of the Flowing Flame. What is its strength?"

Lindon took another vial of purple water and his thoughts sharpened. He concentrated on that memory of their fight, as the dragon-girl flowed like a coiling snake around his attack. She used whips, and her Striker technique curled like a stream.

"Flexibility," Lindon said. "Adaptability."

"The usual strength of water artists," Orthos said, a touch of scorn in his voice. "They will avoid or redirect your attacks, and use that moment to attack. How do you maintain pressure on such an opponent?"

Ekeri's movements were clear in Lindon's Dream Well-enhanced memories. "She becomes predictable," he realized aloud. When he left a gap, he could count on her taking it. Meaning he could see where she would attack him. "I can anticipate her."

"Show me," Orthos said. And he rushed at Lindon.

Two days of constant, sleepless training later, Lindon left the cave again.

Thanks to the water, Lindon felt as though it had been much longer. He was able to train for twice as long as before—when his body or spirit couldn't recover, he instead discussed strategy and theory until he was ready to move again. And what training he had was twice as effective, because he was always ready to give it his full concentration.

The level of water in the well had now shrunk significantly. Orthos' thirst was not to be underestimated, and the water was only replaced by a few drops a day. Lindon was already wondering if there was some way to take the well with them when they left, or at least recreate it outside.

He snuck out of the cave under a veil with no complications, and the Silverfang Carp died easily under his Remnant fist. His body felt lighter and stronger than ever, after digesting the power of the sacred beast meat from before. This one had only managed to scream once before he crushed its skull, then shredded its Remnant.

He had barely recovered any pure madra over the last several days—he hadn't realized how much he'd relied on Eithan's elixirs to refill his pure core. As a result, he'd only been able to make one low-quality scale for Little Blue. She hadn't been able to use any madra, so Orthos' spirit was growing worse and worse.

Even if he managed to bring back this whole Carp, they couldn't stay in the tunnels forever. Fortunately, his Blackflame core was in top condition.

He made it all the way back to the tunnel and opened the door, tossing the fish inside, before Ekeri showed herself.

His perception caught her descending like a meteor from the rock tower overhead. She blazed with power, aiming for him while he still held Dross in the keyhole.

Lindon released the Eye of the Deep and ignited the Burning Cloak.

He struck overhead, launching a punch along with a pulse of Blackflame madra above him. It wasn't a true dragon's breath, but it should at least singe her.

She was falling headfirst, her eyes blazing gold, her teeth bared. She slapped his punch aside with one claw, the other sweeping at his head.

Lindon caught it.

His Remnant arm seized on her wrist. His strength couldn't compare to hers—not only was she a Truegold, she was a dragon. But he had gravity on his side. With all his strength, he hauled her down. She twisted in his grip, slamming into the ground braced on her feet and tail. Sand blasted away in a ring.

Lindon had already triggered his arm.

Intense heat flowed into his limb along with a flow of orange madra, sending spiritual pain shuddering through him. He gritted his teeth and continued even as she pulled back, trying to break his grip.

She snarled, turning, whipping her tail at him. He had to release her and jump back before her tail lashed him in the chest.

Without missing a beat, he vented the madra in his arm. Her own molten madra sprayed at her from only a few feet away, causing her to raise one gold hand to protect her face.

Seizing Dross again, Lindon dove through the gap and slammed the door shut.

Ekeri's rage burned so hot that the nearby aura ignited. Even through the overwhelming power of water, the edges of the nearby stalks began to smolder and release smoke. The distant fish shrieked, but Ekeri wished they would close on her. She needed something to vent her frustration.

The other Truegolds would have moved on to other habitats by now, or to the wreckage of those that had collapsed. They would be reaping a rich harvest. And here she was, clawing at a treasure chest that remained stubbornly locked. No longer.

Raising her hand to her chest, she activated one of her necklaces: a chain of silver with a single thumbnail-sized bell on the end. The bell rang once. No matter how far away her attendants were, they would hear it and return.

The next time that door opened, they would kill everything inside.

Lindon leaned his head against the wall of the tunnel, his arms trembling. Blocking the Truegold's attack directly had cracked bones in his left wrist, which his Iron body rushed to repair, and fractures had appeared in the madra of his right arm. He patched them over with pure madra, though he'd have to perform real maintenance with hunger madra when he left.

Even that brief exchange with Ekeri left him strained and bruised, but it also left him grinning like Eithan. He had traded blows with her and come out ahead.

Orthos had already torn the head off the Silverfang Carp, and was crunching happily through its skull. "I hope you've prepared yourself," Orthos said through a mouthful of food.

Lindon nodded to the door. "I know. She won't let me walk away next time."

The turtle grunted. "No. Next time, *you* won't let *her* walk away."

Over the next few days, the fish became easier for Lindon to digest. It still kicked him like a horse, but it took him less time to process the energy, and he started to see a clear improvement in his body. Every time he cycled more of the sacred beast's power was another round of tempering everything from his bones to his skin.

Orthos was clearly seeing the benefits too. He moved more easily than Lindon had ever seen him outside a fight, and even the fissure in his shell had started to close. Mentally, he reported feeling clearer than he had in years, so his mood was bright. Relatively speaking. However, his soul was still damaged and weak. He couldn't use a single technique without treatment, which Little Blue was in no shape to give him. Lindon's pure core recovered at a snail's pace without help.

Every day, Lindon ate as much of the Carp as he could and trained Blackflame under Orthos' supervision.

"You have been practicing a broken Path," Orthos told him. "How many techniques were taught in the Blackflame Trials?"

"Three," Lindon said. He knew where this was going, but he had no choice but to humor the sacred beast.

"And how many have you been using?"

"Two."

"All Blackflame artists mastered those three, and incorporated them into their fighting styles. Most of them developed at least four. When you have greater insight into the use of your Path, you usually create other techniques to sharpen your strengths and cover your weaknesses. This is how you form a Path," Orthos said, nodding at the wooden chest of Lindon's belongings.

Lindon was surprised to see him allude to the Path of Twin Stars. He often seemed to ignore Lindon's pure core entirely.

"You look at the purpose of your Path and you cultivate

techniques to accomplish that purpose. You do not neglect one-third of your abilities because the other two-thirds seem easier to practice."

Lindon had ignored Twin Stars for too long. The Empty Palm was the only real technique in his Path; the Heart of Twin Stars had no practical use in battle. What else did he need? Some way to close the gap with his opponent in order to land an Empty Palm, certainly. He was relying on the Burning Cloak for that so far, which meant he needed to switch cores too often.

Orthos thumped on the floor, sending a slap echoing through the hall. "You've taken the wrong point, I can see it in your eyes. Stop thinking and listen to me: we're going to practice the Void Dragon's Dance."

This wasn't the first time Lindon had heard this argument. While preparing to fight Jai Long, Orthos had argued that Lindon needed to master the Dance. But because their practice grounds had been both small and devoid of much fire aura, and because Eithan insisted that the duel would occur in a place with very little fire aura, they had abandoned the idea. As a result, Lindon had never used it in a real battle.

And rarely in practice; in his opinion, the technique seemed too large and unwieldy to use in an actual fight. It seemed like the sort of thing you'd want if you were burning down a forest or attacking a village.

He and Orthos gathered all the flammable trash in the hallway and spread it all around the huge, empty warehouse room that Lindon had found before. They intended to train both the Dance and his other clear weakness: it took him too long to form his dragon's breath. They had made great progress on that before Jai Long, too, but they had never reached a point that satisfied Lindon.

The fires they ignited while training served as sources of aura for Lindon to cycle. A natural fire generated more fire aura than destruction aura, so Lindon's advancement was much slower than it had been in the Blackflame training grounds of Serpent's Grave, but it was enough to keep his core full for training. As long as they rationed themselves; they only had a limited amount of garbage in the hall.

With piles of trash as targets, water from the Dream Well to support him, and Orthos watching, Lindon dove into focused training. Cycling aura, processing fish meat, practicing dragon's breath, and learning the Void Dragon's Dance swallowed every day and every night. All his sleep was replaced by the Dream Well.

He lasted two weeks.

That was as much time as they could afford. By the end of it, Little Blue was listless, thin, and pale. Even Dross— who assured him that Ghostwater was intact enough to last a few more months—had retreated into his gem to try and minimize madra loss. Though Lindon still rinsed out his madra channels with pure madra while training, the damage from the Path of Black Flame was adding up. His channels were scarred, and his Bloodforged Iron body was taking longer and longer to heal him after he channeled Blackflame for too long. He had to get out and find a way to refill his pure core.

None of them could stay here any longer. Dross needed a better vessel, Little Blue needed food, and Orthos needed her treatment. They had finished the Silverfang Carp almost a week before, and if Lindon waited any longer, his condition would only get worse.

He stood behind the door, Dross' gem in his hand, steadying his breathing to smooth out the flow of his spirit. Ekeri would come at him with everything she had. She wouldn't be trying to persuade or rob him, but to kill him. Orthos had assured him she would use a weapon, she would position her two Lowgold assistants to prevent him from running, and she would have no mercy.

"Dross," Lindon asked, "how often do Lowgolds defeat Truegolds?" That was the question he'd avoided asking for two weeks.

He had taken off Sandviper Gokren's hand while Lowgold, which meant he could certainly wound Truegolds. And he had fought Jai Long, knowing that victory was a long shot, so he should be used to this by now.

But he'd lost that fight.

"I wouldn't worry about it," Dross said, purple light flashing from the gem in Lindon's hand. "Just focus on doing your best. Don't think about the massively improbable odds, or what will happen if you fail. She's probably killed *scores* of people stronger than you, but you can't think about that, because an instant of distraction will spell your certain death."

"...gratitude," Lindon said, his breathing coming a little quicker.

Orthos shoved him aside and walked around Lindon, standing between him and the door. He glared at him, eyes circles of red on darkness. "Listen to me. The black dragons were the kings of this continent. In their day, their power dwarfed the Akura family. The gold dragons were just a servant family beneath them, scraping and clawing for every scrap."

He raised one leg, tapping Lindon's stomach with a claw. "That is the spirit that flows through you. She is two realms above you? Good. You need at least that much of a handicap to make it a challenge."

Orthos snaked his head down and seized Dross in his jaws, then lifted the gem and pressed it to the keyhole. The door melted away, revealing the blocky structure of golden madra that was Ekeri's shelter.

The turtle released Dross, turning back to Lindon. "Go out there and show her the power of a true dragon."

With the Path of Black Flame flowing through him, Lindon felt his eyes warm as they turned black. He marched out without another word, not looking back as the door closed behind him.

In the blue light, Dross flashed brightly. *"Wow, you really set him on fire, didn't you? He didn't look very encouraged after I talked to him, but wow, you knew exactly what strings to pull. If I had hands, I'd be applauding you right now. Picture me applauding."*

Orthos ignored him, settling down on the ground. The Sylvan Riverseed gave him a worried look and a peep, and he extended a paw so she could climb up and wait with him.

"Now, be honest with me," Dross went on. "What do you think his odds are? He's not here, he won't hear you, I just want to know what you think. Turtle-to-gem."

"He is my partner," Orthos growled. The construct talked too much. He just wanted to wait in silence.

"No, sure, I understand that, but what do you think his odds *really* are? Ten to one? A hundred to one? Maybe just two to one?"

Orthos locked his eyes on the purple-lit gem. "One hundred percent."

"...optimism! Oh, that's a good one, it really is. False courage really does wonders for keeping the spirits up."

"One more word, and I will eat you."

第九章

CHAPTER NINE

Lindon stood in front of the gold shelter with no veil, staring up at the highest window. Orange curtains hung limp in the still air.

Seconds after he stepped out of the hall, the dragon's pair of servants walked out of the front door. Lindon tensed, tracing their movements, but each of the plain-looking men walked in a different direction and took up a post near the edges of the closest stalks. As expected they were there to prevent him from running. Though they felt like Lowgolds, his spiritual perception had trouble reading them. It was like trying to hold a handful of mist.

At the highest window, Ekerinatoth appeared. The dragon-girl glared down at him, golden scales flashing in the light. She had traded out her layers of fanciful colored clothes for something that looked more like a sacred artist's robe of jade-colored silk. Necklaces still hung on her chest, and she carried a weapon at her side. It looked like a long, thumb-thick needle with a sword's hilt.

Lindon looked up at her, focusing his perception on her, afraid to miss a single movement. She stood watching him.

Then she fully unveiled her spirit.

To his eyes, nothing changed, but his soul trembled. A

faint weight pressed down on him, and she felt like a wild-fire raging toward him. The Blackflame madra in him was nothing but a candle before a hearth. She dwarfed him.

Lindon gathered his madra together anyway and ignited the Burning Cloak. Orthos' words bolstered him: this was just a handicap.

And this time, he wasn't trying to sneak past her.

He kicked off the ground, launching himself up to her second-story window. Even with the reflexes of a True-gold, she hesitated an instant when she saw him suddenly appear in her face, and ripples of light started running in waves from her feet as she activated her own Enforcer technique.

Lindon's fist almost caught her, but she twisted enough to avoid the impact. She slammed into her own wall, leaving a web of cracks.

Black dragon's breath followed from Lindon's hand an instant later.

She slipped beneath, and the bar of dark fire punched a hole in the wall. He wrenched the technique to the side, following her, the beam carving a long gouge in her shelter. Orange-gold essence drifted up in sparks like the rising dawn.

She flowed up to him, pulling her weapon from her side, but he dropped his dragon's breath and closed the gap with the Burning Cloak. He knocked her wrist aside with his left hand, and this time his bones didn't crack. Days and nights of pain, cycling the energy of the sacred fish, had forged his body anew.

Before she brought her weapon to bear, he grabbed her shoulder in his pale right hand and began to consume her madra. She slashed at his Remnant arm with her needle, forcing him to let go, creating a step of distance between them.

Then she thrust a claw forward. Orange light burst from it like a waterfall of blazing heat.

It was far more raw power than he could conjure in an instant. The beam was as wide as his torso, and while it wasn't as focused or as destructive as Blackflame, its raw power overshadowed anything he could produce.

Lindon held out his white hand. He and Orthos had tested this as much as they could without risking Lindon's life, and it should work in theory. But there was every chance that the Flowing Flame madra would pass over him like a tide and leave him helpless.

As the Striker technique hit his palm, he triggered the hunger binding.

Unleashed, his arm started devouring the technique. It reached its capacity almost immediately, and orange lines began to stain the limb, searing Lindon's soul and filling his arm like a sack stuffed to bursting.

But he'd consumed the technique.

Without giving Ekeri an instant to recover, Lindon held his white arm out as though holding a shield. Flowing Flame madra gushed out of his forearm.

It wasn't as focused as her original technique, and it had lost much of its potency, but she still had to cross her arms and bear it. Liquid fire splashed out of the holes in the house.

Cutting off the technique, Lindon launched himself forward with the power of the Burning Cloak. He hit Ekeri foot-first, stomping her back.

For once, he landed a clean hit. Whether she thought she could endure the blow or just failed to dodge, she took the kick on her crossed arms.

And she blasted back through the wall of her shelter, hitting the sand like a falling star.

Lindon dashed after her while she was still in the air, the corona of the Burning Cloak turning him into a black meteor. He landed in front of her, sending wide, sweeping slashes of dragon's breath scything into the waving sea-stalks around her.

Stalks toppled, smoldering and smoking, but because of the water aura, none of them burst into flames.

Shrieks rose in a chorus from all over the habitat. He

sensed cold, savage power approaching from every direction as the Silverfang Carp closed on them.

A great roar echoed over the sand as Ekeri's shelter collapsed. The blocks tumbled to the ground as though they were made out of real stone, a great puff of essence rose into the sky like dust. At last, flames licked up from the wreckage as bits of smashed wooden furniture caught fire. That was one of Lindon's worries eased.

But she had been waiting too.

The fire aura from around the flame gathered behind him, flames pulling themselves into a river. He sensed it happen, whirling to face the Ruler technique she was conjuring behind his back.

It was like staring down a dragon made of orange flame. He extended his own madra to the aura, contesting her control, but he felt like a child throwing his whole body weight against the arm of a warrior. The snake of fire washed over him, instantly igniting the edges of his clothes. If not for him using fire aura to push the fire away, and the water aura weakening flames, his robes would have burned away entirely.

Still, fighting against her Ruler technique took everything he had. His soul blazed, his Blackflame madra rolling like a whirlpool, and his teeth were gritted as he threw his whole concentration into it. With his right hand, he fumbled at his pocket.

The hand ignored him.

Not now, Lindon begged. *Please, not now.*

The hand lurched in Ekeri's direction. Lindon split his attention, and the fire pressed closer, searing his skin. He screamed, but forced his hand to listen to him.

It reached into his pocket and withdrew a sealed vial of baked clay. He broke the seal with his thumb, dumping glowing purple water into his mouth.

Instantly, his concentration sharpened. His vision cleared, and his control over the aura firmed. His training with Orthos had showed them both that reaction speed and focus were both noticeably improved under the effects of the Dream Well.

But his newly enhanced reactions weren't enough to stop the golden tail from catching him across the chest.

He flew back, tumbling across the sand, trying to scramble to his feet. Fear spiked in his chest.

He only had one chance of winning: keeping Ekeri on the defensive. Orthos had lectured him at length, but it was a principle he'd learned from Yerin. The strength of an offensive Path, like the Path of Black Flame, was its ability to put pressure on the opponent. Without that pressure, he would crumble like a dry leaf.

And now she had him on the back foot.

With the power of the Burning Cloak, he ran, trying to put some distance between them. She followed him as though tied to him with a string, holding out the needle in her hand.

A long string of orange madra extended from the end, and Lindon recognized it for what it was. Not a needle, but a whip. This would be a tool to enhance the whip-like Forger technique she'd used before.

She spun it over her head, and the line of flexible madra spun in all directions, slicing stalks open. The aura around them was mixed with spots of visible red, as fires started to ignite, and the air was beginning to choke with smoke. The screams of the fish grew closer as Lindon ducked and dipped through the stalks and the occasional boulder, trying to increase the gap between them.

A man in white appeared out of nowhere in front of him, sending a kick at his feet.

Lindon leaped over him, driving his fist at the servant's face, but he ducked his head slightly to one side. Lindon followed up with a kick, but the servant moved back a step.

Lindon's gut clenched. The man wasn't trying to fight him, just to tie him up until Ekeri reached him. Though he didn't want to waste the madra, he gathered black fire in his left palm.

Silver flashed from within the smoke, and a Silverfang Carp came for him with fangs open.

Lindon seized the fangs with his Remnant arm. After feeding on their meat for so long, Lindon could hold it back much more easily than before; even his replacement arm had been strengthened by the power in their flesh. However, it was still massive. As it swam through the air, it pushed him back through the sand.

A burst of pain exploded next to his shoulder blade, and he screamed, hauling the fish with him as he twisted to see what had hit him.

The servant stepped back, bloody knife in hand.

Rage flowed from his Blackflame core. Still gripping the massive Carp, Lindon extended his hand of flesh and fired his dragon's breath.

Ekeri leaped over her servant at the same time. If she wanted to save him, she would have to land and take his Striker technique, which would give him time to push away the fish. His Bloodforged Iron body had already started to drain madra to heal the wound in his back, so he needed to end this quickly.

But the dragon-girl ignored his technique. The bar of fire punched into the Lowgold's side, instantly taking a chunk out of his ribs and igniting his clothes. His body bucked, and the wound flashed with green light—he must have had a treasure to preserve his life.

It wouldn't be enough. Three more Carp darted over, descending on him.

Then Lindon could no longer pay attention to the Lowgold, because there was a Truegold on top of him.

She whirled her whip at him, and as he struggled to cut off the flow of his dragon's breath, the glowing orange weapon wrapped around his leg.

It seared like red-hot metal against his skin, and Lindon knew with rock-solid conviction that it was about to tighten and tear his limb away. Instead of cutting off his dragon's breath, he poured more madra into it, slicing down like a burning executioner's blade onto her head.

Before she could cut his leg away, she had to raise a hand to defend against the dense bar of Blackflame. With her attention distracted, he kicked the weapon away.

As the whip slid back down his skin, it burned him, and he choked back a scream. He wrenched his leg free, stumbling back.

The Silverfang Carp had truly gathered now, flashing everywhere, so he and Ekeri fought in the middle of a school. The air was so hazy that it looked like they were swimming through smoke. With the Burning Cloak active, he knocked them to one side and the other, leaping and kicking off of a fish that hovered in the air.

He looked down, seeing the sliced and broken sea-stalks smoldering on the sand.

And, as he watched, they burst into open flame.

Until that point, the greatest source of fire aura had been the furniture in the wreckage of Ekeri's shelter. That generated enough red-hot aura to fuel her Ruler technique.

But the Void Dragon's Dance also required destruction. The more the fire consumed, the more destruction aura it released along with the heat. Now, there was enough for him to work with.

Extending his spirit, he gathered threads of black and red energy, controlling it with his madra, wrapping it together, coiling it around himself. The air rippled with heat, his skin tingled, and the edges of his robes started to dissolve as though under the effect of invisible flames.

Holding her larger whip in one hand and a Forged whip in the other, Ekeri rushed after him. She leaped, grabbing onto one Carp with her tail and swinging over a second, snapping sacred beast. She kicked off another, slapped the next in two, and came down on him with both whips descending. All the while, fires dimmed nearby as she gathered fire aura to defend herself.

He was almost out of madra. He couldn't compete with her in endurance, in physical strength, or in technique.

The longer this battle went on, the more options he'd lose.

She'd undoubtedly survived more battles than he had. She'd read his Ruler attack the second he started preparing it, gathering up aura to prepare a defense. By the time Lindon played his last card, she'd still have a full hand.

But, as Orthos had taught him, the Path of Black Flame had some good cards.

When the red and black vital aura had been wrapped together in roughly equal measure, Lindon braided it according to the Ruler technique he'd learned almost a year before.

He turned and faced Ekeri's whips. His left hand flowed with the power necessary to control the Void Dragon's Dance, so he couldn't move it, but his Remnant arm reached out and seized a nearby fish. He dragged it in front of him, using its body to shield him from her attack.

Before it hit, he pushed his left arm forward. With it, he pushed out the tightly coiled aura. It wrestled against his madra, trying to spring free, and his arm and spirit trembled.

Golden light sliced the Silverfang Carp in half, and the second whip descended. He raised his right hand to catch it, though it burned his Remnant palm with a piercing pain that shot through his spirit. At the same time, visible only in his Copper sight, a tightly wound disc of red-and-black aura reached Ekeri.

She pushed against the fire aura with her own spirit, and in only a moment she would unravel the technique.

Instead, Lindon clenched his left fist.

And unleashed the Void Dragon's Dance.

The aura exploded into a cyclone of spinning flame. It stretched from the ground to the ceiling of the dome, and the heat scorched his face. The column of swirling black-and-red fire swallowed Ekeri, then the Carp around her were consumed, followed by those farther away as the technique grew larger and larger.

But this was not just a fire technique. Empowered by

destruction aura, the flames devoured material in a blink. What would normally take hours for the fire to burn instead disappeared instantly.

Every Silverfang Carp touched by the flame was consumed in a snap, becoming little more than ash that drifted down. Lindon projected Blackflame madra around himself as the technique expanded, but the Void Dragon's Dance was over in only a second.

All of the nearby fish, the remaining stalks, and the yellow-glowing plants had been completely destroyed in a circle around him. Losing the lights left him in shadow, but he couldn't feel the attendants anymore either. Everything within a hundred yards had vanished, leaving Lindon in a world of sand and ash.

Except for one other survivor. A dragon could not be so easily burned.

Though he *had* hoped.

Ekeri was only singed, her clothes damaged and smoking, her scales charred. She knelt on one knee with whips crossed before her, spirit trembling. As the ash cleared, her eyes snapped open. They blazed gold.

He braced his knees to keep from collapsing.

There were only a few scraps of madra left in his Blackflame core, but he released a quick, sloppy dragon's breath to keep her at bay.

It didn't help. Enforcer technique rippling around her legs, she flowed around his attack, letting her Forged whip vanish in order to strike with her weapon. He ducked it, but she was clearly prepared for him.

Her tail slipped around behind him, locking him into place. Then her clawed hand struck for his chest.

Lindon was past the scope of his plan. They had practiced for everything they could, but no fight could be fully anticipated. At some point, he had to lean on his experience and training.

He only had enough Blackflame madra for one more technique, so he let it go.

And took the hit.

Her claws pierced his chest around his gold badge. They plunged through his skin, sending blood flowing down his stomach.

The pain tore at his consciousness, but he hadn't accepted the hit by accident. If she wasn't this close, so close that he could smell the ash on her skin, he would never have been able to hit her himself.

So he shoved his Empty Palm into her core.

Her Enforcer technique vanished and her whip went dark, reverting to nothing more than a needle-pointed silver hilt. Gold eyes widened, and her reptilian lips parted.

Heat crept back into Lindon's eyes as he pulled Blackflame for one last time.

The dragon's breath was only the width of two fingers, but it drilled straight through her heart. Severed, her necklaces fell to the ground, leaving loose pearls and chunks of jade and links of gold chain tumbling over the sand.

Lindon shoved her away, stumbling backwards, trying to conjure up enough madra for a Burning Cloak. He should have gone for her head. Now he had given her enough room to recover. She would be coming for him any second, but he couldn't scrape any more power together.

A full breath of time passed before he realized she wasn't coming after him.

Instead, she dropped to her knees, scrambling in the sand for her jewelry. Blood leaked from her lips, and she wheezed as though trying to speak, but she ended up coughing blood over the ground instead.

Lindon limped forward. His right arm wasn't obeying him, but he had to try something. If he left her alive...

Her hand closed over a tiny jade rectangle. With one last frightened glance at him, she broke it.

The air shattered.

Lindon held his hands up to defend himself from this new attack, but all the weight on his spirit had vanished. Before him, where Ekeri had knelt before, there was an intricate spiderweb of cracks in the air. He swept his spiritual perception through them, but they didn't feel like madra. They felt like *nothing*, like they were splintered cracks in existence itself.

He did feel something from beneath the web: one or more of those necklaces was releasing an aura like a True-gold weapon. Though every movement sent agony shooting through his whole body, he slowly knelt and slipped his Remnant hand beneath the cracks, reaching for the necklaces.

If they ended up being dangerous, at least he would only lose the same arm.

The pointed tips of his fingers caught on one string... and passed through. This time, he remembered to send pure madra flowing through the limb before he snagged the necklace, pulling the pile of jewelry free of the web and close to him.

He was eager to inspect them, but ash was still falling around him, and the shrieks of distant Carp were growing closer. He could wait until he was back in the safety of the tunnel.

Lindon limped back, passing piles of gray, pressing his robes to his chest to stop the bleeding. When he reached the rock leading into the tunnel, he could only stare at it blankly.

He'd left Dross inside. He had to wait until they opened the door for him.

With a heavy sigh, he turned to lean his back against the stone, sliding down until he was seated. Somehow, the moment of reaction made his pain so much worse, as though all his injuries were waiting for him to let his guard down before they mobbed him all at once.

That only lasted a breath before the wall behind him vanished and he tumbled backwards.

When the agony cleared and he stopped groaning, he spoke. "I forgot you could see out."

Dross drifted out of his gem, a cloud of shifting purple

gears and swimming violet lights. "I don't see Ekeri," he said, bobbing around the entrance. "And I see the earth has been burned and salted. Who saved you?"

"No one," Lindon said. He was still lying on his back, so when Orthos stepped up and looked down at him, he saw the turtle's smile upside-down.

"I won," Lindon told him, and the truth of it seeped into him like warm honey.

Orthos' laugh started as a distant chuckle and grew to a massive, merry rumble that shook the floor. "By the time we get out of here, the Skysworn will be asking *your* permission to speak."

Sopharanatoth, dragon of the gold bloodline, sipped winter-wine from a silver chalice. The wine had weak spiritual properties, but its chill was a pleasant contrast to the heat that usually flowed through her veins. And it was a thousand high-grade scales per bottle, so it was appropriate for her position.

Supervising the entrance of Ghostwater was the most luxurious assignment an Underlord could receive. Especially when the primary portal had been destroyed. She and her retinue reclined in a silk tent planted on a Thousand-Mile Cloud ten thousand feet above the portal, scanning the portal every once in a while with their spirits. The destruction of the other exit had made her job easy; now they barely even bothered to sweep the exit once a day. When Sophara's little sister emerged, she would use her gatestone to leave. Which meant she would appear right here, so there was really no need to keep watch at all.

The other gold dragons, Truegolds all, lounged on beds of cloud madra all around the tent, reading books, consulting dream tablets, or snacking on flaming crickets from a cage. As Truegolds, they looked as much like dragons as like humans, but Sophara's soulfire set her apart. Her face was almost entirely human, but for her eyes and the patches of scales on her cheeks. Scales had fallen away elsewhere on her body as well, leaving patches of skin on her arms and legs.

She looked forward to reaching Overlord, when she would have hair, but she found the strands of loose scales tumbling down her shoulders a pleasing approximation.

Some other bloodlines valued their natural forms most highly, and refused to transform even once they had the soulfire to do so. While the power of the dragon form was useful, golds had a more refined aesthetic sense than their brethren. They shared the tastes of Seshethkunaaz, Monarch of Dragons, who had lived for centuries in human form. And there was no denying that madra moved more smoothly through a human body.

Sophara had emptied her chalice and was trying to decide if she wanted another when she felt a *crack* in her spiritual perception.

In the same instant, a smoking, bleeding golden body tumbled out of nowhere onto her priceless woven rug.

She had kindled a Striker technique before she recognized her little sister. Hurriedly dismissing her madra, she dropped to her knees, pulling Ekeri into her arms.

The Truegold girl stared blankly at the ceiling of the tent, blood staining her lips. A weak cough sent more blood oozing from the scorched wound in her chest.

"Healing!" Sophara commanded, her voice trembling. The other Truegolds shot away to obey, running out for elixirs or reaching into their personal void keys for life-saving constructs.

When her perception delved into her sister's body, her hope shattered. The girl's lifeline was unraveling, green dissipating into aura, and her spirit had already started to congeal. Her Remnant was beginning to form.

Ekeri met her sister's eyes. "I failed," she said. She

coughed up another mouthful of blood and started again. "I failed him. I'm sorry."

An instant later, she was gone.

A golden serpent slithered away from her body, and Sophara stepped away, eyes closed, tears streaming down her cheeks. She couldn't look at her own sister's Remnant.

She heard the Truegolds guiding the spirit away. They would use the Remnant to raise up another student, in honor of her sister, or else they would send it to the Soulsmiths to form it into a guardian treasure for their family, so Ekeri could add to the glory of the bloodline forever.

Or a weapon, to be used against the one who had killed her.

Sophara snapped her eyes open, staring at the wound on her sister's chest. It was black and molten, burned so hot that there was very little blood. On someone other than a dragon, it might not have left any blood at all.

The aura around the wound was black and red, braided together in a recognizable pattern.

Black dragons.

Not even with their bloodline all but eradicated, their authority forgotten, their descendants scattered, would the black dragons leave them alone. Sophara threw back her head, pouring all her rage and her hate into her voice.

When she roared, it was the roar of a dragon. And all the golds roared with her.

CHAPTER TEN

At first, Yerin thought the trip across the island would be quick.

The Sage had marked the basic locations of the other factions on the map. Most of the island was uncontrolled, but there were a few places where they'd have to travel around the territory of the Beast King or the dragons. The portal leading into Ghostwater was on the edge of Redmoon Hall territory. She was tempted to hit them, but forced herself back on track.

To be safe, she thought it might take as much as a week, stepping lightly and using veils. She suspected it would be more like two nights.

The first day, she pushed them so hard that Mercy had to take some elixirs from her storage to stop from collapsing. After midnight passed and they hadn't taken a break, Mercy grabbed Yerin's arm. The Akura's hair was plastered to her forehead, and she breathed like a whipped pack-mule.

"We're not going to get there tonight," Mercy said, a hint of begging in her tone.

Yerin glanced down at the map. She chafed at the delay, but Mercy had a point. They could use some time to rest and cycle.

"Four hours," Yerin allowed, and Mercy sagged to the ground, leaving her staff to topple beside her.

When Mercy had caught her breath, she looked into the darkness around her. Distant howls and whispers on the wind told them that these woods were haunted by predators.

"I've never spent the night in the woods before," Mercy admitted.

Yerin nestled into the crook of a tree, pulling her outer robe around her. "You can thank the heavens it isn't snowing. Some places, this is practically summer." There was a biting chill on the wind, but nothing that would kill a sacred artist above Iron.

She had piled up a little mound of leaves and dirt, and the roots rose high enough around her to break some of the wind. It wasn't an Arelius guest room, but she'd slept through worse.

Mercy fiddled with the end of her hair, looking from herself to Yerin nervously. "I'm not sure there will be enough room for us both."

Yerin's elbows were scraping roots on both sides. Her Goldsigns were folded up over her shoulders. "A hair smaller, and I'd have no room for my arms. You can find your own—"

A small door opened in the air.

It was a square opening about four or five feet to a side, sitting on the ground like someone had opened a box without bothering with the actual box part. Without hesitation, Mercy rummaged around inside, pulling out fluffy padded blankets and a metal box that radiated fire aura. A heater.

"It won't be comfortable," Mercy said, voice downcast. "The tent is really meant for one person."

"The tent," Yerin repeated.

Mercy held up a palm-sized square of dark green Forged madra, which snapped into a pyramid-shaped tent. Scripts on the outside provided an extra veil and warded away spirits. Mercy stared at the shelter like she couldn't imagine how they'd ever squeeze both people inside, but to Yerin it looked like a palace.

"If the heavens gave me one wish, I'd ask to be reborn as a Monarch's kid." Yerin still wasn't sure how she felt about Mercy, but at least the Akura girl came with supplies.

Mercy's brow furrowed. "It's just a tent."

Yerin was already climbing inside.

After a night in the tent, Yerin was certain that the journey would be easier than she had ever imagined. They started well-rested, they made good time that first morning, and they had a map. More than once, on her journeys with the Sword Sage, Yerin would have killed for convenience like this.

Their first delay came when they sensed a Redmoon Underlord a few miles ahead of them. They ended up having to stay in the tent, veiled, for a full day before they could confirm the enemy had withdrawn.

Then a flock of Truegold-level vultures caught their scent, forcing them off the path.

Then there was the mammoth that grazed on trees. They had to go around him.

A zone of shadow and darkness covered another hillside as Redmoon Hall skirmished with servants of the Akura family, and they had to sneak past.

Before she knew it, the days flowed like water and they still hadn't reached their destination.

Their speed dropped to a crawl, and they were forced to wait for hours at a time. So Yerin did what she always did when the hours pressed in on her: she trained.

As he fell through the air, the Sword Sage continued to fight.

One of his opponents flew on currents of air, his Ruler technique commanding the wind aura as he soared with no wings. That one produced halfsilver darts, whipping them at the Sword Sage to try and disrupt his madra.

The other rode an eagle like a horse, carrying a long spear in one hand and a shield in the other. Her eyes blazed the same color as her sacred beasts, and sword aura gathered around the eagle's claws.

Her lance-strike carried the putrid, sickly energy of death madra. The wind artist hammered him with gusts of wind madra to keep him off-balance, to knock him into the halfsilver darts.

He took a look at the deadly lance an inch from his skin, the furious eagle rearing to strike behind it. He sensed the bludgeon of wind madra from beneath him, the glimmer of sharp chaos as the halfsilver darts closed from behind.

With a tap of his madra, his sword rang like a bell.

As she advanced through the Highgold stage, Yerin had unlocked more memories that had been ingrained into her master's spirit. Some of them were personal or too short to make anything out of them, but some contained the insights into the Path of the Endless Sword that he'd never been able to share with her. She chewed on these like a cow with a mouthful of grass, meditating on them morning and night.

In this case, the Sword Sage's Endless Sword technique had met every attack at the same time. The eagle's claws, the deadly lance, the halfsilver darts—they were all knocked aside at once as though deflected by invisible swords.

Only the green column of wind madra was unaffected, and the Sage sliced that in half with a wave of madra from one of the six sword-arms on his back.

The rest of the scene faded, leaving Yerin to replay it over in her mind.

The Endless Sword was the Ruler technique for which her whole Path was named. It was the root and branch of her master's fighting style. But she hadn't even used it in her fight against Bai Rou.

The truth was, hers was a pale shadow of her master's. Her master could use the Endless Sword to cut one page from a closed book. She just hit the aura around her weapon as hard as she could with her madra. It spread out like ripples in a pond, cutting everything in its path, and when it passed through another source of sword aura, that aura burst too. Her master had called it aura resonance, and with enough madra behind it, it could start a cascading reaction that could tear a city to pieces.

But in her case, it didn't pack enough punch. She could only use it effectively against enemies weaker than she was. And what good was a weapon that couldn't be used against real opponents?

She'd focused on other pieces of her Path instead: advancement, her other techniques, physical swordplay. For too long, she had neglected the namesake of her Path. She had hoped that, as she grew in insight and experience, the Endless Sword would begin to make more sense to her.

Now Yerin was out of time. She needed more power... and her Blood Shadow was *right there.*

If she didn't find a new weapon, she'd be forced to rely on the Shadow every time the battle became tough. It had tormented her for too long; she couldn't lean on it. Frankly, it turned her stomach when she so much as thought about it for too long. If she never had to use it, that would be the real victory.

Which meant she needed to win without it.

In that vision, the Sword Sage had demonstrated the second level of Endless Sword mastery: sword like the wind. Yerin was stuck at the "storm" stage. Her aura exploded out from her weapon in a furious, uncontrolled storm.

But he'd revealed a much greater level of control. His sword-aura was quiet, invisible, and everywhere.

There were three higher levels of mastery.

He'd barely mentioned any of this to her before his death. She'd discovered most of it from the visions he'd left behind in his Remnant, paired with some of her own memories of him in combat. Technically, her skill in the technique wasn't connected to advancement. She could reach Archlord if her Endless Storm still looked like a hurricane. With enough power behind it, it could do damage.

But her madra was already dense enough to cross the barrier to Truegold. A deeper connection to her master's Remnant could give her that last nudge she needed to get there.

She hoped.

From the branches above her, a brown leaf drifted slowly to the ground. With a deep breath, she delicately tapped the sword in her lap with her madra. The dense silver aura around it flared, pushing out into one direction.

She could control that much, at least. Directing it one way or the other was an advancement for her. Now, her goal was to cut that falling leaf in two.

The leaf exploded into shreds. It fell to the ground as a fistful of dust.

After another hour, she gave up, stretching her legs and standing up. "We clear to move on yet?" she asked.

Then she saw that Mercy had begun training of her own.

The Akura girl was hanging upside-down from a limb at the top of a tree. She held a short wooden bow, arrow nocked, and her eyes were closed. Her breathing was even, and though Yerin was close, she couldn't sense the girl's presence at all.

After she had held that position for several minutes, three leaves fell from her tree at once.

Purple eyes snapped open, and she slipped her legs out of the branch.

She fell, arms blurring as she released the first arrow, pulling a second from the air, stringing it, and loosing it. Then a third.

Only then did the first arrow pierce the first leaf, pinning it to the ground several yards away. The second followed suit. The third arrow brushed by its target, sending the leaf spinning in the wind of its wake.

Mercy's head cracked as it hit the ground, and she crumpled.

Yerin folded her arms and waited. Iron bodies could take more punishment than that.

Mercy hissed as she sat up, cradling her head with one hand. "Aaaahhhh ow ow ow." Through watering eyes, she looked up to Yerin. "When I do it right, I land on my feet."

"You expect to fight upside-down a lot?"

Mercy examined her bow to make sure it hadn't broken. "Do you not practice Striker techniques this way? Trains accuracy, precision, reaction time..."

"Pain tolerance," Yerin suggested.

"Only when you miss." She stood up, brushing herself off. "I had a few more rounds to go, but now you're awake. Dinner?"

"Is the barrier gone?"

One of the factions—Yerin hadn't been able to determine who—had raised up a barrier of blue light that stretched across half the island in front of them. It was hard to see through the tree cover, but if you went far enough forward, you could see nothing but a sapphire wall. She wasn't sure what the barrier formation would do to people inside, but she wasn't curious enough to find out.

Mercy's eyes widened, and she snapped two blackened fingers. "Oh, that's right! I have news!"

Hurriedly, she scrambled over to their camp. They had spent three days in this place, so it was starting to look a little too permanent for Yerin's liking.

As she looked over the stump they used as a table and the stone-lined firepit they'd dug, the impatient itch returned to her heart.

Lindon could be running from Truegolds, and here she was locked out.

Mercy tripped over a root, landing belly-down in the dirt, but she held the Sage's folded map over her head in triumph. "Got it!" she said into the ground.

A moment later, she was explaining her excitement to Yerin. "I was at the top of the tree, checking on the barrier, and I realized what we *thought* was a hill was just that mammoth sleeping. And the mountain is farther away than I'd thought."

Yerin's stomach fell. Every time they'd made a mistake navigating, it had resulted in days' more delay.

"So, we're not here, we're *here*," Mercy said, stabbing her finger at a spot on the map.

A spot just below the portal.

"If the wall wasn't there, we could see it from the tree," Mercy said brightly. "It's fading away. You can see through it now, and you couldn't this morning."

Yerin leaped.

Her Steelborn Iron body drew thirstily on her madra, fueling her flat-footed jump so that she launched herself to the top of the tree. She bent the top of the tree as she landed, but she had no trouble keeping her balance.

The wall of blue light still rolled on the horizon, but if Mercy was right, then it was covering the beach and the edge of the island more than another expanse of forest. When the boundary came down, they would be only a few hours' run away from the portal.

She strained her eyes to try and see if there was some change in the boundary, but she could tell nothing. She hopped back to the ground, and was surprised to find that Mercy was starting a fire instead of packing up.

"You cracked in the head? Let's go!"

"Dinner first," Mercy said firmly. "It won't come down any faster just because we're closer."

Yerin paced like a tiger in a cage. She just wanted to feel like she was making *some* progress. Even moving an hour closer would mean an hour's less travel time when the light did disappear.

She started to say so, but a deafening, bestial scream covered the island out of nowhere. It was joined by more and more, until it sounded like a choir of raging spirits howling at the heavens. A furious, burning presence lit up her spiritual senses like a flying bonfire.

"It's not the vultures again," she muttered, opening up her perception. The roars had been deeper than that, and she thought she felt fire. But that sense could be slippery.

Mercy grabbed her staff, which hissed into the sky. Its violet eyes flared. "Not vultures. Dragons."

As she said so, a golden cloud descended from heaven, bearing a complex of palaces on it. The Thousand-Mile

Cloud that had hovered outside the Akura fortress about two weeks before, from which a woman had argued with Old Man Lo.

"What's rustled their scales?" Yerin asked. They were still roaring, and she thought she saw golden flames rising from the Cloud.

Mercy shivered. "I think we should get in the tent."

A second later, Yerin felt it too: someone's spiritual sense was sweeping the forest. The Cloud was still many miles away; to search them from that distance would take an Underlord at least.

"I'd contend we should," Yerin allowed with a sigh. She took a last, regretful glance in the other direction. Hiding was the smart thing to do, but she'd rather move closer to the boundary.

After all, it wasn't like the dragons were looking for *them*. The heavens couldn't hate her that much.

"You're just having a little break? Having some time to yourself? That's okay, nothing wrong with that. You've just been through a fight, haven't you? But now you're rested, you're refreshed, you're ready to get yourself up and move on! The road doesn't get any shorter while you wait, as they say."

It had been five minutes.

Lindon was still sitting cross-legged on the floor, cycling his madra to try and bring power back to his spirit before his Bloodforged Iron body took it all and left him spiritually drained and helpless. Little Blue lay sprawled on top of his head, sleeping, and he held his spine straight to avoid disturbing her.

Now Dross was growing impatient.

"I told you about the Spirit Well, didn't I? I'm pretty sure

I did. Well, that's our next stop! No need to waste time trying to restore your madra now, when the Spirit Well will do it with just a sip! Well, I mean, I suppose you *should* strengthen yourself just a bit. There are quite a few giant, hungry beasts between us and our destination, but uh...it sounds worse than it is."

Lindon held out a broken necklace with a copper key dangling from the center. It was only the size of a fingernail; too small to unlock anything bigger than a dollhouse. But it was a sacred treasure, he was sure of it.

Using as little madra as he could, he reached his spirit out and activated it. He was confident that this was the device that he'd sensed before, and his curiosity was too ravenous to wait until he had finished stabilizing his soul. If he really did run out of madra, he might not be able to trigger this for hours. And that would be unacceptable.

Fortunately, it didn't take much effort to start. Little more than flipping a switch.

A doorway bloomed in front of him, seven feet tall and about three wide. It led into a closet, hanging there in midair.

The closet was only a few feet deep and mostly empty. A few chairs were stacked in the center, with pillows and blankets stuffed beneath them. Three sealed clay jugs sat in the corner, and based on a quick glimpse of their contents, they seemed to contain water. He was still on his knees, weak and injured...but not too weak or injured to rummage through a closet that he'd summoned out of nowhere. A few scripted bundles were revealed to hold dried meat.

Rations, water, furniture, and bedding. Practical things to hold in a magical storage space, except perhaps for the chairs.

Orthos walked around the other side of the portal, speaking with a tone of awe. "A void key! I've only glimpsed them from afar. It's rare for even an Underlord to have such a thing. It contains a private space, accessible only by the one who holds it. Whatever you keep in here, no one can touch it unless they steal the key."

Lindon wished there was a tear running down his face so that he could wipe it away. "I've never seen anything so beautiful." Even Little Blue woke up, sitting up on his head and cooing in wonder. He almost wanted to thank Ekeri.

Besides the more mundane objects, there were a few eye-catching treasures shoved into the corners of the closet. A sculpture of a woman in smooth white jade, a mirror of pure gold, a jeweled star, and a teacup that seemed to be made from a paper-thin eggshell.

None of them gave off the slightest aura of power, but Orthos suggested they were valuable enough that they could fund Lindon's entire advancement to the end of Truegold. Assuming they could escape this pocket world and find a buyer.

"The real treasure is that necklace," Orthos said, and Lindon fervently agreed. "If you were lucky enough to find anyone willing to sell one, that would cost as much as half the Arelius family. Sages are the weakest beings who can create void keys."

"There was a void key storage room in this habitat," Dross told them. "Room upon room full of them, each key filled with specialized equipment."

Lindon seized him.

"...yes, it was the first thing the Heralds looted," Dross continued, and Lindon's heart crashed back into his chest.

His spirit and body were both still unstable after his fight, but he wobbled to his feet. "We should leave soon. As soon as we're prepared."

As it turned out, their preparation took two days.

The first thing Lindon did, once he could move his arms freely, was to smash the chairs and toss them back into the closet. He didn't need furniture, but as a fire artist, he could always use kindling.

He placed the chest with all of his belongings next to the bundle of kindling, then emptied all the water jars and filled them with water from the Well of Dreams. The well was only a few inches deep now, but that was still far more water than Lindon wanted to leave behind. He filled all twenty-four vials they'd found in the storage room, placed them in their racks, and stored them in the void key as well.

A few of the Silverfang Carp had been killed by his battle with Ekeri without being reduced to ash by the Void Dragon's Dance, so he found their corpses and stripped some meat. Thanks to the fires burning all over the habitat, he was able to roast them without tainting them in the flavor of Blackflame, then wrap the fish steaks up in leaves he cut from the remaining forest of stalks.

Even after two days of preparation, he was reluctant to leave. There was still water in the Dream Well, and plenty of food from the Carp. He and Orthos could cycle easily in the smoldering wasteland they'd made, and the return to regular cycling was helping heal Orthos' spirit.

Dross kept up a steady complaint, but he couldn't go anywhere without Lindon. He wasn't what finally pushed Lindon to leave.

Yerin was out there, somewhere. He had no way of knowing what she was doing, if she was safe, if Bai Rou had attacked or abandoned her. He wondered about her sleeping and waking, and whatever he did, the worry stuck in the back of his mind like a splinter.

But if she knew this place was good for his advancement, she would surely tell him to stay here as long as possible. Little Blue was more urgent.

He was using everything he could spare from his pure core to feed the Sylvan Riverseed, but she was still pale as a winter's sky and he could see straight through her. She spent most of her day sprawled on his shoulder, silent. He was no expert on spirits, but she couldn't stay here much longer.

Even Orthos, despite his good humor, couldn't fully recover just from cycling. If he could, he would never have gone insane in Serpent's Grave. He needed to move on.

But there was one last reason that shook him enough to push him out of this habitat.

The cracks in space, which once had been the size of Ekeri's body, had now spread to the size of a room. The web of nearly invisible fissures was growing. Dross said it had to do with the decay of the pocket world. Any forced spatial movement would fracture the world's boundaries until the whole thing decayed.

And, as usual, he turned that into an argument for reaching the Spirit Well as soon as possible. This time, Lindon happened to agree.

He tied the tiny copper key to the shadesilk ribbon around his neck, so that it hung behind his gold hammer badge. Opening it one last time, he walked into the closet and pulled Little Blue from his shoulder.

"Wait for me in here," he said, lowering her to the ground.

She scrambled up his arm, chirping in distress.

"I'll let you out as soon as I can. We're going through dangerous waters; if I lose you, I might not be able to find you again."

She clung to his forearm and chimed like a bell.

Lindon sat down in the extra-spatial closet, lifting his arm so he could look Little Blue in the eyes. Her pale face was the picture of panic.

"I'll come back for you," he assured her.

She shook her head.

"You want to come with us?"

Silver bells rang.

"Are you more scared of being locked in here than coming with us?"

Another long, sad note from a flute.

Lindon couldn't blame her. He'd been locked into tight spaces...too many times.

So he walked out and tucked her into his pocket, next to Suriel's marble. "Try not to fall out," he told her.

She was already playing with the glass ball.

Another wisp of madra shut the door to the closet, and Lindon was ready to leave. He looked over at Orthos, who held Dross in his mouth.

"Great, we're ready to go! Fantastic! Don't worry about the two days worth of essence I lost, each of which was a memory. As I decay, I lose more and more of who I am, but don't you worry about that now, because we're leaving!"

Lindon ducked his head to the construct. "Lead the way."

Purple light sketched a line out of the bubble, into the dark water outside. The line extended into the darkness, then sank lower. And lower.

"The tablet library, and the Spirit Well it contains, is a tad deeper than we are," Dross explained. "Not to worry, though, because I am both map and key. It will be a straight shot from here."

A line of bright blue spots slid by the bubble, close enough that Lindon could have reached his arm through and touched them. In the light of the still-burning fires, he saw a glimpse of silver scales between the blue.

Dross cleared a nonexistent throat. "There's the one complication. Diamondscale Sea Drakes. You remember when I told you the Silverfang Carp were raised like cattle? Well, this is what those cattle were meant to feed."

The last blue light slid around the bubble, and Lindon traced its path until it moved out of sight. It was circling the whole habitat.

"The refiners kept them in captivity, but the facility records say they broke free decades ago. They've been breeding in the wild ever since."

Lindon reached a hand out to the bubble-wall. "Was this meant to keep them out?"

"No, the boundary formation is meant to keep out the water. It doesn't keep them out at all, they just prefer it out there."

Lindon took a few steps back.

"Is there any way to avoid them?"

"Some believe that *hope* is the strongest force in the universe," Dross said. "Although that is objectively untrue."

Lindon looked back. He couldn't see the blue lights anywhere in his vision.

"Can we form some kind of—" he started to say, but Orthos had already stepped into the water.

With a deep breath, Lindon joined him.

第十一章

CHAPTER ELEVEN

Dross' purple light and the deep red of Orthos' shell were the only sources of illumination out here, in the icy deep. Swallowed by cold and dark, Lindon almost turned back on instinct, but the red and purple were his only guides. He swam after them, reaching a hand into his pocket to make sure that Little Blue was secure.

Satisfied that she was, he pulled out Suriel's marble, adding a faint blue candle-glow to their procession. To his surprise, Orthos was a capable swimmer; the turtle's feet acted more like flippers in the water, and he outpaced Lindon in seconds. Lindon had to strain to keep up, and only because he suspected Orthos was waiting for him.

They had only swum a few yards before they reached the edge of a cliff and looked down. Warm, inviting light spilled up from below: a new habitat. The bubble was shaped a little differently than the previous, like a wide circle rather than a dome, but the top was only a dozen feet straight down. The relief was like a breath of air; he could swim that distance. No problem. He was honestly surprised that they hadn't seen the light from this place before, when it was so close.

He glanced back to judge the distance between himself

and the habitat, and saw two points of blue light coming at him out of the darkness.

He looked for the other lights instinctively before he realized they weren't spots.

They were eyes.

Blackflame madra raged through him, and the Burning Cloak ignited. When he couldn't breathe freely, controlling madra was like pushing mud through a straw, and it strained his channels to bursting. Primitive, crippling survival terror made it easy: he'd tear his soul in half to defend himself from those approaching eyes.

The Diamondscale opened its maw, revealing even more saber-sharp teeth than the Silverfang Carp, as well as a light welling up from its throat like a blue furnace.

Lindon kicked off the sand, twisting desperately, hoping that the Enforcer technique would give him enough speed so that the great serpent wouldn't just turn and snap him out of the water.

It twisted, but he scratched at its face with both hands, seizing ridges on its head and plastering himself to it like a monkey clinging to a tree branch.

The Sea Drake bucked like an earthquake, rumbling with a fury that Lindon interpreted as a roar. Every quake threatened to shake Lindon loose, until he was holding on only by the pointed tips of his Remnant hand.

Red light shot through the darkness, and Orthos sank his jaws into silver scales.

Now the serpent's ferocious twist threw Lindon free, and for a moment he was lost in an aimless blur of bubbles and darkness. Lost, disoriented, he clawed in the direction he hoped was the ocean floor.

He found himself staring down at a purple light from ten feet above: Dross lay on the sand, helpless in his gem.

Lindon pulled through the water, scooping up the jewel in his left hand. He faced a wall of dust kicked up by two massive, thrashing bodies. Red and blue lights flashed from within the cloud.

His lungs were starting to burn as badly as his madra channels, and now he was faced with a choice: forward or back?

The choice was made for him when Orthos came hurtling out of the dust cloud, righting himself in the water and charging back in.

The Diamondscale Sea Drake flipped back to stare at him once more.

Then it rushed at Orthos, seizing him in its jaws. Orthos wrestled with it, sinking his own teeth into its snout, and they struggled in the water for a long instant before plunging over the cliff.

Lindon followed them. If he could reach the bubble, he could use his madra properly, and then maybe he could help Orthos.

Through the bubble, the dream tablet library looked like a series of stone shelves, resembling bookshelves, only instead of books they contained points of soft multicolored light.

Orthos and the Drake fell into the center of the ring, kicking up another cloud of sand, and Lindon pulled himself to the edge of the habitat. He clawed through the bubble, pushing his head through, getting a deep gasp of breath that brought life back to his madra.

His head was sticking through the ceiling of the bubble, and he looked down onto the stone libraries. After a disorienting moment of shifting gravity, he started to fall through into the air.

He allowed it, Blackflame still flowing through him, and twisted in midair to land on the floor. Unlike the ground in the last habitat, this one was laid with polished tiles.

And it wasn't empty.

From down the curving row of shelves, a man stared at him. Bright green horns grew from his forehead, pointed up, and he wore a road-stained cloak of gray. His expression was so worn and weary that he initially looked older, but a second glance made it clear that he wasn't much older than Lindon.

Lindon recognized him as one of the young Truegolds. The one who had saved him back in the portal room.

He heaved a sigh as he saw Lindon, reaching out to a hammer leaning up against a nearby shelf. Its haft was as long as he was tall, its head the width of his body, and Lindon braced himself for sudden battle.

Instead, the stranger pulled the hammer behind him as though it weighed as much as a mountain. The head dragged against the tile with a horrible scraping noise. Each step cost him visible effort. There had once been an emblem dyed into the back of his cloak, which Lindon thought resembled a lotus flower or perhaps a web, but it was too faded with age to be clear.

Lindon pressed his fists together and bowed, saluting the man's back. No need to be unnecessarily rude, even if the man couldn't see him. After all, Lindon was the one who had burst in out of nowhere, dripping water all over the tile.

Then he shot off. Orthos was still in trouble.

When he cleared a few rows of bookshelves, he saw what the center of the ring looked like from the inside. It appeared to be a column of dark blue water in the center of the facility, extending from the floor to the ceiling as though it supported the weight of the ocean overhead.

Now, that column was filled with flashing scales, billowing dust, and leathery skin.

Lindon watched for a moment. Dross was babbling something, but Lindon was too focused on the battle to hear it. The Burning Cloak burst into being around him again, its power flowing through him much more easily. He started gathering dragon's breath in his hand. If he got a clear shot, he was sure he could turn the fight in Orthos' favor.

Then the water exploded in his direction, drenching Lindon as Orthos and the serpent spilled out of the bubble and into the library.

Orthos smashed into one of the shelves shell-first, cracking stone and releasing hisses of colored light from two of the broken tablets. The Sea Drake flopped around in midair at first, but after only a second it righted itself.

And started swimming through the air.

Sure, the Carp had done it, and they were huge. But this creature was ten times bigger; it didn't seem fair that its mastery of water aura was great enough to allow it to swim through air so easily.

It struck at Orthos as the turtle forced himself upright, and Lindon extended his dragon's breath.

The stranger was standing there, between Lindon and Orthos, holding the haft of his hammer in both hands while the head still rested on the floor. Lindon hadn't seen him arrive, but now he had to abort his Striker technique to avoid hitting the newcomer. He stood before the serpent with eyes closed, like a man embracing the approach of death.

For an instant.

A blink later, the Drake slammed to a halt like a fist hitting a steel plate. There was a sickening crunch that echoed through the library and a brief flash of green light, and the huge serpent's head *exploded* under a titanic hammer-blow.

Blood and gore sprayed over the floor, gushing over Orthos and splattering the tablet shelves behind him. The stranger was only speckled in dark red; a floating script-circle hovered in the air in front of him like a shield Forged out of green light. It pushed the tide of carnage to either side, preventing the man from becoming drenched in blood.

The rest of the Sea Drake's body sank to the floor, twitching, and its tail slid out of the column of water to land on the tile with a meaty slap.

The stranger's eyes were still shut. He lowered his bloody hammer to the floor and, without a word, started dragging it off again.

Orthos shook himself like a dog, spraying yet more blood everywhere, and laughed freely. "You hit with the strength of a dragon! What is your name, human?"

The green-horned man stopped. He wiped blood from his eyes with a thumb, though he didn't bother cleaning the rest of his face. "Ziel," he said.

Then he kept walking.

"Ziel," Orthos said to his back. "I will remember you." He continued chuckling as he walked past the body of the Diamondscale Sea Drake, taking a bite of its meat as he passed. He was still chewing when he walked into the column of water, washing himself off.

Dross, keeping his voice to a whisper, spoke as soon as Ziel was out of earshot. "Ziel of the Wasteland. We're not exactly flush with records about him, sorry to say, but there are plenty of rumors. I *can* tell you he's under the Beast King's protection, and you know what that means."

"I don't," Lindon said. He was still in awe at what Ziel had done with a single blow from his Enforcer technique. And he was supposed to be on a level with Ekeri.

"The Beast King," Dross said, as though it was something obvious. "He's been a legend for centuries. A crippled boy who befriended some ancient sacred beasts and eventually rose to the level of a Herald. He's one of the guardians who stands in the Wasteland between Akura territory and the land of the dragons, protecting human civilization. Or so they say. Without him and others like him, the Black-flame Empire would be a war-torn desert."

"So what does it mean that Ziel is under his protection?"

"The Beast King spends all his time in a wasteland of endless battle. He cares about nothing but his war. If he's taken on a human, then that means he thinks this kid will be a critical weapon against the dragons. Not too surprising, seeing how he dealt with that Diamondscale. Maybe that was a secret anti-dragon technique."

"A dragon hunter," Lindon mused aloud. It sounded exciting, like the myths he'd heard as a child, but he had trouble putting the pieces together. Ziel hadn't turned on Orthos, though Orthos was clearly using the power of a dragon. And he hadn't showed any hostility toward Ekeri in the portal room, nor had he followed her when she left.

He didn't *act* like someone whose sole purpose in life was a war against dragonkind.

Orthos emerged from the water clean and radiating satisfaction. However, his soul told a different story: the battle had scarred him further, his spirit throbbing with deep pain.

"Not that this will surprise you," Dross said, "but Ziel headed in the direction of the Spirit Well. Just follow the bloody footsteps."

Those footsteps led past shelf after shelf of dream tablets, some of which had gone dark or flickered with age, but most of which shone brightly. After a few minutes, they reached a vast gray wall, featureless but for a keyhole identical to the one in the other facility.

The door must once have been hidden, but now it was shattered, revealing another blue hallway. Rubble had been sprayed all over the downward-sloping floor, almost as though someone had smashed their way in with a hammer.

"Ah, why don't you hold up for a moment?" Dross said as Lindon was about to enter. Ziel's footsteps led into the hall, and Lindon had intended to follow them.

"I don't know much about how these facilities were constructed, but I can tell you that they're not supposed to be something that a Truegold can break." Dross slid out of his gem, drifting across the space as a floating purple cloud of light and phantom gears. "If we're not dealing with a Gold, but a Sage in disguise, that would be...less than ideal."

Orthos kept walking, crunching over the pebbles in the doorway. Clearly, he didn't intend to cower at the entrance.

Lindon stopped. He hadn't done anything to antagonize the stranger, but it still seemed prudent to let Dross investigate first.

After sinking himself into the keyhole, Dross let out a sound imitating a breath of relief and floated back to Lindon. "We're okay! False alarm! The protective scripts in this wall were already failing. Good thing that didn't happen back in the Dream Well facility, eh? That dragon-girl could have just blasted her way in to us."

Lindon shivered. His hand moved unconsciously to the still-healing wound on his chest.

"Now all we have to worry about is the facility crashing down around us," Dross said brightly. "Should be several weeks before that happens, though. We can be fairly certain. At least...let's say sixty percent."

This storage facility was much smaller than the one in the other habitat. It only had four rooms besides the one at the end of the hall, where Lindon soon saw Orthos drinking deeply from a shining blue well.

Though nothing had happened to the turtle, Lindon still entered hesitantly, looking around for Ziel. His footsteps led to the corner, where he sat with his back against the wall and his hammer propped next to him. He sat with arms on his knees, saying nothing.

Lindon bowed to him over a salute. "Ziel of the Wasteland, this one thanks you for your protection."

Ziel waved a hand. He was staring at the floor as though watching a memory.

"We humbly request your permission to drink from the well, if you don't mind."

The Truegold, still stained in blood, looked to the well and then raised weary eyes to Lindon. "Plenty to go around," he said.

It was true. The Spirit Well was at least ten times bigger than the Dream Well, and looked more like a pond than what Lindon would call a well.

"Gratitude," Lindon said. "We will try not to bother you more than necessary."

Ziel stared at the floor again.

The well gave off a blue glow brighter than the hallway outside, and hazy purple shapes drifted through the air above it.

At first, he thought they were constructs meant to defend or inspect the place, but they looked vaguely like ghostly animals. Fish swam in schools with spirits like butterflies and some like snakes. They were all pale pink or purple with no fine details, and they all pulsed slightly as though on the verge of shifting shape.

Little Blue pushed out of his pocket and cheeped at the sight.

"Sylvan Dreamseeds," Dross explained. "Just like River-seeds are pure spirits that are born in areas with a strong balance between water and life aura, these little guys are born under the influence of dream aura. From the dream tablets, you see. The library and the Well are here purely to create the right conditions for their birth. Right now they're weak. Not much better than pure madra *acting* like dream madra. They only wish they could hold all the memories I can."

He darted aggressively at the nearest Dreamseed, which ignored him, drifting through the air like a frozen bird.

As interesting as the Dreamseeds were, it was the Spirit Well that held Lindon's attention. He dipped both cupped hands into the water and lifted them to his lips.

While the Dream Well had carried a slight mineral taste, this water was sweet. The mouthful went down easily, and he cycled its power to his pure core.

The effect was instantaneous. His core crackled with lightning, reminding him of the orus spirit-fruit Lindon had consumed back in Sacred Valley. Only this was a hundred times more powerful. It felt like a whirlpool had formed in his core, refining his madra with every revolution. It was almost like his madra was cycling itself.

Not only that, but the water's power seeped into his madra channels like rain on dying grass. He gasped at the sudden pain, which reminded him of splashing icy cold water on a burn. Only when this hit his channels, it left them stronger than before.

Lindon didn't hesitate to dunk his face into the well.

It was like a high-grade madra-refining pill mixed with Little Blue's touch. Every drink rinsed his spirit, helped his core refill itself, and refined his madra. He could feel his pure power growing denser, richer, thicker.

He came up for air, gasping. "Jars. We need jars."

CHAPTER TWELVE

The Spirit Well was Lindon's greatest dream made real.

It was like a heavenly feast set before him; an endless spring of power from which he could literally drink. Cycling had never been so rewarding or so effortless. He and Orthos moved into another room that was filled with garbage—the wreckage of long-abandoned crates and barrels that smelled like vinegar and had been smashed years if not decades before. They set the garbage on fire, leaving Dross to open the vents and get rid of the smoke. It became their cycling room for Blackflame. After a mouthful of Spirit Well water, each revolution of madra produced twice the result for half the effort. Lindon missed his parasite ring; the scripted halfsilver ring would have filtered his madra even further, resulting in even faster growth.

But the water was just as much of a boon for Blackflame as it was for his pure core. After the first few hours, he was pushing the barriers of Lowgold. If Lindon ever met Northstrider face-to-face, he was going to prostrate himself at the Monarch's feet in gratitude for building this place.

Ziel left the well room for an hour or two at a time, but always returned to sit in his corner. When he came back, he would dip his bowl into the Spirit Well, take one half-hearted sip, and then dump the rest over his head so that it washed the blood away in finger-thin rivulets.

Lindon almost choked at the waste.

"Forgiveness, but why don't you drink more?"

Ziel didn't open his eyes, but gestured at his abdomen. "Take a look, then tell me if you think it'll do any good."

Lindon opened his Copper sight. A venomous, toxic green ravaged his body, dimming the aura of his blood and life. He extended his perception, scanning the man's spirit; he didn't resist at all.

His core, a hazy green light, had been destroyed. Something had *deliberately* sliced it into pieces, then stitched the pieces back together. Half his madra channels were dark, and the other half were twisted and knotted into chaotic patterns.

Lindon closed off his perception, horrified. A Truegold with that much damage to their spirit should either be dead or Unsouled. But he had the power of a Truegold *now*.

How powerful had he been before?

Lindon bowed to him in silent apology and turned back to the pool. Little Blue's touch could cleanse and reinforce madra channels, but the Spirit Well had a similar effect. If it wasn't helping Ziel, neither could she.

At this point, Lindon wasn't sure if a team of spirit healers could help the man. He was ashamed to have looked.

Outwardly, Orthos wasn't as thrilled with the well as Lindon was, but he went back and guzzled deeply whenever he could. Slowly, Lindon felt the turtle's spirit improving, like a knot unraveling or a stain shrinking.

Little Blue was hesitant to leave Lindon's side at first, staring warily at the newcomer and the Dreamseeds overhead. But after she dipped a hand into the Spirit Well, she cooed in wonder and then dove in headfirst. She had taken to it like a fish, swimming around happily and growing deeper in color with every passing minute. A night in there, and she would be back to normal.

Dross had returned to his vessel and demanded to be dropped into the pool, just as he had been in the Dream

Well for over fifty years. Lindon didn't spare any more thought for him until the first night—which was what they had chosen to call the half of the day when the overhead scripts dimmed. The water outside the habitat was just as black as always, and of course the dream tablets and Spirit Well glowed constantly.

Lindon was just starting to wonder if he should drink a vial of Dream Well water to shake off sleep when he heard a loud sigh from the azure pool. Dross' spirit-form drifted up from the water, an ethereal ball of slowly turning gears and spinning violet lights.

"It's great in there, it really is, but uh...I don't know that I want to spend fifty years in there again. Do you know what I mean? I wasn't conscious for most of that time, but once I was, it got *very* boring very quickly. Not sure I want to do the whole thing wide awake."

Lindon rubbed his chin, looking at the Spirit Well. "What do you think this will do for you?"

Dross made a coughing sound. "That's the question. The Soulsmiths who made me tried to make a construct that could work alongside a person's brain, but they failed, didn't they? Ended up just making better memory constructs.

"Well, this facility was run by a collection of scholars after the same goal. They theorized that they could create a kind of super-spirit, an advanced hive of Dreamseeds that would handle thoughts so that Northstrider didn't have to. It would make it so that he wouldn't have to *think* to solve a problem, but he would always know the answer, bam, just like that. The Dreamseeds would do the mental work for him."

"And it failed," Lindon said. That wasn't a guess; if it had succeeded, Northstrider would never have abandoned Ghostwater in the first place.

"Like a snow fort in the desert," Dross said sadly. "Turns out, when they pumped power into a Dreamseed, what they got was a more powerful Dreamseed. Not sure how else they expected that to go, really." He waited a breath

before continuing. "I may have been born a little differently than these little guys, but surely a construct that's come
to life can't be too different than a natural spirit."

That made sense to Lindon. And he wanted to see what
Dross was becoming; it might end up useful. This was the
chance to learn something that even Northstrider's expert
Soulsmiths hadn't understood.

"We could try and come up with a script that might
focus the power on you," Lindon said doubtfully. If he was
a more knowledgeable scriptor, it might work, but he had
never done much research on that front. "It's a pity you
can't just drink it."

Dross glowed brighter. "That's it! I can borrow your
body!" He saw the look on Lindon's face and hastened to
add, "Don't worry, I'll share."

"You can do that?" Lindon asked. That was intriguing.
Could he send Dross to take over other people's bodies?

"Don't see why not. There's a Remnant inside you right
now, or at least all the ingredients to make one when you
die. Plenty of room inside your spirit, so I'll just *squeeze* in
there." He pushed into Lindon's chest, but bounced off the
madra running through Lindon's skin. "Excuse me, you have
to move aside. Just for a minute. Don't worry, it shouldn't
hurt. Me. I don't know what it will feel like to you."

Orthos pushed past Lindon on the way to the Spirit
Well. "There are some sacred artists who take in the power
of natural spirits as part of their Path. It is safe."

"See! Perfectly safe, he says." Dross tried to push into
Lindon's head this time, but slid off.

Lindon wanted to see what Dross would become, but he
was still uncomfortable with the idea of letting a self-aware
construct inside his soul. "Is this the only option we have?"

"Don't worry," Orthos said. "If the tiny spirit tries some
mischief, I will burn him out of your body."

Now Lindon had more worries, but his curiosity won out.

Lindon extended a hand to Dross. "I'll still my madra as
much as I can until you're inside."

Dross whooped in excitement and zipped into his palm almost before Lindon had withdrawn his spirit.

It felt like something swimming up his left arm, and Lindon instinctively recoiled. He focused his spiritual sense on his own body, and in the blue-white loops that normally represented his spirit, now a purple ball slid around his madra channels and settled into the center of his pure core.

"Wow," Dross said in his head. *"Roomy in here. Were you born with two extra-large cores? I'm sorry, that sounds rude. But do feel free to answer."*

Since Lindon had used the Heaven and Earth Purification Wheel to advance, it still had an influence on his cores even when he wasn't actively practicing it. His madra recovery was slow, but he had much more madra than he would have otherwise. And a good thing, too; his Iron body and his techniques took a lot of power. If Eithan was any indication, his cores would only get deeper as he advanced, until he had a truly ridiculous amount of madra.

But he suppressed the Purification Wheel as much as he could, with Dross inside. It was inconvenient, but Eithan's warning still made him hesitant to let the technique's existence leak.

Orthos eyed him. "Seems like it worked."

"It's messy in here," Dross sent to him. *"You're so...squishy."*

Lindon walked over to the pool, scooping up some shining blue water in a cracked teacup. He drank it and cycled it straight to the construct, who instantly let out an excited whoop.

"It's working! My memories have so many connections I didn't see before; this must be what having a brain feels like! Only, you know, less...mushy."

Lindon had cycled all the power to Dross, leaving none for his own channels or core.

He spoke aloud, because he wasn't sure if thinking the words would get through to the construct. "How is it? You need more?"

"I'll chew on this for the rest of the day," Dross said. *"At that*

rate, maybe...two more weeks? Three? Compared to fifty years, it's like a drop of water in the ocean, isn't it?"

"Three weeks? Do we even have that long?" Lindon gave an aching glance at the Spirit Well; he wanted to take as much time in this room as he could, and didn't want to waste a minute of it on Dross' advancement. Yerin would kill him if she knew he'd found an inexhaustible source of power without her, and would kill him twice as hard if he didn't take advantage of every second.

A weary voice spoke up from the corner of the room. "If nothing else accelerates the decay in the pocket world's structure, we have at least a month." Ziel spoke from his position leaning against the wall, eyes shut. "Could be longer."

Lindon didn't have any reason to believe a Truegold's word about the structure of a pocket world, but he spoke with the utter confidence of an expert, so Lindon thanked him.

"There you have it," Dross said, relaxing himself into a more comfortable position within Lindon's core.

And so Lindon settled in. He was looking forward to seeing Dross' transformation, but he couldn't deny a little bitterness about having to share the power of the Spirit Well. How much would this delay his advancement? A week? A month?

Lindon reached Highgold on the Path of Black Flame in two days.

Surrounded by burning trash, he was cycling fire and destruction aura as usual, regretting that he couldn't use the Heaven and Earth Purification Wheel with Dross sitting in his soul. Without warning, his madra started running back from the rest of his body into his core like he'd opened a plug and it was starting to drain out.

"Hey, would you look at that!" Dross said, from his vantage inside Lindon's pure core. *"Are you trying out a new cycling technique?"*

Lindon couldn't open his eyes, struggling as he was to focus on his madra, but he heard Orthos rise to his feet nearby. Suddenly, madra poured into him from outside, guiding his power and easing the burden on his spirit.

All of his madra pushed together, squeezing to occupy the same space, and it seemed to shrink together. After several minutes passed, he had only a third of the madra he'd started with, but it was more dense and potent. If his madra before had been water, now it felt like syrup.

When it finished, all of his Blackflame madra concentrated into a thick drop at the center of his core, a pulse of uncontrolled power rippled out from him and activated the aura. Fires flared up all around the cycling room, consuming their fuel in an instant, creating a cloud of smoke.

Lindon let his new Highgold madra run through his veins. At last, he was on the same level as Yerin.

She had years of practice and experience he didn't have, but finally, they were standing on the same ground.

"Highgold," Orthos announced. "It is the role of a Highgold to think more deeply on the purpose and nature of your Path. At this stage, sacred artists that have bonded Remnants often begin to inherit insights from their predecessors."

"There's no need for insight before Underlord," Ziel said. He stopped in the doorway on his way down the hall, as though he were a construct that had simply run out of power. Green horns were cast in shadow—his Goldsign was so condensed as to look completely real. "Highgold only indicates a certain density of madra. You could go from Lowgold to the peak of Truegold with two pills."

"*Shortcuts* are for the weak," Orthos said. "You walk a Path one step at a time, and this is the step of a Highgold."

Ziel raised two fingers as though holding something very small. "I used to have those pills. They were this big. They smelled like fresh berries and summer leaves..."

He cast his glance down at the floor and dragged himself down the hallway.

"Really brings down the mood, doesn't he?" Dross observed.

Not Lindon's. After reaching Highgold, his smile was

iron-plated. He didn't care *what* the stage meant, just that he had taken another step.

And there was plenty of water left in the blue well.

Orthos and Ziel carved every meal from the corpse of the Diamondscale Sea Drake, but one bite of the cooked meat had knocked Lindon out for six hours. It nourished his body even more than the Silverfang Carp had, but it was at the brink of what his body could tolerate. After eating it, his Iron body had consumed so much madra that it delayed his training, even with the Spirit Well's help.

After reaching Highgold, he could keep himself conscious while cycling one bite of the Drake's meat to his body, but it took everything he had. He couldn't afford to have more than one bite a day, so the rest of his meals came from Carp steaks stored in his void key. He was clearly reaching the limit of what that meat could do for his physical condition, but food was food.

Other than spending his time in the corner of the Spirit Well room, Ziel wandered the shelves of dream tablets. Each of the shining, multicolored stones was labeled with a name, a stage of advancement, a Path, and a subject.

After a few days, Lindon began following him. He touched six dream tablets while Lindon watched, and all of them belonged to Archlords. Those were the most advanced subjects in the library, and Ziel seemed to have no interest in anything beneath them.

For Lindon's part, he didn't try anything above Underlord after a single touch of an Overlord tablet had left him flat on his back and sweating, with no memory of what he'd seen.

When he activated a dream tablet with his spirit, he was taken into a memory of a particular scene, as though he were living it. The devices were less useful for recording information than he had imagined, but they were ideal for containing experiences. He had heard of portable dream tablets before, but these were either of a different sort, or were secured to prevent thievery: each dream tablet was sealed to the stone around it.

She held out one palm, Forging a spear of red ice. From her vantage point among the clouds, she looked down on the great spider that crouched over her city, spreading its webs from building to building. She let soulfire bleed into the Forged spear, its gray fire tempering the technique, smoothing it, nourishing it.

Now, the spear shone like a polished shaft of diamond. This was the strongest technique she could conjure.

She only hoped there was anyone down there to survive this.

Meiyen Teia, Underlord on the Path of Glacier's Birth: the Devastation of Whisperbark.

Lindon came out of the memory gasping, his last sight a storm of bloody ice shredding a great spider...and the city over which it lurked.

He sat down and focused on the vision, drinking down a vial of Dream Well water he'd brought with him.

"What do you call that feeling she was having?" Dross asked.

"Grief," Lindon responded absently.

"I don't like it," the constructed decided. *"It's too heavy. Go back to the one with the man who had just cured his daughter's disease."*

Lindon couldn't spare the effort to reply, instead focusing on the Underlord's memories. How her madra felt as it ran through her, the rhythm of her cycling technique, the feel of pulling soulfire from the center of her soul.

Buried in these memories was the key to developing his own Path.

The Path of Twin Stars needed a real Enforcer technique, he knew that. Over the last week, he'd checked dozens of dream tablets, and he'd discovered a greater variety of Enforcer techniques than he'd ever imagined. Full-body Enforcer techniques were the standard, but they were only one type. Many of the techniques he found were single palm-strikes or sword slashes, concentrating their Enforcement on a single blow. Those gave him the shadow of an idea to improve the Empty Palm, but they weren't what he really needed.

He focused on another category: movement techniques. He needed something to close the gap between him and his opponent if he wanted to land an Empty Palm. Until this point, he'd been forced to rely on letting his opponent come to him.

Some of the memories contained single steps or leaps that ate the gap between opponents in one burst. Others held full-body Enforcer techniques focused entirely on speed, or Forger techniques that carried their users where they needed to go.

After viewing several of them, he'd started trying to apply the principles of the Burning Cloak to his pure core. The Blackflame Enforcer technique burned his flesh and spirit for a contained explosion of madra, which resulted in a burst of power.

What he learned was that pure madra was about as combustible as a snowbank. It felt like a still pond, only even *less* substantial.

So, since he'd found no records of anyone on a pure Path, he started looking up water artists.

These were almost all scenes of battles or intense training, so none of them were designed to explain the principles behind the techniques the subjects were using. He had to extrapolate based on the feeling of the technique.

His image of Ekeri helped as much as anything. He had a clear understanding of what her Enforcer technique looked like from the outside; when she had fought with it active, she had bent and flowed effortlessly, like a stream.

Blackflame was furious, and he had to match that fury and give it an outlet in order to control it. Pure madra, like water, had to be slowly guided and gathered until it had enough momentum to become a raging river.

Time fell away as Lindon focused on his madra, building it up and up to a rushing crescendo through his veins. When he thought it had reached its peak, he controlled it into a new pattern.

He had spent days theorizing this technique, based on

adapting pure madra according to the principles of the Burning Cloak. But this was the closest he'd gotten to a real test.

Finally, *something* happened. Madra flooded through his body, giving him a sense of steady strength, and blue-white power flared in the air around him. His excitement soared along with it, until the madra dissipated a second later and his pure core returned to stillness. It had taken half of his Twin Stars madra to activate even that much, and it had only lasted a breath. He sighed and started stretching his legs—meditating on his madra so long was a good way to get cramps.

Only then did he notice Ziel sitting across the aisle from him, on the floor, back leaning against another shelf of dream tablets. His eyes were closed, his head tilted back, and his green horns glimmering in the light of the tablets.

"There's no one around to see," Ziel said. "You can take a break."

Lindon looked down at his outstretched legs. "That's what I'm doing."

Ziel opened his eyes as though his eyelids were heavy. He looked as though he hadn't slept in days. "You push yourself to the brink of collapse, then you drink your potion and you keep going. Almost two weeks now, and I've never seen you stop working."

"This is a rare opportunity for me," Lindon said. "I'd hate to miss it."

"You're killing yourself for nothing."

He didn't look any older than Lindon, but he spoke like he carried the burden of ages.

"The prize is an illusion," he continued. "The mountain has no peak. You keep climbing and climbing until you fall off and break yourself at the bottom. Highgold is one step, Truegold is another step, but there's no end to it. You could walk forever, but every Path ends in a fall."

His bloodshot eyes pierced Lindon, who shifted uncomfortably.

"...two years ago, I started at the bottom," he said at last.

He told Ziel about his life in Sacred Valley as briefly as possible, skipping over Suriel and making it sound like they had a dream artist who had caught a glimpse of the future.

"Now, I have a chance I never had before. I would be a fool to waste even a second of it."

Ziel watched the dream tablets shifting over Lindon's head. "Just make sure you have something else to keep you going. Sacred arts are not enough to live for."

With that, he pushed himself to his feet and started shuffling down the row of shelves. When he reached the end, he turned and looked back to Lindon.

"Keep up," he said.

Lindon followed.

Dirty cloak fluttering behind him, Ziel paced down the shelves until he found the tablet he wanted.

The Script Lord, Archlord on the Path of Whispering Wind: the Creation of the Seven Principles.

Ziel nodded to it. "For you."

Lindon hesitated. "Gratitude, but I am not advanced enough to tolerate the memories of an Archlord."

"Try it."

He had not been swayed at all, so Lindon took a swig of water from the Dream Well. His thoughts sharpened, and he braced himself, inserting a thread of pure madra.

He stroked his long, white beard, his body tender and aching in the chair. He would have to stand soon, but inspiration was upon him, his quill pen scratching feverishly on the scroll in front of him.

For too long, the Foundation children had used the same cycling techniques. Now, he had applied his long years of experience to revising his sect's Foundation theory, and he had found it an unexpectedly rich area of research. No one with any knowledge had ever reevaluated the principles of pure madra; why would they? No one advanced without harvesting aura. As a result, the children used inefficient techniques.

Now, his principles would revolutionize how the sacred arts were taught to the least disciples.

Lindon's eyes snapped open, his mind racing with thoughts. He fell to the floor in a cycling position, focusing on his pure core.

He wished he had a book on the Seven Principles; the Archlord in the vision hadn't spelled out his thought processes for a stranger. Why would he? This was his own memory. There was much more to the vision that Lindon didn't have the insight to catch.

But he understood enough. Even a brief glimpse into an Archlord's revision of pure madra cycling techniques gave him a better sense for the mechanics involved.

That vague, intuitive feeling was invaluable. He tried running the technique again, this time modifying his cycling pattern based on the Archlord's thoughts. He had been trying to cycle pure madra like water, but it *wasn't* water madra. It simply felt more like it than like Blackflame.

Pure madra was lighter, more delicate, more adaptable. But it still strengthened the body naturally. It was the foundation on which all other aspects of madra were layered.

This time, he gathered up the momentum in minutes. Rather than a furious white-water froth, his madra now flowed smooth and steady. He began executing the new pattern, making alterations wherever it felt wrong; he would have to write down these insights later, but for now, he had to seize this moment of inspiration.

When he opened his eyes, white-and-blue haze hung in the air around him, billowing like steam. Strength pooled in his body, steady and calm.

He walked down the hall, marveling. He was just *walking*. When he activated the Burning Cloak, he had to suppress its power with every step, lest it launch him ten feet into the air. With this technique, the strength waited until needed.

He punched the air, and his body moved like a dream. His every movement was smooth, easy, perfect, as though his brain had absolute control over even the tiniest change in balance.

It didn't have the explosive strength or speed of the Burning Cloak, that was certain. The technique dissipated in five or six breaths this time, and it guzzled his pure madra. But this was the first time he'd used it. He could do better.

"What will you call it?" Ziel asked. He was seated nearby, hands on his knees, as though he'd been cycling himself.

Lindon had given this some thought. "The Soul Cloak," he said.

"I used to have poets name techniques in my honor," Ziel said distantly. "They would never have allowed such a plain name. Each character was a poem in itself. My bed was stuffed with phoenix feathers."

"Your insight is appreciated," Lindon said, bowing over his salute. "This dream tablet was invaluable. I am overwhelmed with my own weakness; advanced sacred artists must have a thousand techniques." If Lindon could come up with a new technique in a few days, even with the help of a tablet library, an Underlord would surely have hundreds of techniques at their disposal.

Ziel shook his head. "They develop a thousand ways to use the same seven or eight techniques. When you practice a technique, it becomes engraved in your spirit in the form of a binding. With use, it grows, until it is far stronger than any new technique you could learn." He flipped his palm up, and a ring of green runes bloomed over his hand. It flickered and fuzzed for a second before disappearing.

"A Monarch might invent a new technique every five seconds," Ziel went on, clenching his now-empty hand into a fist. "They do not spread themselves so thin. A new technique would be a thousand times weaker than an ability they have spent centuries honing. For this reason, old Truegolds are often stronger than young Truegolds; their techniques are so practiced that they are faster, more flexible, more powerful...superior in every way." He rubbed his wrist as though pained. "However, young Truegolds are more respected. They have a better chance of advancing farther."

Lindon bowed to him. "Thank you for your instruction." It was valuable information, but he was aching to withdraw his Twin Stars manual and take notes.

Ziel waved a hand, dismissing him. "Time grows short. Advance your second core."

第十三章

CHAPTER THIRTEEN

Longhook staggered through the rain, limping on his twisted knee, cradling one ruined arm. He could only see through his left eye; his right had been all but blinded. His Blood Shadow coiled inside him, burned and twisted. He had fed it everything he could, but it would need days of uninterrupted treatment to recover. So would he.

Since they had come into the Blackflame Empire, everything had gone wrong.

To begin with, the Phoenix's awakening had caught them all by surprise. She wasn't expected to stir for years. When she rose, sending her compulsion through them all, they had scrambled to follow.

Not only did their Blood Shadows prefer it when they listened to the Bleeding Phoenix, but following a Dreadgod was a simple pathway to power. The Shadow grew quickly in the Phoenix's light, and she left plenty of wreckage behind her. Redmoon Hall was largely made up of scavengers, feeding in the wake of a greater predator, but the idea had never hurt Longhook's pride. Sacred artists always pursued power.

And this time, the Bleeding Phoenix had sought a prize. She pushed for something that filled her with hunger, a treasure she desired above all others. The Phoenix's long-ing had echoed inside her children, and they had rushed to fulfill her commands. Both for her, and for themselves; whatever was inside the Blackflame Empire's western laby-rinth, Longhook wanted a piece of it.

They had encountered resistance, but nothing serious. Not until Akura Malice took up arms against the Dreadgod. By then, Longhook and his fellow emissaries were at the gates of the labyrinth; they could taste success.

When the Bleeding Phoenix fell apart, scattering her pieces across the land, it had ruined them.

Their army of bloodspawn had fallen apart. Their Blood Shadows weakened, and their great protector abandoned them. The Phoenix had returned to her slumber without warning, and then they were hundreds of miles deep into enemy territory.

He had thought he was going to make it. These Under-lords couldn't stand up to his Shadow.

Then he'd faced that smiling Underlord. The streak of light had caught him out of nowhere, burning his flesh, practically crippling him. He still didn't remember how he'd landed.

Now, days later, the same storm raged overhead. Their battle had unbalanced its aura, and it growled with unnat-ural fury, lightning flashing red and green. The rain sizzled against his skin, but his body had been reborn in soulfire. Something like this wouldn't faze him.

But every bit of discomfort was adding up to a blinding haze of pain that covered his thoughts with every step. He focused his eye on the range of mountains in the distance. There was a pass there; it was normally guarded, but he and his fellow emissaries had destroyed its defenses when they came through the first time. He could slip out and make it to the Wasteland in only another day or two.

Redmoon Hall had allies there. Their Sage of Red Faith was occupied, pursuing another project in the Trackless Sea, but they could find other protectors. It was their best chance.

Assuming he wasn't the only survivor.

He shook off that thought as he always had: by focusing on his destiny. His Path did not end here. The Hall had dream-readers, and they had singled him out years ago. Fate would reward him for his sacrifices, they told him.

Even now, he did not doubt them. The sacred arts were all about sacrifices—the more you put in, in time or resources, the more you got out. And he had given up everything: his friends, his former sect, his children, even his name.

He would continue walking this road he had paved for himself. And someday, the dream artists had promised him, he would become Redmoon Hall's second Sage.

Longhook's weapon fell from his sleeve with a thud. He strengthened his grip on the chain again, dragging it behind him. The endless rain had churned the dirt road to mud, so his hook dug a trench as he pulled it along. He didn't spare the effort to pull it back up.

Squinting, he fixed his one eye on the mountain peaks in the distance. Soon, he would be out of this Empire for good. After he escaped and recovered, he could meet back up with the Sage and the other surviving emissaries. Then, they could figure out what had gone wrong.

He couldn't extend his spiritual perception far without dropping his veil, so his Blood Shadow was the first to notice his enemies. It flinched and coiled up around his core, like a beaten dog flinching back from a raised fist.

Longhook raised his weapon to defend himself from an attack from above, but it didn't come. He looked up at an emerald green Thousand-Mile Cloud floating a hundred feet up.

He cycled the Path of Rolling Earth, funneling the strength of boulders through his arms and his weapon. He hadn't seen what happened to Gergen, but if all three Blackflame Underlords had survived, he would stand no chance even if he were at full power.

He looked forward to seeing how he escaped this one.

"Excuse me!" someone called from behind him, and Longhook spun instantly, whipping his hook-and-chain in an arc.

Eithan Arelius leaned back, letting the hook pass in front of his nose. He held a blue umbrella of waxed fabric over his head, and even when he dodged Longhook's attack, he angled the umbrella so not a drop of rain fell on him.

It was clear from his appearance that he'd never worked for his sacred arts. His blue robes were pristine, sewn with dragons in green thread wrapping up his sleeves and around the hem. His long, blond hair flowed smoothly down his back, and his smile was bright and unstained by worry.

Longhook wished he'd killed the man the first time.

"Slower than last time," Eithan noted. "Wounds catching up to you?"

Longhook didn't respond, releasing the veil around his spirit, scanning his surroundings in an instant. As he'd expected, there were two more Underlords on the cloudship above him.

But why hadn't they come down with Arelius?

"I'd like you to know that it was a Highgold who operated the launcher construct that almost killed you. I reinforced it with my soulfire, of course, but even so. Sometimes the simplest of tricks can bring down the largest game."

"What do you want?" Longhook asked. It would be hard to hear him over the roar of the rain; the old injury to his throat had not even been repaired by his ascension to Underlord. Maybe one day, when he reached Archlord, he would be able to speak normally again.

Eithan gestured upward with his umbrella. "They have agreed not to interfere. It was easy to get them to agree; I think they want to see me suffer." His smile brightened. "And you get to fight me in single combat! It's a win for all of us, isn't it?"

"...why?" Longhook asked.

No matter how he looked at this, it made no sense. This had to be another ambush. He had beaten Eithan Arelius in combat before without even unleashing his Blood Shadow. Now they had him at a three-to-one disadvantage, and they weren't using it.

"On behalf of the Emperor of the Blackflame Empire, I charge you with the slaughter of innocents. He has judged you and found you guilty, and I am here to execute his will."

For a man delivering a notice of execution, he sounded too cheerful. Especially for one who was so weak.

"Why alone?" Longhook clarified. This was definitely a trap; there was no other explanation.

Eithan cast his eyes up for a moment, then leaned in as though to share a secret with Longhook.

"I want to show you something," he said.

His umbrella snapped shut, and he rushed to close the gap with Longhook. The emissary had prepared for this since the instant the cloudship had appeared overhead. He pulled his chain back so he was holding the hook, driving its point up for Eithan's shoulder.

The other Underlord slipped the point of his umbrella through one link of Longhook's chain. He pushed down with surprising strength, jerking Longhook's hand aside so his attack slipped through Eithan's hair.

The Arelius Underlord seized the collar of Longhook's robe in one fist. Before he could respond, Eithan turned, heaving with all his strength.

Longhook found himself hurtling through the rain. How had that happened?

He landed on his feet a hundred yards away, but his left knee screamed and buckled, leaving him standing on one leg. The rain matted his hair to his neck, and thunder cracked overhead. He stretched out his perception, searching for the Arelius.

A finger tapped him on the shoulder.

This time, his Blood Shadow unfolded from behind him, striking out with a copied Rolling Earth technique. A fist of blood madra, dense as a hammer, struck out from his back. Longhook turned to follow up, but saw only darkness and rain.

Something hit him in the back, and he was flying through the air again.

He landed with a new pain in his spine added to his collection. This time, he held nothing back. Rolling Earth madra flooded through him in the Mountain's Fist Enforcer technique. Power of force and stone gathered in his hands, and his Blood Shadow flew out into a rough red copy of him.

It was still wounded and broken, but the Shadow could do its job for a short time. Certainly enough to take care of one pure madra Underlord from a backwoods country.

Longhook hurled his hook with the power of the Mountain's Fist, strong enough to crack bones. His Blood Shadow mimicked him. Eithan arrived, holding his folded umbrella to one side like a sword, and the two Enforced hooks crashed into him.

The Blood Shadow's red hook burst apart into madra as it hit; Eithan had dispersed it. But his own hook landed on Eithan's arm.

It should have crushed the man's bone and caved in his ribs, but the Arelius just grunted and shoved away the hook. He winced, rolling the arm.

"That's going to bruise," he said, looking back to the sky. "Now, I think we have a moment. In this storm, they won't be able to sense us clearly. And it will take them a minute or two to catch up."

The rain had already soaked through Eithan's hair and robes, but he didn't seem to mind, giving his umbrella a few test swings.

The Arelius gave a sigh of relief. "At last, I don't have an audience."

Longhook hurled his Striker technique: the Meteor Breath. A comet of earth and force madra flew out from his fist, a rolling yellow ball of pure power. His Blood Shadow echoed him with a red copy of the same technique.

In the brief instant before the madra hit him, Eithan leaned forward on the balls of his feet, his left hand coming up to the side. Madra flooded out of him, bending the air so it looked like he was covered in a transparent bubble.

It wouldn't work. He couldn't stop Longhook's technique with a shield of pure madra. He wasn't strong enough; Longhook's power would crumple his defense like a hammer hitting rotten wood.

The Meteor Breath hit the edge of Eithan's shield...and was caught like a leaf in a whirlpool.

The madra was *spinning*. Eithan seized the Meteor Breath with his madra, whirling it around and around his body like he stood in the eye of a hurricane.

Then he released his grip, sending the Meteor Breath hurtling back at Longhook.

Longhook met his own technique with an overhand strike fueled by the Mountain's Fist, punching the ball of yellow madra. It exploded against his fist; he felt like he had struck a plate of lead, and shards of his own broken madra pelted his face and arms like debris.

When his sight cleared, the Blood Shadow's copied technique was hurtling at him too.

This one hurt worse, breaking the skin on his knuckles and sending blood spraying into the air. Its power sank into his arm, striking his bones like a gong. Blood madra affected living bodies directly, so the Blood Shadow's copy of the Meteor Breath caused him much more pain than his own had.

His breathing turned ragged, but he tapped the last of his soulfire, pouring it into his Enforcer technique. The strength of soulfire soaked into him, empowering his limb and his weapon.

Eithan was Forging stars of pure madra in the air. They sparkled in the flash of lightning like birds of glass, but Longhook swung his hook through them, crushing the Forger technique before it was born.

Arelius batted the hook away with his umbrella, but the Blood Shadow had reached him from behind. Its arm morphed into a hook, and it was filled with its own version of the Mountain's Fist. It slammed its hand into Eithan's back.

The Blood Shadow's hand shattered like a hammer made of ice striking rock. The Shadow screamed, its agony flowing into Longhook's soul. Eithan stood untouched.

This time, Longhook could feel what Eithan had done. He'd projected a layer of pure madra armor, dense enough to stand against the Blood Shadow. It would do him no good against a sword, but against any spiritual attack, it would be a solid defense.

But Longhook could hardly bring himself to believe it. Eithan would need to *flood* such a technique with madra. It was one of the biggest wastes of power he could imagine; no one would be able to maintain a defense like that for longer than a few seconds.

When that armor fell, Longhook would have his last chance.

His Blood Shadow was weak, falling apart. It would help him no further in this battle. He had one wisp of soulfire remaining, to empower one last attack. The cloudship—now a few hundred yards behind and above them—was starting to move. And Eithan stood in the rain, umbrella in one hand and a grin on his face.

Longhook reached deep into himself, seizing the Blood Shadow with his will. It struggled, sensing what was coming.

He had sworn he would never do this. It would set his growth back by years, especially after the damage the Shadow had sustained. It might never recover to its current level.

But he needed an edge.

Flexing his spirit, Longhook devoured his Blood Shadow. The red spirit let out a silent scream that cut into Longhook's soul, and from its position behind Eithan, it began to dissolve into sparkling particles of red essence. As though caught in a swift breeze, the blood essence gusted toward Longhook.

The power flooded into him, supplementing his madra, knitting his wounded body back together. Blood madra stitched the muscle and bone in his broken arm, accelerating his healing. He stood tall, full of power, eyes flashing red.

There was a gap in his spirit where once his Blood Shadow had rested, but for now, he was fueled by its power. His core was stained red, and it burned hot.

Eithan watched, an infuriating smile still on his face. Longhook had been prepared for his interference, but he hadn't moved an inch.

That would be his last mistake.

Longhook lifted one foot, gathering up a Ruler technique and cycling it down. He stomped onto the ground, splashing mud onto his ankle and delivering the pulse of madra into the ground.

Golden earth aura flared beneath him, responding to his call.

Fingers of stone rose from the earth, each the size of a man's torso. They closed around Eithan, grasping at him. He twisted to avoid each one, leaping and turning as new pillars of rock broke the mud and tried to grab him around the waist.

Longhook felt the armor around Eithan fade away as the Arelius shifted his focus.

Now, the Redmoon Underlord seized his chance. Holding his two palms a few inches apart, he crafted one final Meteor Breath. It gathered, a chunk of yellow earth madra tinted with the red of blood, and he poured the last wisp of his soulfire into it. The colorless flame soaked in, empowering it, and the technique became brighter and more solid, almost as dense as a Forger technique but raging with power.

The rest of his madra, and the residue of his broken Blood Shadow, all of it went into this technique. The ball of power shone red and gold, brightening the shadows of the stormy night. It radiated such force that the mud and rain flew away from him. A Lowgold might have been struck dead with the spiritual pressure alone.

Eithan jumped, avoiding Longhook's ongoing Ruler technique. The pillar of stone brushed the edge of his robe, but failed to find purchase, and now the Arelius was in midair.

With the last remaining vestige of his spiritual strength, Longhook launched the Meteor Breath.

It streaked through the night, trailing red-and-gold light, bright as dawn. It moved like a bolt of lightning, the force of its passage tearing a line in the ground beneath.

With the technique only inches away, Eithan extended a hand.

Longhook saw what happened as clearly as a painting. Pale gray soulfire swirled in Eithan's palm for an instant, vanishing as it soaked into a technique. Pure madra gathered, condensed and empowered by soulfire so that it shone blue-white. It drew to a point in front of Eithan's hand, then fired out in a finger-thick line.

The bar of pure madra pierced his Meteor Breath, punching through without resistance.

Longhook's technique burst like a bubble, exploding in a devastating wave of force that knocked Eithan off-balance and tore a crater in the earth. But it hadn't hit. Eithan spun once in the air, but landed on his feet, umbrella braced on his shoulder.

At first, Longhook thought the shooting pain in his spirit was a side effect of exhaustion. It was only by chance that he glanced down to see the line of pure madra spearing him straight through the center.

It did nothing to his body, but his core shattered. A cold pain started sharp and only got worse, spreading through his spirit. His Ruler technique faltered and failed, stone fingers crumbling to the ground.

He tried to cycle his madra, but nothing happened. He might as well have tried to catch a handful of air.

Eithan's umbrella caught him beneath the chin, and his vision faded.

A moment later, he was lying on his back in the mud, staring into the rain. Eithan Arelius looked down on him, umbrella unfolded and held over his shoulder.

Power erupted from Eithan, rising like a pillar into the sky. He was gathering up a technique of such magnitude that it could shake the ground for miles around, though outwardly he was doing nothing but standing still. How could one man have so much madra?

Longhook turned his good eye to Arelius. "My fate... does not...end here..."

Eithan's smile softened. "Everything ends."

The power rising from him tapered off, leaving a mass of pure madra hovering in the sky far over Eithan's head. He looked down on Longhook and pointed.

The pure madra in the sky, vast as one of the stormclouds, gathered together into a single point. It was so dense it looked blue-white instead of colorless, like a newborn star.

Longhook stared into it for a moment, enjoying its beauty. Then he closed his eye.

Like a heavenly sword of judgment, the madra stabbed down into him, obliterating his spirit. And he knew no more.

Highgold-level dragons were just big lizards. In the days she and Mercy spent running from dragons through the woods, Yerin never saw them breathe fire or use any flame arts at all. She only saw them use three weapons: their claws, their fangs, and their tails.

"What is burning *them* up?" Yerin said for the thousandth time, as they crammed themselves into a tiny gully and drew a scripted blanket over themselves. The script only dispersed spiritual senses, so it worked on top of the veils in their spirits to keep them hidden.

The blanket was starting to tear around the runes; the script had put too much of a burden on it. It would last a few more hours, if they were lucky, before the force of the activated script tore the fabric apart.

One of the dragons, a gold-scaled lizard the size of a horse stopped nearby. Its head was barely visible in the crack of open air they could see. These weak dragons didn't look anything like the huge sky-crawling serpents her master had mentioned, but she supposed they changed as they advanced even more than sacred artists did.

It sniffed, eyes flaring with light. It started snuffling around the forest floor like a hunting dog, looking for them.

Some sacred beasts were no smarter than normal animals, but dragons were different. This one would be able to speak and use the arts of any Highgold sacred artist. But it was hard to remember that as it snarled and hunted by scent.

Yerin braced herself, reaching for her sword. It almost took her by surprise when she realized she *wanted* the dragon to find them.

If it did, there would be no more hiding. No more running.

They weren't running from this thing anyway. They were running from its big sister; the Lord-stage dragon they'd felt coming after them.

The barrier of cloud had faded days ago, and they had tried to make their way closer to the beach. But every time they did, dragons tracked them down in the time it took to boil a pot of tea.

Yerin was about ready to throw the dice and dash for victory. She wasn't built for hiding and creeping.

Her Blood Shadow agreed.

While she was holding herself back, her Shadow slipped out of her back. It actually looked like a red-tinted shadow this time, sliding along the ground and closer to the dragon. If the sacred beast didn't notice, it was going to spring out of the ground and get the first strike.

Yerin grabbed it.

A chill of terror passed through her as she caught it. Not because it had almost alerted the dragon; a large part of her welcomed that. It had almost escaped *on its own*.

When else would it decide to do that? When she was with friends? When she was asleep?

She hauled back on it with one hand and the full force of her will. Just touching it made her feel degraded, like she'd lost somehow, but she dragged it back.

When she wrestled it back into her spirit, it boiled around outside her core, lashing at her from the inside.

She sat there panting as the dragon moved a little farther away. That had been too close. Too close to her losing control.

It tempered her will to steel: she needed to be stronger. Stronger *without* this thing.

From beneath the scripted blanket, Mercy looked at her with concern. "Are you feeling alright?" she whispered.

Yerin threw the blanket off and stretched all four arms. It felt good to stand up again.

The gold dragon stared at her.

She took a deep breath, feeling madra cycling freely within her spirit. Veils were a necessary sacred art, but they felt like tying yourself in a sack.

Yerin hopped out of the tiny hole in the ground where they'd hidden. Mercy stared up at her from inside, eyes wide.

Still stretching her arms, Yerin used one of her Gold-signs to beckon the dragon. "All right, you ready?"

The dragon glanced from side to side, ready for a trap. But after a moment, heat flared in its eyes again, and it roared.

Yerin put a hand on her master's sword and concentrated on the aura.

She needed power that didn't lean on the Blood Shadow. Power that was hers alone. And she'd always learned better when she was pushed to the brink of a cliff.

The dragon rushed at her, sword-aura gathering around its claws as it swept them in a powerful strike.

The sound of a bell echoed through the air as she activated the Endless Sword.

The sword-aura around his claws exploded, causing shallow white slashes to appear on his scales all over his body. His strike wasn't slowed at all, and Yerin threw up her Goldsigns to block.

When the claws met the steel of her Forged madra limbs, the impact pushed her back. She let it happen, falling back several steps.

Then she tried again, focusing this time.

Her technique should look like the wind: it should surround her, unseen except for its effect. It should be like she was defended by a thousand invisible swords.

As she triggered the Endless Sword again, it looked more like a thousand invisible swords flailing wildly.

Its tail slammed into her, though she got her sword in the way just in time. It knocked her backwards, and she had to use her Goldsigns to brace herself before she hit a tree spine-first. The silver madra limbs stuck in the trunk like axe-blades, catching her just short of slamming into the wood.

Mercy emerged from beneath her, using her staff to lever herself out of the hole. She'd tied her hair back into a tail again, and her purple eyes were fixed on the dragon. "I'm sorry, she's training. I'm Mercy! You are..."

The dragon drew in a breath.

Black madra stretched away from Mercy and stuck onto the limbs of the tree just above Yerin's head. She pulled herself away just in time, as a spray of fiery golden madra incinerated the grass, leaves, and scripted blanket she'd left behind.

Yerin glanced up at Mercy as the Akura girl dangled from a limb. "You want this to go faster, then you could help. Hit it with your stick."

Mercy sighed, giving the dragon a sad glance, before she gripped her staff in both hands. "It's not a stick."

The dragon was gathering itself to leap into the tree, but Mercy's weapon came to life in her hands. It looked like a bundle of flexible black tendons worked into the shape of a staff, except for the violet-eyed dragon's head on its end.

That snarling head slid from the end of the staff down to the center. The staff itself bent like a wooden limb under pressure until it was shaped like a crescent, and a single black string slid from one end to the other.

A bow. It was a bow, almost as tall as Mercy was.

Mercy drew the string back, Forging a jet-black arrow as she did so. The point emerged between her weapon's jaws.

"This is Eclipse, Ancient Bow of the Soulseeker." She loosed, and the arrow stuck in the dragon's palm. "It was my mother's weapon from Lowgold to Archlord. Made from the Remnant of a shadow dragon who became a Sage." Another arrow took the dragon in the other hand, but it had already burned the first one free. "With this bow, my mother sealed the living volcano of Shara Kahn." Two more arrows, and this time dark madra spread like a web from the point of impact. It started crawling over the dragon like living ropes.

"She destroyed the Sunlight Rebellion with this bow, and bound together the thirteen islands into one." The dragon went crazy, tearing and clawing at itself like it was trapped in a net. But as Mercy continued firing arrows, the web kept drawing tighter.

"I know it's just a bow, but I call her Suu." Mercy patted the bow on its dragon's head. "Good girl, Suu."

The bow hissed.

Yerin hopped down, inspecting the dragon. It still struggled, but it was wrapped in a dark cocoon and didn't look like it was going to escape anytime soon.

This way, at least they didn't have to deal with its Remnant.

"What about yours?" Mercy asked politely, dispersing her madra and dropping to the ground. She missed her landing and fell in a heap but didn't seem to care. "Did you get that sword from your master?"

Yerin ran her fingers down the hilt. "...yeah."

"So what's its story?"

"I don't know."

The Sage had never referred to his weapon by name. She didn't even know if it had one. He had made her use it to chop firewood by hand when he was trying to build up her muscles. He used it because he was too lazy to hunt down an axe.

Instead of talking about that, Yerin asked Mercy another question as they walked away from the cocooned dragon. "How about your Path? Aspects of shadow and force, if I'm not wrong."

She'd felt Mercy cycling over the last few weeks, so she was pretty certain about that.

"Oh, this is just a restriction technique."

Yerin glanced back. "I can see that. I've got eyes. You don't want me poking my head into your Path secrets, say so."

Mercy gave her a surprised look. "I don't keep secrets. Bad for your heart." She held out one hand, and a Forged book of shining violet madra popped into her hand.

The cover was entirely covered by the most intricate script-circle Yerin had ever seen. She suspected she could keep staring at it forever and finding new secrets, and the scripts seemed to *turn* like wheels within wheels. It was a disturbing sight.

And that didn't even count the way it felt in her perception. It gave off a menacing pressure, like the shadow of a shark circling beneath the waves.

"The Book of Eternal Night," Mercy announced, holding her book up proudly. "I'm on the Path of Seven Pages. And the first page, the Lowgold page..."

She opened the cover, revealing the first page. It looked more like a thumb-thick tablet than a piece of paper. Yerin wondered if it contained a binding.

This page was choked with more incomprehensible script-circles instead of plain writing. Not that Yerin would have been able to get anything from it either way.

"It's the central technique from the Path of the Chainkeeper," Mercy said. "Strings of Shadow. There are seven techniques in this book, one for each page. The Path of Seven Pages unites seven techniques from seven different shadow Paths into one."

She let it fade away, and this time Yerin traced it with her perception. "You stock that thing in your spirit?"

Mercy patted her stomach like she'd just had a full meal. "When I bonded with this book, they opened up my soul-space early. It's one of the requirements of my Path."

A screech echoed through the woods. Either another dragon had caught up, or the first had gotten free.

"All right, that's enough friendly time," Yerin said, drawing her sword. "We've been too soft on these things. Now, we punch through. I'm getting through that portal before the sun sets, or I'm bleeding out."

Mercy's eyes sparkled, and she hopped out in front of Yerin. "Did you say we're friends now?"

Yerin stared at her.

Another Highgold dragon waited for them ahead, and spots of heat in her perception told her there were more Lowgolds and Highgolds ringing them. They were getting sewed in.

But they were making progress. After an hour of running and dodging through the trees, Yerin spotted something that brightened her heart: the sparkle of light on the ocean.

According to the map, the portal was at the very edge of the island. They were close.

The Highgold dragon roared at them, spraying fire.

A Rippling Sword technique split the fire down the middle. Strings of Shadow dragged its claws to the ground, and Yerin's sword plunged into the back of its neck.

Its scales actually managed to deflect most of the blow, but blood gushed up, and it shrieked.

Mercy bound it to the ground a few more times as they kept running. She frowned at Yerin. "It wasn't going to hurt us."

"It was *trying*," Yerin said.

Mercy continued to argue, but Yerin looked ahead. This side of the island ended, not in a sandy beach, but in a strip of dirt overlooking a cliff that dropped to the ocean. She pulled out the map, examining it and pointing.

"Farther north," she said.

She had to guess the jade doorway would be in the same place as the first one had been. If it was, that meant it would be at the edge of the treeline.

They were getting close to Redmoon Hall territory, but that couldn't dim her spirits. According to the map, they were within minutes of the Ghostwater entrance. At last, they could leave this boring rotten island behind and join Lindon in the Monarch's pocket world. It was about time.

A golden shadow passed in front of the sun.

Yerin knew what it was even before she stretched her perception up and felt the presence of the Thousand-Mile Cloud. She knew before the pressure of an Underlord pushed down on her spirit, before dragons roared in triumph and a woman jumped down from the golden cloud, landing easily a hundred feet down.

This was where the Highgold dragons had been meant to lead them. Right into the claws of their leader.

The woman wore a sparkling sacred artist's robe of intricate red, gold, and purple. Her eyes were golden and vertically slitted, and patches of gold scales remained on the pale skin of her cheeks. Her nails looked like claws, and there were patches of scales on the backs of her hands as well. A thin, gold-scaled tail lashed behind her.

She was doing nothing to restrain her spirit, or the rage that was obvious on her face. The Underlady's fury hit Yerin only a few steps from the trees, and she fell to her knees, gasping for breath. It was like a bear sitting on her chest.

Mercy fell flat to the ground, in even worse shape than Yerin. She looked like she'd been pinned in place like a corpse prepared for study.

The Underlady was flanked by Truegolds who looked like a cross between humans and dragons. They were scaled, their face reptilian, but they stood upright and wore clothes just like humans would. They spoke to the Lady from behind, but she had furious eyes only for the humans.

"...then they can *give me back my sister!*" It sounded like she was responding to one of the dragons, but her voice raised to an angry roar in mid-sentence.

Sunset-colored light gathered around one clawed hand, and that technique gave off heat like a scorching bonfire.

Yerin used her sword to push herself up a hair, straightening her back a little bit. "Don't know...your sister..." she pushed out.

The dragon tossed her head, and Yerin realized she didn't have hair, but rather a veil of loose scales hanging down from her head so that it looked like hair. "You will meet her now."

Mercy struggled on the ground. Yerin braced herself.

One of the Truegold dragons lunged at the Lady's arm, holding her back for just a moment. Madra shone in her hand.

Yerin forced her own sluggish madra to move, lifting her sword in arms that felt a hundred times heavier than usual. She gathered power, Enforcing her weapon, holding it against the Striker technique that was about to come. It wouldn't be enough, but she had to try something.

"Second page," Mercy whispered, through gritted teeth.

A phantom image flickered behind Mercy for a second, so quick that Yerin thought she might have imagined it. The violet book, turning from the first page to the second.

Light dimmed about ten feet around Mercy, as though she'd cast a bigger shadow than normal, and suddenly she was giving off the aura of a Highgold. It was the quickest, most casual advancement Yerin had ever heard of.

Not that it would save them. The Lady shook off the Truegold, hurling her Striker technique at the two humans. The liquid madra surged like a river after a storm, carrying the raging heat of a wildfire.

The full-power strike of an Underlord.

Mercy shoved herself in front of Yerin, holding up an arm as though she carried a shield. Another time, Yerin might have been impressed with the spine that took, but in that instant, she was horrified. Was she cracked in the head? Yerin had a better chance of weakening the technique by facing it with her own madra head-on; all Mercy could do was get herself burned to ash a little early.

Violet crystals started to form all over Mercy's arm, and then the madra washed over them.

It detonated as it hit, scorching every inch of Yerin's exposed skin. She couldn't tell how much of it had been pushed away by her Enforced sword, but it hit her weapon like a hammer, slamming it back into her, driving her back into the trees.

Yerin lost herself for a second. She saw only light and motion, heard only a formless roar.

When she came back, she was looking at the sky. Her face, her arms, her head—in so much pain she could barely breathe. She pushed herself up to sit, her Steelborn Iron body draining madra, and the flash of pain was so intense she almost passed out.

Pieces of her robe crumbled away as she moved. The skin of her right arm was red-and-black, twisted, almost melted. Her master's sword lay not far away. It was unharmed, and she crawled for it.

Then she saw Mercy.

The girl's left arm was covered in a violet crystalline armor the same color as her book had been. Slowly, the armor faded to essence, revealing an arm that looked totally untouched.

It was the only part of her body that looked that way.

Most of her hair was scorched off. Her robes were half-melted to her body, and all her skin was red and burned. She cradled Suu in her arms.

At first sight, Yerin was sure she was dead. Only her spiritual perception said otherwise.

Another sunset-colored light bloomed, and Yerin turned slowly to face it.

If anything, the Underlady looked even more furious now. Tears streamed from her eyes, and she gathered this Striker technique in both hands.

A Truegold dragon leaped in front of her.

The man fell to his knees and spread his arms, clearly pleading with her.

Yerin understood. She wasn't the only Underlord on this island. The dragons knew they had come from the Blackflame Empire with the Skysworn, but they also must see the two of them as members of Redmoon Hall and the Akura family.

If she, a Lady, struck down two Golds, the other Lords would do likewise. It would be an invitation to tear the dragons apart.

But Yerin wasn't going to stick around and see where the dice fell.

Her Steelborn Iron body was drawing on her spirit to keep her limbs moving, and she positively flooded it with madra. She hauled Mercy onto her shoulder, skin screaming and tears flooding her own eyes in the pain.

She gathered her master's sword and the ancient bow under one arm. Then she started jogging into the woods.

If they got far enough away, she could pull the tent from Mercy's void key and hide in its veiling script. That was their only hope.

For now, though every step was agony, she had to run.

第十四章

CHAPTER FOURTEEN

At the end of the second week after reaching the Spirit Well, Lindon advanced to Highgold in his pure core.

It struck him again how much longer it took to raise the Path of Twin Stars. If he had focused on only one Path, he would surely be Truegold by now, thanks to the miraculous properties of the Well water.

Even with the distractions of raising Dross and his pure core, his Path of Black Flame had advanced significantly into Highgold. He wasn't knocking on the door of Truegold yet, but he could at least see it in the distance.

This was the easiest his advancement would ever be, and he relished it. Every sip of the Spirit Well water felt like a victory.

Orthos' spirit burned brighter than Lindon had ever felt it. If the Dream Well water had helped him to stay focused, his newly cleansed spirit meant that Lindon no longer had to feed him pure scales or keep him calm. He spent his days cycling with Lindon, drinking from the Spirit Well, or swimming around the habitat. Lindon was fairly certain he'd been fighting with Sea Drakes, because sometimes he returned from his swims with an exultant look in his eye and scratches all over his skin.

Little Blue was once again a deep ocean blue, and she scampered around like a child in a field. She played with some of the more advanced Dreamseeds, the ones who had taken a more solid form. The less-advanced spirits were hazy and ever-shifting, and they didn't seem to have minds at all.

Though it still knocked Lindon sideways when Dross said he wanted to eat some of them.

"It's not eating as you do it," Dross said from within Lindon's core. *"No, thank you—that's disgusting. It's more like a...merge. A merge in which I take in everything and they cease to exist."*

Lindon supposed there was nothing different about that than using Remnant parts, but he couldn't help but think of some construct devouring Little Blue.

"The little ones don't have minds. They're like plants. If you wanted to feed them and raise them for a few years, sure, then they'd be all cute. And then you'd feel like a monster. But you haven't done that, so we're all clear!"

Lindon gave in. Dross was confident that this would be the last stage of his growth, and that after this, he would qualify as a living spirit rather than a construct. Lindon was curious to see that, and just as importantly, he wanted the construct out of his spirit. Dross was taking up far too much of his time and water each day.

Unfortunately, that meant he had to do the job of consuming the Dreamseed himself.

"You've got an arm for it!" Dross said. *"Just walk over there and slurp it up."*

"it won't work. My arm can't draw anything into my core."

"Get it into your madra channels and I'll do the rest."

When Lindon tried to consume the first Dreamseed, which clung to one of the nearby walls in a translucent purple blob, his arm of hunger madra drained something out of it and left it a lifeless husk of dissolving dream essence.

The next time, he restrained the limb, pulling the Dreamseed into his core as delicately as he could. It swirled into his spirit, a mass of impressions that felt surprisingly compatible with his pure madra. Dross had been right; these spirits were less like real dream madra and more like pure madra pretending.

That was interesting, but not as interesting as what happened to Dross when he absorbed the Sylvan.

He shivered inside Lindon's core, his essence shifting, and some of the sparks inside him gathered together. It looked like he was forming a core of his own.

"Oh yeah, that's it. That's the right stuff. Now grab the one that looks like a flower."

It took six Dreamseeds before Dross stopped talking. Inside Lindon's spirit, the construct spun, turning in faster and faster loops.

Lindon funneled as much power from the Spirit Well to Dross as he could. He didn't know if it was helping, but he reasoned that it couldn't hurt.

Dross started pushing at Lindon's core. It was only a little pressure at first, but it grew stronger and stronger, until Lindon had to extend his left hand and push the construct out like he was releasing a Striker technique.

The ball of purple light spun into the air, wobbling. He was more solid now, a more clearly defined orb. Now, twisting lines of light formed a web through the mechanical spokes at his center, all leading back to a single spot of bright light.

A madra system. He had grown madra channels and a core.

"Oh, this is brilliant! Brilliant stuff! It's like all my thoughts and memories are crawling together and breeding new ones! I'm having *ideas* now!" Dross spun excitedly around Lindon's head. "We don't have to go to the portal at all, do we? We could harness fish and ride our way up! No, wait, we're in a pocket world. We could harness fish and ride our way *through space.*"

He stopped in front of Lindon's face. "I can activate the tablets myself now! Don't be surprised if I return as a master of the sacred arts."

He whizzed off, out of the Spirit Well room and down the hallway.

Ziel watched the whole exchange with a complete lack of interest, sitting against the corner and staring at him from beneath emerald horns.

"Forgiveness," Lindon said. "I did not mean to disturb you."

Dead eyes drifted over to the Spirit Well.

"If you don't mind, how long until I reach Truegold? In your estimation."

"Two more weeks," Ziel said without looking over.

"And we have that long, don't we? You said a month..."

"You don't want to stay here."

Lindon wasn't sure if that was a warning or not. "This is my new favorite place in existence. I want to stay here forever."

"And you want to leave." Slowly, Ziel's eyes returned to Lindon. "Don't you?"

Lindon stood there for a long moment before he moved and took a seat beside Ziel. "Well, I have this friend. She—"

Ziel held up a hand. "No. Stop. We don't know each other well enough for this."

"Of course, I'm sorry."

"You'll reach Truegold. Whether you do it in two weeks or two years, it won't make much of a difference in the end."

"Actually—"

"Stop. It's my turn. I have nothing against easy advancement, but don't let it blind you." He raised a finger, pointing to the ceiling. It took Lindon a moment to see what he was pointing to: a long cobweb stretching from one corner to another.

"The decay has already begun. That is a naturally forming spatial crack. You still have three weeks or so before this world collapses, so long as nothing accelerates it. By the time they form fast enough that you can *see* space cracking, you should have left already."

He pulled his worn cloak around him. "If you're going to a deeper habitat, you'll have plenty of time if you leave now. You don't want to be racing the hourglass with a collapsing world."

Lindon thanked him, though he was part relieved and part disappointed. He had already been apart from Yerin for so long; he found himself wondering more and more what she was doing on the outside. He had expected that to fade with time, but it had only grown worse.

On the other hand, he felt like a fool for leaving the Spirit Well without milking every second.

He filled every spare container he could find with the blue water: all of the vials he'd emptied so far and everything he could scavenge from the junk rooms in this facility.

He'd opened his void key and prepared to leave, Little Blue on his shoulder, Orthos at his side, and Dross in the Eye of the Deep. Still, he looked over the pool of blue water like he was abandoning a fortune.

Ziel waited for them at the entrance to the room, leaning on his hammer like an old man on a cane. He hefted a bag in one hand and tossed it to Lindon. It clinked as he caught it.

"Six bottles," Ziel said. "Should be enough to get you to Truegold in at least one core."

Lindon held the bottles for a moment before placing them into his void key. He actually teared up.

Ziel ignored him.

When they were ready to leave, they stood lined up in front of the wall of black water. Dross assured them that this was the way to the final habitat, the one containing the entrance to Northstrider's quarters.

It was filled with the swirling blue lights of Diamond-scale Sea Drakes.

Orthos chewed a mouthful of stone to gravel and swallowed it. "Hmmm...I left too many alive."

He and Ziel had consumed far more of the original Drake's corpse than Lindon thought should be possible, but when it started to decay, they had tossed it into the ocean. Had that attracted the others?

Little Blue chimed like a bell from his shoulder, and he patted her tiny shoulder with one finger. Together, they stared down a wall of flashing silver scales and blue lights.

"Do we have time to swim around?" Lindon asked.

"That depends," Dross said. "Do you still need air?"

A loud scraping grew closer and closer, and they all turned to see Ziel dragging his hammer two-handed over the tile. "They focus on the biggest threat in their territory. I will punch through, and you head to the habitat. This is no task for a Gold."

He hesitated and glanced down at himself. "...although I guess it is, isn't it?"

With a heavy sigh, he pushed through the bubble and into the sea, his cloak billowing behind him. The faded symbol on the back reminded Lindon of spread wings this time.

"You could learn from him," Orthos said, eyes blazing red. "He has the spirit of a dragon."

"I'm not sure he would take that as a compliment."

An instant later, a green script-circle bloomed above Ziel's head. It was big enough to swallow his body, but then the ring expanded. And expanded again.

A second later, it exploded. Water rushed up in a violent column from his hammer, carrying most of the Diamond-scale swarm with it. The bubble-wall of the habitat rippled with the force.

The other strings of blue lights converged on Ziel in an instant, but Lindon and the others had already ducked into the water.

The ocean of Ghostwater was a chaos of blood and dust, with nearby impacts shaking the ground. They pushed forward, guided by a purple light projected by Dross. Occasionally scales flashed silver or blue lights shone in front of them, but none of the Drakes attacked them.

Lindon's lungs were starting to ache by the time the water cleared, and then the new habitat was already in view. It was a dome of bright light packed with green; it looked like a slice of a jungle transplanted to the bottom of the ocean.

He hung onto Orthos' shell as the turtle swam toward it, but after a moment he felt a spike of battle-hunger from his contracted partner. The sacred beast turned, cycling Blackflame.

A pair of blue lights headed toward them out of the darkness.

The Burning Cloak had let Lindon down the last time he tried it underwater, the aura and the water dampening his movements. Now, he was a Highgold, and his body had been reinforced by weeks more of feeding on sacred beast meat. And this time, he had a new technique.

The Soul Cloak swirled around him, and he kicked forward, joining Orthos in battle.

Ziel waited until the last moment to use his gatekey.

Unlike a gatestone, the gatekey could be used without breaking it. The key was many times more valuable than the stone, but once he had been able to afford these things. Now he had to rely on his patron.

One moment he was using the last of his madra to swing his hammer in the face of a Sea Drake, and the next he was dripping water all over the grass, staring that patron in the face.

The Beast King sat on a log, tearing a hunk of meat between his teeth, grease sliding down his unkempt beard. A campfire crackled in front of him, casting long shadows. He showed no surprise at Ziel's appearance. Silver eyes looked the Truegold up and down as he took another bite.

"Lot of blood in that water," the Herald observed. "Do I have the Lord of the Dawnwing Sect back with me once again?"

Without his Enforcer technique active, Ziel's hammer was too heavy for him. He let it sag to the ground, where its weight pushed into the soil. "The Spirit Well didn't work," he said, his hammer digging a furrow behind him as he walked to sit against the Vastwood Mammoth that lay across the landscape like a hairy hill.

The wall of fur gave a welcoming trumpet as Ziel leaned against it. He patted the sacred beast, though he doubted the mammoth could feel it. It would be like a human feeling the touch of a single ant's leg.

The Beast King had seen through the state of his spirit with a single glance. He shrugged, speaking through a mouthful of roasted meat. "It was a long bet. We can still try it in the form of an elixir. How much did you bring me?"

Ziel tossed him a bottle, which he caught balanced on one finger. Silver eyes moved from the bottle to Ziel. "One? Had the Well run dry?"

"No." Ziel leaned his head back, resting against the mammoth's hair. The sacred beast smelled like warm fur, and he found it comforting. The stars glittered overhead, distant and uncaring.

The Herald grunted as though he understood, and the bottle of water vanished into his void key. "How long does the pocket world have?"

"Three weeks, maybe less."

"Shame. Built by Northstrider, and it's gone so quickly." He shrugged, tearing the rest of the meat away and tossing the bone behind him.

Ziel could hear the dogs fighting over it:

"You got it last time!"

"Ah, but you forget about the squirrel that you did not share with me."

"A squirrel's bones are tiny and snap easily. It is hardly the same."

The Beast King leaned closer to Ziel, ignoring the dogs. "Since you seem so willing to help others, I have something to occupy your time. I put a couple of Golds on a task for me, and they seem to have gotten themselves stuck. How about you swing by and un-stick them."

Ziel had just gotten comfortable.

He reached a hand out to his hammer and gave a long sigh. "Where?"

"Under the gold dragons. I'll send you close." He snapped his fingers as though something had just occurred to him. "Oh, and there might be an Underlord in the mix."

Ziel heaved himself to his feet an inch at a time, like an old man. "Then maybe I'll die."

Lindon walked through the outer wall of the new habitat hauling the corpse of a Diamondscale Sea Drake behind him. He held one fang in his Remnant hand, dragging the serpent's long, silver body behind him as he walked. The blue-and-white light of the Soul Cloak still drifted through and around him.

Orthos followed, roaring with laughter. "You'll need to eat a dragon's portion of this one. It'll put some scales on you, that's for sure."

Lindon's stomach twisted at the thought as he pulled the Drake the last few feet and released it. Each bite of the Sea Drake's flesh had been a new exercise in agony, and it had required his full willpower and not a little bit of madra to avoid vomiting up every meal he'd ever made of the sacred beast. At least it showed results.

"What we have here is the refiner's garden," Dross said from the gem in Lindon's pocket. "They tried to refine an elixir, from rare plants and the blood of certain sacred beasts, that would make a mental breakthrough in the same way people make spiritual breakthroughs. They kept all the rare plants on hand here, but uh...according to our records, it's not supposed to be this much of a mess."

If this was a garden, it was one that had been abandoned for years and then infested by monsters. Flowers that glowed like full moons were trampled by diseased, frog-like creatures the size of cows. Two hideous insects bigger than dogs wrestled in a patch of grass, surrounded by a pile of bones arranged into a nest. Whispers, cries, and twisted laughter rose in the distance, as did a pillar of smoke.

In his spiritual perception, the powers of life and blood reigned in equal measure, all infected by a poison that reminded him of the Desolate Wilds. As he looked closer, he saw black spots on nearby trees.

As soon as he noticed, he returned his attention to the giant frogs with patches of wet rot on their skin. They were dozens of yards away, but their stench carried.

"Dreadbeasts," Lindon said at last.

"They kept a few samples safely imprisoned in this habitat," Dross said. "Not quite safely enough, as it turns out."

Orthos growled, and Lindon let the Soul Cloak drop to switch to his Blackflame core. "Which way to the portal?"

"Life Well first," Lindon reminded.

Dross slipped out of his gem and bobbed in front of Lindon. "To our good luck, it's on the way."

Lindon and Orthos marched forward. Without discussion, they burned more dreadbeasts away.

"The Life Well was really just a side effect of their work here. It bolsters the line of life aura inside everyone's body, and can even restore youth to the elderly. This was the most rare and expensive of all the water; you'd be lucky to get a spoonful after a successful project." He flashed bright light in Lindon's face. "I used the word 'spoon' correctly there. Just thought you ought to notice."

After the Spirit Well, Lindon was looking forward to this one. What could the Life Well do? Could it bring back youth? Heal injuries? Whatever it did, he could find some use to it.

Lindon and Orthos destroyed the remaining dreadbeasts on their way to the Life Well, though Orthos had to use a

Ruler technique to quash a few fires that they started in the process.

This time, the Life Well facility was actually a building. It was the size of a large barn, its walls iron-gray. The huge door on the front was decorated with a skeleton cupping its hands; he recognized the pattern on the skeleton's palms from the previous keyholes.

Dross slid into the keyhole without instruction, and slowly the door began to grind open, spilling green light.

"Where is the portal?" Lindon asked, while the door slid from one wall to the other.

"Right below us," Dross said, zipping back into his gem. "Good thing that the ground hasn't caved in here, or we'd be falling right now. There's a shaft inside that leads down to his quarters, but it's a one-way trip."

"How did he make it up?"

"He was a Monarch. He jumped."

By then, the door had opened enough for Lindon to see the Life Well. It reminded him of a laundry tub more than an actual well, and though it released bright emerald light, it wasn't nearly as large as the other two wells.

The reek of decay wafted out of the door, and Lindon waited with his hand over his nose until he figured out what he was seeing inside. The green light revealed tall, cylindrical tanks lining either side of the room; they contained bloated corpses of every species and description. There must have been two dozen of them along each wall, and the subjects ranged from hand-sized fish to coiled serpents that barely fit in their tanks. None of them had survived.

The tanks were surely airtight; the stench came from the ones that had broken. Three or four of the glass tanks had been shattered from the inside, shards scattered on the floor, covered by the rotting remainders of their former inhabitants.

Lindon caught a new whiff of something dead, and at first he wondered if something had died recently. By the time he realized the sensation was coming from his spirit rather than his nose, Orthos had already turned and let out a roar, the Burning Cloak springing up around his shell.

Yan Shoumei stood there, hair falling in front of her face like a veil, Blood Shadow clutched around her like a cloak. Her eyes, barely visible through the black locks, glistened with hatred.

"You even followed me to another world," she hissed. "Tell Anagi that he was too late! I have everything I need."

Lindon glanced down at Orthos to see if he had followed that, but the turtle had already unleashed his dragon's breath.

The flow of black-and-red flame streamed from his mouth, but Shoumei punched out with a fist covered in a globe of crimson force. Orthos' Striker technique hit the globe around her hand and split apart, sending fingers of Blackflame splashing into the undergrowth. Tongues of fire licked up immediately.

She gave a wild laugh, withdrawing a stoppered bottle and waving it at them. "You were days too slow! I have all the blood I need! I look forward to seeing your bodies buried beneath Hearthway!"

Still laughing, she crushed a gatestone in her hand and vanished in a blue flash.

Surrounded by burning undergrowth, Lindon turned to Orthos again. "Do you think she had the wrong people?"

"I think she should have stayed and fought us," Orthos said, taking a mouthful of undergrowth. "But yes, as they say, she was crazier than a nest full of squirrels."

Dross piped up curiously, "So Anagi didn't send you?"

"Do you know who that is?" Lindon asked.

"I don't know anything that didn't take place inside this pocket world. But I *do* wish she hadn't done that."

Where Shoumei had once stood now waited a web of cracks. Falling leaves, passing through that space, were effortlessly sliced in half by nothing more than the weight of their fall.

Slowly, the cracks expanded. It wasn't obvious, but if he

looked closely, Lindon could see them inching forward.

"Let's hurry," Lindon suggested.

Back at the Life Well, Lindon cupped his hands and drew out a mouthful to take a sip. It had a faint taste like a very weak tea, and he could feel it spreading to his body without his encouragement.

But unlike the meat of the Silverfang Carp or the Diamondscale Drake, this didn't carry with it a burning sense of strength. Lindon felt a little more relaxed, a little refreshed, but otherwise he didn't notice much of a difference.

Well, his expectations of the Life Well hadn't been high to begin with. He started to open his void key when Orthos dipped his head in for a drink.

Pain shot through their spiritual bond, and the turtle bellowed in agony.

His legs collapsed immediately, shell slamming to the ground, and his head curled back into his shell. His eyes rolled into his skull, showing all black.

"Tell me what's happening," Lindon demanded of Dross, lowering the Sylvan Riverseed from his shoulder. Little Blue hopped over, placing both hands on Orthos' neck, letting her power flood into him. She gave a little cheep of distress almost immediately; whatever was wrong with him, it wasn't in his spirit.

"The water of the Life Well *can* have...more of an impact on older subjects," Dross said. "Usually it's very healthy for them. Very healthy. Only in a small percentage of cases do they lapse into a coma and die."

Green light oozed from Orthos' skin. It beamed like a beacon from the crack in his shell, shone from his mouth, and spilled from beneath his belly. Lindon readied his arm; if this was excess power overflowing from the Well's power, maybe his Remnant binding could devour it.

But when he took his first step forward, he noticed that the wound in Orthos' shell was closing.

The verdant light dimmed slowly over several minutes, and by the time it did, Orthos had gone through a clear transformation. His skin was less of a worn gray and more of a glossy black. The edges of his shell now glowed bright red, and when his eyes snapped open, they were bright.

Orthos' voice was recognizable, but deeper. Smoother. Younger. "I...I feel..."

He laughed, bounding to his feet and running in a circle like a puppy. Lindon had heard more laughter out of him since coming to Ghostwater than in the last year.

He galloped away, leaping and kicking off a wall, then backflipping and landing with surprising grace.

Orthos turned back to Lindon, mouth open as though to say something. But he only laughed again and bounded out the door. Going to hunt some dreadbeasts, Lindon assumed.

Lindon looked down at Little Blue, who had tumbled onto the ground while Orthos frolicked. He picked her up and glanced at Dross, who brightened.

"I'd like some of that," Dross said hopefully.

Lindon absorbed him into his core.

Over the rest of the day and into the night, Lindon cycled the fire and destruction aura released from the burning undergrowth, using Dream Well water to stay awake and cycling power from the Life Well to Dross.

Though the Spirit Well had taken him weeks to absorb, this started to change the construct immediately. He cheered as he spun inside Lindon's core.

Orthos still hadn't returned, but the roars in the distance and the satisfaction radiating from his soul told Lindon the turtle was having a good time.

This place had been at least as much of a blessing for Orthos as it had been for Lindon. Not only had it helped heal some of the damage that Blackflame had done to his spirit, but it had sharpened his mind and now restored his body.

"Dross," Lindon asked, "If this place existed while the Blackflame family was in charge of the Empire, why didn't they use it?"

"Oh, they did. They used to buy as much Well water as Northstrider would allow them. It was one of the ways this facility maintained itself." Dross squirmed inside Lindon's core, absorbing some more green water. He was becoming opaque, as though he were growing skin.

"It was more an issue of quantity. A single cup from the Spirit Well cost a fortune, and it was the cheapest of the three. You've been drinking a fifty-year stockpile. And you really dove into it headfirst, too. You should bow down in gratitude for every mouthful."

Absently, Lindon took another sip of the green water. "It will all go to waste when the world collapses."

"Yeah, that's...yes. It will." Dross' words were distant. "You know, I spent a long time in the Dream Well. And now I won't get to go back ever again." He was quiet for a moment. "What do you call this feeling?"

"Sadness," Lindon said, sitting against the Life Well.

"It feels a lot like grief," Dross observed. "I don't like it."

"It's not my favorite either." He spun quietly for a while, processing the water. "Here's some better news: I only needed a taste of this well. I'm coming alive by the second! How does that make me feel? Excited!"

A sudden sound, like a distant clink of metal on metal, drew Lindon's attention to a rounded hatch in the floor opposite him. The clink came again, and again, louder as it continued.

Lindon pointed to it. "What's that?"

"The way down. We shouldn't go yet. There are some spirit-fruits in here that I think you'd really enjoy."

Lindon rose to his feet, cycling Blackflame. The ringing sounded like a bell-tower now. "I'm not worried about going down. I'm worried about what's coming *up*."

"There's nothing down there," Dross said confidently. "It's been sealed for decades. You'd need an Eye of the Deep."

"*An* Eye of the Deep?" Lindon asked.

"You didn't think there was only one key to this place, did you?"

With a sound like a ringing gong, the hatch crashed

open. Darkness spilled out, shadows oozing from the entrance.

Lindon pushed Dross out. "Go get Orthos."

Dross spun as he emerged from Lindon's palm, blinking in the light. *Blinking.* "I have an eye!" he exclaimed.

This time, Dross' evolution was even more pronounced. He was covered in what looked like purple skin, with one huge eye in the center of his body. He was speaking with an actual mouth now, which Lindon could see was lined with tiny teeth. He looked like a very advanced Remnant, or a cross between a spirit and a sacred beast.

Blunt tendrils extended from his sides. "And I have arms! Well, I have little pseudopod tentacle things, but I'll *take* them!"

Under any other circumstances, Lindon would have been delighted with the possibilities of a construct coming to life. He would have started speculating about what could be accomplished with other constructs, about whether long-term exposure to dream madra was the way to turn a construct into a living spirit, or whether there was something special with Dross' circumstances. If it was so easily replicable, the expert Soulsmiths would have tried it before.

However, Lindon's spirit warned him clearly about that darkness. He turned red-hot eyes on the construct. "Dross. Now."

"Oh, right." He spun away, flailing his stubby little arms as he flew. None too soon.

A moment later, Akura Harmony rose from the dark.

He looked as well-fed and comfortable as a man who had spent the night in the palace, his skin clear and smooth, his purple eyes bright. Hair flowed straight down his back, and the black disc of his Goldsign hovered behind his head. His black-and-white sacred artist's robes were spotless and pressed.

He drifted up until Lindon could see the dark purple Thousand-Mile Cloud on which he was standing. Casually, the Akura hopped off and strolled closer.

Lindon cycled madra, preparing to ignite the Burning Cloak.

Harmony didn't even look at him. Every step brought him closer, but he had eyes only for the Life Well. The Akura produced a shallow bowl, and brushed past Lindon to dip it into the pool of shining green water.

Lindon supposed he should be grateful the man wasn't hostile, but his spirit was still warning him. He pressed his fists together and gave a shallow bow. "Greetings, Akura representative. I am—"

Harmony cut him off with a sigh. "Quiet."

Like a painter raising a brush, he raised two fingers.

Madra gathered within his hand, dark and sharp, and Lindon recognized the technique.

The Burning Cloak sprang into the air around him, and he struck at the Akura's wrist with the explosive speed of Blackflame.

Harmony's left hand intercepted his, pushing his punch aside with apparent ease. Lindon opened his Remnant hand, trying to grab hold of the Akura's body.

Harmony stepped back, still graceful, and lowered his fingers.

A black blade flickered down, slicing a line in the stone floor.

Lindon managed to throw himself to one side, the blade cutting only into his outer robe. He rose to his feet, conjuring dragon's breath, but Harmony was once again looking at something else.

This time, he was looking at the corner of Lindon's robe, which had fallen to the ground. It had included his pocket.

Harmony first drew out a blue-glowing glass ball, which he tossed aside. Lindon almost wished he'd taken it; Suriel's marble would return to him without fail.

Then he withdrew the other blue orb that had been inside Lindon's pocket before it was severed by the shadow-blade. This time, it was the cracked, damaged sapphire that had once housed the Eye of the Deep construct.

Harmony examined it for a moment, then reached into his own pocket and pulled out a sapphire that shimmered with a gradient of other colors.

Another Eye of the Deep.

Lindon launched a bolt of dragon's fire at Harmony, but a black wedge appeared in the air in front of him. The Blackflame madra split along the wedge, one half drilling into the wall on the left and the other half cutting a glass cylinder in two.

Unconcerned, Harmony raised the dead sapphire. "The construct. You removed it."

"It cracked," Lindon said, gathering madra again. "The construct dissolved."

Harmony nodded to the door. "You opened the door not six hours ago."

Lindon leaped at him, powered by the Burning Cloak. He grabbed for the gem with his Remnant arm.

Harmony stepped away, but that step carried him half-way across the room. "Let's see, then."

He held up the unlit gem, sending his spirit into it. A blue light flickered deep within, and Lindon's heart fell.

There was a script inside the sapphire, which Harmony had just activated. And Lindon suspected he knew what it did.

Soon enough, he heard Dross' shouts growing closer.

"What's happening? What is this? Something's got me! Help!" As though drawn back by an invisible fishing line, Dross was hauled into the room and straight into his sapphire.

Brows drawn in confusion, Harmony held both gems next to each other. One was blue, though it rippled with other colors, and smoothly glowing. The other was now purple, with Dross inside it, and was begging to know what happened.

After a moment of examination, Harmony simply turned and walked back to the hatch.

Where Lindon was already waiting for him.

Empowered by the Burning Cloak, he lashed out with his Remnant fist. Harmony met the blow with the back of his hand.

It was a casual gesture, as though Harmony were waving him away, but it carried the weight of a hammer. Lindon flew back, turning in midair and cycling madra to his legs. He landed against the wall in a flare of black-and-red madra.

He leaped away, dragon's fire gathered in his palm. He shoved the half-formed Striker technique into Harmony's face, but Harmony's fingers pierced through it, shrouded in darkness. The ball of fire burst in Lindon's hand, and the momentum of his lunge carried him past Harmony and into the middle of the floor.

The Akura turned, crooking his fingers as though beckoning a dog.

Black swords stabbed up from the ground.

Lindon slid aside, avoiding them, but they kept coming. He started drawing Blackflame into his palm, glancing up to judge his distance from Harmony.

Icy pain flashed through his spirit as a sword shoved through his Remnant arm. He staggered, his technique disappearing, gripping his white arm around the dark blade that emerged from the forearm.

Without another word, Harmony turned and hopped back into the tunnel. Taking Dross with him.

第十五章

CHAPTER FIFTEEN

Lindon wrenched his arm free of the Forged blade, biting back a scream. He rushed over to the hatch, grabbing it one-handed and trying to haul it open with the strength of the Burning Cloak.

Orthos raced in at that moment, skidding to a halt in front of the hatch. He looked around at the burns in the walls, the sliced floor, and the newly damaged glass cases. "Where is the enemy?" he demanded, excited.

Right arm hanging limp, Lindon slapped the hatch with his left hand. "Down there. He took Dross."

The turtle's spirit swept over the hatch. "...it was the Akura?"

Lindon nodded.

"Then thank the heavens you are still free," Orthos said gravely. "The Akura do not kill honorably. They take prisoners."

Without warning, Lindon gathered power in his left hand. The dragon's fire congealed in seconds, and he drove it at the domed lid of the hatch.

Hidden rings of script shone on the lid and on the ground all around, the runes glowing the orange-white of heated metal. In seconds, they faded to orange and then to red.

"Can't follow him," Lindon muttered, looking around the room. The refiners had left so much behind; had the Heralds stripped this place decades ago, as they had the other habitats? If not, there could be something he could use.

"If you followed him, what would you do? A dragon does not walk blindly into the devil's lair."

"I know you see the problem here," Lindon said, walking over to a cabinet next to the glass tanks. He threw open the doors—empty. "Without Dross, we are stuck here. Locked in a dying world."

"Keep a calm head, boy," Orthos said quietly. There had been no heat in Lindon's words; even Yerin might not have heard any anger. But Orthos had a direct line to his spirit.

Lindon slammed his fist down onto the cabinet.

It stood as high as his chest and wider than his shoulders, but under his blow, it burst. Wood chips flew everywhere as the two halves of the furniture collapsed inward.

"He took Dross from me. From my *hand*. More easily than taking a bone from a dog."

Lindon's rage stirred his Blackflame madra, which called fire aura to him from outside; he could feel the red power flowing into him. The shards of the cabinet started to smolder.

"Swallow that anger," Orthos said. "Use it to fuel the fire in your belly. Dragons sometimes lose, but they learn from their losses and come back stronger."

"If I accept this loss, there *is* no coming back!"

"That's not what's setting your tail ablaze. If you had a choice between leaving alive and staying to compete with the Akura, what would you do?"

"Leave," Lindon said immediately.

Orthos grunted thoughtfully, then heaved himself to his feet. "Give me a moment. Cycle your pure core."

That was unusual. Normally Orthos would tell him to cycle Blackflame. But then, normally Orthos wasn't the one telling him to keep his temper and think through a problem first.

At first, Lindon paced in restless frustration, irritated at having to follow instructions. But eventually he sat down in a cycling position and focused on his pure core.

He soon lost himself in a meditative trance, so he wasn't sure how much time passed before Orthos returned. In his mouth, he carried a fist-sized chunk of what looked like shimmering blue chalk.

The turtle rolled the lump of chalk across the floor so it bumped into Lindon's knee. "This," he said, "is a gatestone. They come in different shapes and sizes, but crushing one will allow you to instantly return to one place. It is how the others have been escaping Ghostwater."

Lindon's eyes brightened and his heart cleared. This was the answer to all of his problems. He reached out for it before hesitating. "Where did you find this?"

"In one of the dreadbeast nests. A sacred artist must have died before using it."

"Why didn't you bring it before?"

"We didn't need a way out before," Orthos said, holding his gaze steady. "Now, you can decide: use this stone, or not."

Of course he would. Lindon almost laughed out loud. But something else came out of his mouth.

"...why do you think he took Dross?"

Orthos said nothing, but Lindon's mind started churning. Harmony already had an Eye of the Deep, so he had access to all of Ghostwater. What would he need a second one for? There was the possibility that he wanted Dross specifically, but there would have been no way for him to know that Lindon's Eye was special before he stole it. Not unless he had access to the bloodline ability of the Arelius.

Maybe Harmony could have accessed the same observational security constructs that Dross had, but Lindon had no idea how likely that was. He had to assume that Harmony just needed another Eye.

Or perhaps he was acting to keep Lindon and Orthos locked inside Ghostwater as the world crumbled around him. Maybe he was just that cruel.

Lindon didn't have enough information to speculate. But using the gatestone would leave Dross to whatever Harmony wanted to do with him.

And Lindon recognized that an Akura wouldn't move for a cheap prize. He benefited from this in some way.

Lindon scooped up the stone...and slipped it into his one remaining pocket. Suriel's marble glowed there, though he didn't remember putting it away.

"Whatever he wants, we can't leave Dross to him," Lindon said at last. And whatever the Akura was after, he wanted a piece of it.

Orthos nodded as though he'd expected nothing different. "Once, you were weak. That boy is long dead, but his Remnant still haunts you." He turned to drink from the Life Well. "Your weakness, Lindon, is thinking you are weaker than you are."

Lindon opened his void key, reaching in and pulling out a tiny vial of purple water. He drank it down quickly, feeling his focus sharpen.

"I think I can see a way to break the script on the hatch," Lindon said after a moment.

Orthos shook his head firmly. "No. We're too weak."

"You just said—"

"Prudent caution," the turtle said. "That is where you should find yourself."

Lindon spread his one remaining palm. "If we stay here, we're leaving Dross to his fate."

"Convince me we can defeat the Akura without him escaping to his family," Orthos said. "Then I will allow it."

"I can repair my arm with the hunger bindings inside the dreadbeasts," Lindon said.

"That arm didn't win you the last fight, did it?"

"We have some fresh Diamondscale meat. It will strengthen us both."

"Slowly," Orthos said. "If we're going to wait another two weeks, we might as well use the gatestone at the last moment and be done."

"There are supposed to be some spirit-fruits in this garden, and I still have water from the Spirit Well. I could reach Truegold, but that will take just as long."

Orthos shifted in place. He glanced to the side, snapping up another piece of debris and eating it.

"...Orthos."

"It doesn't have to," he admitted. "I have the power of a Truegold. I had to share it with you in small doses before, as neither your spirit nor mine could handle the burden."

A light dawned in Lindon's mind. "But now we *can*. And whatever madra you expend, you can replace with the Spirit Well water. Let's go!" He sat down in a cycling position immediately, ready to begin.

"Listen, boy. You're only a few weeks from Truegold on your own. Don't rely on me for this last step." He hesitated. "And nothing good comes from opposing the Akura family."

Lindon rested a hand on the turtle's head. "Dross has traveled with us for four weeks now. Would a dragon abandon an ally in time of need?"

Orthos grumbled.

Then he opened his spirit.

Harmony knelt before the jeweled tree, calming his madra, stilling his mind.

The two Eyes of the Deep sat in his pockets, one silently, the other one chattering. He ignored them both equally.

The Akura family had known more than the others all along; they ensured that their disciples got the *real* prize in this pocket world. Of the other factions who had joined them to periodically plunder Ghostwater, only the Nine-cloud Court had the knowledge they did. But the Nine-cloud delegate hadn't made it inside this time, so Harmony would be the final recipient of Ghostwater's treasure.

The tree that loomed over him was made of scripted metal, spiraling from the floor up to the ceiling. Instead of leaves, its branches held metal cages, and inside each cage: a sapphire.

Only about a third of the cages were filled, but the chamber still sparkled with light from the Eyes of the Deep.

Harmony withdrew the silent jewel from his pocket. There was a ritual necessary to prepare the construct before coming here; he had to carry the gem around the outside world, then give it a thorough tour of the state of Ghostwater.

For the previous month, he had carried the Eye around with him as he cycled and trained, letting it absorb information about the world. About him. It would add its knowledge to the collective in the tree.

In return for his efforts, he would be rewarded.

He knelt before the tree, holding the shimmering jewel before him like a supplicant. "Harmony of the Akura clan returns the Eye of the Deep to the place of its birth."

Without his power activating it, script flared to life all over the tree. One branch bent down toward Harmony, its cage creaking open.

Carefully, Harmony placed the gem within. His family wasn't sure to what degree the tree was aware of his behavior, but it had been known to punish rudeness. When the cage carried away the Eye of the Deep, Harmony bowed.

The jewel was restored to its state among the others, and a whispering voice echoed through the chamber.

"Ask..."

"What is the fastest path that I may use to reach Underlord?" Harmony asked. He had struggled with this question for weeks, regretting that he didn't have a second chance to ask another question.

Then he had sensed the delegation from the Blackflame Empire next to the Life Well. It meant they had an Eye of the Deep of their own.

The heavens, it seemed, were looking out for him.

The tree trembled for a moment, its script shining and its jewels shaking, as it contemplated the question.

Then a sparkling wave of blue-and-purple light washed over him, and he *knew*.

The shock of the sudden knowledge left him panicking and disoriented, as though he'd woken up from a dream and not recognized the room around him. When he regained control of himself, he pressed his fists together and bowed to the tree.

"Akura Harmony is grateful for your wisdom," he said, his voice still rough.

Then he waited.

In front of him, at the base of the tree, was a scripted basin like a birdbath. He stared at the basin hungrily.

The answer was only half the prize.

A few breaths later, a clear tube slid out from the tree and hovered over the basin. A twinkling white pearl rolled through the tube, splashing into the center of the basin.

A drop of ghostwater: the substance for which this world had been named.

Abandoning dignity, Harmony leaned over the basin and lapped the droplet up with his tongue. Lords and Ladies would kill for this.

A moment of cycling later, and he realized why.

The droplet of ghostwater traveled through his madra channels to his head, where it fused with his channels and nested at the base of his skull. It shone there like a distant star, a tiny pinprick compared to the full moon of his core.

He tapped it, and it was as though his mind was refreshed. He stood, Forging his Nine Blades of the Underworld technique. Ordinarily, the technique struck nine times at a target, and it took his full concentration to control it otherwise.

Now, he caused the blades of dark madra to rise in a perfect circle. Once again, and they appeared one at a time on the same spot, delayed by a perfect second each time.

It was like he'd struggled all his life to juggle nine balls at the same time, and suddenly it had become as natural as breathing. One of his older cousins, who had earned a droplet of ghostwater twenty years before, had described it to him as 'strengthening his mental power,' but he hadn't pictured what that meant.

The power faded after only a breath of time, the point of light in his skull dimming. The ghostwater was tapped out, but it would draw from his body and spirit and restore itself over time.

One breath of increased control meant the difference between victory and defeat in a fight. Now, he could consider himself invincible among those of the same stage. And soon he would step into a new realm entirely; the tree had made his steps clear.

He pulled out the second Eye of the Deep.

He would be the first Akura since the Herald who found this place to return more than one Eye. Only a handful of people in history had attained ghostwater at all, and he would have more.

...assuming the tree accepted this one. It shone purple, thanks to the light from the construct inside the gem, and it was *talking* to him.

"Oh, this place is amazing! I'm a little insulted I didn't know about it, but you know, I guess they couldn't tell me everything. I mean, they could, because I do exist to store knowledge, but it's fine. It doesn't hurt at all. Although now that you mention it, I do feel a sort of connection. Like that is the place I'm *supposed* to return to. You think that's the Eye talking?" He paused for a moment, considering. "Hey, how about this for a plan: let's not put me in there. I know you've sealed me inside this vessel, but how about you let me go? Hm? I don't trust mysterious compulsions that are telling me to go somewhere."

The construct pushed against the script keeping it locked inside, and the script flared. Harmony reinforced it with his madra again.

The Blackflames had corrupted this Eye somehow,

maybe fusing it with a Remnant or the memories of one of their dead sacred artists. He knelt and held it up, hoping the tree would accept it anyway.

But before he could open his mouth to ask, his spirit whispered a warning. Instinctively, he looked up to the ceiling.

A dark, furious sun had dawned above and behind him. It was like feeling a dragon's birth.

The aura was only Truegold, but it carried such fury and destruction that his spirit trembled. It surprised him; he hadn't thought any Truegold could be a threat.

"Did you feel that? Is that Lindon? I tell you what, let's wait for him. I'm sure we could talk this—"

A cage drifted down from the tree, and Harmony shoved the Eye inside.

The construct shut up as though choked off. The cage started to rise, but it froze only a few feet up.

The branch trembled, and the gem shone purple. The ring of script inside glowed as the spirit pushed its way out, and suddenly Harmony could actually *see* it emerging from the crack in the sapphire.

It spoke as though through gritted teeth. "...not going to...stay...here..."

The tree's light shone brighter.

When it did, the cage continued to move. The spirit was drawn back inside the gem with a yelp, and the cage settled into place.

The jewel shone purple for another few seconds, and then its light dimmed.

The spirit was finally, blessedly, quiet.

Lindon held up his hand of flesh, and the madra of a Truegold Blackflame burned the dreadbeast's blood away.

He'd done some quick surgery on a few of the monsters in the garden, extracting the twisted corkscrew bindings in their body. They were hunger madra, the same as his arm, and he'd been able to patch up the hole in his skeletal limb.

It was still scarred, and you could tell where the different sources of madra butted up against one another, but it worked. That was all that mattered.

And he was Truegold.

With Orthos' power running through him, and the water from the Spirit Well to guide it, he was filled with a sense of strength he'd never felt before. Orthos told him that it was always best to spend a few days practicing and cycling after advancement in order to get used to his new power. He'd heard such advice before, and generally agreed.

But not only were they out of time, something felt different about Truegold. He felt complete, as though he were a bowl that had been completely filled.

He suspected that was partially overconfidence, but it was partially that he was approaching the limit of his Blackflame core. When he reached the end of Truegold, he would have advanced as far as he could normally.

After that, he'd have to reforge his body and spirit in soulfire.

Even minutes after advancing, he was looking forward to the next step.

Lindon opened his void key, the closet doorway appearing in the air. This time, when he pulled Little Blue off his shoulder, he handed her a pure scale.

His pure core was still Highgold, but that was higher-grade than he'd ever fed her before. She smiled at him before tilting her head back and swallowing the coin whole. Her blue body rippled for a moment until she let out a drifting hiss of satisfaction.

He reached into the void storage, placing her inside. She squeaked, just as she had last time, clambering up his arm.

Now, he met her eyes. "I can't take you with me this time," he said.

Little Blue let out a sad note.

"I know. But we have to bring Dross back. You remember Dross?"

She whistled.

"I'm going to have to fight for him, and I'm afraid I can't look after you at the same time. You understand?"

She frowned for a moment, but then turned and walked to the edge of his fingers. She was six inches tall now, and he actually felt her weight as she leaped off like a diver, landing lightly on the edge of a jar filled with Dream Well water.

Little Blue sat down on the jar and gave him an impatient peep.

"I'll be back as soon as I can," he said, and closed the void key.

Outside, Orthos gave the hatch a sideways glance. "This is not wise. I've changed my mind. The courage of a dragon is valuable, but it must be balanced by the *wisdom* of a dragon."

Reaching into his pocket, Lindon withdrew the gatestone. The chalky ball shimmered in the light as though it were made of crushed blue glass. "Then you'll be relieved to know that I have decided to use the gatestone."

Orthos brightened. "Really?"

"Yes." Lindon lobbed the stone so that it landed a few feet away from the hatch. Before Orthos could ask what he was doing, Lindon extended a finger. A quick beam of dragon's breath struck the gatestone dead center.

The device let out a blue orb big enough to swallow a person, then disappeared. The stone was unharmed, a man-sized web of cracks hovering in the air.

Orthos rounded on him in a fury. "What have you *done?*"

"The scripts around the Spirit Well were disabled, and I thought about why. The cracks must have sliced through the runes and interrupted the script." Lindon pointed to the ground, where many of the silk-thin cracks ran into the stone. "Even if that's not what happened before, I'm fairly certain it would work that way now. Look."

He extended a palm, and a much thicker bar of dragon's breath punched through the hatch.

There was no flaring script to defend it. This time, it blasted through the metal, and Lindon moved it from one side to the other to obliterate the hatch. The edges of the tunnel now glowed white-hot, but there wasn't as much melting metal as he'd expected. That would be the destruction aspect of Blackflame at work.

He walked over to the edge and prepared to hop in. Orthos peered over the edge.

"That's a long way down," he said.

"Look at it this way: the entrance is plenty big enough. You'll fit just fine."

"What if it gets narrower as you fall? My shell is not meant for tight spaces."

Lindon looked down into the darkness, swept it with his spiritual perception, and then took a deep breath. "I'll let you know," he said as he jumped.

There was a rush of air and darkness, then he hit the ground. Even without an Enforcer technique active, he absorbed the impact lightly: the benefit of the meat from the Silverfangs and Diamondscales.

He would probably look back on this month in Ghostwater as one of the most profitable of his life...assuming they made it out.

"Nothing down here," Lindon called up. "You can jump."

"Are you certain?" Orthos shouted back.

"I'm going to start exploring. If you don't think you can join me, you can leave it to me, and I'll let you know what I find."

A moment later, a dull red meteor crashed into the ground as Orthos hit shell-first. He swung from side to side to right himself, marching over to Lindon.

"A dragon doesn't hesitate."

Orthos had hesitated for quite a long time, but Lindon said, "I'm glad for that. I think we should head this way."

The room at the bottom of the shaft was nothing more than an open space with three dark tunnels leading in different directions. Since advancing to Truegold, Lindon's spiritual senses had immediately expanded, so he headed through the entrance where he most clearly sensed Harmony's shadow madra.

They walked through a dark hallway with rooms on either side. The hall reminded him of the Dream Well facility, except it was lit only by the subtle glow from Orthos' shell.

The sense of Harmony's madra pulled them straight down the hall, and Lindon started to pick up speed.

Until a man appeared next to them.

He was a hulking figure a head taller than Lindon, packed with muscle, his golden eyes vertically slitted like a reptile's. Black scales covered his arms up to the elbow, and he loomed like an executioner.

Lindon had ignited the Burning Cloak and gathered up a handful of dragon's breath when he recognized the figure.

Northstrider, the Monarch on the Path of the Hungry Deep. Creator of Ghostwater.

He was shocked for a moment, but hurriedly dropped to his knees.

"What are you doing?" Orthos growled. "Get up."

"Don't you see..."

"No, I see it. It's a projection."

Lindon swept the image of Northstrider with his spirit. It reminded him of the White Fox madra his family had always used; a blend of light and dreams.

Northstrider's projection surveyed them both, or seemed to, and then spoke. "For you who travel here after my departure, I have left this message."

"Let's hurry," Orthos said, and trotted off. Lindon followed him, with Northstrider's image floating along next to them.

"I poured years of effort into this world and its research projects," he went on, undisturbed by their jog down the hall. "None of them delivered what I wanted: a mind, subordinate to my own, that could manage a small portion of my powers. The messengers of the heavens use such con-structs, so perhaps they can only be created beyond this one small world. But I still left behind the greatest mind a man could create."

Some of the doors had small windows, and the shining lights or shifting movement he saw inside made him want to look inside. But a new sensation from up above had drowned out the trail of Harmony's madra: it was a surge of power that felt like the Eye of the Deep, only many times more powerful.

They picked up the pace.

"I dismissed the researchers, but scattered keys all over the world. Over four thousand memory storage constructs, each gathering knowledge on their way back here. When they return, they contribute to a greater whole. Eyes of the Deep record and gather knowledge, all with the purpose of returning here. To add their information to the collective."

Now the world was crumbling. This would be the last delivery Ghostwater ever received. It only had a few weeks left, at most.

Lindon extended his perception behind him, sensing a disruption in space that felt like cracks in existence. The spatial cracks were crawling after him, down from where he'd crushed the gatestone.

Maybe they had less time than he'd thought.

"I will allow a few beggars into this world to fight over the other scraps, but you who bring an Eye of the Deep, you will receive the true prize. A drop of ghostwater. If you have tasted of the other wells, you should know they were only prototypes. By-products of our attempts to create this one power. It no longer benefits me, but what is trash to a Monarch may still be treasure to all others."

The hallway opened up onto a huge chamber, like an artificial cave. A metal tree filled the far wall, with cages instead of leaves and Eyes of the Deep hanging like glow-ing fruit. Two-thirds of the cages were empty, but it was still bright.

To the right of the tree, there was a jade doorframe. Identical to the one Lindon had destroyed in the first habitat.

And in front of the tree, Harmony stood in front of what looked like a stone birdbath. His Goldsign hovered behind his head, so all Lindon saw was a circle of darkness on his shoulders.

"Return the Eye of the Deep to the tree," Northstrider instructed, golden eyes turning to the massive scripted device. "You may ask one question and receive one drop of ghostwater. And for the rest of your life, know that you are in my debt."

Then the Monarch vanished, and Harmony turned to meet them.

第十六章

CHAPTER SIXTEEN

The dark green madra of the tent flickered and fuzzed like it was losing reality. For Forged madra, it had lasted a long time.

Light trickled in through the entrance; Yerin had cut open a hill and buried them in it. All the better for hiding. She'd scratched basic script-circles into all the nearby boulders to help veil them, but the one on the tent was still their best. When it went out, it was only a matter of time until they were found.

She opened a case that had once contained healing salves. As she'd expect from a rich girl, Mercy carried an herbalist's shop worth of pills, elixirs, and sacred herbs around with her.

Or she had. They had delved deep into her stock to fight off the burn wounds the dragon Underlady had left them.

There was one vial left in the case, its contents glowing like blue diamonds. Yerin removed it and tossed it to Mercy.

"Last one," she said. "Make it count."

Mercy tried to push the vial back to her. "What would I use it for? Look at me, I'm good as new!" She stood up and twirled in place to demonstrate, but she didn't have enough room to stand up straight.

Yerin wouldn't have jumped straight to 'good as new.' The liquid fire madra had burned the hair off half of Mercy's head. You wouldn't know it now. Her salve was specially made to get rid of burn wounds; apparently the Akura family dealt with dragons more than mosquitos. Her hair had even started to come back in, faster than was natural, but Yerin had cut the girl's hair all over to match. Now it was cropped close to the skull; it would be months before she could tie it back into a tail again.

The faint shadows of burn scars remained on her left cheek. Those would never heal on their own, but this salve should take care of them. Her leg was in worse shape. She hadn't been able to put any weight on it for days, but a blood elixir had restored most of the meat. A sacred herb, sealed in a jade box like some kind of treasure, had taken care of the rest.

They had burned through most of the healing elixirs Mercy had brought with her from the Akura family. She wouldn't be able to restock anymore, cut off as she was, but Yerin couldn't think of a better thing to use them for.

So long as Mercy kept getting attention, she'd recover.

Yerin was in a brighter spot. She had a sturdier Iron body than Mercy, and she was more advanced. Whatever Mercy had done by summoning armor onto her arm, it took the lion's share of the blow. Without that, they'd both be dead.

"Use it," Yerin said. "Don't make me break it over you."

She'd almost had to do that already. After Mercy had first woken, incoherent from her wounds, she had refused to take anything until Yerin did first. Yerin had forced a healing pill down her throat.

At first, Mercy's spirit had scared Yerin worse than her injuries. She had advanced to Highgold during the fight, clear as glass; after waking up, she was a Lowgold again. Yerin had thought it was some kind of spiritual damage, and had avoided bringing it up for days, but Mercy explained that it had to do with her Path.

She could push to open a page beyond her reach, and that book inside her would lend her the power to use it. For a time.

After that, she went back to advancing like normal.

Yerin had immediately asked if she could push to Underlord. Not that far, Mercy had told her. But she could hit Truegold for a minute or two.

That was more than Yerin could say for herself.

The gold Thousand-Mile Cloud was hovering over the edge of the island, and now there were Truegold dragons mixed in with the Lowgolds and Highgolds. Even if the Underlady stayed on her cloud, they were cornered. And the tent had only a day or two left.

Yerin had spent the whole time in this self-made cave cycling and practicing the Endless Sword. She had started touching on the next stage of mastery, but the hourglass was running out like it had a hole in it.

Mercy reluctantly started to apply the salve to herself, but Yerin was staring at the flickering tent. "I need to hit Truegold. Now."

"We have plenty of time," Mercy said. That was something Yerin had learned quickly about the Akura girl—if they were about to be buried in an avalanche, she would point out that at least it wouldn't be hot.

"Even if I use my...guest..." Yerin still wasn't comfortable talking, or even thinking, about her Blood Shadow. "...I can't punch through any Underlords. If I don't advance, we're stuck on a raft with sharks all around. I've packed my madra to the brim, so I need something to draw more out of my Remnant and push me over the edge."

Absently, Mercy rubbed some salve over a scar on her right arm. Her left was still clear, protected by the armor that had—briefly—stood up to an Underlord's attack. "When we reached a bottleneck in our progress, we were taught to find someone to guide us through."

"My master told me something like that."

He had said, 'You'd be amazed how much faster you run

when there's a hungry wolf behind you.' His way of saying that danger could bring out new depths of strength. Also, his approach to training foot speed.

"I'm headed outside," Yerin said, bracing herself for Mercy's arguments.

Mercy's hand froze. "I guess we have to go sometime." She rubbed the remaining salve from her fingers, grabbing her bow—which was still in staff form—and pushing herself to her feet. Using the staff to brace herself, she picked herself across the crowded tent.

Yerin didn't move. "Thought I was going to have to wrestle my way past you."

"You want to put yourself in danger to push your advancement, right? Not a bad idea, but it would be safer with someone watching you." Mercy started to run her fingers through her hair again, but stopped and pushed it back down to her side. "I'm not eager to take more fire madra to the face, but we can't stay here forever."

With a deep breath to cycle her madra, Yerin moved to push debris away from the entrance. Mercy stopped her.

"One Highgold," she said.

"Not looking to bleed, am I?" Yerin said. If she lured in a Truegold—or worse—then she'd get no chance to advance. There was risk, and then there was stupidity.

"*One* Highgold. If there's more nearby, we back out."

In Yerin's judgment, two Highgolds would be safe enough, but still she agreed.

She pushed her way out, into the clearing outside their handmade cave. After stretching out the last week of cramped muscles, Yerin knelt in the middle of the clearing. She breathed deeply, cycling sword aura to every limb.

"Keep their breath off me," Yerin said. Her sword-aura couldn't deflect madra, but it would do a decent job with everything else. So long as she handled it right.

Mercy bent Suu into a bow, nervously fiddling with the bowstring. "You can do this. One Highgold, you start to advance, and I'll tie him up. Then we run."

Yerin tore the veil from her spirit.

Her perception immediately extended; the veil dampened her spiritual sense like wearing a cloth over her eyes. Golden spots of heat flared into existence nearby.

The closest one started moving toward her. Perfect.

"They're all around," Yerin reported.

"Plenty of targets," Mercy said, but her voice was higher-pitched than usual.

Yerin focused on aura. Her sword shone silver at her hip, though she didn't draw it. Her Goldsigns were dimmer, but still useable. She summoned the image of the Sage's Endless Sword, keeping it focused in her mind.

A delicate, controlled touch. Like plucking a string instead of hammering a drum. Aura like the wind.

The first Lowgold dragon veiled himself as he approached. Yerin saw him before she sensed him, a rustling in the brush followed by a flash of golden scales and silver claws that flashed in the sunlight. It happened so suddenly that it didn't feel real.

But Yerin was prepared.

As a Lowgold, this dragon was more ruled by his instinct. He attacked like a beast, pouncing on her with fangs and claws extended.

She tapped the aura around her sword, and sparks exploded from the dragon's claws like he'd run into an invisible steel bar. He was slammed back, twisting in midair to land on all fours, staring at her with clear surprise.

Not enough.

That had *looked* fine, but Yerin could feel that something wasn't right. It had taken too much concentration to deflect one clumsy attack.

She met the dragon's eyes. "You waiting for sunset?"

The beast leaped at her again.

Once more, Yerin knocked him away. It wasn't enough. What was missing?

Extending her perception, she found that the nearest dragon was a Highgold. Abruptly, she stood up. "Let's take this on the road. Mercy, I'm done with him."

Mercy nailed him to the ground with several arrows, but Yerin didn't stay to watch her work. She was already headed for the Highgold.

When Mercy caught up, she was out of breath and leaning on her staff. "You know, I don't have unlimited madra."

"Good thing you're not fighting, then."

They were walking away from their cave, but if Yerin failed here, they couldn't defend themselves. When your back was against a wall, you had to bet it all.

She found the Highgold dragon eating a deer. It turned and saw them, then lazily licked its snout clean. "Humans," she said in a feminine voice, her speech surprisingly clear. "You should have stayed holed away."

Yerin knelt again. Though dropping to her knees before a fight felt wrong, she was putting herself in a place where she had nothing to rely on but the Endless Sword.

Mercy waved to the dragon. "My name is Mercy. What's yours?"

"Derianatoth," the dragon said. Her eyes flared. "The girl you Skysworn killed was my cousin."

She leaped over Yerin, then. Straight at Mercy.

Yerin kept her breathing steady, and her sword rang. The dragon staggered in mid-pounce, like something had struck her a glancing blow, but she wasn't knocked backwards. She landed next to Mercy, gathering up her breath.

Yerin drew on the Steelborn Iron body. In one jump, she closed the distance between herself and the dragon, planting her foot in its ribs.

Combined with her momentum, the kick sent the cow-sized sacred beast tumbling into a tree. It crashed into the wood, giving it a healthy dent.

Mercy froze with an arrow half-Forged on her weapon. "Nice hit!"

"Not enough pressure," Yerin muttered, walking closer to the dragon.

Derianatoth was enraged now, shaking debris from her

scales like a dog after a bath. She swept a razor-sharp claw, and Yerin could already feel that there was a second coming. She felt the pressure from a dragon as advanced as she was, born with a body no human could match. Unstopped, this blow would tear Yerin in half like a piece of bread.

Perfect.

Yerin struck the Endless Sword, the weight of battle keeping her mind tightly focused. The claw bounced away, struck aside by a blade of sword-aura, but a second had already closed, a hair's breadth from tasting blood.

Another pulse of the Endless Sword knocked it back, but the claw had been so close that it nicked the side of Yerin's chin.

She'd done it twice, and that second technique had been both faster and more precise.

"Are you...practicing a technique right now?" The dragon asked. As she spoke, Yerin could hear her disbelief turn to fury.

She roared, swiping with both claws.

Yerin stopped them both with one pulse of the Endless Sword, but it still wasn't fast enough. Not sharp enough. She could do better.

Another claw was deflected in a spray of sparks, and Yerin stepped closer. The sense of danger in her spirit spiked, but that was what she was looking for.

After a second flurry of blows was met by invisible swords, the dragon backed up.

Yerin, still with her sword in its sheath, stepped forward.

The dragon may have been furious, but she wasn't stupid. She recognized sword aura and filled her mouth with orange-gold light.

A black arrow slammed into her from above, tying her jaw shut.

Madra sprayed from the sides of her fangs, and the arrow dissipated, but it had done its job. Yerin turned her attention to offense.

Her sword rang again, and three white lines appeared

across the dragon's throat. That was a step forward; only three lines meant she was more controlled. But when it was like the wind, her Endless Sword would leave only one line. And those scales would be nothing.

Now the dragon was truly infuriated. She dashed away and pushed her madra to its limit, shining in Yerin's spirit.

"You should run farther," Yerin advised.

"Who's running?"

A Truegold aura flared in the distance, taking to the sky immediately.

Yerin regretted the loss; she could tell she was only a finger away from a real breakthrough in her understanding. But they couldn't play any longer.

"Truegold," she called to Mercy, dashing away. "Game's up."

That burned. This was an opportunity she hated to pass up, but she'd pushed it too far already. There was a line between flirting with death and throwing yourself at him.

Then another light dawned in her spirit, much brighter. The Lady.

She was close.

Yerin skidded to a halt, Mercy right behind her. The Lowgold's senses weren't as sensitive, and she gave Yerin a look of confusion.

"Underlady," Yerin said.

Mercy instantly drew her bow back and loosed an arrow. There was a screech from Derianatoth. "To the tent?"

That was the decision. They could try and hide again, but the Truegold and the Lady were close. If they were found this time, that would be the end.

"No," Yerin said.

There was only one way out now.

She rushed back the other way, running for the approaching Truegold. As she ran, she pushed deeper into her spirit, reaching out to her master's memories.

Give me something, she begged silently. *Anything.*

Madra flowing through her Steelborn Iron body, she ran like a rushing river. The Highgold dragon was waiting for her, but she leaped over the giant golden lizard, still aiming for the Truegold.

There was one great thing about the Endless Sword, however she used it: it didn't take much madra. She had plenty left for her Iron body.

A stream of orange madra spewed out behind her, but she flipped around a tree and kept running, focusing on her spirit.

This was it. She was in the final, no-escape corner that her master had always said was the best for forcing an advancement. She'd advanced to Lowgold after her show-down with his spirit, and Highgold in the middle of the battle with Jai Long. It was time to go beyond herself again.

She had to make it if she wanted to reach Lindon.

But as she thought of it, that reason rang hollow. It wasn't *wrong,* but it also wasn't *enough.* There was more. Something deeper.

If she didn't advance, she'd have to rely on her Blood Shadow.

That wasn't it either. She knew she'd have to get used to the Blood Shadow soon. As much as it sickened her, she couldn't run from it forever.

She dug for more.

If she didn't advance, everyone else would leave her behind. Lindon would keep growing, she'd never catch up to Eithan, and even Mercy had her advancement written out for her.

The Truegold appeared over the treeline, glittering in the sun, standing on a small golden Thousand-Mile Cloud. His draconic face turned down to her.

A memory boiled up, and Yerin couldn't tell if it came from her or from her master's Remnant.

She was maybe ten years old, standing with her master beside a stream. Every morning, he would bring her a boulder and have her try to cut it in half with the Rippling Sword. Every morning, she failed, and he took the stone away, only to bring a new one the next day.

She'd thrown her training sword aside in disgust. "I can't do it," she had said.

"Been waiting for you to say that," he'd responded.

He had taken her to a cave behind a waterfall, where he had kept all of the stones she had tried and failed to cut. There were the marks of her failure: slashes in the rocks where her madra had cut. The scars started faint, but they got wider and deeper. And the stones got bigger.

"This is what you did yesterday," he'd said, pointing to the largest rock, the one with the deepest cut. "I can't wait to see what you do tomorrow."

At the time, neither could Yerin.

Now, she stood under the dragon, feeling the echoes of her master's spirit inside her.

"Surrender yourself, Highgold," he said. "We will not make this painful."

Yerin's sword rang like a bell.

He reacted to the sword aura, striking with the back of his hand against the rush of silver. He knocked away the blow, but one tinkling scale was knocked free.

It took with it a drop of blood.

This time, the technique had felt right. It resounded in her master's spirit, resonating between the two of them. She basked in that feeling, memorizing it.

Then the barrier in her spirit crumbled.

Her madra faltered, slipping from her fingers. This was the hazard of pushing for advancement in the middle of battle; it tended to throw you off your game. And this time, her opponent wasn't sweet-minded enough to give her some time for herself.

Scenting blood, the Truegold dragon jumped down from his cloud.

"Page three," Mercy announced.

Yerin had time to wonder why Mercy had said that out loud before an arrow the thickness of her arm pierced the dragon through the gold-scaled chest. Mercy's Truegold aura blanketed the clearing in heavy darkness, and this time, the arrow didn't feel like one technique. It felt like three different techniques crammed into one arrow, and two of them were not friendly.

The force of the arrow carried the dragon back, so he fell to the ground far away from Yerin, but he burned it away almost immediately. His scales oozed blood—so at least this technique did some damage, unlike the arrows Yerin had seen her use before, which didn't even break the skin.

But now, the darkness that crawled over his skin felt like poison. He screamed, breathing fire on himself, but the darkness kept creeping.

That was all Yerin saw. Rivers of silver aura rushed to her, blinding her, filling her spirit. They flooded into her veins, far more than she could ever cycle, rushing to her core.

Her master's Remnant blurred, soaking more completely into Yerin's madra. The sense of his presence weakened again, as it had when she'd advanced to Highgold.

Then, like a deep breath released, the sword aura burst from her in a wave.

Every tree in the clearing exploded under the strike of a thousand axes. Mercy wasn't spared; violet crystal covered her chest in a breastplate, taking the brunt of the force, but scratches still appeared all over her body.

The Highgold dragon Derianatoth had been webbed up by Mercy at some point. Yerin guessed when she was focused on the Truegold. She couldn't defend herself, and her black cocoon burst into sprays of blood.

Blood spurted from the Truegold's scales too, but it wasn't enough to kill him. Not until she followed it up with a Striker technique.

Seconds after the wave of sword aura passed through the forest, his body fell into chunks of flesh and bone.

And then the forest was quiet.

Sunlight streamed down on them, unfiltered by branch-es. A chill wind blew through now that it wasn't blocked by trunks. Mercy's presence faded back to Lowgold, and her bow relaxed to a staff. She hobbled closer to Yerin.

"Congratulations! Should we run?"

"Not yet," Yerin said, eyeing the bodies. "Can't leave the Remnants to follow us. And we can't look like cowards in front of our new guest."

Guided by her Truegold perception, she turned to look into the forest.

A young man stood there, emerald horns shining very slightly in the shadow of the trees that still stood around him. He wore a faded gray cloak, leaned on a hammer as big as he was, and wore an expression like he'd died two days before.

"Looking to pick off the winner?" Yerin asked, her sword starting to shine with the Flowing Sword Enforcer technique. It hummed with a might she'd never felt before; the strength of a Truegold.

He took a long, slow breath, letting it out like it was his last. "...no," he said.

It looked like it had taken him a week of effort to force out that one word, but she had Remnants to deal with. They rose like sunset-colored serpents from the bodies of the dragons. At least in death, they looked like proper dragons: flying, serpentine creatures of flame.

As she'd expected, they both turned to Yerin.

Sword aura wouldn't do much against these non-physical Remnants, but madra would. She whipped a Striker technique at the Highgold, dashing at the Truegold herself. A few strokes of her master's blade left the Remnant in a few hissing puddles on the ground.

The whole time, she'd kept her perception locked on the newcomer. He didn't feel like he was ready to step in. He felt like he would fall over at any second.

"We have to go," Yerin said to Mercy. She didn't like running past an unknown threat, but the Lady was coming from the other direction.

Wait...no, she wasn't.

Yerin's spirit crawled. In the instant she'd taken her perception off the dragon, the woman had covered miles.

Dreading what she would see, Yerin looked behind her.

The Underlady stood there, a sword in hand. It crackled with orange lightning. "On my blood and my name," she whispered, "I swear that you will suffer as none have suffered."

Perfect.

Yerin's Blood Shadow spun out from behind her, and this time she didn't try to stop it. Like a red Remnant copy of her, it spread its Goldsigns. Its right hand flattened into another sword, and it leaned forward, ready to fight.

"Don't suppose you have another one of those shields," Yerin said. Mercy gave a flat, lifeless laugh.

The stranger stepped out of the trees, dragging his huge hammer behind him. It carved a furrow in the soil as he walked, as though he barely had the strength to pull it. "I am the Beast King's witness," he said with a sigh. "I witness a Lady attacking two Golds. Fall back, or he has cause to intervene."

The dragon's shrieking laughter pierced the forest. "And who are you?"

"Underlady," he said, "believe me when I say that I am no one at all."

Her eyes narrowed, and she took him in from the tips of the horns to the bottom of his time-worn cloak. She bared fangs. Then more.

"No," she said at last. "I will not bow to you. Nor even to your master."

With a sweep of her sword, she whipped a rush of liquid flame at Yerin.

Yerin had expected it all along. Together, she and her Blood Shadow both launched a Rippling Sword at the incoming Striker technique. The Blood Shadow's technique did about as much good as a kitchen knife against a tree. Her own wave of silver energy crashed into the flow of orange flame.

But the Underlady's technique, like a river of fire bursting through a dam, pushed right through.

Yerin met the madra with the flat of her master's blade. It pulsed with the power of her Enforcer technique; though it felt like pushing against an ocean's tide and the heat of molten metal all at once, she gritted her teeth and braced herself.

Mercifully, the onslaught ended, leaving smoke rising from her arms—singed again—and her madra dangerously low.

She'd stopped it.

The green-horned man watched the whole thing with flat, dead eyes. "Remember you said that, Sopharanatoth." Yerin guessed that was the dragon.

Yerin's spirit trembled as another powerful soul was unveiled somewhere on the island. Yerin couldn't put a name to its advancement level, but it felt impossibly ancient.

Then the mammoth rose over the trees and raised its trunk, trumpeting into the sky. She could see it mostly as a pile of fur in the distance; it looked like a mountain's pet dog.

The stranger pointed in that direction. "My friend was listening. He's not happy."

The golden Thousand-Mile Cloud rushed in as though blown on a storm's wind. Two Truegold dragons dropped from it, right in front of Sopharanatoth.

"Sophara," one said. "We have to leave."

The mammoth blasted another note.

"We have to leave *right now.*"

The Underlady raised her sword again, but was tackled by her retainers. She struggled against them, and though she could surely overpower them if she tried, they managed to wrestle her onto a smaller Thousand-Mile Cloud.

"Skysworn!" she howled. "I will come for you! Your Empire cannot protect you! You cannot hide from me!"

She kept wailing as the cloud carried her into the sky.

When she vanished, the giant Thousand-Mile Cloud started to slide away. It moved quickly, for something so huge.

Yerin took a deep breath of relief as the pressure was lifted, letting herself be soothed by the Truegold madra flowing through her. Mercy looked to her, and then to the newcomer.

"Hi!" she said brightly. "I'm Mercy."

第十七章

CHAPTER SEVENTEEN

Lindon sensed no Eyes of the Deep in Harmony's possession, and his Goldsign was even more dense than before. It seemed like a hole hovering behind his head.

"He's only a step away from breaking through to Underlord," Orthos rumbled. "He'll have a weapon in his soulspace, and he'll have soulfire in his body, but he won't be able to infuse it into his techniques yet."

"Then we have nothing to fear," Lindon said. He should have been terrified, but the Blackflame running through his channels was stronger than ever, and he felt nothing more than eager.

Harmony raised two fingers, and Lindon activated the Burning Cloak. He had seen this technique before.

Fingers fell, deceptively slowly, and a blade of shadow flickered between Harmony and Lindon. The blade sliced a shallow gash in stone, but a sidestep powered by the explosive Burning Cloak put Lindon five steps to the side. It would be hard to avoid if you didn't know how it worked, or if your body wasn't fast enough to keep up. But shrouded in the burning black-and-red of his Enforcer technique, he was ready for anything.

Harmony's eyes flashed, and his fingers moved in a complex pattern.

Half a second later, shadow-blades flashed at Lindon from every angle. His eyes widened, but he didn't have enough time for panic. He kicked forward, slid on his knees and bent backward to avoid a horizontal slash, rolled to avoid one coming from above, and raised his Remnant arm to seize the technique coming from his right.

The blade was thin as a string and not solid—it was a Striker technique, not Forged. The hunger madra crushed it easily.

Orthos slammed into Lindon's side, knocking him away, as a blade came from behind that he hadn't noticed. Orthos disappeared, his own Burning Cloak taking him away from the technique.

Harmony hadn't moved, looking at his own fingers curiously. "It's truly incredible," he said. "I can see as Monarchs do."

Lindon gathered dragon's breath into his left hand, but he didn't release the technique. "We have no grudge against the Akura clan. I serve on a Skysworn squad with Akura Mercy. Let's leave together."

At the sound of Mercy's name, Harmony's expression twitched. Lindon couldn't read his expression, but the young man's spirit grew darker.

"Shouldn't have said that," Orthos muttered.

Harmony pulled his hand up, and Forged black blades erupted beneath Lindon and Orthos. They split, dodging the technique.

And without discussion, they both rushed for Harmony.

They came at him from either side, and Harmony glanced from one to the other. He spoke as they ran at him, shaking out his sleeves. "Come, let me show you."

Lindon struck with his Remnant arm as Orthos bit down on Harmony's left hand.

In an instant, the purple flooded out of Harmony's irises, filling the whole eye. It looked as though he had smooth gemstones in both eyes.

Gauntlets of purple crystal covered his hands, and he

seized Lindon's arm in one and the back of Orthos' neck in the other.

Their charge stopped as though they'd been locked in stone.

Orthos struck with his front leg, Burning Cloak flaring, and Lindon slammed his half-formed ball of dragon's breath at Harmony's chest with his left hand.

Harmony spun in place, releasing them and avoiding their attacks. In the same motion, he struck each of them with the backs of his fists.

Orthos took it on the shell, skidding back a few paces.

Lindon flew across the room.

His ribs throbbed with pain. A month ago, the strike would have caved in his chest. But his Truegold Enforcer technique and weeks of eating sacred beast meat made him tougher than that.

Lindon hit the floor on his feet, but Orthos had already engaged Harmony one more time. He cycled Blackflame to his feet, ready to dash back in.

Until he looked up.

The jeweled tree shone down on him, the Eyes of the Deep soothing his spirit with their placid, thoughtful presence. Dross was up there, somewhere. He'd been too late.

Blackflame turned that failure to anger, and once again he prepared himself to return to battle...

Until he caught a glimpse of purple among the tree's cages.

He looked closer to make sure he wasn't seeing things. Dross wasn't as bright or violet as he'd been before, as though blue madra had seeped into him, but he was still a different color to all the other Eyes of the Deep.

Maybe he could still be saved.

"Hold on, Orthos," Lindon shouted, and with the assistance of the Burning Cloak, he leaped into the iron branches of the tree.

Orthos gave him a wordless shout of frustration. Harmony had kicked him into the ceiling, and was now launching a series of shadow-blades at him. Only a few weeks ago, Orthos would have died there.

His mind, body, and spirit had been rejuvenated by his time in Ghostwater. This place had remade him just as much as it had Lindon. He twisted in the air, agile as a snake, not only avoiding the blades but flashing out with dragon's breath that scorched a line along the floor, forcing Harmony to raise a sword and to leap back.

But Lindon could still feel the turtle's frustration. He wouldn't win on his own, so Lindon would have to be quick.

He flipped open the cage, which was surprisingly easy. He had thought he might have to burn it open, but it didn't even seem to lock. Then he reached in with his left hand, pulling on Dross' vessel.

It was locked in place.

Lines of light ran from the rest of the cage to the gem as madra sealed it inside. Dross mumbled something from the jewel, like a man mumbling in his sleep.

Lindon reached out his Remnant arm, hesitating before he touched the lines. He didn't know what severing this connection would do to Dross; as far as he knew, it might be the only thing sustaining the construct's life.

But Orthos cried out behind him, and he hooked a white finger around the line of madra. He didn't have time to examine this carefully.

With his finger, he cut the line connecting Dross to the other Eyes of the Deep. Dross gasped, and Lindon quickly sliced through the other connections and pulled out the gem.

Dross mumbled sleepily for another minute. "...I dreamed I was a thousand birds," he said at last.

Lindon let out a breath of relief, turning back to the battle. "Dross, we need to leave. Can you activate the portal?"

The light in the gem shivered, as though Dross were shaking himself. "I can if we can get to it. Will Harmony let us, do you think?"

A wave of swords stabbed up from the floor, seeking Orthos, as the turtle flipped and spat fire over them.

"I don't think so."

"Well, that should be fine. I have another idea."

A purple spark flared over the stone basin at the base of the tree, and Lindon followed Dross' direction, hopping down in front of it.

"I know so much now," the construct said in wonder. "More than I ever thought possible."

"What do I do here, Dross?" Lindon asked. Blackflame blazed behind him.

The spirit flowed out of his vessel. Dross was slightly transparent again, as though he'd lost some substance, but he still looked the same as he had after the Life Well: a round body with one eye and a mouth. He extended two tendrils like arms, pressing them to the script around the stone basin.

The script flashed purple, and after a moment, a clear tube extended from the tree. A white pearl rolled down the tube.

"This is what Harmony drank," Dross said. "Ghostwater."

"Did it really give him the vision of a Monarch?" Lindon asked, watching the pearl greedily.

"Ha! No. He's a Truegold; the true sight of a Monarch would pull his mind apart like clay."

The drop settled into the basin, and Lindon leaned for it.

"Wait! You kept samples of each Well, didn't you?"

"Only one vial from the Life Well."

"That should be good enough. Probably. Open your void key."

Lindon did, and the closet door appeared out of nowhere, Little Blue squeaking happily.

And Harmony's spirit locked onto Lindon.

Lindon ignited the Burning Cloak again, turning to face the Akura. He kicked Orthos away to glare at Lindon.

"You can handle this, Dross," Lindon said, waving to the basin. Then he kicked off, launching himself at Harmony.

"Yes, of course I can," Dross said behind him. "Of course. Handling it, that's what I'm doing."

Swords shoved up from the ground, almost as tall as

Lindon was, but he tore them apart with his right hand. While they tangled him up, a shadow-blade flashed at him at neck height.

Orthos plowed into Harmony from behind. The Akura turned, catching his shell with one gauntlet, but Orthos spun and whipped his tail into the shadow artist's chest.

Harmony flew back, gauntlets dissipating to essence and violet crystal boots appearing on his feet. They bit into the stone, stopping him instantly, as he fired another Striker blade at Orthos.

So he wasn't watching when Lindon broke through the techniques and landed in front of him, Burning Cloak blazing around him. He punched Harmony with his right hand, but white fist met purple as Harmony got his gauntlet up.

Lindon was pushed back by the force of the attack, but Harmony was only feet from the stone wall. He crashed back into it, his black halo eating into the stone even as his gauntlets cracked the rock.

Orthos landed at the same time as Lindon steadied himself, and once again they acted as one. Lindon brought his hands together in front of him, gathering a ball of black-and-red fire between his palms. Orthos cracked his jaws, dragon's breath forming in his mouth.

Two burning bars of Blackflame met on Akura Harmony's body.

Dross struggled, panting like he had lungs, to pull a single vial of Life Water out of the void key's open storage.

"You're not going to help, are you?" he asked Little Blue.

The Sylvan cocked her head at him and whistled.

Before his union with the other Eyes of the Deep, that would have been incomprehensible to him. It was still *mostly* incomprehensible to him, but there was clearly a pattern in the Sylvan Riverseed's communication. He had started to see it, so he could make out what she was saying. Mostly.

"It's not about carrying heavy things, it's about your attitude. Do you hear what I'm saying? Willingness to help, that's all I'm looking for. Moral support."

Little Blue raised her arms in the air and gave a cheer that sounded like wind chimes.

"See, that's all I'm asking."

With superhuman effort, Dross stretched the vial in his arms over the basin. Shining green liquid splashed around the ghostwater pearl, with the white swirling inside the green. They hadn't mixed.

And they wouldn't. Not yet.

"The truth is," Dross said to Little Blue, "all the hard work happens in the Wells. This tree just gathers it and uses it to fuel our thoughts." He paused as he grabbed a vial of Spirit Well water, his mind drifting back to what it was like to be part of the collective.

It had been...expansive. He was far more now than he had ever been before, but when he was connected to the tree, he was a drop of water in the ocean. There was something empowering about being an ocean.

Little Blue squeaked, and violent power flared nearby.

Right, the fight. Time limit, and all that.

Dross heaved the second vial into the air. Each time he lifted one of these, he strained his physical substance. It didn't eat into his memory anymore; now he had an outer membrane that took on all physical strain. But sooner or later, that membrane would be exhausted.

Sooner rather than later, if he was reading his own body's condition correctly.

The blue water swirled in with the green and white, creating a pleasing whirlpool. The aura above the basin twisted like a storm as the powers clashed, and Dross lurched closer to the void storage again. "Just...one...more..."

He was having trouble dragging his body through the

air. He moved his stubby arms in front of his eye, and he could see straight through them.

That wasn't ideal.

He drifted closer to the ground, and Little Blue hopped down from her perch. Her dress-like lower body twirled around his eye, and she looked down on him.

Dross tried to speak, but he was having enough trouble holding himself together without losing any of his real essence.

The Sylvan Riverseed dipped down, looking him straight in the eye, and her expression firmed. With the solid ringing of a bell, she walked over to one of the few remaining vials from the Dream Well.

With both hands, she pushed it out. It was almost half her body's height, and surely twice her weight, but she tucked it under one arm and dashed for the basin.

Dross looked up at the stone device, which loomed over him like a tower. "Why...didn't you...do that before?"

By the time he reached the top, Little Blue had already upended the purple water. All four colors now whirled in the basin, the air around them crackling with power. She was as wary as he was; that power could tear them apart, or change them fundamentally.

Of course, that was almost the idea.

Dross stretched one of his arms beneath the basin, activating a hidden circle with a bare spark of madra. "North-strider left some of his very own soulfire stored at the base. It's the last ingredient."

Pure silver fire, like a mirror stretched into the shape of flames, flared up from the center of the basin. It spread to the water like a natural fire spreading through a puddle of oil, but it consumed nothing.

Rather, the water grew brighter. And it started to blend.

The swirl of white at the center extended out, staining the rest of the liquid, as the silver fire grew smaller and smaller. Sparks of blue and green and purple essence drifted upwards; soulfire burned away impurities, refined the physical vessel, and empowered madra.

Yet another thing he'd learned from the collective.

The silver fire was exhausted as it sunk into every drop-let of the water. It was solid white now, but it glimmered with a metallic sheen.

Dross gathered himself, looking for Lindon. One more step, and he needed a physical body for this part.

Then the grand work would be complete.

The dragon's breath met in a furious conflagration over Harmony's body, an inferno of black and red. The ball of fire devoured the nearby stone, so that it looked like they'd scooped out chunks of the wall and floor with a massive shovel. The rock glowed cherry red, but thanks to the destruction aspect of Blackflame, it left no molten stone behind.

Lindon and Orthos released their techniques together.

"Do we have a way out?" Orthos asked.

"Dross is working on it."

"He should work faster."

Harmony stepped out of the fading black-and-red madra, clad from head to toe in armor of violet crystal. The black disc hovered behind his helmet, and light shone where his eyes should be.

He extended one armored hand, and a metal axe shim-mered as it appeared from his soulspace. It had a shaft as long as he was that looked as though it was made of one long bone, and its broad, curved head glistened with a red light.

When he gripped the weapon in both hands, Lindon felt Dross behind him. He clapped Orthos on the shell.

"Hold him back. I'll open the portal."

"Hold him *back?*" Orthos repeated, but the axe was al-ready descending on him. Snarling, he leaped away.

Dross panted as he arrived, even fainter than before. Lindon could see the wheels turning inside him, his madra channels looping around his core.

"Let...me...in..."

Lindon didn't ask questions. He seized the spirit, drawing him into his core without hesitation, dashing toward the portal.

"How do I start this?" he asked, as the chamber quaked with Orthos' and Harmony's battle.

"Wrong way, wrong way!" Dross shouted inside his head. *"Turn, turn, turn!"*

Confused, Lindon turned so that he was facing the jeweled tree. Orthos leaped away from a crater of cracked stone, and Harmony was a violet blur as he pursued.

"Back to the basin!"

Despite his frustration, Lindon obeyed. "What are we doing?"

"That is called ghostwater!"

Lindon saw the shimmering diamond-colored liquid and understood. This was the fourth well.

"Will this help us beat Harmony?"

"Eh, well...it will help you fight *Harmony, I can guarantee that much."*

Lindon stopped in front of the basin. Little Blue saw him and cheered like jangling coins, hopping back inside the void storage. Tapping his void key to close the door, Lindon looked down at the shimmering milk.

"Northstrider's grand work failed because this collective mind he created had no initiative or creativity, you see. It did only what it was told. Not to brag, but as it turns out, all they had to do was let a memory construct soak in the Dream Well for fifty years."

Lindon ducked his entire head into the white water.

"You could take this yourself, if you wanted," Dross continued. *"Your mind would be enhanced far beyond Harmony's. But if you give it to* me, *we'll have finished Northstrider's project."*

As the water rushed through his body, it started to gather at the base of his skull.

Lindon seized it.

As tempting as it would be to see what the ultimate product of Ghostwater could do for his advancement, Orthos could only last so long. A Monarch artifact would go a long way here.

He guzzled down the ghostwater, cycling it all to Dross.

Orthos crashed into the ground next to him, Burning Cloak dying. He struggled to rise to his feet, but failed. There were new cracks in his shell, smaller but leaking light.

"I'm at my end," he said, voice low.

Lindon couldn't turn enough to see Harmony, but he could feel the Akura behind him, like the shadow of death. Edged darkness gathered, approaching him as the scythe approached the wheat.

Dross was spinning in his core. The ghostwater started to draw him up, through Lindon's channels, until the spirit rested where his neck met his head.

Lindon finished the last of the ghostwater, taking a deep breath. "What do I do?" he demanded.

There was a brief, sharp pain in his spirit, like a pinprick on his neck that cut straight to the soul. And then Dross was part of him, seared into his madra channels like he'd been nailed there.

Dross' voice echoed in Lindon's mind and soul.

[One battle plan, coming up.]

INFORMATION REQUESTED: COMBAT SOLUTION AGAINST AKURA HARMONY.

BEGINNING REPORT...

Now, you're going to want to get right on this, because there's a Striker technique about six inches from your spine that will split you like a fish.

One thin edge of shadow, a line stretching from floor to ceiling, approaches Lindon's back. As it streaks away from Harmony, it cuts a line in the floor.

That armor of his is the bloodline legacy of the Akura family. That's an advantage for us. He didn't make it with his Path, so he doesn't have full control of it. He's not supposed to use the full armor until Underlord, anyway, so his movements will be wide.

The violet crystal armor encasing Harmony feeds on his madra. Lindon can feel it in his spiritual perception; it's draining Harmony's spirit and most of his attention. His core is on the edge of empty, and he has to Enforce himself to even move.

That axe is an Underlord weapon too. He can't bring out its power. Silly, isn't it? He thought of it as an emergency measure, but he would have been better off taking a weapon he could handle. It will still take your head off, though.

The binding isn't active. Now, with all this information flowing through him in one surge of images and emotions, Lindon can feel it. He's shocked he didn't notice it before.

The weapon itself is still powerful, but Harmony can't activate the binding.

First, get rid of the Striker technique. Shouldn't be too hard for you.

Lindon turns, the technique in his white arm activating, and he sweeps the shadow-blade aside. His hand devours the madra, staining slightly dark.

Distract him. Throw sand at him or something.

The stolen madra vents into Harmony's face, confusing his eyes and his perception at once. Unshaped, the madra forms a handful of black needles. The shadow and sword aspects fight one another, so they're not deadly, but they are a distraction.

Right, now block his blind strike.

The red-edged axe swings at him, and Lindon reaches for the haft. He's not fast enough. The axe cleaves through hand, arm, shoulder, blood spraying into the air. The pain fades quickly as the cold haze of death closes in.

Er, sorry, I mean dodge it.

Lindon ducks, and the swipe of the axe passes over his head. He is unharmed, and Harmony is off-balance.

Disrupt his footing.

He reaches for Harmony's armored ankle, heaving with a Burning Cloak-empowered pull. It's too soon for Harmony to steady himself, and he's hauled from his feet.

Take that weapon away.

Harmony's spirit surges as his attention shifts from the fight to keeping his armor from fading. His grip weakens.

Lindon's hand of flesh closes around the haft of the axe, and he wrenches it away.

When he hits the ground, he'll strike out, so be prepared for that.

His back slams into the stone, and Harmony draws two diagonal lines in front of his chest. An X-shaped cross of shadow blades slashes upward at the place he last felt Lindon.

But Lindon has already moved. The Burning Cloak carries him beyond so he stands over Harmony's head.

You can't crack the armor, but you can make it too expensive to keep on.

With both hands, Lindon lifts the axe over his head and plunges it down on the crystal breastplate.

It strikes sparks without penetrating, but the burden of madra is too much for a Truegold. The armor bursts into essence, purple light retreating back into Harmony's irises.

Watch out for your allies.

Arm-thick dragon's breath roars from Orthos, and Lindon sidesteps. The madra consumes Harmony's body.

And that's one dead enemy. It's simple. It's clean. And there's only minimal chance for failure and a horrific death.

Now, go out and do it.

REPORT COMPLETE.

Reality returned as though Lindon had moved five seconds back in time.

He spun, slashing the Striker technique apart with his hand, absorbing its madra and immediately venting it into Harmony's face. He ignited the Burning Cloak, ducking the blind slash of the axe and wrenching Harmony from his feet.

He snatched the axe and dashed from Harmony's feet to his head in one movement. The cross of shadow-blades passed through the space where he had been standing.

Lindon plunged the axe down on the chest of Harmony's armor, which burst instantly. Now he only had to stand aside and wait for Orthos' breath to obliterate the Akura's body.

Instead, he kicked Harmony to the side.

Blackflame carved a trough in the stone, but Harmony tumbled to one side, his Goldsign slicing the stone.

Orthos tracked Harmony's movement, turning the dragon's breath to the side, moving the stream closer.

Lindon stood in front of him, raising a hand. Orthos slammed his jaws shut, madra spilling from the sides of his mouth.

Finally, Lindon relaxed. That had been a risk. He could deflect a certain amount of Blackflame madra, but it wasn't as though he would walk away unharmed.

"Kill him!" Orthos demanded. "What are you thinking?"

Lindon's Burning Cloak faded away, and Lindon tapped his pure core. His madra channels were sore and aching after the fight, and he'd used up quite a bit of his madra.

He looked down into Harmony's eyes, and he saw there only anger, humiliation, and exhaustion.

"We're leaving," Lindon said at last. "As a gesture of goodwill to the Akura family, I would be happy to take you with us."

Without waiting for a reply, he walked over to the jade arch of the portal. Orthos followed him, speaking as low as he could. "If we bring him back, he will bring word to his family. The Akura family has more Underlords than you can imagine, and they do not suffer disgrace lightly."

"Will they see this as shame?" Lindon asked curiously. "I would think they would see it as mercy.

He held out his left hand, conjuring Dross. The spirit rushed out of him, spinning into existence as a hovering purple head with one giant eye. Their connection did not weaken at all with distance.

Dross drifted over to the scripted panel next to the portal. [Hm, yes, this will be tricky. It will require all of my skill and enhanced knowledge.]

"Will it take long?" Lindon asked.

The script lit up, and suddenly a portal rippled swirling blue and green in the center of the arch.

[Honestly, that was much easier than I thought it would be.]

Fractures spread immediately from the portal, crawling away from the frame at visible speed. Clearly, the world wouldn't last much longer.

Scuffling from behind told Lindon that Harmony was climbing to his feet. Dross' mere existence helped him sort through sensory information much more clearly. It didn't expand Lindon's senses, like the powers of an Arelius might, but it helped him organize everything neatly with only a moment of focus.

Yerin would be jealous.

"The pride of the Akura does not bend," Harmony said, his voice heated. "The next time we meet, I will be a Lord. And I will raze your home and burn your family, root and branch, until your name is used as a curse."

Lindon turned to see Harmony reaching into space, pulling out a lump of chalk that glittered blue.

The Soul Cloak, which Lindon had already prepared, flared around him so that he shone in a cloud of smooth blue-and-white light.

Harmony's core was all but empty, and Lindon sensed nothing Enforcing his limbs. The Burning Cloak lent itself to sudden, violent bursts of movement, but that also meant it was difficult to control.

The Soul Cloak, on the other hand, helped his body move almost before he thought of it. No sooner had he activated the technique than he stood before Harmony, clasping his wrist in one pale hand.

"That seems a little extreme," Lindon said, plucking

the gatestone from his hand. He hurled it against the wall, where it burst into blue light and another mess of spatial cracks.

The room was crawling with hairline fractures now, and they were getting faster and faster.

Harmony lunged for him, swirling the last of his madra to Enforce himself.

Lindon slammed an Empty Palm into his core.

As the Akura dropped, Lindon walked back to the portal. "He has refused our offer of a way home, so we'll leave him to make his own way back."

Dross drifted back into Lindon's body, and his madra didn't block the spirit any longer.

Orthos glanced back, but walked through the portal. They didn't know where the doorway would take them, but at least it would be somewhere on the outside.

Lindon followed.

For one blink, they were buffeted on all sides by textured blue light. Then the air tore around them again, and they were standing inside a shallow cave.

Moss and bright mushrooms filled the space like grass, and the jade arch was set against the wall. Sunlight spilled through the mouth of the cave, and he could see it shining on an endless field of waves.

Lindon heaved a deep breath of salty air, feeling as though he had crawled out of a hole for the first time in weeks.

The portal, which was transparent from this side, showed a steadily cracking image of Harmony scrambling over the pocked and pitted floor left behind after their battle. He crawled for the portal as Ghostwater collapsed around him.

Lindon watched, locked in a debate. On the one hand, Harmony had made it clear that he wouldn't cooperate. On the other hand—

Orthos blew a finger-thin stream of dragon's breath through the arch, and the portal disappeared.

Lindon stared at the spot where the portal had been for a long moment.

"He asked for that," Orthos said.

"...I can't argue with that." Lindon turned back to the ocean. "Now, Dross: where are we?"

[Oh, I don't, ah, I don't know. Is that the sun?]

第十八章

CHAPTER EIGHTEEN

The green-armored guards lifted their spears and stepped to the side, allowing Eithan to approach the tall doors to the Emperor's audience hall. He was expected.

Fisher Gesha fussed with her hair, bowing to both of the Truegold guards as she walked in Eithan's wake. She had left her drudge behind today, so the top of her head was barely above Eithan's waist.

"This will not go as you expect," she muttered. "Did you ask me what I wanted? Hm? No. You just *drag* me along, like luggage. He will not see me. Do you think Highgolds go before the Emperor every day?"

"Don't worry," Eithan said, marching forward. "He's not as intimidating as you think." Wind aura swung the door open before he touched them.

The doors opened onto a long hallway, decorated with enough opulence to shame the halls of heaven. Everything was sheathed in gold: the dragon statues hanging from the ceiling, the pillars lining the hall, even the floor tiles.

At the end of the hall, the Emperor sat on his throne of gold and jade. Naru Huan, Emperor of the Blackflame Empire, was the picture of a hero: he was powerfully built, with piercing eyes and a short beard that emphasized his square chin. His hair was pinned back by an ornate crown, and his wings spread to either side, flanking him in shining emerald feathers. His Overlord spirit spilled freely through the halls, pushing down on them with the weight of true power.

A shirtless man on one side of the door rang a massive gong as they entered. The air trembled as the deafening tone broke the silence.

A crier stepped forward before the throne. "You enter the presence of Emperor Naru the Second, Overlord and Patriarch of the Naru clan, Guardian of the West and Protector of the East, master of this land. Prostrate yourself before him, and show him your gratitude."

Fisher Gesha threw herself to the ground, and even Eithan lowered himself to his knees. Though he wanted to roll his eyes at the useless ceremony.

The Emperor raised one finger.

"Stand!" the crier ordered, and Gesha scrambled to her feet. Eithan followed, brushing off his knees; there was a thin layer of dust on the ground. He would have to speak to the cleaning crew.

"Gesha, Highgold of the Desolate Wilds, approach the throne." Trembling, each step a burden, Fisher Gesha pushed forward. She dared not raise her head enough to look directly at the Emperor, and she was clearly torn between obeying quickly and walking with a stately, respectful pace.

Eithan yawned.

When she was within a few paces of the bottom step, the crier held out a hand. "Stop! To your knees, and prepare to receive the word of the Emperor. Let all ears and hearts attend to his wisdom."

She fell back to the ground, and Naru Huan looked on her.

"You have pleased us, Fisher Gesha," he announced. "You have served us with distinction, standing even against an enemy Underlord. For this, we will reward you."

One of the servants to the side of the throne stepped forward, carrying an ornate wooden chest. He squared his shoulders and cracked the box open for Fisher Gesha's inspection.

Gold and purple light spilled out. The box was filled with rows of high-grade force scales, as well as three pills like shimmering balls of gold.

"Daughter of the empire, we grant you the path to True-gold," the Emperor said. "Advance your Path and continue to serve us."

Fisher Gesha pressed her forehead to the floor. "Forgive this old woman, Your Imperial Majesty," she said, and Eithan's eyebrows rose in surprise. He hadn't expected her to speak. "I am too old for such a gift, you see? My family... they have followed me from the Wilds. They have just arrived, but they are young. Please, grant me permission to share these gifts among them instead. They will serve their people longer than I will, hm?"

Gesha's family had joined her only recently. Eithan had found them with Gesha, setting up a Soulsmith's shop in the floating city of Stormrock.

A smile flickered on Naru Huan's face, but it was quickly gone, replaced by the mask of an emperor. "Though your request is admirable, we will not grant it." On the floor, Gesha flinched. "These rewards are for you alone. You will serve us better as a Truegold."

Two more servants, carrying identical boxes, stepped out. "Your concern for your grandchildren does you credit," the Emperor continued. "We will not forget them."

Gesha raised her head, and her wrinkled face was wet with tears. "Heavens grant long life to the Emperor," she said, her voice cracking.

"Go in peace," Naru Huan announced. He looked up to Eithan, still standing at the far end of the hall, and his expression hardened. "We must have an audience with our Underlord alone."

Gesha bowed her way out, flanked by three servants carrying boxes. As she left, she glanced at Eithan.

He winked.

When the doors slammed again, signifying that Gesha had left, the whole room relaxed. The Emperor pulled the crown from his head, withdrew his wings, and let out a breath. The crier knuckled the small of his back, stretching. Some of the servants started chattering among themselves. Even the gong attendant slumped down to the floor, leaning his back against the wall.

"Last audience for the day," Naru Huan said, and his voice no longer echoed through the hall. He had been holding it with wind aura, probably all day. "At least you brought some good news. Panic and fear threaten to do more damage than the Phoenix did."

"The Overlord still got away," Eithan reported, strolling up to the throne. "And we saw no sign of their Sage, for which we should be grateful."

Naru Huan folded his wings and hopped down from the throne, handing his crown to a servant. "He is currently on an island in the Trackless Sea, where he is matched by the Sage of the Silver Heart. If he were to leave to save his subordinates, she would follow him."

That was interesting news. What was in the Trackless Sea to attract the Akura family and Redmoon Hall both?

"Then he's in no position to threaten us now, but he will eventually. He doesn't strike me as the sort to take the loss of half a dozen Underlords lightly."

Eithan hadn't learned that number until he'd reached Blackflame City. He, Naru Saeya, and Chon Ma had eliminated two Underlords, but the other teams had done as well. Six of the Underlord emissaries that had entered the Blackflame Empire had been killed, as well as many more Truegolds. They may have missed an Underlord or two, but considering the Blackflame Empire had suffered no losses, this was something to celebrate.

"This is a victory," the Emperor said firmly. "We have won, and the Empire must see that. I allowed Gaien Arelius to revoke your position because he told me that you were not performing your duties as the head of the family, and

I wanted to remind you that your service to the Empire is what matters. You have served me well, so I will allow you to return to your former position."

Eithan waved a hand. "No, thank you."

A bit of the Imperial authority returned to Naru Huan's eyes. "This is the attitude that gets you into trouble. You do not have the standing to refuse."

Eithan slipped hands into his pockets and walked alongside the Emperor as he strode away from the audience hall. "Huan, how long have you known me?"

"Long enough to know that you do what you want."

"Do you suspect that I am not loyal to the Empire?"

Naru Huan gave him a sidelong glance. Servants pushed open a door for him, and he led the way through. "I suspect that, in your heart, you acknowledge no authority greater than yourself."

That was close to accurate, but Eithan brushed it aside. "If I am allowed to do as I please, it will only benefit the Empire. I consider this place my second homeland. But I must be allowed to act freely. Especially considering what is coming."

The Emperor halted, turning in the hallway. Servants around him bowed. "The Akura family might compete, but we won't. We *can't.*"

"When the Dreadgods begin to act strangely, the Monarchs look to one another. This upcoming competition will be a battle between Monarchs, and the Akura family will not allow us to stand aside."

Naru Huan stared off into the distance, light rippling in his wings. "What can you do?"

"I have two, maybe three prospects for young Underlords. Given the opportunity to coach them directly, I believe I might be able to raise two of them in time."

"You think they would impress the Akura family?"

"Huan," Eithan said, "I think they could do a little better than that."

The Emperor studied him. He spent a moment in deep

thought, examining Eithan's expression. "All the more reason to reinstate you as Patriarch."

"No. All the more reason to let me join the Skysworn. I don't know if you've heard anything about my training methods, but I like to supervise. Personally."

The Emperor folded his arms. "You will operate according to Naru Gwei's orders."

"Of course!"

"And under no circumstances will you be granted any additional authority over the Skysworn."

"I would never dream of it."

Naru Huan thought for a moment longer. Then he nodded.

Using the Soul Cloak and his newly reinforced body, it was no problem for Lindon to climb up the cliff on the side of the island. Or it wouldn't have been, except that he had to drag Orthos behind him.

In his flesh-and-blood hand, he grabbed the rocky edge of the island, body and spirit straining. His Remnant fingers were under the lip of Orthos' shell; the turtle had retreated inside when he realized they had to climb up.

"Let me go," the turtle commanded, his voice echoing from inside the shell. "Drop me into the water."

Lindon heaved, the blue-and-white haze around him flaring for one last burst of strength. His spirit and body were already exhausted from the fight with Harmony, but now he needed a final step.

He dragged Orthos up, one-handed, muscles straining and face hot with effort.

Black madra oozed out the side of the cliff.

He released the cliff immediately, letting himself fall. If there were new enemies up there, it would be better to hit the water.

Dark, shadowy tendrils snagged him, stopping his fall, catching him in a quickly woven basket. More strands grabbed Orthos, who snaked his head out of his shell and looked up.

"We could have used you a few minutes ago," the turtle rumbled.

Lindon looked up.

Mercy stood at the edge of the cliff. Her hair was cut close to the skull, and she was matted and dirty, as though she'd spent the last several weeks living outside. She ground her staff into the sand with both hands, channeling her madra through it, eyes closed and spirit straining.

He could feel her Lowgold power, and it struck him how weak she now seemed.

With long, deliberate breaths, Mercy controlled her madra. The limbs of shadow lifted them up, spilling them onto the grass at the edge of the cliff. Lindon landed on his feet, Orthos rolled over and over, and even Mercy collapsed to catch her breath.

She opened her eyes and gave him a bright smile. "We came to save you!"

We.

Lindon looked toward the trees, opening his spirit to feel for Yerin's presence. He felt only a flash of power as a black-and-silver blur crashed into him.

He stood his ground as Yerin threw her arms around him, squeezing him so tight that his ribs would have cracked a few weeks before.

"You're solid," she said, from somewhere around his shoulder. "You made it."

Slowly, hesitantly, he put his own arms around her. He had to avoid her Goldsigns, and he pulled his Remnant arm back when he realized it was about to touch her. Instead, he embraced her with his real arm.

"Forgiveness. It took me too long."

She shook her head, squeezing tighter. If not for the month of eating sacred beast meat, his body would have...

Actually, his ribs were starting to crack.

"You're not missing any more pieces," Yerin said, still not looking up.

Lindon tried to take a breath and couldn't. He tapped on her shoulder, trying to get her attention.

"Your cores still..." His spirit shivered as her perception passed through him, and she looked up at him. Her eyes were red, and they widened. "...Highgold? *Truegold?*"

Whatever she saw in his face startled her, and she released him so he could heave a desperate breath.

"That's what...took me...so long..." he panted, trying to give her a confident smile through the sharp pain in his sides.

She turned to look over the cliff. "Must have a dragon's worth of treasure in there. I'll be burned and buried before I leave that behind."

Lindon grabbed her wrist as she started to walk away. "The portal's closed. And..." He felt the power of the madra running through her arm. "You too?"

She grinned back at him, scarred face beaming. "Looks like we're standing on the same ground. About time. I was sick of waiting for you to catch up."

He realized he was still holding onto her wrist and started to let go, but she twisted her hand around and grabbed his in turn, so they were clasping each other's arms.

Lindon let himself relax. He was here, he was alive, and he was advanced enough to stand shoulder-to-shoulder with Yerin. Everything had worked out.

Mercy leaned in, eyes sparkling. She threw an arm around each of them. "Let's *all* be excited! We made it!"

"You changed your hair," Lindon said. "I like it." He still didn't know Mercy well; he wasn't sure what else to say.

She grimaced. "I don't. Makes me look like a twelve-year-old boy. Hair growth elixirs are pretty cheap, but I need to find a refiner I can trust."

Yerin and Lindon released each other's hands. By then, Orthos had walked up, closing the circle. Yerin eyed him up and down, eyebrows raising. "You look all polished up. You get a new shell?"

The turtle raised his head, and Lindon felt a flash of smug pride through their bond. "I feel a hundred years younger. Now I can show you what a true dragon is capable of."

Yerin shot another glance at the cliff. "You're sure that portal is—"

"Definitely closed," Lindon said. They wouldn't want to travel back through it even if it was open.

A cloud passed over the sun, but the ocean still glistened, and for a breath of time Lindon just enjoyed that he was still alive. Little Blue crawled out of his pocket and sat on his shoulder, watching the ocean.

[That *is* the sun!] Dross said, popping up onto his other shoulder.

Mercy let out a quick scream. Yerin had backed up, her sword halfway out.

Lindon held up a hand. "Forgiveness! Forgiveness, please. I forgot. Everyone, this is Dross. He's a memory construct that I found inside."

Yerin's eyes narrowed. "Memory? He's talking in my head."

[I'm a special case,] Dross said, focusing his eye on her.

Mercy's purple eyes were only an inch from him, and she extended one finger to poke him in the side. She seemed surprised when the finger passed through him. "I like your color," she said.

Dross turned to her, then yelped and leaped an inch back. [You, ah, you remind me an *awful* lot of the young man we just left to die.]

Lindon turned away before he had to face any questions. He'd tell Yerin what happened later, but he had to think Mercy would disapprove of him leaving an Akura to dissolve with the breaking world. "I suppose we should see if the Skysworn cloudship is still there. Where's Bai Rou?"

"Left him," Yerin said. "I can tell you sure and certain: it takes longer to walk across this island than you'd think."

"We could go find hammer guy," Mercy suggested.

That hooked Lindon's attention. "Hammer guy?"

Yerin waved a hand. "He won't help. Ran back to his Herald without so much as dropping his name."

Orthos pushed forward, looking into the woods. "Lindon is right. We should be heading for a way home. We will see if the ship is still there."

Yerin and Mercy did not look forward to the prospect of marching through the woods, but Lindon was strangely excited. Everyone was together, he was Truegold, and he was ready to dive into the woods filled with the unknown.

"Just have to hope the dragons are gone," Yerin muttered.

"Dragons?" Orthos asked.

Lindon remembered a wounded Truegold dragon passing through the blue flash of a gatestone. Had Ekeri survived?

"Tell us about the dragons," he said.

Sophara knelt before the image of her master, cheeks still wet with tears.

"They took so much from us," she said, her chest tight with pain. "So much."

The Monarch's body was built from sand. It was a projection of his will; his true body was halfway across the continent, but this sand took his form. He looked like a human boy of twelve or thirteen wearing a mantle that covered him from neck to ankles.

Sophara was not worthy to look upon him directly. Instead, she studied his bare human feet.

"They took nothing from us," her divine ancestor corrected her. "You gave it all to them."

Her throat seized up, but she didn't dare argue with a Monarch.

"Your sister cornered a mouse and was nibbled to death. She was a shame to my blood." He spat to one side. "I wasted my words on her."

Sophara's claws gouged trenches in the wooden floorboards.

"You set Derianatoth and Nagatonatoth to hunt, and they too were killed by their prey. If their Remnants had not been destroyed already, you should have done it yourself. They do not deserve to be used in death. They were useless in life."

She could hold her words no longer. "Divine king, whose wisdom spans the ages, please...please have mercy on me. They were my family."

A finger of hard-packed sand slipped under her chin, tilting her face up. She squeezed her eyes shut so she didn't accidentally see his face.

"Look upon me," he commanded.

His face was round and smooth, with no hint of its true nature. Unlimited power, hidden in a frail package. Perfect beauty, as Sophara had always thought.

"Truth does not care for your feelings," he said. The sand-sculpture was so fine, she could see every nuance of his icy expression. "The truth is, they were stronger. You were weak. And thanks to your weakness, this trip to Northstrider's laboratory has gained us nothing and cost us much."

Fresh tears oozed from her eyes. "I will accept my punishment with a glad heart."

"What do I gain from your punishment? We face the facts. Aside from the Tidewalker sect and the Ninecloud Court delegation, we achieved the least of everyone in Ghostwater. And the Court cares nothing for any of this. Redmoon Hall retrieved what they came for, and the Akura family went to great lengths to hide their child's fate from me. He must have succeeded."

He gripped her chin with his whole hand, and she knew that even with the strength of this projection, he could tear her jaw from her head without effort. "I looked weak. The difference between perceived strength and actual strength is smaller than you would believe."

He released her, folding his hands behind his back. "Hear me, Sopharanatoth. You have begun a hunt. There can be only one outcome: success, *overwhelming* success. You must bring me glory that overshadows my shame."

"Tell me how," she begged. "Tell me and I will."

"Soon, there will be another competition," he said. "On a much grander stage. This year, it means more than it ever has before. Even their tiny, insignificant Empire will be forced to compete. You will face their champions, and you will kill them with the world watching.

"Only then will I smile on you."

In a distant corner of the world, a dragon's corpse lay stretched across an icy mountain range, its blood flowing in swiftly freezing rivers. Blood aura boiled up, covering the horizon like a cloud bank, rising from miles of sapphire scales. The sacred beast had died only minutes before. Its Remnant—the size of a city—was already dispersing back into aura.

On that corpse sat Northstrider, Monarch on the Path of the Hungry Deep. He sat cross-legged, in a cycling position, as the blood aura rose around him.

With a breath, he cycled it into his core. The vitality of dragons seeped into him, strengthening his body and his spirit. A spark within his soul carried the image of a dragon, majestic and roaring; it fed upon the imprint of the dragon's life that remained in this aura. Every part of him was nourished by this creature's power.

And now there was one fewer dragon in the world.

This moment of cycling after the kill was the closest to

content that he ever came. That satisfaction was suddenly interrupted by an irritation in his spirit.

He opened his perception, stretching it across the planet to the source of that irritation.

It was the anchor he'd planted to keep Ghostwater tied to this world. It had failed. Ghostwater was seconds from destruction.

He spent a moment weighing whether recovering the information remaining in his pocket world was worth breaking away from his cycling, but that only irritated him further. If the Ghostwater project had succeeded in the way he'd wanted, he wouldn't have had to think about the question at all. A Presence would have told him the answer.

Mood broken, Northstrider rose to his feet. He might as well go salvage what he could.

With a brief effort, he stepped out of space.

The irresistible blue currents surrounded him, buffeting him and trying to push him back to the world, but this was a battle of wills he'd fought many times. He kept his focus locked on his destination, and in seconds he reached it. There was no change in his surroundings, just the sensation of being carried in overpowering currents and then a certainty that he had arrived.

Relaxing his will, he allowed himself to be carried back into Cradle. Or, as he preferred to think of it: into the miniature world he'd tacked onto Cradle like a spare room onto a house.

The prime chamber of the Ghostwater facility was much as he'd left it decades before. It was a cave he'd hollowed out with one scoop of his hand, with an exit on one wall, his oracle tree on the other, and not much else of note.

It had splintered like glass on the edge of shattering. Some of the cracks in space were so wide that he could see the void through them; endless black like the depths of space, speckled with lights like spinning, colored stars.

Reaching out, Northstrider extended his will to every corner of the pocket world.

"Hold," he commanded.

The spatial cracks froze.

Compelled by his presence, space slowly stabilized, knitting back together. Reality reasserted itself, and Northstrider paced across the stone floor.

As he walked, part of him noted the boy on the ground. It was a Gold, a battered young man with an empty core on a Path that felt like shadow and swords. Bits of violet crystal armor clung to him, as though he expected armor to protect him from spatial cracks. One of Malice's brood, then.

There were only two things worth noticing about the boy. First was that he had managed to drink two drops of ghostwater. Northstrider could feel their weight between the boy's spirit and his mind.

Second: he was still alive.

The boy gasped as the cracks that had pressed against his neck vanished. He caught sight of Northstrider and his purple eyes widened. Without another sound, he bowed until his forehead pressed against the floor.

Northstrider reached the oracle tree, the collective where his Eyes of the Deep compiled and compared memories. Out of four thousand and ninety-six possible Eyes, two thousand, four hundred and thirteen had been returned.

Not bad. A better harvest than he'd expected.

He produced a smooth black orb. It was based on the same principle as the Eyes of the Deep, but this construct was many generations more advanced. Someday, if his wish was ever granted, this would be his second mind.

He held up the orb, activating it. The oracle tree felt its pull and surrendered itself gladly, the hive-mind of constructs rushing out of its branches in a stream of ghostly light.

"Master," the worm on the ground said, "I am unworthy to make a request of you."

There was a brief flash of purple in the river of light. It felt like a wound, as though something had been added and then gouged out.

Northstrider froze the transfer. He focused his perception on the oracle construct, reading its history.

Something *had* been added. A mind. One of his constructs had become an interesting anomaly.

"If you take me from this place, I will forever be in your debt."

The oracle's memories told him most of the story. A Lowgold, raised to Truegold thanks to his Spirit Well. Nothing special about that. The children of many Monarchs enjoyed such resources, if they were worthy.

But he'd ended up cobbling together a living construct made from pieces Northstrider had left behind.

Well, at least someone had made something useful out of this trash heap.

The Monarch finished drawing the oracle out of the tree. He would check on the results of this rogue construct someday, if fate allowed. He might learn something, even from a failed product.

Until then, he would continue on as he had before.

"Though my service is worth nothing, my family would help repay you. Any of my achievements in the future would belong to you. And future generations would tell tales of your legendary mercy."

The halo of shadow behind the young man's face lent him the aspect of a specter. Determination was carved into every line of his smooth face. His purple eyes smoldered with resolve, and with the fires of vengeance. Northstrider honored this young man by meeting those eyes.

"No," the Monarch said.

Then he stepped back out of space, leaving the world to collapse.

THE END
of Cradle: Volume Five
Ghostwater

LINDON'S STORY CONTINUES IN

UNDERLORD

CRADLE : VOLUME SIX

ΛΝD ΝΟШ THIS...

Mercy drew the string back, Forging a jet-black arrow as she did so. The point emerged between her weapon's jaws.

"This is the weapon my mother carried from Lowgold to Archlord: Bowey McBowFace."

Purple eyes snapped open, and she slipped her legs out of the branch.

She fell, arms blurring as she released the first arrow, pulling a second from the air, stringing it, and loosing it. Then a third.

Only then did the first arrow pierce the first leaf, pinning it to the ground several yards away. The second followed suit. The third arrow brushed by its target, sending the leaf spinning in the wind of its wake.

Mercy's head cracked as it hit the ground, and she crumpled.

Yerin folded her arms and waited. Iron bodies could take more punishment than that.

She waited. Mercy's body rested, bent and broken, on

the ground. Empty eyes stared into the forest.

Yerin walked up to Mercy and nudged the girl with her foot. "Mercy? You playing with me?"

A black Remnant peeled itself away from Mercy's corpse.

The air ripped like a torn page.

Lindon stepped through the portal into a dry, dusty sitting room filled with ornate furniture. Sword-racks hung on the walls, some holding curved, single-edged swords, others sitting empty. A tall standing mirror reflected Renfei's surprised expression as she, Lindon, and Orthos emerged from the portal together.

Renfei stared down into the Eye of the Deep, the sapphire dead in her hand. "This isn't right," she said. "Ghostwater is supposed to be..."

A shadow flowed from beneath the only door in the room, unfolding into a hunched figure wearing a dark gray cloak. The fabric was worn and tattered with age, and breath hissed from the darkness in his hood.

"I think we opened the wrong door," Renfei said.

Back at the Life Well, Lindon cupped his hands and drew out a mouthful of emerald water to take a sip. It had a faint taste like a very weak tea, and he could feel it spreading to his body without his encouragement.

"Yes, this water will restore your youth," Dross continued. "Unless you're too young, and then it will overwhelm your life-force and instantly kill you. How old are you, again? I have the worst time telling humans apart."

Lindon's heart seized up, and he collapsed to the floor, dead.

Eithan leaned closer to Naru Gwei, Captain of the Sky-sworn, and stared him straight in the eyes. "Look at me. Look at me! I am the Captain now."

INFORMATION REQUESTED: COMBAT SOLUTION AGAINST AKURA HARMONY.

BEGINNING REPORT...

Now, you're going to want to get right on this, because before I can tell you how to beat Akura Harmony, I'm going to need you to slap that Like button and subscribe to my YouTube channel! Donate to DrossTheRobotGhost on Patreon, and at the $5 tier, I'll tell you how to defeat one enemy once per month. At the $10 tier, I'll share clever quips during combat. And at the $20 tier, you get access to my erotic fanfiction: 'Humans Mating: a Tale of XxxCitement'.

DENIED, REPORT COMPLETE.

ШILL ШIGHT lives in Florida, among the citrus fruits and slithering sea creatures. He's the author of the Amazon best-selling *Traveler's Gate Trilogy*, *The Elder Empire* (which cleverly offers twice the fun and twice the work), and his new series of mythical martial arts magic: *Cradle*.

He graduated from the University of Central Florida in 2013, earning a Master's of Fine Arts in Creative Writing and a flute of dragon's bone. He is also, apparently, invisible to cameras.

He also claims that *www.WillWight.com* is the best source for book updates, new stories, fresh coriander, and miracle cures for all your aches and pains!

CPSIA information can be obtained
at www.ICGtesting.com
Printed in the USA
LVHW011709020419
612699LV00017B/340